Clash of Legions

Also by Anthony Riches

Empire
Wounds of Honour
Arrows of Fury
Fortress of Spears
The Leopard Sword
The Wolf's Gold
The Eagle's Vengeance
The Emperor's Knives
Thunder of the Gods
Altar of Blood
The Scorpion's Strike
River of Gold
Vengeance
Storm of War

The Centurions
Betrayal
Onslaught
Retribution

About the author

Anthony Riches holds a degree in Military Studies from Manchester University. He began writing the story that would become the first novel in the *Empire* series, Wounds of Honour, after visiting Housesteads Roman fort in 1996. Married with three grown up children, he now lives in Suffolk. He is also the writer of the '*Protector*' thriller series.

Clash of Legions

Empire: Volume Fourteen

Anthony Riches

**HODDER &
STOUGHTON**

First published in Great Britain in 2024 by Hodder & Stoughton Limited
An Hachette UK company

This paperback edition published in 2024

1

Copyright © Anthony Riches 2024

The right of Anthony Riches to be identified as the Author of the Work has been asserted by him in accordance with the Copyright, Designs and Patents Act 1988.

All rights reserved. No part of this publication may be reproduced, stored in a retrieval system, or transmitted, in any form or by any means without the prior written permission of the publisher, nor be otherwise circulated in any form of binding or cover other than that in which it is published and without a similar condition being imposed on the subsequent purchaser.

All characters in this publication are fictitious and any resemblance to real persons, living or dead, is purely coincidental.

A CIP catalogue record for this title is available from the British Library

Paperback ISBN 978 1 399 70149 5
ebook ISBN 978 1 399 70150 1

Typeset in Plantin Light by Manipal Technologies Limited

Printed and bound in Great Britain by Clays Ltd, Elcograf S.p.A.

Hodder & Stoughton policy is to use papers that are natural, renewable and recyclable products and made from wood grown in sustainable forests. The logging and manufacturing processes are expected to conform to the environmental regulations of the country of origin.

Hodder & Stoughton Limited
Carmelite House
50 Victoria Embankment
London EC4Y 0DZ

www.hodder.co.uk

For Helen

ACKNOWLEDGEMENTS

The usual suspects have provided inestimable support in the writing of this book. My editor Carolyn exercised her usual exemplary patience in waiting for me to get on with it, and actually deliver a completed manuscript. My agent Sara was as encouraging as ever. And my wife Helen, without whom all things would be so much harder, was steadfast in making me get on with it, when a myriad of distractions continually enticed and blandished an author possessed of the attention span of a goldfish away from the path of discipline and delivery.

I am sincerely grateful to all concerned that you all so generously continue to facilitate the doings of the imaginary people whose lives seem so real inside the confines of my head – and hopefully in the imagination of the readers too. And on that note, thank you, dear readers, because there wouldn't be much point doing this without you.

And just to reassure those of you who write to wonder if there are any more in the series to come, please rest assured (or alternatively rend your garments and gnash your teeth), there are a good deal more stories about Marcus and his friends washing around in my head. I currently plan to continue into the end phase of Severus's war with Niger before heading off to the east to put the Parthians back in their place – after which there's the small matter of Clodius Albinus, a character from some of the earlier books, and a real life 'emperor', to be dealt with. So we could be here for a while yet.

THE
WAR IN ASIA

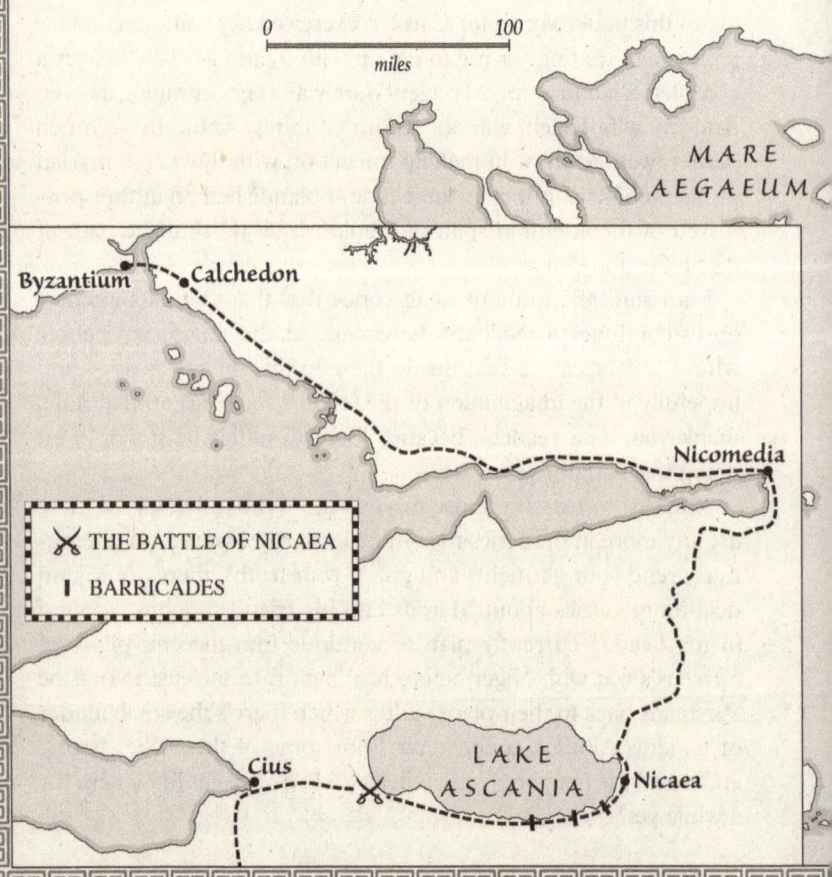

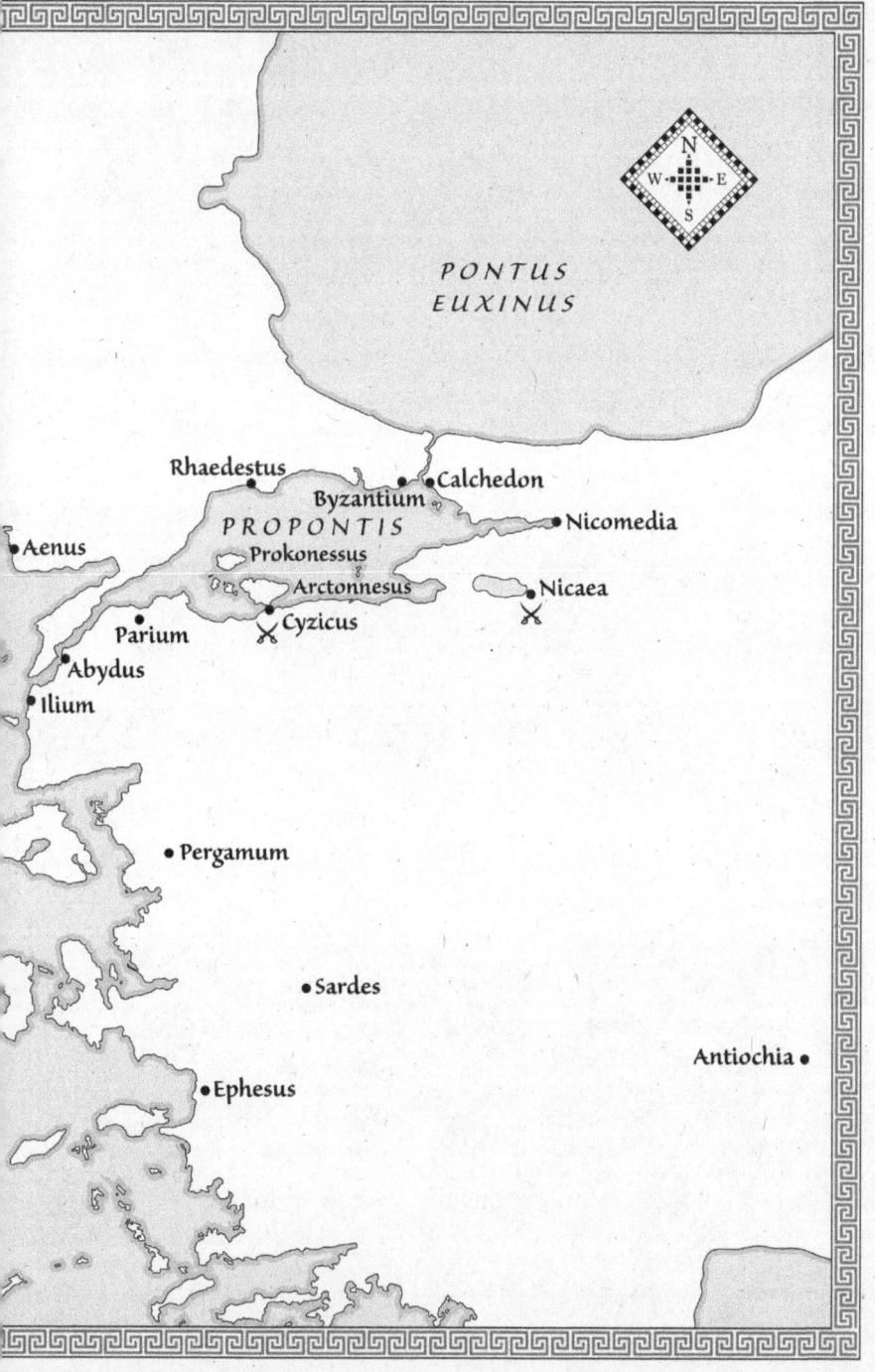

Prologue

Calchedon, Bithynia, September AD 193

'Gentlemen!'

The assembled officers of four imperial legions turned to face the entrance to the hall in which they had been called to gather, simultaneously coming to attention and waiting for the emperor's chief lictor to announce the arrival of their master. A heavily built former legion first spear, he and another eleven of his fellow officials accompanied the great man with great pomp and no little physicality at all times in public, carrying ceremonial axes wrapped in bundles of fasces – rods traditionally indicative of the emperor's power – as the symbol of their duty to maintain public order in the imperial presence, and prevent any risk to the safety of the empire's ruler. The man in question snapped to attention, a reflex from his legion days, barking a warning at the gathered officer in a tone of voice he might have hitherto used to bellow orders across parade grounds and battlefields.

'Imperator Caesar Gaius Pescennius Niger Justus Augustus! Rome's chosen man, and the one true ruler of the empire!'

Niger swept into the room through the doorway from an antechamber in which he had been waiting for his consilium to gather, the generals who had already gathered about his throne standing to attention as he took his seat. He had claimed imperium, for the eastern half of the empire at least, upon hearing news of the previous emperor Pertinax's brutal assassination by the praetorians in violation of their oath to protect him, and their subsequent shockingly brazen auctioning off of the throne's imperial power to a disappointingly inept highest bidder, Didius Julianus. The new and short-lived emperor, a hapless incompetent, had in turn been easy meat for Septimius Severus, the military strongman whose power base on the rivers Danubius and Rhenus had gifted him with sixteen legions at just the right time to take advantage of the resulting power vacuum.

Severus had been dressed in the ritual purple cloak by his soldiers almost immediately upon their receiving the news of Pertinax's death, and had, naturally with the required modest reluctance, declared his willingness to take on the burden of imperium only at their continued insistence. With that formality out of the way, what had followed had been a swift march on Rome with all the military strength that could be spared from frontier duties, the murder of Julianus in his palace by the new emperor's men and the straightforward strong-arming of the senate into ratifying his place on the throne under the watching eyes of his legions, whom he had marched into the city in defiance of all convention. It has been at much the same time that Niger had taken his own momentous step to claim the empire, having received the same momentous news of an imperial assassination and auction of the throne, and declared himself emperor in Antioch, the Syrian capital of everything Rome's boots bestrode east of Byzantium.

All of which made Niger, at least for the time being, the de facto master of half of the Roman empire. Emperor of everything east of the Pontus, the sea that separated Europa from Asia, and with six legions at his back, he was a worthy contender for the throne in Rome. But even such a powerful army paled by comparison with the force possessed by his opponent. Severus had seized command of every legionary and auxiliary soldier from the lengths of both the major rivers that ran across Europa, thereby claiming everything else in the empire other than the isolated and strategically unimportant island province of Britannia, which was held by a third contender for the throne, Clodius Albinus. Which meant that Niger, as all men present knew, almost certainly lacked the military power to extend his rule to the remainder of the lands possessed by

Rome, unless he was willing to gamble on the great bloodshed of a successful war fought against the odds or was blessed by greater luck than had been the case in the preceding months.

'He looks dreadful.'

Asellius Aemilianus nodded at his neighbour's whispered comment as he watched the master of their world take his seat on the throne that was waiting for him. Recently the former governor of Syria, Aemilianus had been the proconsul of Asia until the death of Commodus, the increasingly unhinged emperor who had ruled for thirteen years until the reputedly dubious bath-house incident that had seen the ill-starred Pertinax ascend to and briefly hold power at the beginning of the year. Aemilianus and the emperor had recently returned from the province of Thracia, where the first battle of the campaign against Severus's army had, rumours had it, ended inauspiciously. The shadows under Niger's eyes spoke clearly as to the pressure that he was under, in the wake of what was being described, in whispered conversations around his court, as having been much worse than the mild setback that his closest allies were attempting to call it. Aemilianus, having actually been present on the battlefield at a critical moment which had rocked Niger's army back on its heels with its sheer and unarguably symbolic power, privately considered it to have been little better than a full-fledged disaster. He replied to the man next to him, keeping his voice equally low to avoid being overheard being in any way disloyal to their master.

'We fought a battle at Rhaedestus, on the coast of Thracia. And *certain* people close to the throne' – he tipped his head to indicate the former frumentarius Sartorius, who was standing behind the seat in question – 'told us that it could only result in the swift and efficient destruction of a single enemy legion sent to the province by sea as Severus's strategic gamble. He promised Niger an easy victory to blood the troops, and to get the wheels of our campaign turning. Instead of which we were forced into a bloody and attritional fight under the less-than-ideal circumstances of being forced to attack a determined and forewarned enemy.'

He shot Niger a glance, and seeing that the emperor was still composing himself and arranging his garments, ventured a little more information.

'It ended not with the inevitable collapse of a single, outnumbered enemy legion, as had been the promise, but by an apparent intervention by the gods in support of Severus. It was beyond shocking, colleague, a blow to the gut from which he is still to recover.'

Even two weeks after the battle, Aemilianus still shuddered inwardly at the memory of the moment that had rocked both his master and his legions to the core. Added to which, Niger, as Aemilianus knew all too well, had learned of unhappy personal news, tidings of the worst possible kind with regard to his family, from the officers of the legion that had opposed them. The information that his children were held prisoner by Severus had been imparted to him in a battlefield negotiation, and only moments before the divine intervention that had forced him to allow the enemy general to leave with his men's honour intact and their weapons unforfeited, where the minimum he had hoped for was to send them away in defeat and having sworn to take no further part in the war.

The emperor gestured to his chief strategist, the former grain officer he had promoted for the man's known guile and cunning as demonstrated in his role as a member of the feared imperial frumentarii, and whose plan had led them to the brink of victory only for that triumph to turn to ashes in the blink of an eagle's eye.

'Very well, Sartorius, you say you have a plan for the next stage of this war. Let's hope it ends more successfully than the last one did.'

The man in question bowed deeply before replying in his usual level tone.

'As you say, Imperator . . .'

To the watching officers it seemed as if a shadow had fallen across Sartorius's face, if only momentarily, and Aemilianus recognised the look that momentarily clouded his colleague's expression, largely because it was founded on a set of emotions that he too was prey to in the wake of the disastrous battle. Emotions to which he suspected the emperor was equally susceptible, after such a blow to his cause. Put simply, he could see all too clearly that the former grain officer regarded what had effectively been a defeat at Rhaedestus as being much less a military setback, and far more about the gods' apparent lack of favour for his master. Although, like Aemilianus himself, he was far too wise to say anything so likely to see him dragged away and either imprisoned as a traitor or more likely executed.

'Gentlemen, your attention to the map, if you will.'

Sartorius took a pointer, and indicated the central point of the map of Asia and Thracia that he had had painted on the consilium chamber's wall.

'This, gentleman, is the strategically vital city of Byzantium, across the strait from here. It controls the Bosporus, the narrows that are the easiest place to cross the Pontus, which makes it the most likely point for an enemy army to make an entry to Asia via our province of Bithynia.'

And, Aemilianus thought, it is currently besieged by Severus's legions from Moesia. A siege which Niger's legions had no means of lifting given the withdrawal of the army from Thracia, to avoid the risk of their being pinned against the coast and destroyed by the superior strength of Severus's fast-approaching army.

Sartorius continued.

'Yes, we have chosen to withdraw across the narrows in order to deny the enemy the temporary advantage of their greater numbers, but the garrison of the city is well supplied, and its walls are thick, and deeply founded. Byzantium can and will hold in the face of an enemy siege for months, perhaps years. And while the pretender Severus is preoccupied with taking it, we will have the opportunity to regain the initiative and strike at him where he least expects it.'

Aemilianus frowned at what he suspected the former frumentarius might be about to propose.

'You propose for us to recross the Pontus and fight in Thracia again, Sartorius?'

'Not immediately, Legatus Augustus.'

The strategist's tone in answering the question was respectful, Sartorius recognising the general's strong influence over the emperor and knowing that, with his own children held hostage by Severus alongside those of Niger, the highly influential senator was a man whose world was crumbling around him, and who had little more to lose. All of which would make him a dangerous enemy in the imperial court's scheming environment, at least in the short term. He continued in the same measured tone.

'We plan instead to the use the time we have to regather our strength, to recruit from the local population in order to bring the legions to their full strength, and generally ready ourselves to retake the offensive. Which we will achieve either by crossing to the Thracian side of the sea – when the time is right – or simply by baiting a trap and awaiting the moment when our enemy blunders into it.'

Aemilianus nodded, recognising that, despite the failure of his previous plan, the former grain officer was right.

'I concur. We need to see just how the usurper Severus plans to crack the nut that Byzantium represents, and rebuild our strength so that we can attack at the moment of his maximum vulnerability. But tell me, Sartorius, how exactly is it that you will know when the enemy is ready to either strike or be struck, and where they will plan to land the blow?'

The master spy pointed at the map behind him, drawing their attention to the Propontis, the sea that separated the eastern and western halves of the empire to the south-east of the Bosporus's narrow channel.

'Before we pushed forward into Thracia, I spent time carefully preparing a network of men who are loyal only to our master, former soldiers for the most part and with one of my former colleagues to lead them. I intended them to be the backbone of an intelligence operation, to discover our enemy's intentions for the next steps in this war, should we find ourselves temporarily excluded from Thracia and facing the enemy across the Propontis. They are trustworthy men, dedicated to—'

'You prepared for us to *fail* in Thracia?'

Sartorius turned an unreadable expression on the legion commander who had asked the question.

'I acknowledged the *potential* for us to end up needing to prevent an enemy from crossing the Propontis successfully, Legatus. A potential need which I discussed with the emperor, who deemed such preparation to be prudent.'

Niger nodded, waving a dismissive hand at the senatorial officer.

'Continue, Sartorius. I am grateful that at least one of my senior officers has exercised some forethought.'

The former frumentarius kept his face carefully composed, avoiding eye contact with the red-faced legion commander.

'Thank you, Imperator. As I say, my informers are trustworthy men whom I have known for years, dedicated to the emperor and well rewarded for their service, and whose families are the surety of their loyalty. And now that my preparations prove to have been a wide precaution, they will enable us to place spies inside the enemy camp, military men who—'

The same legatus, irritated by his earlier put down, bridled at the spymaster's words.

'You have made *informers* of soldiers? Reduced men from a noble calling to be no better than the basest of gutter-dwelling liars?'

Sartorius raised a tired eyebrow.

'I make *informers* of whoever I find is willing, colleague. And these centurions, when called to a new and challenging duty, were eager to serve their emperor in any way that they could.' He waited for any response, but the senior officer, faced with an unrepentant Sartorius and a clearly irritated emperor behind him, nodded with a show of acceptance, and the spymaster continued. 'They are now being sent across the narrow sea, and once they are in position they will watch and wait, feeding critical information back to us by a means that the enemy will never be able to detect, much less prevent. What information, you might ask? The answer is that it will be impossible for Severus to move his legions into Asia at the obvious point, across the Bosporus, because Byzantium dominates the narrows where such a ferry operation might be easy, making any such attempted crossing by his legions vulnerable to a sally from the city. Instead, he will have to gather a naval force to cross elsewhere, and approach the task in a more careful and calculated manner. This will give us all the time we will need to be ready and waiting, should his men attempt to come ashore on the coast of Asia before the time is right for us to retake the offensive.'

Aemilianus nodded his understanding, shooting a glance at the emperor to find him still looking sullen and preoccupied. As well he might, the general mused, were he still pondering the fateful moment in which the actions of an innocent bird of prey had taken the realities of a finely poised battle and turned them upside down. He turned to the throne, speaking respectfully but with sufficient firmness for his counsel to be both unmistakable and heard with the appropriate respect.

'I believe that our colleague Sartorius has the right of it, Imperator. We must indeed rebuild the strength of our army, even at the risk of ceding the initiative to the usurper Severus and allowing him the next move. He has to cross the Pontus, and if he attempts to do so we will be waiting for his ships, forewarned by our spies on the other side of the sea. We will attack them even as they attempt to come ashore, sink their vessels and slaughter their men in the surf as they struggle to fight their way onto dry land! And with the usurper's claws pulled out, we will be able to go back on the offensive in Thracia, and rid the empire of the dangers of his false imperium for good!'

Niger stirred on his throne, raising his gaze to meet his most senior general's eyes and speaking in a near whisper that bespoke the horror of what he had learned from the enemy officers on the battlefield at Rhaedestus, when they had paused the fighting to negotiate the terms of an expected surrender that had never come to pass.

'He has our children, colleague. He has my *children*!'

Aemilianus nodded soberly, walking closer to the emperor in order to whisper in his ear.

'Indeed, he does, Imperator. And if that sad truth is enough to kick the legs out from under your reign, then I am bound to suggest that you would be as well to admit it to yourself, and to the rest of us, so that we might at least attempt to make our peace with Severus, rather than further antagonise him with continued resistance.' He stared levelly back into the other man's outrage, as the emperor swivelled his head to glare at him, speaking again before Niger's rage could boil over. 'And if that makes you want to have me executed, you have only to give the command and I will fall on my sword, here and now. If we lose this war then there can be no doubt that Severus will have me killed, if only to punish my disrespect in initially indicating that I might side with him before I eventually took my current position at your side. Either way I am a dead man, either at that time or here and now, but were I to take my own life he might just decide to spare my children, deeming them as being of no threat to him, since he will not have had to order my execution.'

Niger thought for a moment before making any response, visibly swallowing his anger as the reality of his general's predicament sank in. At length he spoke, pitching his voice to be heard by all in the room.

'My trusted and esteemed adviser Asellius Aemilianus makes an excellent point, gentlemen. We are committed to the path on which we have started out, no matter what obstacles we encounter or personal sacrifices we have to make. And so we must strive to our utmost in order to overcome this latest setback, and we will fight on in the knowledge that we can only be on the right side of events when the histories are written.'

He stood, putting a hand on the hilt of his sword for martial effect.

'I command you all to go about the task of bringing our army to the maximum possible strength. Recruit, resupply and train our legions, and make our men ready to stand toe to toe with Severus's army when they attempt to sully the shores of Asia with their boots. And you, Sartorius . . .'

The master spy turned to his emperor with an expectant expression.

'Imperator?'

'You failed to bring me victory at Rhaedestus largely as the result of the acts of one man.'

'That man being Gaius Rutilius Scaurus, Imperator?'

Niger grimaced at the memory of the hard-faced tribune's imperturbability when they had met on the battlefield, on blood-soaked ground stamped into ruin by the boots of the combatants and surrounded by the dead and dying men of both sides. His face hardened at the memory of Scaurus's absolute refusal to grant him the prize of his legion's surrender, an outcome that had seemed so inevitable at the start of the battle, and thereby buying time for the random act of a passing eagle to shatter Niger's legions' morale simply by dint of its random but heart-stopping choice of perch.

'Yes. *Scaurus*. Lucius Fabius Cilo would never have trained that legion of his to anything like the perfection of the men we faced, or positioned them as well or even inspired them to fight in so bestial a manner and for so long, without that young bastard's assistance. I curse the day that I met him in Dacia all those years ago. So, among your other preparations to disrupt our enemy's preparations to invade our provinces, you are to make sure that you find and capture Scaurus, and the equestrian Aquila who fights at his side. I want them both to be dealt with once and forever, and in as protracted and painful manner as possible. Let them learn just how unwise it is for any man to stand in the way of an emperor!'

I

Marching camp of the army of Septimius Severus, Roman province of Thracia, September AD 193

'Fourth Legion, halt!'

The first cohort in the column of marching men came to a slightly untidy stop, the rapping of the hobnails that remained on their badly worn boots dying away with a jumbled staccato rattle, rather than the precise massed stamp of what in a time of peace would have been hundreds of right feet. But then to be fair to the legion, Marcus Valerius Aquila mused, shooting his friend Dubnus, the Fourth's first spear a sympathetic glance, there were a good deal fewer than the usual five thousand men marching behind their eagle. Even more of a mitigation for such a poor showing of the expected military discipline was the fact that a good third of those who had survived the battle they had fought a fortnight before were still carrying wounds and injuries, disabilities that were likely to see them discharged from the service before their twenty-five years were fully served.

The Briton Dubnus, a heavily built bear of a centurion only recently promoted to legion first spear, after the death of the man under whom he had served for fifteen years, looked equally unlikely to seek out any miscreants to blame for his men's evident lack of polish. He turned and looked down the legion's sadly reduced line, as each successive cohort stopped marching in a similar display of exhaustion, a look of sadness crossing his face at the sight of so many men holding their tent-mates upright. Raising his voice to a parade ground roar he shouted a command at his brother officers standing at the head of each cohort.

'Stand at ease! If you need to fall out, do so with some decorum! Let's show these barrack room flowers what a legion that's seen off three times its strength is worth!'

The big man turned back to face the centurion of the guard who had walked out of the massive camp's eastern gate while he had been speaking, tilting his head back to look down his nose at the man in a way that Marcus knew often presaged trouble for the stare's unwitting recipient.

'You're the Fourth Legion, right?'

Marcus stepped forward, his fellow tribune Vibius Varus at his shoulder, the two men's rank evident in their bronze armour and gilded helmets, and pointedly waited for the centurion to salute him before replying.

'Yes, we are, Centurion. The Lucky Flavian Fourth, returned from battle victorious and in need of some rest and recuperation. Did you receive our message advising of our arrival, and advising that tents and food would be needed, and the necessary medical aid for five hundred wounded men be ready?'

The other man nodded, with the look of a man trying to work out how to best show obsequious respect to a superior he was about to disappoint.

'Yes Tribune, your camp is ready and waiting.'

'Very well, you may lead us to it. And while you're doing that, you can also send a runner to the medics and *remind* them about the message we sent ahead of us, and that we have *at least* five hundred men who will require their attentions.'

'Yes Tribune.'

The Fourth's legionaries straggled into the camp's sea of leather tents under the hard eyes of the men already encamped on either side of the Via Praetoria. The men watching them progress past their well-ordered sections of the marching camp were legionaries who had marched east from Rome and were yet to see battle, whereas the battered troops limping past them had been transported by sea to play the part of a regrettable but strategically necessary sacrifice. Marcus tapped the centurion on the arm, gesturing to the weary, hungry and wounded men straggling past them.

'Let me tell you, Centurion, how it is that my legion came to be in what I'm sure you've already decided is a "shit state". We were selected to disrupt the enemy army's preparations for war, by the device of our arriving unexpectedly in their rear by sea, with orders to attack them out of the blue and cause as much disruption as we could. Our legion was loaded onto a praetorian fleet in Misenum, near Vesuvius, and shipped all the way here as fast as an arrow from a bow by comparison with your leisurely march, then dropped off on a beach with orders no more detailed than to go and find the enemy. It was a plan that was always likely to end up with us fighting a desperate battle against overwhelming odds, and in fact it brought three of the enemy's legions down on us like wasps onto spilt honey. Three legions to our one, Centurion.'

The officer had the good grace to look embarrassed, but Marcus was already continuing.

'It was a strategic masterstroke by the emperor, of course, to disrupt their preparations so rudely, but you can probably guess the predictably heavy price that we paid to delay Niger's plans. We were only ever expected to suffer a bloody defeat, you see, a loss from which an honourable return, without our being forced to swear an oath to take no further part in the war, was probably considered an impossibility – albeit one we would be punished for, of course. But we didn't lose, and we weren't humiliated. We made Niger's legions swallow that humiliation instead. These men staggering into your well-organised camp, wounded and hungry, they were the victors, the heroes of a battle they had no right to win. And now, when we expect to receive some respect in return, I'm not really getting the feeling that there's any on offer.'

The centurion, clearly embarrassed, remained silent, and Marcus and Dubnus exchanged glances as they were led further through the temporary fortress. The Briton's look of puzzlement hardened as they approached the western gate and marched back out into open ground, where a line of carts loaded with leather tents awaited them.

'Here? We're expected to camp *here*?'

The officer of the watch had the good grace to look embarrassed at Marcus's question.

'Yes Tribune.'

'Men who took on three legions and emerged victorious are expected to camp *outside* the walls? As distant from the camp hospital, the supply tents and the river as it is possible to be, and yet in most need of all three? Is this some kind of joke?'

'I was ordered to—'

'It's all right, Centurion, we understand perfectly well what's happening here.'

The hapless officer came to attention again as two more officers approached from further down the column, realising from the finely tooled bronze armour and white linen cloak worn by the older of them that he was in the presence of the Fourth Legion's commander.

'Legatus sir, as I was telling your officers, the order for you to be placed here—'

Legatus Cilo raised a hand to silence him, sharing a look of dark amusement with the equally splendidly equipped younger man beside him before answering.

'We were half-expecting something of the sort, Centurion, and it really isn't important. You could go and enquire of the hospital when the medics will be making an appearance though? And intimate to the chief medicus that if I lose any of the men who have lived until now from the lack of care, then he will have made a powerful and dangerous enemy of a man who is likely to be commanding a good deal more imperial favour than you people might be expecting. Dismissed.'

'Sir! We will do what is ordered, and at every command we will be ready!'

The officer gratefully hurried away from their ire just as another, older officer came out of the camp gate and made his way over to them, saluting Cilo in a perfunctory manner and looking about him with a cold stare that told the newcomers exactly who it was that had made the decision to place their tents in such an ignominious position.

'Are you *gentlemen* the officers of the Fourth Legion?'

Cilo looked him up and down for a moment before responding, gesturing to his officers.

'Yes, we are. I am Lucius Fabius Cilo, and these are my tribunes, Rutilius Scaurus, Vibius Varus and Valerius Aquila. And you, I presume, are the camp prefect.'

'Indeed I am, serving under Legatus Augustus Laetus, and I bid you welcome to my camp, gentlemen. We—'

Scaurus, having shot a glance at Cilo and received a nod of encouragement, overrode the official with the ease of long-practised social superiority.

'Are we to presume that your appearance here so soon after our arrival is solely intended to allow you to bask in the pleasure of having placed us at the arse end of *your* camp, Prefect? Or is there some genuine if somewhat hard to discern purpose involved in this outrageous – and quite possibly dangerous, for you I mean – display of rank disrespect?'

'What? How dare you threaten me, I'm—'

Scaurus put a finger on the older man's chest, freezing him into silence with a shake of his head.

'Threaten you? I'm not threatening you, and if I were, my dagger wouldn't be in its sheath. I'm simply pointing out that the camp can be a dangerous place after dark, and you're just about to make a large number of enemies who are now not just trained to kill but proven as expert in their chosen profession.'

The older officer looked around to find Dubnus staring at him with an expression that combined menace and disdain, while Marcus's eyes seemed to look straight through him, as if his existence was of no importance to the man. He shrugged off the unnerving feeling, falling back on the feeling of superiority to be derived from the knowledge that Cilo and his officers would soon enough be on their way home in disgrace, or possibly worse, and addressed the older man directly.

'What I came for, Legatus, is to inform you that your presence is commanded by the emperor's staff, and immediately now that you have arrived. You should probably bring your tribunes with you, as I believe they are to be subjected to the same orders, once you have formally confirmed your failure to defeat the enemy.'

Much to his discomfort the legatus smiled, turning to walk back towards the gate without waiting to be shown the way and speaking over his shoulder as the camp prefect hurried to catch him up.

'You really ought to be more careful, Prefect. A man like you, only recently promoted from the plebeian ranks, is still somewhat vulnerable to the potential dislike of men of my class who are less tolerant of commoners getting above themselves than I am. You'll leap astride that high horse you like to ride and find that you're on your back on the beast's other side, and taking receipt of a painful kicking from its hoofs, if you're not careful.'

Unsure of what to say, given the thinly veiled nature of the threat, the prefect kept his mouth shut, and Cilo turned back to stare at him with unconcealed disdain.

'Of course, I'm hardly bothered by the fact that you've chosen to form a judgement without any knowledge of the *actual* events. Or that the outcome of a battle we fought has been misreported to the emperor by couriers bearing incorrect tidings of the battle we fought last week, for that matter. A battle in which many of our men died, or suffered grievous wounds in the name of the emperor and at his direct command, all of them doing their duty unto death or physical ruin. Because I know that when my old friend Severus hears the truth of it then men like you, who were swift to trumpet the false news of our defeat, will find themselves very much on the wrong side of the coin when it lands. But then it isn't me that you need to worry about. Is it? Now, since I presume the command tent will be in the usual place in this very much standard camp layout, you can leave us to it from here and go about your business.'

He turned away again, but the three tribunes were too quick for the prefect as he made to do as he was bidden. Marcus gripped him by the arm, while Scaurus leaned in close enough for the rank smell of his unwashed body to be obvious and their colleague Varus shook his head in disgust.

'You would be well advised to organise food, medical care and assistance in getting those tents up, Prefect. Because when the emperor hears what those men went through for him, and the way the gods showed their favour for their efforts, you're going to want to be on our good side. Mine *especially*.'

They pushed him away and followed the legatus into the camp. In the antechamber to the audience chamber their hard stares and rough, unwashed appearance discomfited the other officers waiting to be shown into the imperial presence, making them somewhat relieved when the staff officer who had vanished into the inner chamber with news of their arrival came back to fetch the four men.

'The emperor will see you now, gentlemen.'

The praetorian led them into the imperial encampment's innermost sanctum, Severus's most private domain other than for the royal family's living quarters, the throne room in which audiences were held and decisions were made. But if Cilo had been hoping for a private audience with the emperor his wishes had gone unanswered. The space around the throne was occupied by several men clad in gleaming ceremonial armour over pristine white tunics, all of whom turned to regard the four newcomers with the less than friendly demeanours of competitors who saw an opportunity to gain an advantage for themselves.

'Fabius Cilo.'

Septimius Severus's tone of voice was no more encouraging than the expressions on the faces of his generals.

'Imperator!'

All four men bowed deeply, and waited to be summoned from the extended gesture of obeisance they had been advised by the praetorian was now expected from all men who came before the emperor. After a moment's pause Severus spoke again, his voice no less acerbic.

'Very well, Lucius, perhaps you should elucidate for me as to how it is you have returned with less than half the strength of the legion that Rome entrusted to your command. I should warn you that the news that you found it expedient to surrender to Niger's army, rather than fight to the death, has beaten you here by several days.'

The emperor sat back in his wooden chair with an expectant expression, waiting for the legatus to speak, and Cilo, having been very clear with the two younger men that he would be the one doing the talking, remained silent while he took a calculated moment to reply. Too fast an answer would appear desperate, while being too slow to answer would risk the appearance of impudence with the one man in their world whose response to such an insult could be immediately fatal. Just as Marcus was sure the emperor was on the edge of asking the question again, and in a less controlled manner, Cilo spoke in a calm and measured tone.

'As to why the news – or at least the *purported* news – of the battle beat us here, Imperator, the answer is simple enough. The usurper Niger has horses to spread his lies, while we had none to carry our truth, due the nature of our swift deployment to Thracia from Italy by the praetorian fleet. Added to which, we have marched a hundred and fifty miles with a quarter of our remaining number wounded, without very much by way of food after the first two days, other than what we could forage, and without any certain knowledge of where your army was to be found.'

Severus nodded noncommittally, which Cilo took as his cue to continue.

'You will recall, Imperator, that the stated objective of our mission to the east was to confront the usurper Niger with an attack into that part of the territory he has occupied in Thracia. It was to be an audacious stroke of strategy, sending a legion by sea and landing it behind the enemy army to sow confusion in their ranks, and in the usurper's mind to boot. And in that objective, Imperator, you have succeeded in more ways than you might have intended.'

He fell silent and waited for Severus to consider his words, perhaps hoping that the emperor's curiosity to know how his gamble in effectively sacrificing a legion had paid off would outweigh any irritation at having to enquire as to how. The response, when it came after a longer pause than Cilo might have desired, was crisply acerbic.

'So I am more successful than I had hoped for, even though my legion was battered half to death and left to limp back to camp, was I? How so?'

Cilo, recognising that he was at risk of needlessly irritating the emperor, answered in a brisk, matter-of-fact manner.

'We were landed by the praetorian fleet at the port of Aenus, Imperator, and made our way from there towards our objective, Byzantium, by means of tracks through the country rather than the main road, the Via Egnatia. We hoped to avoid detection, and thus to fall on the enemy unexpectedly. But our approach was most assuredly not unexpected.'

Severus leaned forward, his face darkening and his game of verbal cat and mouse with Cilo forgotten.

'You believe that your mission was *betrayed*?'

Cilo shook his head.

'As to whether the usurper had advance knowledge of our orders, Imperator, I am unable to speculate. What did become clear, whether it was the result of betrayal or effective intelligence work on their part, was that we were clearly expected to land on the Thracian coast. One of our officers was ambushed in the port of Thessalonika when he went ashore for information with which to scout for a beach to land on, in an abduction attempt led by the man who seems to have the role of being Niger's spymaster ... his chief *informer*, if you will.'

He allowed a moment for the most distasteful term possible for the role played by Sartorius in the attack to sink in and then continued.

'This clearly shows us that Niger's officers had worked out that our attack was likely, and were on the lookout for our fleet.

Although the usurper gave no hint that he was possessed of any such intelligence from Rome, when we met him on the battlefield.'

Marcus smiled inwardly, guessing exactly how the emperor would react to his general's words. Severus started forward in his chair, locking a direct stare on Cilo.

'You *met* with Niger?'

'Yes, Imperator, we did.'

Severus's eyes narrowed, and the thinness of the ice that the legatus had walked onto, deliberately or not, became evident as the generals standing around his throne held their breath in expectation of an outburst. The emperor, however, simply asked a question, his voice pitched softly but with unmistakable threat.

'Explain this meeting to me, Fabius Cilo. How did you come to be in conversation with our greatest enemy?'

The legatus smiled sadly.

'It was a day that was both bitter and sweet, Imperator. We had been ambushed by three enemy legions in our approach to the city of Rhaedestus . . .' He paused for a moment, allowing the size of the disparity in fighting strengths that his legion had faced to sink in with the men around the throne, then resumed his account in the manner he had warned his colleagues to expect. 'Which means, Imperator, that your plan had worked to perfection, does it not? To throw confusion into the mind of the enemy, and to distract his forces from their main objectives, even if purchased at the risk of losing a legion? That *was* your intention?'

The emperor looked up at him for a long moment before answering, perhaps weighing his general's words for any hint of frustration or anger. At length he answered, but not before flicking glances at the three men behind Cilo in search of any sign of dissent.

'Indeed, it seems to have done so. Three legions, you say, and led by Niger himself?'

'Yes, Imperator, or at least the strongest possible vexillations from all three. The Third Gauls, the Sixth Ironclad and the Twelfth Thunderbolt. Over twelve thousand men.'

'And did you have the time to prepare defensive positions?'

One of the emperor's generals, Julius Laetus, a man known to Marcus and Scaurus, had interjected without asking Severus's permission, but if the emperor was irritated he managed not to show it. Cilo shook his head.

'No, colleague, we did not. We were in our approach march to the city when tribune Aquila here detected their presence, waiting in ambush, doing so by dint of his cunning and courage and without himself being detected. We barely had the time to assume a hasty defence at the edge of the road and with the olive grove at our backs before they came at us. So no, we were not afforded the time needed to dig out a ditch, or to build a defensive wall with the cut turves, before they were upon us.'

Severus elbowed his way back into the discussion, with a warning glance at Laetus that Marcus decided the general would do well to pay heed to.

'So, you were ambushed on the march and still managed to survive an attack by three times your own strength. And better yet, to leave the battlefield with your weapons and armour, from what I am told about the state of what's left of your legion as it made its way through the camp. There were *conditions* attached to such a fortuitous turn of events, I presume?'

The men standing around the throne went very still, all eager to hear the words that they expected would see Cilo lose either his command or his life. Affecting not to understand, he answered the question with one of his own.

'Conditions, Imperator?'

Laetus almost shouted his reply to the question, beating his master to the punch.

'The emperor wants to know what oath you were forced to swear to be allowed to leave the battlefield with you swords! What did you promise Niger, to escape with your lives!'

Cilo answered the impatient question in a tone that by contrast was purely conversational.

'You might do well, Julius, not to judge every man by your own yardstick. There is a reason that we returned from this strategic masterstroke of the emperor's with less than half the men we sailed with, which is the fanatical resistance that the outstanding men of my Lucky Flavian Fourth put up against such overwhelming odds. Your men, Imperator, fought like wild animals in *your* name, and saw off three times their own number. It was a slaughterhouse the likes of which I pray I never see between soldiers of Rome again, and when the usurper realised he could not win he sent his spy Sartorius to negotiate instead in the hope of saving both his fighting strength and his dignity. Twice his messenger entreated us to swear not to fight in this war again, and twice we declined, suggesting he might instead tell Niger that his army's losses were disproportionate to our own, and that it was him that needed to escape the battle to preserve his strength, not us. Neither side would back down, it seemed, and we therefore prepared to sell our lives in our emperor's name.'

He paused, nodding as if at the memory of the battle's horror, and his pride in his men.

'But the third time it was Niger himself came to talk, and with the nerve to parade his legion standards in front of him as if he had already won the battle and it was all over but for the burial of the dead and our submission to his terms. Which was of course a challenge that we met with our own eagle. We discussed matters between us for a while, the usurper and I, without reaching any agreement. And then, when it was clear that neither side could back down with any honour, and it looked as if we'd be fighting to the death, a real eagle flew down, ignored Niger's shouts that it was a sign from the gods in his favour, and landed on our standard instead of any of their three! Better still, when the usurper tried to make it fly away, it simply called out in defiance and defecated on our standard-bearer's shoulder.'

Emperor and generals alike were now staring at him in amazement.

'By all the gods! You have witnesses to this' – Severus savoured the word with all the pleasure of a drinker tasting a fine wine – '*omen?*'

Cilo nodded at Severus.

'Over two thousand of them, Imperator, the legionaries of your own Lucky Flavian Fourth. Plus, of course, all the legionaries of Niger's army who know the truth of it. And who will tell that truth when their so-called emperor is nothing more than a memory and some disparaging lines in the history books. It was the strongest of omens, straight from the gods. And the gods, Imperator, favoured *you*!'

Marcus watched in carefully concealed amusement, as the men around Severus's throne realised that their rival had just stepped out of the hole in which circumstances seemed to have dumped him, and was probably about to be hoisted up onto a pedestal by the man who had been deliberating whether to execute him only a moment before.

'By *all* the gods . . .' Severus's voice had fallen to a whisper. 'A sign of such unmistakable power must have shaken the poor fool to his very being.' He pondered for a moment. 'Lucius Fabius Cilo, you truly are a worthy *comes imperator*! My dear friend! I had hoped that your legion would manage to inflict some delay and uncertainly on Niger's army by appearing unexpectedly in their rear, but in successfully predicting my roll of the dice he opened himself up to the judgment of the gods, and their disdain for his hubris in taking up arms against the true master of Rome has been stated for all to see! And in your steadfast and loyal refusal to consider any form of surrender, you have persuaded the masters of our fates to show their favour! Do you not agree, gentlemen?'

He looked around at the army's generals, who were swift to voice their agreement and congratulation of their esteemed colleague, compliments which went unheard as the emperor turned back to the four men before him.

'Such a result demands a reward, I believe.'

Cilo inclined his head fractionally.

'My reward, Imperator, lies solely in the joyous memory of that moment when the eagle alighted on our solitary standard. But my fate was ever yours to command.'

Severus smiled indulgently, although to Marcus's eye there was a hint of calculation in his outwardly effusive praise.

'And yet your fate must be lauded in Rome for your deeds, Lucius. You will return to the city with a strong escort of my praetorians to keep you safe from any brigandage, and when you reach Rome you will report on the progress of the war to the senate, sparing no details as to the divine omen you were privileged to witness. You can tell the city fathers that I will be celebrating a full triumph on my return, one for each and every battle that we win and most certainly one for this momentous event! You can also take counsel with those of the senate you consider to be *our* friends, and determine the depth of their regard for their emperor now that he is far from the city. And, perhaps, you might choose to counsel them as to my likely reaction to any lingering temptation to disloyalty. Serve me well in this matter and I am minded to request your service further in the governance of one of my richer provinces, once this matter of the usurper is dealt with.'

Cilo bowed deeply, keeping his expression carefully neutral as he replied.

'It would be my greatest honour to do as you command, Imperator. And in return, I ask only for some small favour for my men.'

'For my glorious legionaries of the Fourth Legion, whose steadfast resistance led to such a powerful gesture of the gods' favour? For those men there is no request within my power to grant that is too great! Lucius, you have only to ask.'

Cilo gestured a hand at the camp beyond the tent's walls.

'The men who fought to afford you this victory are currently camped outside of the walls, Imperator, unprotected by any rampart. A third of those who survived the battle and the ten-day march here are wounded, but they were without any medical care when we left them to brief you. This is shabby treatment, when the height of their valour in your name is considered.'

Laetus's face darkened, as he realised the mistake he had made in ordering the Fourth to be quartered in so ignominious a location. Severus shook his head in a carefully confected display of surprise.

'My heroic legion has been quartered *outside* the camp?'

'Yes, Imperator. It seems hardly fitting for the most experienced and successful legion in the army, given their demonstrated devotion to you.'

Severus nodded briskly.

'I agree! Laetus, have them moved to the most prestigious position immediately. They can dwell next to my own guard, until the time comes to move on, and others can move to make space for their tents, and raise their own turf wall to defend the camp's extension. Further, every medicus in the army is to labour night and day until every wounded man has been treated, and they are to be supplied with rations and wine sufficient to restore their spirits and enable them to celebrate their victory. Make this happen immediately, Julius, and do not take the risk that I will not visit our new arrivals soon enough to raise a cup of wine to their heroic performance, because if I find anything not to my liking I will know where to place the responsibility!'

He watched in amusement as the discomfited general hurried to do his bidding, then turned his regard on Cilo and the men behind him.

'And now, with that wrong put right, let us turn our consideration to the matter of the Fourth Legion's command, now that my good friend Lucius is leaving us for Rome . . . and, of course, how to reward those men who were most instrumental in such a signal from the gods as to the legitimacy of my rule.'

'So, what did the big man say? And where's your young aristo friend who insisted on coming to war with us, despite knowing that all you two can ever achieve is to find the biggest fight to be had and pitch us right into the middle of it?'

Dubnus was warming his feet by the warmth of a camp fire in the cool of an autumn evening when Scaurus and Marcus found the Fourth Legion's new place at the heart of the sprawling camp, the latter carrying a saddlebag that was clearly laden with significant weight. Cilo had bidden them both a good evening and gone off to find his fellow officers of the senatorial class, presumably to receive their congratulations on his successes in battle and the resulting politics and to exchange news and gossip over whatever would pass for dinner in the temporary camp, and had taken a still reeling Varus with him to effect the appropriate introductions. The Briton's bear-like frame was dressed in a freshly washed tunic, his skin's pores clean of the last two weeks' accumulation of mud and blood, and his armour had been placed in the care of Khabour, the eastern slave he had purchased from a farmer at the roadside during their march, as a symbol of his newly elevated role in life as a newly promoted legion first spear. The Thracian was sitting in the tent's doorway, working with the frayed end of a softwood twig to scrape the ubiquitous and faintly disgusting mix of hard baked mud and blood from the most difficult crannies of his new master's *lorica squamata*, the armoured shirt whose thumbnail-sized iron plates overlapped each other to protect the wearer from the sharp-edged blades of swords and spears.

The young Briton Lupus, barely out of his boyhood but already highly skilled with a sword, was sitting beside him with a blue sharpening stone, carefully polishing a fearsome edge into the centurion's gladius. Self-appointed as Marcus and Scaurus's bodyguard after the death of the latter's former slave Arminius, his hard eyed presence at their backs was something to which both men were still getting accustomed after the German's somewhat more relaxed if still vigilant attitude to their protection.

Marcus and Scaurus exchanged glances, the older man leaving his friend to explain their suddenly revised circumstances and walking into his tent, already unknotting the linen strip that held his bronze cuirass in place. Marcus took a seat at the fire and warmed his hands for a moment before answering.

'There's no easy way to tell you the news. The emperor has decided that the Fourth Legion's standard-bearer should be promoted into your current role, for having the nous not to move a muscle when "that forever blessed eagle" perched on his standard, making him in turn the equally blessed recipient of its message from the gods when it defecated on him. He also said that the man should be given a golden *vitis* as well. He really was in a *very* generous mood once he understood what had happened.'

The big Briton stared up at Marcus in disbelief.

'You're joking.'

The Roman shook his head wearily.

'No, I'm really not. We did manage to convince the master of the world that a vine stick made of gold would be next to useless, being too soft to take to an armoured legionary's back, but he was immovable on promoting the man into Julius's boots.'

'But . . .'

The Roman shrugged.

'I know, the man's not even fit to be a centurion, never mind *the* centurion, but the whims of an emperor are not to be gainsaid. And what you have to bear in mind is that the eagle which landed on our standard not only put the fear of the gods into Niger, and enabled us to walk away from the battlefield on which he had us pinned, but in doing so also made the emperor as happy as a dog with the proverbial pair of phalluses. It's exactly the sort of thing that can convince one man that he cannot lose, and his opponent that he cannot win. And, given that it enabled us to avoid either having to fight to the death or being executed for not being able to beat three times our own number had we escaped the battlefield, I'm somewhat inclined to share that joy he's feeling.'

Dubnus grunted morosely.

'None of which changes the fact that I woke up as the most powerful centurion in the legion and will go to my bed as . . .' He looked across at Marcus in disgust. 'Well, as what? As a centurion? As a citizen? As a man who may not even be able to afford to feed my slave?' Khabour looked up at him, shook his head minutely and returned his attention to the mail shirt while his master continued. 'So, tell me, what will we be doing to earn our gold, if not shouting at all the new recruits this tattered remnant of a legion is going to need to put itself back into the field? Or are we being thrown into yet another collection of thieves and half-wits that's been allowed to go soft and needs beating into shape? And what's in that saddlebag the tribune was carrying?'

Scaurus walked out of his tent, having divested himself of his armour, washed his face and changed his sweat stained tunic for a clean garment.

'The quick answer to that last question is gold, and plenty of it, with which to grease the wheels of our next task if so needed. But before we speak of that, am I right in thinking that you're not sure what would be worse, actually being the anonymous citizen you longed to be only a few months ago, or being expected to whip yet another legion into shape, prior to risking your life in yet another battle for a cause you really don't care about. Is that the size of it?'

Dubnus shrugged at the head of their familia, respectful but long familiar with the spirit of open and vigorous discussion Scaurus liked to encourage.

'What would I like to do next, Tribune? I'd just like to feel like I have control of my own life, at least to some degree. The way I was feeling until a moment ago, as it happens, and not forgetting that the money that a first spear gets paid is more than generous. So hopefully you've been directed to do something I will find a bit less risky but equally well rewarded?'

'Ah . . .' The tribune smiled at him sardonically. 'You're taking the Morban approach to life, are you? Nothing matters unless you're being paid.' The faintest hint of a murmured protest reached his ear, and he shot Dubnus's tent a knowing glance. 'And yes, Morban, I was fully expectant that you'd be hiding in there, hoping to glean some useful information with which to construct a wager that will once again empty the purses of your companions. Which is why I'm not telling the centurion here the answer to his questions until I know you're no longer listening! Your skills with turning inside information into gold won't be getting any unwitting help from me this time! Come along, on your way!'

After a moment a short and rotund man in his sixth decade pushed his way out of the tent and walked away, muttering to himself in a distinctly unhappy manner. Scaurus waited for a moment, then called out again, his tone a little less forgiving than before.

'And *you*, Sanga. It doesn't need a genius to work out that where your partner in crime is lurking you won't be far away.'

A second man, perhaps ten years younger than the former standard-bearer and very much active oddsmaker Morban exited the tent, his complaints less muted than had been the case with his older comrade.

'A man can't even innocently volunteer to help clean a much-respected officer's armour?'

Dubnus shook his head in disgust.

'You were no more cleaning my armour than I am! Obviously, I had no idea they were there, Tribune. You'd think that my new slave would have made some comment.'

Khabour looked up for a moment and then bent back over the armour that he was painstakingly cleaning, speaking quietly but distinctly.

'When you have been a slave your entire life, Master, you learn to see and hear as little as possible. As long as they were not stealing from you, I saw no reason to make enemies.'

Scaurus nodded at the man.

'He has a point, Dubnus. Our colleagues are all new to him, and the safest way to deal with that unfamiliarity is to keep himself to himself until he knows who is who in our world. Do we have any wine left, or has Sanga managed to gain access to my tent as well as yours?'

Dubnus laughed tersely.

'I saw that potential disappearance coming a mile away, so I asked Lupus to keep an eye on it, in return for a fair measure when we came to finish what's left from last night. Would you do the honours, Lupus?'

The young Briton nodded, fetching a jug and a handful of wooden cups from the tribune's tent and pouring each of them a measure. Scaurus took a drink, winced at the wine's bite and then raised his cup in salute.

'Thank you, Lupus, well guarded. You seem to have avoided the worst traits of your grandfather; no insult intended.'

The young Briton shook his head.

'And none taken, Tribune. Morban can be a good man on occasion. Indeed, he can sometimes almost be the father I lost ten years ago. It's just the *daimon* that overcomes him whenever the opportunity to take money from other men's' purses presents itself that can make him so irritating.'

Scaurus acknowledged the point with a nod.

'Could you perhaps go and find Centurion Qadir for me? I'd prefer to recount the tale of our meeting with the emperor just the once.'

Lupus agreed good naturedly and walked away, and the tribune sat back to enjoy the fire's warmth for a moment.

'He's a good man, and a testament to all that training you and Arminius invested in him over the years, Marcus, but I still miss Arminius most of all at times like these, to unlace my armour and jibe at me until I realised that I am far from the most important man in the world.' He sighed. 'But I find the idea of taking a new slave on quite demoralising. How is your man Khabour working out, Centurion?'

'I do have ears and a tongue, Tribune sir, if you will permit me to have an opinion.'

Ignoring his master's outraged stare the Thracian got to his feet and bowed, and Scaurus waved away Dubnus's irritation.

'Allow the man his say, Centurion. It was the key to a long and usually harmonious relationship with my own slave.'

Khabour bowed again.

'And it is my opinion that I am doing very well, thank you, Tribune. I am very happy with my new master, who shows no inclination to beat me for imagined offences, and who provides adequate food and shares his wine with me . . . on occasion.'

All three men stared at him in surprise, then Dubnus guffawed with amusement, then waved a hand to Marcus.

'Give him a cup, he's earned it if only for his nerve. And how's he working out? You can see for yourself! If I had known what sort of a man he was I might have chosen differently. The man who sold him to me said he was quiet and respectful in nature, instead of which he does nothing but comment on everything he sees, and share his opinions with anyone who'll listen. Already he seems to be a kindred spirit with the Sparrow, and I've seen the two of them consorting with that other dangerous intellectual Lugos, talking about book stuff and other nonsense.'

'Speaking of whom . . .'

Lupus walked back into the firelight with the Hamian centurion Qadir, the diminutive Aegyptian scholar Ptolemy and his constant companion the giant Lugos close behind them.

'You requested my presence, Tribune?'

Scaurus cocked a wry eyebrow at Ptolemy and Lugos.

'I did. I didn't expect that you would be quite so closely shadowed by these two, but I suppose their curiosity is innocent and can be forgiven, this once, as long as they guarantee not to let Morban and his sidekick into the news I am about to impart to you.'

Both men promptly and a little indignantly vouchsafed their silence, the Aegyptian Ptolemy in the usual piping tones that had led Dubnus to give him his avian nickname, while Lugos's promise was a bass rumble by comparison. Scaurus nodded.

'Very well. Once the facts of the matter had been clearly communicated, that we did not surrender or give any oath to refrain from fighting on in this campaign, the emperor was somewhat mollified.'

Lugos leaned over and spoke in a rumbling stage whisper in Dubnus's ear.

'This means happy.'

The Briton's answer was as indignant as always when his giant compatriot sought to needle him from his relatively newly minted intellectual standpoint.

'I *know* what it—'

Scaurus ignored them and kept talking.

'Whereas the news of the eagle landing on our standard positively delighted him. With the result that legatus Cilo is declared a Roman hero, and has been sent home to give the senate the good news about the opening battle of the campaign being a resounding success, at least when measured in eagle shit sent by the gods to fall on an aquilifer's shoulder. His replacement in command of the Fourth will be our friend Vibius Varus, who is currently sitting at a table with his fellow legati and wondering what on earth he's doing there. And we, gentlemen, since we're deemed to be not entirely useless, will be moving on to a fresh task. Which means that the Lucky Fourth not only gets a new legatus, but also a new broad stripe tribune and a fresh first spear. May the gods preserve them from the dubious capability of the latter.'

Dubnus pulled a face at the confirmation that his new and elevated rank wasn't permanent.

'I just hope that young Varus has the nous to work out that his new senior centurion is an oaf.' He shrugged. 'So, where are we going then? And why do you have enough gold that you need a saddlebag to carry it in, rather than a purse?'

Marcus smiled.

'There's good news and not so good news. You know how much you like riding, and travel by sea . . . ?'

'So we are heading for the coast again, right?'

Dubnus raised an eyebrow at Morban, who was mounted alongside him, then called out to Scaurus, who was riding in front of them with Marcus. The remainder of the familia were strung out along the road in pairs, Qadir's Hamian archers for the most part on the smaller of the beasts that had been provided, the centurion riding alongside Khabour and conversing in their own language, while Dubnus's heavily built pioneers were mounted on more heavily built horses bred to pull heavy supply carts and artillery pieces. The Via Egnatia's long ribbon of cobbles stretched out into the distance before them in the usual straight line that was the hallmark of the army's construction methods, the grove on either side cut back to provide a wide strip of open land to prevent the risk of ambush, while the now familiar monoculture of carefully tended olive trees provided the backdrop to the road's stark intrusion.

'Tribune, civilian here is asking where it is that we're going. *Again*.'

After breakfasting they had packed up their gear and tents, requisitioned the horses required for their new orders from the military units around them, taking care not to wield the emperor's warrant to do so too heavily with any one senior officer, and made their farewells with their still baffled comrade Varus.

'It should have been you.'

Scaurus had laughed softly at the younger man's discomfiture.

'I think what you meant to say was "it should have been you, *Gaius*". Now that you're a legatus you must treat less exalted officers with that careful mix of familiarity and seniority. Can you see my point, *Legatus*?'

'But . . .'

'Never mind *but*, just focus on doing your job and putting the Fourth back on its feet before they have to fight again. You'll need replacement legionaries, at least a thousand of them and ideally a good deal more, and your men will need boots, hobnails, tunics, cloaks, spades, spears and a dozen other items that the quartermaster will fight tooth and nail not to provide you with. I wish we could stay long enough to help you disabuse him of the idea, but we have our orders.'

Varus had smiled wanly at the daunting task he was still coming to terms with.

'And here's me, the black sheep of the family, obviously destined never to rise above the rank of tribune for my wilful stupidity in insisting on following you both to war, rather than taking the position that was offered to me in Rome, now in the position of doing battle for new swords and shields . . . for my *legion*.'

Marcus had tapped him on his bronze armoured chest.

'Yes, so write to your father today, and get the letter away before the army takes to the road again. Make sure he knows that your persistence and the favour of the gods have won through where quiet acceptance of his wishes probably never would have. And don't worry, I'm sure we'll see you soon enough.'

Their farewells said, and leaving Varus to work out what was to be done with his new first spear, a man with an obvious and new-found superiority in life that somewhat outmatched his abilities, the party had ridden away from the camp towards the east, the direction from which they had come two days before. The soldiers had for the most part been disinclined to question their planned destination, knowing from experience that all would be made clear in good time. What they also knew all too well was that wherever they were going was likely to end up being a disappointment by comparison with the salacious rumours that Morban spreading in support of his gambling, despite his having a total lack of any information to work with.

The tribune shook his head at the oddsmaker's question without looking back.

'It's still too soon. I'll brief everyone once we're so far from camp that the information couldn't leak even if there were a spy among us, rather than just a financial predator.'

Morban snorted derisively.

'It has to be the coast. We're heading east, and there's nothing that way except the sea, and then the empty wastes of Asia.'

Sanga, riding alongside Saratos behind the former standard-bearer, shook his head in denial.

'You have that wrong, you donkey. The last time we was in the east we went to Antioch, remember? The women, Morban, do you not recall the women? Hardly "empty wastes"! Oh to enjoy the tavernas and brothels of that city just once more!'

The veteran soldier sat back in his saddle, shaking his head in what looked to Dubnus like self-disgust.

'Antioch! Of course! Why wasn't I thinking beyond the end of my nose?'

Saratos ventured an opinion from beside his companion.

'Because you don't think like Sanga.' The Briton nodded sagely, preening at the potential for having his intelligence praised. 'All you think about is money. Whereas Sanga only ever thinks about his stomach, and what hangs from the bottom of it.'

Qadir voiced his agreement from behind the two men soldiers, where he was riding with his archers.

'True enough. Every time we pass a taverna without entering I hear the sound of a little piece of his spirit breaking.'

'That's hurtful, Centurion!' Sanga twisted in his saddle and frowned back at the man who was at least formally his superior, and who was also his mentor in the art of covert urban spying. 'I don't just think about women and wine. I think a lot about gold as well.'

They continued to bicker for another five miles or so, until Scaurus deemed it safe to brief the party as to their new orders, gathering them around him at a water stop by a stream so as not to have to raise his voice.

'We are going east again, gentlemen. The emperor needs to send his legions across the Propontis and into Asia, if he is to find Niger and defeat him, because to fail to do so will be to surrender the initiative that we won for him at the battle we fought outside Rhaedestus. The latest intelligence is that Niger has pulled his legions back across the sea to Asia, leaving a strong garrison to hold Byzantium for as long as possible, months at least, making it impossible for our own legions to cross from the Thracian side of the Bosporus strait and follow. Severus's army must therefore be transported by ship across the Propontis, and risk making a landing on a coast that might be teeming with enemy legions, ready to drive any invader back into the sea. And that is where we come in.'

'We're going to be some sort of advance guard for a landing?'

Scaurus shook his head at Qadir's question.

'No, or at least not yet. The biggest concern that the emperor's consilium has is that there will already be spies in place along our side of that sea, informers seeded among the population along any route the army can use to march to embarkation points. And there could also be more spies in each of the ports along the coast, all with orders to warn the enemy when enough shipping gathers to transport an army across to Asia. There might even be men planted in the fishing fleets to similarly keep their eyes open, and report shipping movements back to our old friend Sartorius or to pass on messages from their spies with regard to troop movements. It is these informers that we are ordered to hunt down and remove from the playing board, gentlemen. If we can remove their ability to pass intelligence back across the Propontis then all the spies in the world can watch our legions get ready to cross the sea, but they won't be able to make the slightest difference to the outcome when the time comes to invade. For the next few weeks, brothers, we are hunting that most devious and dangerous of quarries, our fellow men.'

2

'Well, here we are again old friend.'

Marcus squatted by the freshly turned earth of the grave they had dug deep into a hilltop only a fortnight before, the day after the battle that had set Niger's legions back on their heels. Three days of riding had brought them to the spot where the Fourth had camped the night before the battle of Rhaedestus, and to which the legion's remnant had returned before nightfall on the fateful day, Scaurus's familia carrying the corpse of the man whom they had then buried on the crest of the hill overlooking both their campsite and the battlefield on which he had been killed. The burial site was a quiet haven of peace; birdsong and the wind's gentle ruffling of the grass the only sounds in otherwise complete silence; and he smiled to himself in sad satisfaction as he pulled a small engraved stone from his leather bag.

Julius had been struck by a randomly deflected arrow in the course of the vicious fight with Niger's legions, and in a place behind the battle line where he ought to have been immune from any such mishap. The Roman turned to look at the remainder of the familia as they toiled up the hill's slopes, then out across the landscape to the sea, and the distant port city they had intended to capture before their ambush by Niger's legions.

'The view doesn't get any worse, does it? I'd happily be buried in a place like this, when my time comes.' Dubnus had crested the rise in Marcus's wake, with his slave Khabour close behind him and showing no sign of discomfort at the steep climb. He took a moment to bow to his friend's grave and mutter a quiet private prayer. 'And at least burying him properly up here seems to have avoided the risk of wolves trying to dig his grave up.'

Marcus nodded, musing that the veteran centurion's wife Annia wouldn't know that she was a widow for weeks yet, news that they had entrusted Cilo to deliver to her on his return to Rome. The senator had been deeply affected by his first spear's death in the battle that had saved his life, politically at least, and quite possibly in reality as well, given the grim politics of Severus's court. It had been Cilo's opinion, voiced in the days following their having fought Niger's legions to a standstill, that the eagle which had landed on their aquila standard, and so discomfited Niger with its apparent presentiment of his doom, had been attracted by the sacrifice of so many noble spirits. And while the familia's general feeling towards that sentiment had been that they would rather have kept their friend alive, Marcus was grateful that it had inspired the promise of a house and income for Julius's family from Cilo, a man whose patrician dignity would not allow him to fail to provide for them, especially as Marcus's own sons were still in Annia's care.

Scaurus crested the rise, taking a moment to contemplate the grave before turning to look out over the distant sea.

'Shall we put the stone in then?'

Marcus used his dagger to cut away a rectangle of turf, then dug out enough of the soil beneath to allow the bottom half of the memorial stone to fit neatly into the hole created. He packed earth into the gaps to root the grave market firmly in place and then stood back to stare at his friend's newly identified grave. The marker was necessarily small to allow it to be carried to the grave, but the legion sculptor had done a good job of engraving the epitaph in letters small enough to fit.

> To the spirits of the departed, Julius, 45 years of age, a legion first spear from Britannia who fell in the civil war in the service of Septimius Severus lies here. If you wish to understand service and honour, only follow his example in life. We his friends commend him to the gods of the underworld.

The three men communed with the spirit of their fallen brother-in-arms for a moment, then collectively turned away to look out over the view of the land and the sea beyond.

'So, there's the Propontis again. At least this time we'll actually get to the sea. And soon enough the praetorian fleet's ships will be at anchor out there, if the emperor's orders are followed.' Marcus nodded, shooting his friend a swift glance to assess his mood at the prospect of encountering the fleet's commander once more, only to find the older man smiling faintly. 'Yes, I know, we'll be doing business with Titus again. I don't think it'll be any easier for him than for us, do you?'

'Nobody really gives a shit whether it's easy for him or not, Tribune.' Dubnus was leaning on his vine stick and staring out at the distant ships with a jaundiced eye. 'The bastard has put a curse on you, and all most of the men care about is how long it'll take you to put your blade through him.'

Khabour shot his fellow countryman Qadir a look on hearing the word curse, but otherwise remained expressionless, Scaurus raising an eyebrow at the Briton.

'You might advise anyone foolish enough to have placed a bet on such an outcome . . .' he paused meaningfully, shaking his head at Dubnus's look of chagrin. 'Really? Even you?'

The big man shrugged.

'It seems to most of us that you really don't have to tolerate the man's bullshit, not after all that you've been put through over the years. Besides which, his curse was for you to die at the moment of your greatest victory, and yet here you are, still breathing.'

Scaurus pursed his lips, unconvinced.

'It might seem to you and your comrades as if I could kill him with a clear conscience.' The tribune sighed. 'But, in case you had forgotten, he is a fleet commander, and every bit my equal in rank. Were I to kill him, I would almost certainly be executed in short order. Also, it seems to me that there is little point in killing a man who has already cursed me. His death will not avert the gods' revenge upon me. And neither is his curse spent yet. The battle we fought down there,' he gestured to the road to the east below them in the distance, 'was hardly a victory, but more of an exhausted draw with neither side having the upper hand. Added to all of which . . .'

He paused for a moment, and the Briton shook his head in disbelief.

'You sympathise with him?'

Scaurus turned to look at Marcus, who had voiced the question from where he was squatting by Julius's grave.

'Do I sympathise with him?' The tribune nodded. 'Yes, I do. I used information he gave me freely, and in confidence, to save my own skin.'

'And that of every man here, and others besides.'

Scaurus shook his head.

'If it had led to Titus's death then I might be more capable of rationalising the needs of the many against those of the few. But the empire punished him in the worst possible way, not by taking his life but by killing those dearest to him, his wife and children. He has every right to hate me, and to wish the gods to exact his revenge on me.'

He looked down at Julius's grave.

'And if his curse comes to pass? What of it? It sometimes seems to me that all we do in this life is march from one battle to the next, with the only certainties being that every new set of orders will pose us a fresh challenge, and every battle we fight is a roll of the dice, with our lives as the stake.'

'And the only prize on offer is to walk away with our lives and await the next man in the long line of imperial functionaries to order us to make our way to the next battle.' They turned to look at Dubnus, surprised by his unexpected eloquence, but the Briton was lost in contemplation of Julius's grave. 'With those of us left alive forced to adopt the roles played by those of us who rolled the dice and lost.'

Marcus walked over to him and patted his shoulder with something close to affection.

'I know. You wonder how you'll ever live up to the standard he set. But I've known you since I was a wet-nosed teenager, when you were my first chosen man, remember? You've always had just as much piss and vinegar in your blood as Julius did, you were just a few years behind him in knowing how to focus all that anger into making a century, or a cohort, or even a legion, do anything you tell them to, and without question. And we both know you can carry his vitis with pride.'

The Briton looked down at the stout gold capped vine stick in his hands, its shaft curving in a slight spiral from its original growth years before.

'I won't bring dishonour to it. So' – he lifted his head and looked out across the sea dividing Europa from Asia – 'we'd better go and see what the men of Rhaedestus have to say for themselves, now they don't have any legions to hide behind, hadn't we? And on the way we can pay our respects to the men who fell preventing Niger from killing the rest of us.'

The familia reached the city some hours later, having taken their time making a sacrifice to the spirits of their comrades who had died in the battle that had ended in the apparent favour of the gods being bestowed on them. Niger's officers had been true to his word, having gathered the corpses of the dead of both sides, and built a huge pyre with wood cut from large sections of the olive groves on both sides of the road the battle had been fought across, leaving none for the carrion birds to despoil. The fire had raised a column of black smoke that had been visible to them ten miles away as they had trekked eastwards in the conflict's aftermath, but here was proof that the other side in what was essentially a private war between Romans had kept their promise, and been even-handed in giving the dead the dignity of fire, rather than just burning their own dead and leaving the Severan legionaries for nature to deal with.

They had found the spot where the pyre had burned, a blackened, blasted stretch of ground twenty paces in diameter. The air around it had been eerily still, and the more sensitive of the familia had made warding gestures and uttered silent prayers to their favoured gods, while Dubnus, having recovered from the sentimentality that had been triggered by seeing his old friend's grave, had looked around in something close to satisfaction.

'Say what you like about civil wars, at least we don't leave each other's corpses lying around for the crows to peck at. Far better a battlefield that's been tidied up than one where the carrion birds and the rats are fighting over the remains of the dead for weeks after. Even if it looks like nothing will ever grow here again.'

Beyond the fire's blasted and blackened circle the ruined ground across which the legions had fought was now an expense of sharp-edged boot-sized troughs, the once liquid froth of mud, blood and bodily fluids baked to iron hardness by the sun's unceasing glare, marks stamped into the grim terrain by the desperate struggles of the thousands of booted legionaries who had fought across it and in many cases contributed their lives to it. The men of the familia had looked across it in silence, all remembering the chaos and random havoc of a battle fought recently enough for its events to still live on in their dreams and nightmares, and Scaurus had taken out his priest's shawl and ceremonial dagger, shaking his head at the desolate landscape.

'Bring that cockerel to me, and let's get the sacrifice made and push on to the city. I'm curious to see what the locals' state of mind is, now that Niger's retreated and left them to the mercy of his enemy.'

With the unsuspecting fowl offered to the gods, and prayers said thanking them for the eagle's intervention that had saved them from almost certain death, they continued along the road, marching past the farmhouse where Marcus and Qadir had detected the ambush that would otherwise have resulted in a swift and total defeat, rather than the blood bath that had been the result of Niger's attack. Soon afterwards they came to the gates of the city, where Scaurus, having ordered a pause on the road to allow him and his officers to don their armour and helmets, demanded tersely that the city fathers attend upon him. After a pause for the relevant men to gather, peer over the city's low wall at the waiting soldiers and speak among themselves, they tentatively approached the patiently waiting tribune via a small door set in the gate, which remained firmly closed.

After a collective bow which Scaurus recognised in return with a brisk nod, the most senior of them stepped forward and spoke the question that was probably on all of their minds.

'Honoured sirs, you are very welcome to the city of Rhaedestus. I see that you are all armed, and in these troubled times that is to be understood, although I can assure you that you will have no need of your weapons in our streets. We are a neutral city, and—'

'You were not afforded the privilege of neutrality, I presume, when the army that has now retreated east arrived outside these walls? Or were they shipping their food all the way from Asia? Three legions must have taken some feeding, I'd imagine, and now you are wondering what fresh burden might be placed upon you, are you not?'

The older man looked at him for a moment before shaking his head in apparent surrender.

'A fair question, and one from which I deduce that you serve Septimius Severus?'

'Yes. I have been tasked by *the emperor* with determining your city's loyalties. And when I say the emperor, I mean the only man with a valid claim to that title, the vote of the imperial Roman senate, rather than the self-interested scheming of a few senior officers in Antioch. Which is something you would do well to keep in mind, should you ever have cause to speak his name again, whether in my presence or that of someone less forgiving. And, perhaps, exercise a good deal more respect.'

'I—'

The Roman raised a hand to cut the elder off.

'I had not finished telling you the way things are, now that the usurper's army has retreated in the face of the emperor's furious purpose. You have a decision to make, and while it is simple, it is also stark. Your choice is to declare your loyalty to the emperor, whose men stand before you, or to tell me that you are still bound to Niger, whose three legions are on the other side of the Propontis and unlikely ever to return. I know which way common sense should tell you to cast your lot, but you might just be that rare thing in this world, a man whose word is quite literally his life.'

The elder looked around at the men behind him, whose expressions left little doubt as to their opinions, then nodded.

'The city of Rhaedestus is loyal to the emperor.'

Scaurus raised a questioning eyebrow.

'Loyal to the emperor Septimius Severus, and will remain so no matter what the circumstances? Answer carefully, because wars have a habit of taking turns that nobody ever expects until they happen.'

'The city will be loyal to the emperor Septimius Severus, no matter what the circumstances.'

'Very good. And very wise, as I do not expect Niger's army ever to stand outside these walls again. In that case let's have a look around the emperor's newest conquest, shall we? I think we'll start in the harbour.'

They walked through the city's streets, ignoring the citizenry whose appearance at doors and windows was evidently for the purpose of showing disdain for the newcomers, for the most part, although a few women opened their windows and smiled down at them, prompting some among the party to dally, reciprocating the smiles and tapping their purses. Scaurus sighed wistfully as Dubnus took his vine stick to one soldier's calves, prompting both poorly suppressed outrage and the desired compliance.

'Yet another reminder of how I miss Arminius. We would have had to drag him away from the prettiest of them, constantly making the point to him that he was never able to understand, that they would never take him to their beds for anything other than money. Dubnus having to chivvy Sanga along for trying to sneak away to sample their services on a paid basis just isn't the same.'

Marcus tapped the elder on his arm and then gestured to the hostile citizens.

'Your people do not seem happy to see us.'

The elder nodded at the statement, replying in a tired tone of voice.

'They have little cause to love any soldiers, Tribune. Niger's legions stripped us of everything they could carry when they retreated to the north, without any concern at all as to whether they were thereby leaving us to starve. And before you ask, there isn't a single amphora of wine in the city's tavernas, other than whatever their owners might have managed to hide from them of course. And to add insult to the injury, having told us that we could live on the fish caught by our fleet, they also stole every decent ship that was in the port.'

Scaurus stopped as they reached a point with a view of the harbour, which was all but empty.

'So I see. And the remaining vessels are out at sea, fishing?' The elder nodded wordlessly. 'Your people are still hungry?'

'Yes. If not for the catch we're able to take we would literally be starving now, and even with it the position is little better.'

The tribune nodded.

'Very well. I will set up my headquarters in the taverna nearest to the sea, the use of which will be paid for with the emperor's gold.' He smiled knowingly at the sudden interest in the other man's expression. '*And* I'll send a rider to the emperor, telling him that your citizens stayed loyal to him throughout Niger's occupation, and that they are in need of supplies due to the punishment theft of all food in the city.'

The elders nodded gratefully at their failure to resist the eastern legions being erased from the official history, and doubly so at the thought of food being provided, although their leader's eyes narrowed in calculation.

'And what will you ask of us in return for this unexpected generosity on your part, Tribune?'

Scaurus nodded confirmation that there would be a price to be paid.

'I want to see all of the men with boats as they come back into harbour. *All* of them. Without any exceptions, and *especially* the navarchs who don't want to meet me. Just tell them that anyone that doesn't come forward will be declared an enemy of the imperium, and that I'll be stationing archers around the harbour to shoot anyone that doesn't have permission to leave once they're inside the harbour walls. Which, given they will have thereby declared their enmity to the emperor, will be entirely justified. On top of which, permission to leave will not be granted unless you personally assure me, with an oath to the gods, that I've seen all of them and therefore that nobody can be sneaking back out to sea to warn any remaining vessels off. The emperor's friendship, and the supply of food to keep you all from starving, comes with some very robust expectations as to your co-operation.'

As the sun dipped towards the horizon, and the city's meagre fishing fleet straggled back into the harbour. Marcus escorted the boats' disgruntled captains up the quay one at a time, taking them to the taverna in which Scaurus had set up a temporary headquarters. Its owner was still grinning broadly at being paid in gold for his good fortune resulting from the fact that his establishment was the closest to the water, and had somehow managed to procure an amphora of wine whose contents were being dispensed in return for yet more coin.

It was clear to Marcus, from every one of his first impressions of the captains and their crews as each boat arrived, that none of the sailors he had walked along the water's side to the taverna were the kind of man that Scaurus was expecting to sail into the harbour sooner or later. They were all simple men, wedded to the sea, and with no concern as to the doings of emperors, and all presented the same lack of interest to Scaurus exactly as both men had expected would be the case with either all or hopefully only most of them.

And then, close to dusk, a larger boat than anything which had previously entered the harbour docked. The name *Neptune's Bride* was carved into its timbers, and its twenty-five-pace-long wooden hull was filled with more fish than was likely to have been caught in a day, remarkable in itself given the lack of the nets required for its villainous looking crew to have done so. The harbour master cast a wry smile at the ship's navarchus, who was standing in the bows and eyeing Marcus with the expression of a man who not only didn't know the Roman but had no desire to make his acquaintance either.

'You've been *fishing* again, eh Skaiv?'

The subject of his question shrugged, with the furtive look of a man with things to hide, and evidently no desire to be of any assistance to men who, even centuries after his land's annexation by the empire, he probably still regarded as little better than an occupying army.

'You know how it is. When you go out as far as we do, you sometimes bump into fishermen from the other side of the sea, men whom I have always regarded as the enemy and who have proved themselves just that when they came here to steal from us. And since they know where all the good fishing is to be found, and as they seem to enjoy all that sailing around with their nets out, relieving them of their catches can surely be no more than an inconvenience as they can just go and catch some more. Which is pretty much our duty, given *their* emperor's men decided to steal everything that wasn't nailed down when they left, and we've had no assistance from whoever our emperor is these days.'

The official coughed loudly, shooting Marcus a glance intended to warn the sailor to be on his guard.

'Of course, what Skaiv here means is that—'

The Roman smiled thinly.

'I think I know what he means, thank you.'

He appraised the captain, and the men standing behind him with similarly belligerent looks on their faces, every one of them with a long knife at his waist and, the Roman guessed, larger weapons close to hand. Half a dozen of Dubnus's axemen were lounging against the harbour wall behind him, their heavy bladed weapons leaning against the stonework ready to use, pointedly staring back at the sailors in the manner of men spoiling for a fight if only as a welcome break from the monotony. Beside them were four of

Qadir's archers, sitting in a small circle tending to the fletching of their shafts, the polished iron arrow heads gleaming in the evening sun. Marcus pointed at the captain, so that there could be no misinterpretation of his command.

'Leave the unloading to your crew, Navarchus. You're coming with me.'

The captain spat over his ship's side into the water as the harbour slaves tied his ship to the wooden bollards lining the quay.

'And if I decline to be seen consorting with the legions that have already stripped us of all we had? What then, eh?'

Marcus shrugged, gesturing to the soldiers on the harbour wall.

'For one thing, I'm not from the eastern legions who stole your food, I'm from the *western* legions which are going to ask the one true emperor to provide your city with grain, in return for a little well-paid co-operation. But you can stay here and rot on your ship if that's what you want, because you won't be leaving harbour again any time soon if you're not working with us, and neither will anybody else. As you wish!'

He turned and walked away, smiling quietly at the thunderous expression on the harbour master's face, and affecting to ignore the hissed imprecations being directed at the ship's captain.

'Wait!' Marcus turned back with a questioning expression to find that Skaiv had stepped onto the quay, and pushed past the harbour master without giving the man a second glance. 'Did you say *well paid*?'

In the lamplit taverna, Scaurus's bronze armoured finery seemed to impress the sailor little more than Marcus's had, but he had the good sense to remove his greasy cap and adopt an outward show of at least a little respect.

'So, you're Severus's men, right?' Scaurus nodded, not bothering to correct the casual use of the emperor's name as he had with the city's elders, knowing that disrespect was neither intended nor even perceived in the man's simple view of the world. 'And you're going to feed the city?'

The tribune nodded.

'We've sent for grain to be provided, yes. The emperor rewards those who stand for his cause.'

Skaiv nodded, barely interested in the answer once the provision of food had been confirmed.

'Your man here mentioned you'll pay us to help you. What are you paying with, gold or promises?'

Scaurus smiled up at him, holding up a hand in which an aureus gleamed yellow in the lamp light.

'Oh, I have gold with which to pay the right man. When I determine exactly who that is, of course.'

'Well now . . .' the Thracian grinned at the coin, 'that all depends on what you'd be wanting that man to do, doesn't it? What might your pleasure be, Tribune? And do you have any more of that wine, and a seat for a tired fisherman to sit in?'

The Roman stretched his legs out under the table at which he was sitting.

'You can stand, for the time being, and I won't be wasting good wine on *fishermen*, because it's not *fishermen* I'm looking to employ, tired or otherwise. And as to what I'm looking for, I've had a dozen captains walk in front of me in the last few hours, and none of them had it.'

Skaiv's smile broadened.

'That's because you've been talking to the wrong captains. My brothers of the sea are simple men for the most part. The sort who spend all day and every day pulling fish from the ocean, when they can find them. Men who are old after twenty years of such labour, and dead before they get to twice the age, without any ambition to be anything other than a slave to Neptune.'

'Whereas you . . . ?'

The navarchus smirked knowingly.

'Well whatever else I am, I am no fisherman. I have taken to relieving the enemy's boats of their catches, as a means of feeding my city's people, but it is only a temporary distraction from my usual line of work.' He raised a hand. 'Don't ask me to explain, but let us just agree that I am the kind of man you are looking for.'

He shot a significant stare at the jug of wine, which Scaurus ignored with a faint smile. He raised a hand, the yellow gleam of gold between his fingers.

'I'll trade with you, Skaiv. You can react as you wish to my next few questions, and if your answers convince me that you're the right man, then I will pour you a cup and tell you how you might earn this gold coin and some others just like it.' The seaman shrugged, inclining his head in acceptance of the Roman's ploy. 'So . . . you are clearly a man unlike any other that I have seen before me today. Resourceful, for one thing.'

Skaiv nodded.

'It has been said.'

'Unafraid to use violence when needed. Indeed happy to do so.'

'Again, I have been described in these terms.'

'And considering yourself to be above such small details as obeying the law, I'd imagine.'

The Thracian spread his arms wide in protest.

'You could hardly expect me to admit to such a thing. Better just to call me independently minded.'

Scaurus smiled up at him knowingly.

'Of course not. But the very nature of your denial speaks as eloquently to me as an admission of your guilt. You are a smuggler, pure and simple. You trade illegally, avoiding the tariffs that are charged at the borders between provinces.' Scaurus raised the coin, a shining disc in the lamplight. 'And I am willing to bet this gold that you are the undisputed master of navigating the waters of the sea between Europa and Asia, day or night. Am I right?'

Skaiv looked back at him in silence, the two men exchanging stares until the Roman laughed.

'Sit.'

He poured a cup of wine, watching as the sailor drank half of it in a single gulp without adding any water, shrugging at the tribune's grimace.

'It's been a hard few weeks, and those eastern bastards stripped the city of everything they could find, which put the price of even this dog piss so far through the roof that poor men like us cannot afford it. So, now we've established that you think I'm a murderous pirate and smuggler, what is it that you think I can do for you?'

'This sea is what, sixty miles from the European side to Asia?' Skaiv nodded. 'And you more *independently minded* sailors can roam it without much hindrance from either side's navies, true?'

'Yes. There isn't a warship built that could keep up with the *Bride*, as long as there's a decent wind, and even under oar power we can outrun all but the fastest. And besides, why bother with us? We see warships from time to time, but we always just keep our distance and make it look like we're fishing, and they always leave us well alone.'

'Exactly. And there will be others like you, with just the same advantages of speed and anonymity. And I'm guessing that a man like you, with a ship like yours, could easily carry information across the sea to the other side, or perhaps just to meet a contact at sea to pass his message.'

Skaiv nodded slowly.

'I suppose so. Are you saying that you *know* there are men of this city carrying messages to the easterners?'

Scaurus shrugged.

'How would I know? But I have first-hand experience of the devious methods used by a man called Sartorius, who employed a fisherman to spy for him in an attempt to capture us as we sailed here from Rome. He killed a friend of mine on the back of information from that spy, and while his plan failed on that occasion, we believe that using men like you to gather or communicate information is a method he will employ again. After all, the sight of a gold coin is enough to get the attention of even the more successful among you, does it not?'

The Thracian pursed his lips.

'True. But how do you expect that we can prevent such an exchange of information? It's a big sea, after all.'

The Roman took a sip of his wine.

'Put yourself in the shoes of a man who has taken the enemy's gold in return for passing information to the enemy. Let's assume that he meets with a spy who has compiled a report on our movements and likely dispositions, if, say, several legions were to gather around this city, and prepare for a sea crossing. That would be vital information for Niger's generals, because it would give them time to move their own legions to the expected landing point; especially if the spy had somehow managed to find out where it was planned for the attack to be delivered. So, if you were the messenger, how would you go about passing that message?'

Skaiv looked down at his wine cup, as if thinking the task through, and Scaurus refilled the wooden bowl with a smile and waited for him to speak.

'Well, if I were this man Sartorius's messenger I wouldn't want to be seen meeting an eastern vessel at sea, not with the bad blood between us right now. Besides which, knowing where and when to meet would be almost impossible, given there could be information that needs passing at almost any time. It'd be best to have a place somewhere in between the eastern and western shores where the men waiting for their informer's message could make a camp. It would need to be somewhere that it would be perfectly normal for a fisherman to land, to fill water bottles from a spring or to get out of rough seas if a storm rolls in. There is an island to the south of here, close to the eastern coast, called Prokonnesos. It has little population other than the men who quarry marble from its hills, and its shoreline is deserted for the most part. If I were your spymaster, I might well send some men to set up camp on its northern coast, facing this city, and wait for messages to be delivered by this traitor you expect us to catch. You do want us to catch him, am I right?'

'Yes.'

'And doing so will result in a payment in gold?'

'It will. I have five gold aurei to reward such a success.'

The Thracian grinned.

'In which case that gold is as good as mine. Because, Tribune Scaurus, I think I've already met your man Sartorius, and I think I already know who his messenger is.'

At dawn the next day Marcus, Qadir, the soldiers Sanga and Saratos, and several of the familia's archers boarded Skaiv's vessel *Neptune's Bride*. At the last moment the giant Lugos and his companion Ptolemy appeared on the quayside, evidently keen to be allowed to come along on such a voyage of discovery, and Skaiv, at first nonplussed by the Briton's freakish size, quickly enough relented as long as he promised to sit on the deck for fear of unbalancing the craft. The rest of the familia stood on deck watching, as the crew went about taking their vessel out from the harbour, their swift adherence to the navarchus's commands and the general efficiency of the ship's departure from port confirming that they were men who had spent their lives at sea from an early age. Skaiv strolled down the gently pitching deck to join them, grinning as Marcus took a firm grip of the ship's side to steady himself.

'So, how do you like my *Bride*, eh?'

The two men looked down the vessel's length, watching the twelve rowers on each side of the open-decked hull pulling easily at their oars, as the ship skimmed out across the dawn-tinged sea under both her single sail and muscle power. Marcus answered, looking fondly back at the rapidly receding port.

'Much like any other ship, I suppose?'

Skaiv shook his head, looking out across the sea with small smile.

'Hah! Not really, she isn't. The *Bride* is built like a naval vessel of the *myoparone* class, my friends, a design that I copied for its speed across the water and ability to turn in its own length. She is the fastest ship anywhere in these seas, and the most beautiful thing I have ever owned. She cost me a small fortune to build, all of my profits these past five years, but she was worth every penny.' He looked down at Marcus's hand, smiling at the Roman's knuckles which were white in their grip on the ship's side. 'Your first time at sea, is it?'

The Roman shook his head with a wry smile.

'No. It's just that the last captain we sailed with drove us into a storm through his own greed, only just managing to save all our lives; and even then at the cost of dumping us into the lap of the man marching on Rome to seize power. Which is how we came to be here today. So perhaps I'm wondering where *this* voyage will end.'

The Thracian affected to consider the question for a moment, clearly amused.

'It could end in slavery, if those eastern bastards over there were ever to get their shit in a pile and come looking for us in strength. But not if I have anything to say about it! We've been sailing these waters for so long that we know the islands off their coast as well as we know the streets of our own city. Better, for some of my men, since many of them choose to sleep on the *Bride* if they're not spending their coin on wine and the port's whores.'

A pair of the crew had settled down to splice two ropes together, and looked up with disreputable grins at the statement. Each of them was armed with the ubiquitous sailor's knife and both had a stout wooden club at their side, weapons which Skaiv had assured them were far handier for the sort of fighting they were likely to be taking part in, were they either boarded or boarding another vessel. Advising the soldiers to leave their swords for use if they landed on one of the islands for which they were heading, he had handed them all a similar weapon, the smooth wooden batons studded with the round heads of nails driven into the wood, and with a leather loop to put around their wrists.

'You'll thank me for these, if we get into a fight. Your swords are all very well, but you start swinging them on one of these crowded ships and you'll get caught it up in the rigging or take your mate's eye out. A club's far better for stopping a man from fighting you with a single swing, or a straight jab in his face, once you get inside his reach, and it won't kill him or leave him maimed either. At least not unless you want to do permanent damage. We fight to a set of rules out here on the sea, and one of those is not to waste a man's life. Enslave him, yes, if you don't know him, but killing's not what we do unless we can help it.'

Marcus had been surprised at the statement.

'You enslave men? I thought ships' crews were volunteers?'

Skaiv's wry smile had presaged a revelation that the Roman had not been expecting.

'That might be the case on your warships, but in these waters the only thing that makes a man safe from a lifetime of slavery is this' – he raised his own club – 'and the ones like it that we all carry. I was a slave, for several years. The easterners took me when I was a ship's lad of no more than ten, in a raid on a fishing fleet. They couldn't hold me though, not once I grew to manhood. I killed the captain of the boat I was enslaved to one night while he was sleeping off a skinful, and stole the ship's dinghy. Made my way back to Rhaedestus to find both my parents had died of the plague years before, and likely it would have taken me too, so perhaps the bastard did me a favour in taking me, but he still paid for it with a cut throat. And I swore never to be taken again.'

Once the ship was out of sight of the port and heading south he came and squatted next to Marcus.

'Now then, like I said to your tribune, I think I know which ship it is that we're looking for. When the easterners realised that they'd have to retreat over the Ox Ford, while—'

'The Ox Ford?'

Skaiv laughed.

'The Ox Ford! Surely you know this term?'

Ptolemy piped up from his place beside the seated Lugos.

'The Bosporus, the narrow channel between Europa and Asia on which Byzantium is sited, is a name pronounced as βοὸς πόρος in the proper Greek. It is a name which derives from the legend of Io, a mortal who was transformed into a cow by Zeus to hide her from his wife Hera, as he was Io's lover. Or perhaps it was Hera who made her into a cow, opinion is divided.' Marcus coughed significantly. 'Anyway, she was condemned to wander the Earth in that form until she crossed the Bosporus, and it was there that she met the titan Prometheus, who comforted her by telling her that she would be restored to human form by Zeus and become the ancestor of the greatest of all heroes, Heracles!'

Skaiv stared at him in undisguised disbelief for a moment before continuing.

'You and your men are quite unlike any of your kind I have met before. Anyway, when the easterners turned tail and ran for the βοὸς πόρος' – he winked at Ptolemy – 'with the funeral pyre burning their dead from the battle they had lost still sending the stink of burning flesh over the city walls, they came down to the port with a century of legionaries. Or at least what was left of one, perhaps forty or fifty men, all of them dirty and with blood in the seams of their clothing. I was in the harbour buying some pitch for the *Bride*'s hull, and they walked right past me, all looking harmless enough except for one of them who had the look of a right sly bastard to my eye. A man by the name of Sartorius, I discovered. He was dressed like an officer, but he had the dead eyes of a murderer. I was lucky that the *Bride* was on the beach outside the walls rather than in the harbour, having her bottom scraped clean ready for the pitch, so I made a quiet exit, gathered some men and paid them good coin to put her back in the water and let us get her away, before they did what I was expecting.'

'Which was?'

'Just the same as you did. They let the returning ships sail into the harbour and then told them that they couldn't leave. We ran out to sea far enough to be invisible from the shore, and then I went up the mast to watch the fishing boats sail back in, one after another. It was obvious they were going to be requisitioned even before they all set off to the east the next morning, but the interesting thing was that there was one ship that I saw sail in that evening that never went with the rest of them. We sat off the shore waiting to see what would happen, and I went up the mast to see without being seen. Sure enough, the fleet left harbour and turned east, heading for Byzantium, all except one. She came out when they were gone, and instead of heading east along the coast she came south, towards us.'

He paused for a moment and spat over the ship's side.

'It was the *Storm Spirit*, a ship owned by a man called Ardomir. I've always believed that he inhabits a world not that far from my own in terms of our beliefs, but very different in his way of doing things. Of course, a smuggler much like I am, but in my opinion a pirate as well, like the easterner who enslaved me, preying on the innocent when he could take an unsuspecting ship unawares. And so of course I called for sail and oars, nice and quick before she could get over the horizon and see us, and we made our exit to the south and west. We worked our way around her and ended up to her north and west, hidden in the sun's glare as the afternoon wore on, and I watched the *Storm Spirit* make landfall on Prokonnesos. They've been in and out of the harbour in the two weeks since, seemingly bringing back catches, but if they actually caught those fish I'll be a Greek wrestler's man-wife. Plus, the fishwives that do the gutting and scaling tell me that the catch he brings in is always a day or two old and a little stale, not fresh caught, so I reckon it's just a bit of cleverness to distract us from what they're really doing. I was even starting to wonder whether to call Ardomir out on it when you lot arrived and started throwing your weight around.'

'So, this island is Sartorius's courier station, you think?'

The navarchus shrugged dourly.

'It seems likely. I am guessing that dead-eyed bastard I saw in the port recognised Ardomir as a useful idiot, and took him to be his courier. And I think he has found some spies for the idiot to ship across the water and drop off on the western side, perhaps even just in Rhaedestus. They would have orders to sneak around gathering information, and to send it back on the *Storm Spirit* when there's something interesting to be told, or even make the voyage back themselves. It would be a short enough ride from a nice little hidden anchorage on Prokonnesos to the island's port on the southern side, and then a short boat ride to the city of Cyzicus on the Asian shore.'

Marcus considered the sailor's points for a moment.

'So, if we assume that this man Ardomir is the enemy's courier of whatever information their spies can gather to send back across the Propontis, what would you recommend we do?'

Skaiv grinned at him knowingly.

'Surely you're here to make the decisions for us, Tribune? We mere mortals can do no more than obey your godlike commands.'

More than one of the rowers shot the Roman an amused glance, and Marcus shook his head with a hard smile.

'I don't feed a dog and then bother to wag my own tail, navarchus. You work out the best thing to do from a seafarer's perspective and I'll decide if I think it'll work from my own.'

The Thracian nodded equably.

'What would I do? I'd wait for the *Storm Spirit* to show herself, either on the way out to the island or back from it, and I'd sail up nice and friendly, until we were a hundred paces from her.' He waved a hand at the rowers. 'Then I'd set these idle bastards to pulling on their oars as hard as they like to pull their pricks of a night. We'd close with them right quickly, your archers could put a few shafts into her crew and then we'd board, nice and hard, and with plenty of this.'

He raised his cudgel.

'Ardomir is a hard enough man when it comes to robbing the innocent and selling them into slavery, I hear, but I wonder how well he and the scum that sail with him will respond when there's arrows flying across their decks and hard-faced soldiers like you jumping over their side.'

'And having taken them, we do what?'

'Depends.' The sailor grinned wolfishly. 'What do you want to do, stop their messages from getting through or take the opportunity to put a little extra information into the easterner's ears?'

3

As the day progressed, Marcus noticed Skaiv keeping a close eye on the sun's position above the horizon as the *Bride* cruised slowly southwards across the enclosed sea, her oarsmen pushing her through the water at a sedate pace. At length he shook his head and jerked a thumb over his shoulder in the direction from which they had come.

'Time to go home. I don't especially want to be out on the water at night, and what would be the point when they won't be sailing in the darkness and we wouldn't see them if they were.' He shouted to the steersman and gestured for him to turn the ship about. 'Oi, Raskus, time for home! Stir your lazy arse and get us turned around!' With a shout for the oarsmen to play their part the steering oar was pushed outboard to start the ship's turn. 'Hands off cocks, feet on blocks! Let's get the *Bride* pointed north and go home. We can try again tom—'

A piercing whistle from above them interrupted his musings. The man he'd posted to sit on the spar from which the vessel's single sail hung loosely furled was pointing away to the south.

'*Sail!*'

Skaiv gestured for him to come down, shouting a command to his steersman.

'Keep bringing her about and head for home, but keep the sail furled, and row slowly!'

Once the lookout was down, the captain climbed up the mast himself, taking a moment to stare out over the otherwise empty sea from its elevated vantage point. He came down again with the light of battle in his eyes.

'It's the *Storm Spirit* herself! I'd know that ship anywhere. And she's coming at us from the direction of Prokonnesos, which fits what I thought his game might be. Do you want to catch yourself some spies, Tribune?'

Having already discussed the way in which they would make their move on the other ship, were it to make an appearance, both crew and passengers knew what was expected of them. Marcus and his men lay on the deck in the meagre cover of the hull's side to hide them from casual observation, while Skaiv strolled down the deck between the oarsmen barking out orders with one eye on the slowly closing vessel as it came over the horizon.

'We're just cruising back to Rhaedestus, right? We'll leave the sail up, go easy on the oars and let them overhaul us nice and steady! And make it look calm and relaxed, so they don't reckon there's any threat to them!'

He kept up a running commentary, watching as the *Storm Spirit* slowly overhauled them and nodding his head knowingly at his rival's caution, as the other vessel altered its original course to pass the *Bride* at a safe distance.

'He's not comfortable at seeing us, that's clear. Look at the way he's trying to give us a wide berth on the right-hand side without making it too obvious.' He called a command to the man at the steering oar. 'Raskus, alter course to the east *just* enough to close the gap on them!'

The other ship was now close enough for the men on deck to be visible, and Skaiv kept up his description of events for the benefit of the Romans in their concealment.

'Hah! Now he's standing by his steersman, like he wants to take the oar and steer away from us, but then that would look suspicious! And there are at least three men aboard who don't look like they're part of his crew, I can see them trying to hide among the oarsmen!'

He raised a hand and waved languidly, bolstering the appearance of a man at ease and happy to make a slow progress back to port, calling out another command to the helmsman.

'Alter course a touch to the east again, again not so much that it will be obvious! Let's see if we can fool him into letting us get within sprinting range, eh? You oarsmen, the tribune has a silver for each of you if we catch that wallowing tub and board it!'

The rowers grinned at Marcus where he lay, flexing their massive biceps in between the deceptively slow strokes and nodding enthusiastically at the prospect of being rewarded for a few moments of intense work.

'*Ardomir!*' Skaiv was shouting at the other captain, and making a beckoning gesture to indicate that he had news to pass to the other ship, or perhaps needed assistance. He grinned broadly at his fellow across the hundred pace gap between the two ships. '*There's something you need to know before you go back into Rhaedestus!*'

The reply was almost too distant to hear over the wind's gentle sigh and the creaking of oars.

'*What is it?*'

The navarchus looked down at Marcus and winked.

'Let's see if we can put the shits up him, shall we?'

He raised his voice again to bellow across the slowly shrinking gap between the two ships.

'*The Romans are watching out for any of us carrying spies from the east! They told me there's some clever bastard trying to find out what the western emperor will do next . . .*'

He called out a description of the other captain's response to his crew in a low voice, his eyes bright with the excitement of the chase.

'I can't see what he's thinking from here, but he just turned to speak to his steersman. This goes one of two ways: either he comes to find out what we know, or he runs. Whichever it is, be ready to give me everything you have!'

Ardomir barked a command, and the *Storm Spirit*'s rowers took their oars out of the water. Skaiv grinned triumphantly.

'Got him! Rowers, up your pace to the cruise!'

The distance between the two ships started to decrease noticeably, the *Storm Spirit*'s master leaning on the side of his vessel's hull, staring at the *Bride* as she gradually closed the gap. He cupped his mouth in both hands and shouted a question, eager to know what Skaiv had to tell him without allowing the other vessel to get too close.

'*What Romans are these then?*'

Skaiv thought for a brief moment before replying.

'*They marched in from the west yesterday! Nasty bastards who say they're looking for a nest of spies serving the emperor over the water, and headed by a man called Sartorius!*'

Whether the *Bride*'s gradually increasing speed gave away Skaiv's plan, or the other captain simply took fright at the mention of the spymaster's name, Ardomir turned to his crew and shouted an indistinct order that galvanised them into action. The *Bride*'s master barked a command in response.

'Attack speed! Give me *everything*!'

The oarsmen reacted as the words left his mouth, rising from their seats with the effort of each stroke and taking their timing from the bellowed commands of the steersman facing them. Setting their leather-soled feet against smooth edged wooden blocks nailed to the deck for purchase they strained at their oars, and the *Bride* seemed to fly across the waves towards the other ship. Marcus rose from his hiding place and beckoned to the archers to do the same as they closed with their quarry.

'Shoot the steersman!'

The Roman nodded at Skaiv's shout, the Thracian pointing at the knot of men around the other vessel's steering oar, and with a thrum of bowstrings the Hamians loosed their first shafts at the enemy. None of the arrows found a target, but the simple fact of the deadly threat in their whirring passage through the air threw their targets into fresh consternation, more than one of the rowers staring in horror at a shaft protruding from the ship's mast and still vibrating from the impact. While they were still contemplating their peril a second volley found two targets, one of the oarsmen rising from his bench with an arrow in his side and then slumping back, his oar untended, and the ship's steersman falling back against his steering oar with a shaft in his chest, apparently already dead. The *Storm Spirit* wallowed as her course fell away, and the other rowers shrank down under the archers' deadly threat, the *Bride* swiftly crossing the remaining open sea between them.

'Stand by to board!'

Skaiv might have professed not to be a pirate, but the speed with which his crew obeyed his command told the truth of their skills, two of them hauling in their oars and taking up light chains with sharp multi-pointed hooks attached to one end, spinning the heavy iron grapples in the air beside them on short lengths of line, ready to throw. Qadir's archers loosed again, their arrows a deadly scourge at such close range, further intimidating the other ship's cowering crew, and, deprived of control over its steering oar, the *Storm Spirit* wallowed further to its right, presenting Skaiv with an almost perfect opportunity to run his own ship alongside.

'Board!'

The hook men threw their grapnels across the rapidly closing gap even as the oarsmen heaved their oars inboard to prevent them being broken as the two ships came together and leapt to their feet with their cudgels, ready to fight. The other crew were too slow to retract their own oars, and as the *Bride* rode over their shafts the butt ends were smashed into the air, shattering the jaw of one unfortunate who had been bent over his at the moment of impact. Both grappling hooks stuck on the other vessel's rowing benches, their wielders leaning back and reeling the chains in hand over hand to put tension in the knife-proof lines and prevent the hooks from being dislodged and thrown over the side. The two ships' sides touched and parted again, an imperfect union with three feet of space between the two hulls as the hook men strained to haul the *Bride* back into closer proximity, but Skaiv knew he could not wait for the perfect time to send his men across into the other vessel, the other ship's crew still struggling to rise from their benches in the chaos of a fleeting moment of his advantage over them.

'*Into them!*'

He threw himself across the gap between the two ships and, landing on his feet on the *Storm Spirit*'s deck, was instantly laying about himself with the heavy cudgel. Marcus, knowing that the Thracian would be overwhelmed if he wasn't immediately reinforced, ignored his unease and leapt across the gap behind him with Sanga and Saratos close behind him. He landed unsteadily on the other ship's moving deck and fell onto his hands and knees, only his cudgel's leather strap prevented it from rolling away from him. A sailor came at him with a long knife, raising it to strike while the Roman was defenceless, then stopped halfway through the stroke, staring down stupidly at the arrow protruding from his chest. Sanga, having landed more sure-footedly with Saratos at his back, stepped forward and smashed his stave into the skull of a man who had just hit Skaiv in the square of his back, felling the navarchus in writhing pain. The oarsman dropped to the deck unmoving, and the two soldiers stepped forward to protect the Thracian while he was still recovering from the blow to his kidneys.

Getting to his feet and looking about him, Marcus could see that the fight was already effectively over, Qadir's archers having shot enough of the rowers that the rest had declined to offer the boarders a fight. A tight knot of men were holding their own with swords and daggers in the ship's bows, and the Roman shouted a command to the Hamians as they nocked arrows and turned their bows to end the futile resistance.

'*Hold!*'

Obeying his command, the bowmen watched as he stepped through and over the brief fight's human wreckage until he was face to face with Ardomir, who was standing with a sword raised in front of a pair of men dressed in rough tunics and heavy boots, both with pugios in their hands. Another man dressed similarly was lying at their feet with an arrow through his neck, clearly close to death as he fought to breathe against the blood filling his lungs. Marcus allowed a moment for the navarchus to take in the men waiting behind him, and the archers with their arrows aimed squarely at him, before raising the club and pointing it at his face.

'Give it up, Ardomir! Drop that blade and you might be allowed to live! Try to fight and I'll put you over the side myself and leave you to drown! It's not you I need alive, but them.'

He gestured to the informers lurking behind the captain, whose eyes widened as he realised that only they could betray the full truth of his part in the scheme of which they were a part. He turned to strike at the closest of them, then collapsed unconscious to the deck as Marcus hammered a blow from his club into the back of his head. Skaiv was back on his feet and giving orders, both crews combining to do as they were told now that the captured vessel's captain was out of the fight. They stacked the dead in the bows, then sent the terrified prisoners back to their rowing benches under the forbidding gaze of Lugos; Ptolemy making the most of their quiescence to strut up and down with a hand on the hilt of his sword, while the *Bride*'s steersman came across to take over the task of directing her course leaving his deputy to steer Skaiv's ship. Marcus nodded at the Thracian.

'Well won, Captain. Make sure that your dubious colleague Ardomir doesn't get a knife in the back, I think he's going to be very helpful to us once he realises his predicament. And you can tell your men they've earned their silver!'

Ignoring the cheers of the *Bride*'s crew as the two ships floated apart, and their ribald shouts to each other of the ways in which they planned to spend the money, he turned to the two remaining spies who were standing under the threat of Sanga's boarding club and alternating between side-eying him and glancing down at the body of their colleague, who had lost his uneven struggle with the arrow wound in his neck. He sized them up before speaking, noting their weather-beaten faces and, even under the evident threat of death, the confident way they held themselves, unable not to be the men that their lives until that day had made them.

'You don't look like informers, gentlemen, you look more like soldiers to me. You're centurions, right?'

Both men nodded, the shorter of the two pointing to the slumped body of their comrade.

'We are, and so was he. We all served with the cohorts the Third Legion left in the east, until a man called Sartorius recruited us to come back over the water and keep an eye on you lot, so he'd know where to expect an attack. And you're servants of the usurper Severus, right?'

Marcus couldn't help but to smile at the ex-soldier's bullish demeanour despite the circumstances.

'Yes, we serve the man who has been proclaimed emperor by the senate and the people of Rome. Something you might want to bear in mind before venturing that opinion to anyone less tolerant than me. And you seem very confident for soldiers caught spying for the enemy, and without the protection of your uniforms. That makes you no better than common informers, and it means that all the usual niceties with captured soldiers go straight out of the window. So, what is it that you think happens now?'

The taller centurion shrugged, his fatalism evident in the tone of resignation in his voice.

'You'll either kill us or make us prisoners. Not much we can do about that, is there?'

The Roman shook his head, pursing his lips to indicate that all was not quite as the two men might hope.

'Commendably straightforward, Centurion. But I'm afraid that the predicament you've landed yourselves in isn't quite as simple as that. You two might already be in more trouble than you realise. And you have a decision to make that might, *just* might, decide on your fates, if you choose wisely. But only if you're also very, *very* lucky.'

'I'm not sure it's even necessary for us to send those two back to the emperor? I mean just look at them? They're singing like birds in a cage.'

Marcus followed Dubnus's meaningful stare across the dockside taverna to where the captured informers were sitting with Scaurus, seemingly vying with each other to tell the attentive tribune as much as they could about their mission, and the state of matters on the other side of the Propontis. As the two men watched, one of them started pointing to the map that the tribune had unrolled on the table in front of them, the other nodding his head in agreement at the points his comrade was making.

'Yes . . .' Marcus shrugged uneasily. 'It seems that they still think that answering all of our questions will get them off the hook. But, unfortunately for them, it doesn't work that way. Whatever intelligence they are giving him is unlikely to be readily accepted by Laetus, much less Severus, not without their being able to convince themselves that what they are hearing is absolutely the truth by having those men tortured to death. Were the emperor's generals to accept what they were being told without taking such a precaution, and potentially send their legions into a trap that those men might have been sent to bait for them, their risk would be that this war might well be lost in a few hours of fighting. Can you see Severus taking that sort of risk without making very sure that he's not being misled?'

The Briton nodded.

'If you put it like that . . .'

'But there might just be a way to make better use of them by providing their bodies to the chief interrogator's apprentice for his practice in loosening tongues. Ah, here we go . . .'

Scaurus beckoned them over and gestured to the two spies, whose faces betrayed the strain that they were under.

'Our new friends here tell me that they have no orders other than to watch and listen when the army arrives, and to try to predict where and when the emperor might look to send his legions into Asia to hunt down the usurper Niger. They have also told me . . . well, tell it yourselves, gentlemen?'

The spies looked at each other, and then Gracchus, the shorter of them, shrugged and pointed to the map, ignoring his colleague's evident disapproval. His Greek was good for a man whose mother tongue was Aramaic, but his accent was so strong that Marcus was forced to concentrate carefully on what he was saying.

'We were ordered to find your legions, and then mix with soldiers off duty and find out as much as possible about their plans. When we found out where your strength was to be gathered, we were to send that information back to our master.'

Marcus nodded knowingly.

'And your master is Sartorius?'

The spy nodded, seemingly eager to please.

'We did not meet him, but it was on his authority that we were sent across the narrow sea. And these' – he raised his hand to indicate a ring identical to one on his comrade's finger and to one the Roman had taken from the dead man's body on noticing their ubiquity among the three men, its carnelian stone engraved with a miniature representation of a legionary – 'are the means of proving that we are who we say we are, and that the information we send back is genuine.'

Marcus nodded, seeing the moment in which to unveil the stratagem that he and Scaurus had agreed on before starting the captives' debriefing. He raised the ring he had taken from their dead companion.

'You do realise that the very fact that these trinkets identify you as spies is a death sentence in itself? Although I think it's likely to be worse than that. Much worse.'

'What do you mean?'

He looked at Tertius, the taller of the two, shaking his head sympathetically at the soldier's naivety.

'I can't blame you for not understanding, Centurion. Military life is so much simpler than the perilous profession you've swapped it for. And while being a military captive might not be the safest of positions to find yourself in, at least your captor has enough in common with you to have some fellow feeling. But you're not in the legion anymore, are you?' He shook his head. 'Look at you, soldiers impersonating fishermen. More obvious spies I can't imagine, and, in the eyes of the men we will be sending you to, no better than the informing scum who make life in Rome so risky in times of upheaval like this. And to make it worse, the captain of the boat that was bringing you here didn't survive the boarding. It seems I hit him too hard with an unaccustomed weapon and broke his neck. So, as you're the only two sources available, when the imperial command structure gets its hands on you I expect that you will be very roughly treated indeed, because the men making the decisions have lived under Roman informers' threats for long enough that they'll take any opportunity they can to feel like they have the means of revenge.'

The soldiers faces were a shade paler, unable to take their eyes off Marcus as he kept speaking.

'You will be tortured, of course. At length, and with great inventiveness. The emperor always has at least one man with him, hidden facelessly in his retinue, who has served a long apprenticeship in the delicate art of getting the reluctant to be, shall we say, less reluctant to share what they know. They use all the usual means of encouragement that you can imagine plus others whose inventiveness would be a matter of amazement and wonder, were they not being used to subject you to horrific agony. And they always, *always* find out the truth. No matter what lies the subject of their attentions tries to spin, no matter how hard he fights the inevitable, he will always break in the end. But that's not the worst of it.'

The two men stared at Marcus, seeing what looked like genuine sadness on his face.

'The worst of it is that hardly anyone ever survives the torturer, once the decision has been made to loosen their tongues by means of violence. Because once the truth has been tortured out of a man, there still remains the risk that what he swears to you is the truth is really nothing more than a lie, spun in the hope of stopping the torture without betraying the real truth of the matter. A man in your position has much to gain from lying under coercion, and the torturer knows that, and so he just keeps on at his task, often to the point of death – or at least injury that will change your lives forever – until he is sure he has the truth of the matter. Teeth, fingers, toes, knees, elbows . . . there are so many ways to inflict pain, and that's before we get onto the more obvious means of torture. The ones which are guaranteed to kill you in the most gruesome manner that you can imagine.'

He stood, shrugging at their dumbfounded expressions and turning to walk away, then turned back with one last comment.

'Which means, I believe, that the only question you need to ask yourselves is whether there is a way that you might avoid the whole horrible matter of such an interrogation. And perhaps manage to go home to your loved ones as complete men? I suggest you give it some thought. Obviously, you've told us all that you know, and that's not going to be enough to save you, but perhaps you can provide some service to us that might lead the emperor to spare you?'

The two men looked at each other, Gracchus eventually venturing a hesitant opinion.

'We could take false information back across the sea for you?'

Both of them looked up at him hopefully, but it was Scaurus who dashed their faint hopes.

'That would never work, not for us and definitely not for the emperor, were he to find out. Indeed, *we* would be taking your places on the torturer's rack, as obvious traitors for having released you. Because the moment you were freed from our threat, your former allegiances would be sure to reassert themselves; it is simply the way of things. So no, that wouldn't work. But there is a way that you might just avoid the fate that beckons, if you assist us with what we have in mind before you are brought before the throne.'

'I will do whatever is asked of me!' Gracchus shrugged at his colleague as the bigger man shook his head in disgust. 'You can book an appointment with the imperial torturer if you wish, Tertius! I will meet my end in a way that involves a less drawn-out exit from this life!'

Scaurus turned to his companion, raising a questioning eyebrow.

'You will not join in this scheme we have planned?'

Tertius stared hard at his comrade for a moment, caught in a trap from which there was seemingly only one mistake, and then nodded with evident reluctance.

'I can see the point my brother officer here is making, and I do not wish to be taken in front of your emperor without having tried to avoid the fate you describe. What is it that you want of us?'

Later, walking down the harbour wall to where Sanga and his comrade Saratos were sitting with the *Bride*'s rowers in the puddle of light cast by a burning torch set in a gap between the stones, sharing a wine skin and a loaf of bread around the circle of men, Qadir spoke quietly in Marcus's ear.

'It seems that our friend's new slave is a most interesting man, from my discussions with him over the last few days. Not only do we hail from the same region of Syria, but we share a religion. And he, I have discovered is an adept in the cult of the Atargatis to which I also am committed. When he learned of the tribune's curse he promptly interceded on his behalf to the goddess, which I feel may help to sway the gods in his favour, and render Titus's anger impotent in their eyes. And he did this without any thought of favour, much less with any idea of freeing himself as might be suspected. He is a man to watch, for I feel he has more about him than initially meets the eye.'

He paused for a moment before continuing.

'On another subject, it is my belief that the captive Tertius will be an unwilling participant in the tribune's plan only until the moment when he thinks that he will be able to make an escape. Do you really think he can be trusted?'

The Roman shook his head in reply.

'You are as perceptive as ever. And obviously not. But killing him now might shock Gracchus out of his willingness to co-operate with us. And besides, Tertius might yet be instrumental in persuading his colleague to participate in a plan I have agreed with the tribune. So, for the time being at least, he gets to live, unless he is foolish enough to force our hands. Ah, gentlemen, it seems you've taken the opportunity to get to know Skaiv's crew better!'

The two soldiers looked up at him, Sanga waving the half-empty wine skin at him with a grin.

'Have a drink with us, sirs?'

Marcus raised a hand in polite rejection of the offer.

'Thank you, Soldier, but I'd prefer to stay sober as a long day in the saddle seems likely tomorrow. Tell me Sanga, can you swim?'

The veteran shook his head with a smile, not yet realising the thrust of his tribune's question.

'No sir, bless your life! I make a point of staying well out of water!'

'I see. Which makes your willingness to have jumped from one ship to another earlier today all the more impressive. You have my sincere thanks.' He turned to Saratos. 'And you?'

'I can swim, Tribune. I learned as a boy, living by a river.'

'Very good. And, of course, all you oarsmen can swim, I presume?' The amused sailors all nodded, some of them perhaps guessing what was coming next. 'Yes, I thought so. So it's only *you* that can't keep his head above water then, eh Sanga?'

The Briton looked up at him with an expression of dawning horror at what he knew was coming, and was to Qadir's eye tensing himself to make a run for it when Marcus stepped in front of him, cutting off any route by which he might take flight and showing the now grinning sailors a silver denarius.

'I am riding west with the tribune tomorrow, and for the sake of a little peace and quiet we have decided to leave you two here, but that's no excuse for you not gaining a new skill in our absence, one which might become essential. There's one of these apiece for you oarsmen, and one for you too, Saratos, if he can swim when we return. A hundred paces without putting his feet down, and the ability to swim silently and without splashing like a drowning dog will be enough.'

The men gathered around the Briton eyed him predatorily, and Sanga shook his head in dismay.

'Fuck that! Just give me all that silver and I'll teach myself!'

Qadir stepped forward with a broad smile.

'That, unfortunately for you, is not the way that it works. We do not have the time for you to be standing at the dockside trying to gain the courage to get into the water, silver or no silver. Which is why our friend has decided that you need to undergo a swift and hopefully effective course of tuition. Sink or swim, so to speak! You may start the lessons whenever you think appropriate, gentlemen.'

The two men turned away, both listening as the Briton's frantic protests ended with the splash of a man's body hitting the water. After a moment there came the sound of a whooping breath of air, and then a shout of protest as more men leapt into the water to join the floundering soldier.

'*Bastaaaaards!*'

Leaving Dubnus and Qadir in charge of the city, Marcus and Scaurus went west back along the Via Egnatia with the two captive centurions, taking a pair of Dubnus's more intelligent axemen with them both to make sure that the easterners, secured by the temporary expedient of being roped together, didn't get any ideas about escape, and to share the watch-keeping duties. The Roman slept well enough before his turn to stand watch, waking once to hear the sound of the two centurions whispering to each other in the darkness, the words indistinguishable but their respective tones unmistakable. One of them, Tertius from the sound of his voice, was incensed, while the voice he took for Gracchus's replies were defensive in tone. He yawned loudly enough to be heard, and grinned as the two men promptly feigned sleep, laughing out loud.

'Remind me never to select you noisy fools for anything requiring an ability to do things quietly! You can't even have a whispered argument without waking the whole camp. And if either of you think that running away would be any sort of solution to your problems, think again. This area will be riddled with deserters, after a battle of the size we went through only a fortnight ago, and two men like you wouldn't last more than a day before they found you and did to you whatever it is that bandits do to men without food or gold to be taken. I suggest you just go back to sleep and leave any thoughts of escaping to another day.'

They found the army thirty miles to the west of Rhaedestus early the next day, the legions having dug themselves a new marching camp in accordance with the usual practices for an overnight halt, presumably enjoying a rest day from the hard marching that had brought them so far east. The men of the Fourth Legion, Scaurus's former command, were manning the turf wall facing east, and so the party was admitted to the camp without any of the usual proving of bona fides by unexpected arrivals. Escorted to the imperial encampment in the camp's middle with their captives, they saw that a cross had been erected at the enclosure's entrance, a man's body hanging from its horizontal beam with the absolute immobility of a corpse, his eyes staring out sightlessly across the camp from within a cloud of flies. More insects were swarming around his hands, both of which had been reduced to fingerless pieces of meat in what had clearly been a difficult journey to his last resting place. A wooden plaque above his drooping head had the word 'informer' carved roughly into its surface. Gracchus stopped walking and stared up at the dead man with horror, his eyes drawn to the unavoidable absence of either fingers or toes from the corpse's hands and feet.

'I know that man.'

Tertius nodded.

'He is . . . he *was* . . . a centurion with one of my legion's cohorts that marched out with Niger. But how did he end up here, and in such ignominy?'

Marcus and Scaurus were admitted to the command tent, leaving their escort and prisoners outside, finding Julius Laetus sitting at a desk and contemplating the writing tablet on the table before him. The general looked up in mild surprise as they entered.

'Rutilius Scaurus? I hardly expected to see you here given you already have your orders, and therefore there can be no reason for you to return.'

Both men saluted, and Scaurus answered the general's question in a matter-of-fact tone.

'We have secured the port of Rhaedestus as commanded, Legatus Augusti. Further, we have used a requisitioned vessel to capture an enemy controlled ship, and the cargo of spies it was carrying from the far side of the Propontis.'

Laetus, still preoccupied with the map, looked up at them with fresh interest.

'You have captured spies working for the usurper?'

'Yes, Legatus. Two of them, former centurions with the eastern legions. A third man died in the boarding and capture of their vessel by Valerius Aquila here.'

The general stood up and came around the desk with a beaming smile.

'Two spies? Excellent! We've already caught one such weasel trying to work out our strength to report back to Niger, and he was quick to sing once the emperor ordered him to be questioned with the right incentives to talk. We can choose one of them to interrogate while the other watches, and see how long either of them can hold out from telling us everything they know!'

'The man on the cross outside, Legatus?'

Laetus nodded with a hard smile.

'Indeed. I thought it would provide a useful example to the camp as to what to be alert for.'

Scaurus nodded.

'In the case of our captives, neither of them knows anything worth interrogating them for, Legatus. We propose to use them for—'

Laetus raised a hand to silence him.

'Neither of them has *revealed* anything worth interrogating them for, you mean? Which makes having them both interrogated immediately a matter of the utmost urgency!' He frowned at Scaurus, who had tipped his head on one side and raised an eyebrow in silent comment. 'What?'

'We have established an understanding with these men, Legatus. We have been able to communicate to them what will happen if they are not completely open with us. And they have told us that—'

Laetus shook his head briskly.

'I'm not interested, Tribune. These men are *informers*. They are no better than the scheming criminal scum who made our lives so miserable under Commodus. They lie for a living, it is as natural to them as breathing. And more than that, they are traitors to the empire and to their military oaths! We'll see just how much they know once the torturers have loosened their tongues, and then—'

'What is it that they have told you exactly, Tribune?'

All three men turned to the doorway that led to the emperor's quarters, its flap pushed to one side by the man who was standing in the opening, Scaurus and Marcus bowing deeply at the sight of Severus himself. The emperor was wearing a simple white tunic, his dark North African skin contrasting with the pristine wool, the effect of effortless luxury completed by a glossy leather belt and a pair of beautifully polished boots which were in stark contrast to Laetus's bronze cuirass and military cloak. The legatus waved a hand dismissively.

'Scaurus's man here has captured a pair of informers, centurions who—'

'I heard that much, thank you Julius. What I *wanted* to hear was what it was that these men have already revealed? Tribune Scaurus, what is it that you were trying to tell us?'

Lifting his head from the bow that he had adopted on realising the emperor's presence, Scaurus ignored his superior's disapproval and took the chance he was being offered.

'Imperator, we captured these two spies as they were being transported across the Propontis to take up their clandestine roles on this side of the narrow sea. They had no useful information to share with regard to the preparations for war being made by Niger's generals, not even when we warned them as to the nature of the questioning they would face, but they did tell us a good deal as to how they were recruited, and how they were meant to pass any information they gained back to the usurper Niger's spymaster, Sartorius. We have both the talismans and watchwords that he gave them.'

Severus nodded slowly.

'Sartorius? You have a private quarrel with the man, I believe?'

Scaurus nodded grimly.

'I do, Imperator. He murdered a friend of mine in Thessalonika, and I am sworn to kill him.'

'Excellent motivation. And what did these informers tell you about this man Sartorius's operation?'

'There is an island close to the eastern shore of the Propontis, Imperator, by the name of Prokonnesos, on which Sartorius has established a forward base for his spying activities. He has – or had – at least one vessel based in a port on the western coast running to and from the island, taking spies in one direction and information in the other. He means to discover whether you plan to cross the sea, rather than use the Bosporus narrows to enter Asia. We have the ship, which means that any other spies returning to her for passage back across the Propontis are putting their heads in the noose, but with the capture of these two we have a greater opportunity.'

Severus thought for a moment.

'And am I correct in guessing that you want to use these captives to guide you to the island, in order to destroy this intelligence-gathering organisation at its root?'

Scaurus smiled tightly.

'Perceptive of you, Imperator. Although what I was planning was a little more deceptive in nature. And might potentially provide the army with a way to ensure that it has an unopposed landing on the Asian shore, when the time comes to take the war to the usurper.'

Severus turned an amused smile on Laetus, whose expression was unreadable, the fact of his being sidelined by the emperor having sunk in as Scaurus had outlined his plan.

'You see, Julius, there are occasions when the more subtle approach might just be the best way to achieve one's goals. I suggest you have a good look at these prisoners, record the details of their identities and then sign them over to Tribune Scaurus to be his own responsibility. Do you plan to keep them both alive,

Scaurus, or will their deaths be a necessary part of whatever it is that you have planned for them?'

Scaurus shrugged noncommittally.

'I do not plan for their deaths, Imperator, but one or both of them might die in the process of dealing with the nest of spies that Sartorius has established on the island of Prokonnesos.'

Severus nodded, his expression hardening.

'In which case I suggest you bring back the body for tallying with the official record. Otherwise, you might well face the accusation of allowing the man in question to escape. Because while I am empowering you to undertake activities that might result in their deaths, you are not under any circumstance to allow either of them to get away. Is that clear?'

Scaurus nodded briskly.

'Perfectly clear, Imperator. And you have my word that neither of them will be afforded any such opportunity. My aim is to find and kill the spymaster Sartorius, not to show any sympathy to any of his servants.'

'Well now, if that fool wanted to give away his position he could hardly have done any better if he'd just lit a torch and waved it around for us to see.'

Skaiv was standing at the *Bride*'s prow, pretending to supervise the enthusiastic efforts of his crew in putting the fishing net they had brought with them over the ship's side, while at the same time scanning the coastline of the Prokonnesos, less than half a mile distant. A lone figure was standing on the headland above a narrow inlet, clearly watching the ship's slow progress past the small bay with interest, and seemingly unconcerned that he was plainly visible in the soft afternoon light.

'Typical bloody soldier, no idea about concealment. Current company excepted, of course.'

He turned to Saratos with a grin, and the soldier shrugged, still watching the man on the cliff.

'Don't worry Skaiv, Sanga has the skin of an elephant when it comes to insults, and I know exactly what you mean. So, we have them?'

'Perhaps. Except that might just be some poor dumb bastard who likes to wander up the hill from his village and watch the sunset. We need to get a bit closer.'

The soldier smiled knowingly.

'Hey Sanga.'

His comrade looked up from the fish he was being taught to gut and fillet by a member of Skaiv's crew, raising the knife in an unmistakable gesture.

'What? If this is an invitation to another swimming lesson, I'll fight every man on this tub before I go over the side again. I've already had two lessons today and you can stick the idea of a third one right up—'

'Gold.'

'Eh?'

'You heard me.' The Dacian grinned down at his mate. 'There are men in there' – he nodded his head at the inlet – 'who are the key to you and me earning some gold.' He put out a hand to prevent his friend getting to his feet. 'No, don't get up and stare you donkey. And yes, I was thinking we could both go for a bit of a swim, once the sun's down.'

Sanga looked up at him incredulously.

'Go for a swim? In the fucking dark? What new madness is this?'

Riding away from the legion camp, Marcus shook his head in quiet amusement, smiling wryly at his friend. Scaurus nodded, looking back at the legionaries still labouring at the turf wall, obeying their centurions' orders that if they weren't moving on they could at least be usefully employed.

'I know, you're going to tell me how lucky we were that the emperor was close enough to hear our discussion when Julius Laetus was all for putting those two to the hot irons.'

Marcus laughed softly, then shot a grin at the two men riding in front of them.

'I was going to tell those two how lucky *they* were that the emperor was close enough to hear our discussion, when Laetus was already measuring them up for the torture rack.'

'You met the emperor?'

Gracchus's question was stated in a tone of disbelief. The two centurions had been processed by Laetus's staff in an outer tent of the imperial encampment without ever seeing anyone more senior than a centurion, and nobody had taken the time to explain the terms of their reprieve to them, only that they were being signed into Scaurus's keeping. Marcus had made a request of the staff officers, and after a short while a centurion had arrived with a heavy leather bag whose contents the Roman had kept to himself for the time being, simply slinging it over his shoulder with a grunt at the weight inside.

'Yes, it was your exceptionally good fortune that he happened to overhear his general tell us that you would be handed over to the interrogators, and doubly so that he actually chose to intervene in the discussion. He decided not to have you both tortured to death, but only in order to let you prove your loyalty to him by supporting us in what I have planned. And that is the sort of loyalty which can only ever be either whole-hearted or punishable by death and with nothing in between, I'd say. And he was also very clear that if either of you die in the course of doing so then we will be required to produce your bodies, as proof of your deaths, so that he can be sure we didn't just allow you to escape out of fellow feeling. There is no way out of the trap you're in, you have the choice of either co-operating or dying violently.'

The two centurions looked at each other with dawning unhappy understanding.

'So what happens now?'

Marcus nodded knowingly at the more cynical Tertius's question.

'What happens now is that we go back across the Propontis and find a way to put you to use, in the service of the man who just decided not simply to have you both crippled and then crucified alongside that other poor bastard to provide an example to his army of how he treats traitors.'

'We're not—'

'I know, you don't believe you're traitors, just men whose well-paid jobs turned sour on you through no real fault of your own. After all, it's not as if you could easily have said no to Sartorius, is it? And when it comes to the question of one emperor or the other it makes no difference to you, other than for the potential financial benefits if Niger wins. But it *was* you that made the decision to agree to such a hazardous task, and I can only presume that gold was a part of that decision in some way. So, whether you feel as if you deserve to die badly for choosing gold over the comforting anonymity of the ranks, or perhaps that you were just following orders rather than actually choosing a side, you've just dodged an arrow, thanks to Tribune Scaurus here. And if you dare to dream that this is your chance to escape, be very careful, because all the emperor wants back when all this is done with is your bodies, and neither of you has to be breathing to qualify as such. If I have the choice as to whether it's our skins or yours decorating his audience chamber, I think you can guess the way I'm likely to lean.'

Later, as the sun was dipping for the western horizon, they made camp in a secluded glade in the artificial forest of olive trees that stretched away into the distance on either side of the road, and Marcus showed Gracchus and Tertius what was in the heavy bag they had been provided with by Laetus's men. The easterners' faces fell when they realised that it was a pair of heavy iron manacles connected by a short chain, whose links were the thickness of a man's thumb and likely to prove impervious to anything short of a smith's heaviest hammer and chisel. He secured one around each of their ankles to Tertius's open disgust.

'Is this our fate then? To be chained together at every opportunity?'

The Roman nodded equably.

'It is. Because if we lose you then our own lives will take a distinctly miserable turn. And I've had enough misery for this life to have any more of it heaped on by you two thinking you can make a run for it when our backs are turned. This way we might get a proper night's sleep, rather than being disturbed by your whispering about the chances of getting away with it if you try to run.'

One of the soldiers of their escort grinned at Marcus, comfortable with his superior after ten years of campaigning.

'Does that mean we don't have to stand guard tonight, Tribune?'

'No, it does not. There are still plenty of thieves and deserters around, and as it's your turn to watch and mine to get some sleep, I'm very happy to be assured by your watchful presence. If you hear anyone skulking around in the darkness, wake us up so that we can offer them a warm welcome. And if you hear the sound of rattling chain links it'll be these two intent on committing suicide by bandit.'

Once the sun had set, Skaiv ran the *Bride* to within two hundred paces of the shore and dropped anchor, the two soldiers stripping to their loin cloths and easing over the ship's side. Sanga was still complaining bitterly about the lack of sanity involved in the very act of leaving their place of safety in the pitch black as they clung to the ship's side for a moment, growing accustomed to the water's coolness.

'It'll be golden, don't worry. See?' Saratos lifted the reel of thick twine that he was carrying out of the water, the loose end tied to the ship's mast. 'Skaiv has brought us in to within two hundred paces of the shore. And this line is almost twice as long. So all we have to do is tie it to something on the shore and we'll be able to follow it back out to the boat.'

The two men swam for the sound of the surf washing up and down the beach, Sanga's protests silenced by his intent focus on swimming rather than drowning, and within a few minutes they were wading out of the waves and onto a sandy shore.

'See? I told you there was nothing to it.'

Saratos unwound the rest of the line to keep it from being broken by the *Bride*'s movements in the surf, tying it to a tree, then squatted to listen.

'Hear that?'

Sanga nodded, his teeth a white line in the dim light of the moon as he smiled predatorily, his panting indignation of a moment before swiftly forgotten.

'Yes. Voices. I can smell a fire too, so they must be close.'

The two men crept slowly through the trees towards the bright glow of a campfire, Saratos putting a hand on his comrade's arm when they were close enough to discern what was being said. After a few minutes of listening to what sounded as if there were three men sitting around the fire, he leaned in close and whispered in his friend's ear.

'These are no fishermen, all they can talk about is what they'll do with the gold they're earning when the war is over.'

Sanga turned to look at him, devilment in his eyes.

'True, but we'll need some sort of proof. You wait here while I go for a dig around, right?'

Without waiting for an answer, he wormed silently away into the sparse undergrowth, his progress rendered almost noiseless by the fact that the ground around the camp had been cleared of all the usual forest debris for use as kindling, staying in the cover of a fold in the ground between the clearing and the beach. Unable to stop him, Saratos shrugged mentally and resumed listening to the fireside conversation in the hope of hearing something of use among the flow of banalities, all too recognisable as the sort of desultory nonsense most soldiers discussed in their spare time.

After a long wait Sanga crept back in alongside him, opening his hand to show his comrade something shiny.

'There's your proof that these ain't just a bunch of locals.'

The Dacian nodded.

'I swear you could steal a centurion's vine stick from out of his hands without being caught. But this is good, because if it is missed it's a small enough a thing to have fallen off the garment without being noticed. Very nice work my brother. And I presume you took careful note of the camp's layout while you were practising your thievery skills, and where they keep the horses?'

The party rode back into Rhaedestus the next day to find a very smug-looking Skaiv ensconced in Scaurus's impromptu headquarters, a jug of wine on the table in front of him. The Thracian raised his cup in salute, gesturing to the chairs on the other side of the table from him.

'Ah, Tribunes! You're just in time to join me in a cup of this dog piss which the owner of this dive assures me is all he has that might pass for wine, which I am sure you will be delighted to purchase for the purposes of celebration once you hear the good news that I have for you!'

The two officers removed their armour and sat opposite him, Scaurus taking his boots off and lowering his feet into a bowl of water with a sigh of pleasure, while the tavern owner's youngest son rubbed at them with a rough cloth to wash away the pattern of dirt left on the skin by his open-worked caligae.

'A cup of wine and my feet in warm water, just what I needed. Thank you boy, here is a copper coin for your help, now run along and tell your father that we would appreciate a bowl of his stew when he has a moment to set it before us.'

He waited until the boy was out of earshot before turning back to Skaiv.

'So, tell me navarchus, what is it that has you buying wine in the hope of my reimbursing you?'

The navarchus grinned back at him knowingly.

'I'll be earning more than the value of a mouthful of this disgusting brew, I can tell you that. While you've been tenderising your arses on horseback, I've found the location of that secret harbour the prisoners told you about but weren't able to point to on a map. We took the *Bride* out to do some pretend fishing, and cruised up and down the coast of Prokonnesos until we found them, their location given away by an error so basic that the meanest of my rowers could never have been so stupid.'

'Oh really? And you have the proof?'

'Your own man Saratos can vouch for it. His eyes are still young enough to make out a man standing on a clifftop half a mile away, which is what the idiot in question did.'

'Saratos? What was he doing with you?'

'Teaching his comrade Sanga to swim, of course. My crew encouraged me to take them both with us, since they harbour an affection for both the men in question and your silver, and so both men shipped with us for the voyage. One of them voluntarily, and one under a degree of duress. Once he had the basics of not drowning under his belt, we took to throwing him into the sea every now and then, and then helping him back into the ship once he managed to catch us up. He really is quite a good swimmer now, and he has also managed to get over all that childish "salt water in my eyes" nonsense. Anyway, we were casting our nets in a particular spot when we saw a man standing on the headland overlooking a narrow inlet that runs into a small bay, perfect for the landing of a ship like the *Storm Spirit*. He was standing watch, if a little obviously, and so we did our best to convince him that we were fishing, and not hunting for his master's spy harbour.'

Marcus took a sip, grimacing at the wine's sour taste and adding another measure of water to his cup.

'So, you saw a man on a cliff. It's not exactly compelling evidence, is it?'

Skaiv smiled knowingly again.

'In the normal run of things, I would tend to agree with you. Which is why I sent your men ashore that night to do some of that lurking about they tell me they're so good at. They had a quiet look around, apparently without being detected, which, according to your centurion Qadir is something of a miracle in itself as normally they would be straight off to find the closest taverna.'

'And what did they find that makes you so sure that you weren't just looking at someone's fishing village?'

'This . . .'

The sailor put a cloak brooch on the table in front of them, a fine piece of workmanship worth a month of a soldier's salary, finely tooled and gilded with silver.

'Your man Sanga took it from inside their living quarters, the sneaky thieving bastard. No simple fisherman is ever going to afford something like this, much less ever have the need of it, is he? That's a typical soldier's purchase, I'd say, and there aren't usually soldiers sitting around in fishing villages. So, now are you paying for the wine?'

4

'This is definitely the inlet?'

Gracchus nodded emphatically. The *Bride* was drifting slowly with the breeze on a close-hauled sail, with just enough way to be steerable, her crew making a great show of fishing the Propontis's waters close in to the Prokonnesos's shore, only a quarter of a mile distant.

'See that standing rock up on the headland? They call that the watcher. And that's where the man keeping watch will be looking out from until the sun is below the horizon, even if he's not stupid enough to let us see him like I hear his comrade did.'

Marcus nodded, turning briefly to look at the setting sun's proximity to the sea behind them to the west. He was dressed in a rough tunic identical to those worn by Skaiv's crew, only his military boots and the pugio on his belt offering any clue as to his real purpose on the ship. The navarchus followed his gaze.

'It will set soon enough. For now, we are making the most of what little light remains to improve our catch, or at least that's what you really want the man watching us from the headland to believe.'

The Roman nodded at the master's words, looking across the deck to where his own men were huddled in the cover of the ship's hull. Sanga had regained his usual air of disinterest in everything around him soon enough, once the rowers had managed to teach him how to swim well enough to be able to cover a hundred paces without either splashing or sinking. He and Saratos were playing knuckle bones, while Qadir and Lupus were talking quietly next to them, keeping well out of sight of the expected but unseen watcher.

The *Bride* drifted slowly with the gentle breeze, her crew laughing and joshing each other as they hauled in the fishing net and tossed their catch into the ship's bows, working hard to give the impression of complete preoccupation with their task. As the sun kissed the horizon, Skaiv gave the order to turn the ship in a tight half-circle and point it back towards the north, and the narrow sea's far side.

'That ought to satisfy anyone with eyes on us that we're going home for the night. We'll give it until the sun's properly down . . .'

Once the sea was dark, under the blazing river of stars in a cloudless night sky, he ordered the sail to be furled and the crew to their oars, turning the *Bride* back towards the island. His men rowed in slow, gentle strokes intended to give the vessel little more than steering way, and to prevent any hint of their change of course being evident from the interaction of oars and water, were the watcher on the hill to have stayed in place.

'He was probably away down the hill for his dinner a while ago, but let's not trust to the expectation that all easterners are lazy bastards, eh?' Skaiv grinned at Qadir, whose face was dimly illuminated by starlight and who had come to stand by Marcus now that the need to hide from view had passed. 'We'll row in as close as we can, nice and slow, until the moon gets up.'

The slow, patient approach brought the headland's looming silhouette steadily closer, until Skaiv cocked his head and declared that the surf's gentle susurration was loud enough for them to be in the right place.

'Here, and no closer. No doubt we could get her afloat again were we to run ashore, but not without making so much noise that they'd probably realise that something was going on. Over to you.'

Marcus called the raiding party together, beckoning the captives to join them. He shot a glance up at the headland looming over the *Bride*, a stark silhouette in the light of the moon that had lifted over the horizon while they had been waiting for the last of the sun's light to leach from the western sky.

'Either there's a man up on that hill watching us in the moonlight, in which case we'll be sailing into a trap, or he's long gone in search of his bed and we'll have the advantage of surprise. Now that the ship is as close to shore as it can get without grounding, we'll swim in and then make our way in along the shore until we can see their camp. It'll be by the water, right?'

Gracchus nodded, ignoring the silent contempt radiating from his fellow spy as he repeated the information he had already provided to them several times under questioning, albeit without being aware that Sanga and Saratos had already gathered the same information that he believed he was revealing to them.

'They have built a cabin far enough from the water to be dry even in a storm. There were three men when we left on the other ship, taking turns to stand watch and look for ships approaching. They all sleep in the cabin, and the horses are tethered at the back of the building. One man travels back to Cyzicus on the mainland every ten days to report, unless there's something that needs communicating sooner than that.'

Marcus nodded and turned to Sanga and Saratos.

'You two can go first. And try not to splash too much?'

The two soldiers ignored his joke and lowered themselves noiselessly over the ship's side, swimming confidently away into the darkness, and after a moment to allow them a decent head start on the rest of the party he turned back to the easterners and gestured to the ship's side.

'Nice and slowly, without making a lot of noise that'll get you killed – killed by me, if I think you're doing it deliberately – use the line that my man is unreeling to guide you to the beach, and remember that we'll be right behind you. And if there's *any* sign that either of you is trying to alert the enemy I *will* kill you both and take your corpses back to the emperor; your presence here is a luxury rather than a necessity. And that means that your families will never know what happened to you, and no one will say a prayer to the gods for you, or place a coin in your mouth for the ferryman.'

He waited until the two men were in the water, then climbed over the side of the ship, taking a moment to become accustomed to the water's cool embrace, pushing away from the *Bride* and swimming for the shore behind the two spies. The sea's regular wash up and down the beach became louder as they neared the shore, Marcus feeling the waves propelling him towards the beach with increasing strength as the water became shallower with every kick of his feet, until he no longer had to kick but could simply allow the waves to push him onto the sand at the water's edge.

Rising to his feet with water cascading from his soaked tunic, he drew the pugio and paced swiftly up the beach to find the captives arguing in urgent whispers that fell silent when the glittering edge of his blade reflected enough moonlight to gain their attention.

'It's too late for second thoughts. Shut up and follow me.'

He led them along the beach as it curved into the inlet, skirting around a rocky outcrop, with half a dozen of Skaiv's oarsmen at his back. The bar of sand narrowed until there was barely enough of it to form a path, the light of a fire gleaming through the trees as they approached the spot the spies had detailed on the crude map they had drawn at Scaurus's command. Marcus gestured to them to sit on the sand, waving a pair of oarsmen forward.

'You two, wait here. You and you, make sure they do, and if they so as much as fart noisily, you can cut their throats for all I care.'

He led the rest of the party forward, pausing at the edge of the clearing with the sailors clustered close in behind him, watching through the trees as a man walked out of the rough wooden structure the two spies had described, a jug in one hand and a handful of cups in the other. The other two men he had expected sat by the fire, each with a piece of meat impaled on a metal skewer which they were holding over the flames. He turned back to the waiting oarsmen, whispering a command.

'Use your clubs, not your knives. There's a silver apiece for every man we take alive.'

The closest of the sailors grinned at him, his teeth white in his soot blackened face.

'They'll never know what's hit them.'

Marcus signalled for them to attack, and with a silent rush the sailors burst through the trees and into the clearing, their clubs rising and falling as they overran the startled soldiers. The man with the wine jug turned to run and went down before he covered five paces, one of the rowers leaping on him and bludgeoning him to the ground with a triumphant yell. The short struggle was over without so much as an act of serious resistance, their hapless enemy herded together and forced to their knees under the threat of the attackers' knives. Marcus called back to the men he had left guarding the captives.

'Bring them forward!'

The sailors led Tertius and Gracchus into the clearing, their erstwhile comrades staring at them in dazed hatred as they realised who it was that had sold them out to the enemy. One of them attempted to get to his feet, his face contorted with anger, only to fall face first back onto the sandy ground as the sailor behind him tapped him hard on the back of his head with the butt end of his club. Marcus turned to the two men with a triumphant smile, putting on a show for the watching captives.

'Well done gentlemen! Your assistance was critical to our being able to capture these men and render them harmless. And now there's nothing to stop us feeding false information to Sartorius, making him the instrument of our victory.'

The captives stared at him in horror, Tertius shaking his head in angry disgust as he realised what it was that Marcus had intended all along.

'No! I won't be your fucking puppet!'

Punching the sailor closest to him in the face he made a run for the back of the building, but Marcus raised a hand to forestall any pursuit.

'Hold! He has made his choice!'

After a moment the sounds of a brief scuffle came from behind the cabin, and then the short grunting cry of a man in dying a swift and violent death. After a moment's silence Sanga and Saratos carried the dead centurion back around the corner and dropped him at Marcus's feet, the Briton grinning at Gracchus who stared down at his comrade in horror.

'I sent these two around the back of the cabin to secure the horses, and to wait for something like this to happen. It was more than likely he was going to run, sooner or later. I just gave him a reason to show his hand at a moment of my choosing, when he would be running into the knives of my men, rather than condemning us all to death.'

The dejected centurion nodded slowly at Marcus's pronouncement, his lips a tight line as he contemplated his own likely future.

'And now you have complete power over me.' He pointed at the captives, all of whom were staring at him with hard faces. 'If I try to resist your commands in any way, you have the ability to see me condemned as a traitor by any one of these men. But I thought that this was all you wanted from me?'

Marcus shook his head.

'We saved you from an imperial torturer's rack and tools, Centurion, and the fate that will befall any informer captured by our army. Did you really think we'd be happy with you just showing us where these men were waiting for your return? We need more from you, Gracchus. A *lot* more.'

An hour later, with the *Bride* run up onto the beach to collect her crew, the prisoners and Tertius's corpse, Marcus stood watching the activity with the disgruntled captive beside him. Skaiv leapt over the vessel's side and walked over to the two men, gesturing to Gracchus.

'Want me to hang around a while so that this one can make his mind up whether to play by our rules or accept the alternative? It'll be a long wait for us to come back if he decides not to do what you want.'

'No, you ought to get away while it's still dark, and you can evade any patrolling warships, now that you're no longer pretending to be fishermen. If the centurion here decides not to follow through with his promised assistance he will do so knowing that the alternative will always be worse than betraying a spymaster who was always exploiting him in just the same way.'

The navarchus nodded dourly, giving Gracchus a dubious stare. 'It's your funeral.'

The ship was pushed off the beach, turning into the starlit night to head north to Rhaedestus with news of the camp's capture, and Marcus went back to the fire's warmth in the company of Gracchus, Sanga and Saratos, along with a pair of Skaiv's more intelligent crewmen. The captive centurion stared at the fire in brooding silence while Marcus and the two soldiers dressed themselves in the clothing left behind by the camp's former occupants, the Roman putting the carnelian ring taken from Tertius's corpse on his right hand.

'So now you face the truth of it.' Marcus moved to sit opposite Gracchus, staring at him over the fire's embers. 'Until now it's all been so far off the map of what you understand that you've just gone along with events as they happened to you, right from the moment that you were recruited by Sartorius, and done what's been sensible to keep yourself alive. Am I right?'

'Yes.'

The monosyllabic reply was grunted in the manner of a man struggling to come to terms with a drastically revised situation, and the sudden realisation that there was no way out of the trap in which he was caught.

'From the moment we took you both prisoner, all the way to the west to meet the army, and then back here, right up until the moment that your comrade made his bid for freedom and paid for it with his life, you've been playing a double game. Just like Tertius was, only you were better at it than he was, without any sign that you were always desperately trying to work out how to get away, and try to avoid what you know was coming.'

The centurion looked up.

'Was it that obvious?'

Marcus nodded.

'I saw your face when I manacled you to him. He was furious, but your reaction was more contained. He was thinking of nothing more than making a run for it, any way he could, but you had the look of a man who was working out the odds, and whose options were one-by-one disappearing in front of him. You were being forced down a path you knew must eventually lead to this moment, when you cannot avoid the fact that your choices are simple, and very stark.'

Gracchus almost sounded relieved.

'I either do exactly as you ask, or I will be shipped back to your emperor and taken apart one bloody piece at a time. It's not really very much of a choice.'

'No. But of course, in the depths of your mind, you still see one other option. Don't you.'

Gracchus stared back at him, his eyes betraying the truth of Marcus's words.

'Do I?'

The Roman shook his head.

'Nicely tried, but you don't fool me. You're on a hook, but you still hope to find a way not to break the oath you swore to serve Niger, back when you were happy with just being the commander of a century and everything was so much simpler than it is here and now.'

'What's that one option then?'

'Don't play me for a fool, Gracchus. You had two hopes, one of which we just snuffed out by capturing this place. But your remaining potential escape from this trap is probably the better of the two, at least as far as you see it. You plan to betray me once we're in the presence of Sartorius's men. Don't you?'

Cyzicus's harbour was busy with a variety of small craft, but Marcus's eyes were drawn to the warships docked along the eastern side of the slender isthmus that connected the Asian mainland to the Arctonessus, the Island of Bears that jutted out into the Propontis to the south of Prokonnesos. The naval dockyard was at the northern end of the harbour, and Marcus counted four warships and another half-dozen scout vessels, none of which showed any sign of the sort of activity that might presage putting out to sea to patrol the narrow waters between the opposing territories.

'So, there are naval ships moored, but none to be seen on the ocean. Either the local commander is very relaxed about the war or one of life's less committed characters.' He looked over his shoulder at Sanga and Saratos, to find the Briton staring hungrily at the city behind the dockyard. 'You two know what's needed of you, just be ready when the time comes.'

'We'll need—'

The Roman raised an eyebrow at the ever-hopeful Sanga.

'Money? No, not where you're going you won't.'

He turned back to the view, ignoring the Briton's pout.

'So, Gracchus, your real test starts here. Where do we need to put this boat ashore?' He waited, while the centurion scanned the port, his face tense as he sought to recall where he and his two comrades had sailed from less than a week before. 'I'd say you have a count of no more than fifty to work this out, or the men watching us from the dockside are going to wonder why it is that the crew of a boat they've probably seen come and go a dozen times seems clueless as to—'

'Wait! Just . . . give me a moment!'

Marcus fell silent, but slid his pugio from its scabbard and put the blade's tip against the other man's thigh. Gracchus ignored the cold touch of the iron, scanning the shoreline with an intent, almost desperate concentration.

'I remember that the warehouse they took us to before we sailed looked like it was about to fall down under its own weight . . . there!'

He pointed at a disreputable-looking wooden shed whose once jaunty blue paint had weathered to the point of transparency, revealing the flimsy-looking timbers beneath.

'That? That's the hub of a spying operation intended to bring down the emperor?'

Gracchus nodded eagerly, looking down at the dagger as if willing it back into the scabbard.

'It's supposed to blend into the background, and be invisible among all the other warehouses.'

'And what's in there? If we knock on the door, who's there to meet us?'

The centurion shook his head.

'I have no idea. When we came through here we got off our horses, received our instructions on the quayside and got straight onto this boat. I'm guessing that there's a watchman who can call in the big boys if there's anything urgent to report.' He looked at Marcus appraisingly. 'You're sure you want to do this? These are seriously nasty people you're asking me to take you to. The man they're going to call in when we show up was here to meet us when we got here, to give us our final instructions, and I'm happy to admit that I wouldn't want to get on the wrong side of him. And I'm a legion centurion, in case you'd missed what I'm trying to tell you.'

The Roman shrugged at him.

'It would seem like a waste of a lot of hard work just to turn around and run away now. Tribune Scaurus and I have invested a lot of our reputation in this approach to the problem, and neither of us want to get on the wrong side of this emperor. And if we were to give up here, all you'd be returning to would be a short and very unhappy experience of the lowest grade of imperial hospitality. So neither of us have much option but to go through with this, do we?'

Gracchus swallowed, clearly caught between his fear of the man beside him and the men waiting in the city.

'No.'

'There it is, we both have no choice in the matter.' Marcus turned to the sailor manning the small vessel's tiller. 'Take us in as close to that blue warehouse as you can.'

The quayside was quiet, with none of the usual commercial bustle that might have been expected from such a large harbour, only the desultory loading of a cargo ship far enough from their mooring point as to represent no risk of their being detected. Marcus sent Sanga and Saratos to their task, taking a moment to let them get out of sight before making his own move. Gracchus looked over at the decrepit warehouse with obvious unease, and Marcus tapped him on the arm before pointing to the dagger at his waist.

'Just remember, the smallest sign that you're attempting to warn them as to who I am and you'll have a foot of cold metal through your guts. And if they take my dagger off me I can still kill you with a single punch in the throat. And trust me when I tell you from experience that it's no way to die.'

The centurion nodded wearily.

'Very well, if we're going to do this then let's get on with it. But don't say I didn't warn you how bad these people are.'

He led the Roman to the rear of the building and knocked at the door, three swift raps of his knuckles and after a pause, a further two. After a momentary pause, the sound of bolts being withdrawn came from inside, and the door opened to reveal a watery-eyed man in his later years, with a bad haircut and a tunic which had seen better days, looking out blankly at them. With a heavily seamed face and the sort of weather-beaten appearance that most veteran soldiers took on after a lifetime spent outdoors in all weathers, Marcus decided that he was probably more capable than he looked at first glance, noting that the knife at his belt had a handle polished by usage that implied an expertise with the weapon.

'Yes?'

Gracchus raised his hand to show the man his carnelian ring. The doorman's expression changed, and he looked to either side before stepping back to allow them access, past an altar to Mars with a bowl of coals glowing gently and sending the scent of the incense sprinkled on them into the open space. Closing the door behind them he held out an open hand.

'Give me those daggers.'

'Why?'

'Because if you don't I'll be for a kicking when the Nomad gets here, and you'll find yourself handing them over a lot less easily than if I just take them from you nice and quietly now.'

Marcus shrugged, handing over his pugio and submitting to a swift but thorough search. The doorman tipped the contents of his belt pouch out, looked through them for weapons and then dropped them back into the leather pouch as harmless. He gestured to the warehouse's cluttered interior, boxes and amphorae stacked and piled in orderly chaos.

'Make yourselves comfortable.'

Marcus whispered in Gracchus's ear.

'Remember that I can still kill you with a single blow, and I will do so without hesitating. The knife changes nothing.'

The doorman had turned away, and was speaking to a gangly youth who had been sitting in a patch of sunshine coming through a hole in the roof playing with a handful of knuckle bones.

'Fetch *him*. Tell him that one of the watchers has come back, with another man I don't recognise.'

The boy left in a hurry, and the doorman returned his attention to the two men, pointing at Gracchus.

'You I recognise. You're one of the men who went over the water a week or so ago. But you . . . ?' He pointed at Marcus with an expression of distrust. 'You might have the red ring, but I've never seen you before.'

Marcus looked back at him with studied disinterest.

'And? Unless you're running this operation, *you* don't need to know who I am. So if you don't recognise me that's a good thing, and I'm very happy to keep it that way.'

The doorman shrugged, turning away to occupy the patch of warmth the recently departed youth had vacated.

'You won't be sounding quite so tough when *he* gets here.'

After an hour or so the rear door opened to admit the messenger and four more men, the first of them to enter the warehouse obviously in command of the small group from the way the others stayed behind him, one of them taking up a position to block the door while the other two moved to flank their boss. Bearded, and dressed in a well-made tunic and good stout boots, he wore a permanently predatory expression that seemed to explain the doorman's openly expressed fear. While he lacked the bearing of a military man, there was nevertheless an air of command in his demeanour that spoke to Marcus of imperial service. He paced up to Gracchus and barked a pre-emptory question.

'Where are the other two?'

Marcus watched with a show of indifference, ready to strike a killing blow on Gracchus's throat if the easterner's nerve failed him, but the centurion shrugged, his response at once appropriately uninformed and befitting a man in his exalted position within the military hierarchy.

'How would I know? We split up when we landed on the other side and went our own ways. I found some information I thought you needed to know and so I came back. They're either still out there or they've been caught.'

The other man nodded slowly.

'What information?'

'Severus's army is on the march, heading for Byzantium. Four legions at full strength, the same number of auxiliary soldiers, cavalry, artillery. Everything he's got from the look of it, heading for the Bosporus.'

The big man leaned closer to him.

'And you *saw* this? This isn't just some taverna gossip you picked up in a dockyard drinker in Rhaedestus?'

Gracchus hardened his expression, throwing every ounce of his dignity into the reply.

'Your boss chose me for this job because I came recommended by my tribune as a man who can be trusted with important jobs. So no, I didn't pick it up from gossip, and I didn't bother with the tavernas. This sort of thing needs a man to get his eyes on the prize. I stood for half a day and watched the army march past. I even saw Severus, with so many bodyguards that not even you would have been tempted to take a knife to him.'

The big man nodded humourlessly.

'Well now, that is interesting news. *If* it's true that he's marching for the Bosporus.'

He played a hard stare over Marcus.

'So who's he?'

'A centurion from the Third, like me. Another one of your boss's recruits.'

'So how come I don't recognise him?'

'Because you've never met me before.'

The newcomer took a step closer, his interest piqued by Marcus's direct and apparently unconcerned response.

'Let's understand each other, friend. I go by the name of "the Nomad". You know what that means?'

Marcus shook his head, feigning ignorance.

'In Latin it's pronounced *Nomas*. It's the name we men of the frumentarii give ourselves to avoid using our usual title when we're in enemy territory. I am a grain officer. Do you know what that means?'

'Of course I do. You men of the frumentarii are famous throughout the empire.'

The Nomad nodded.

'Then you know that you don't want to piss me off. Now show me the ring.' Marcus lifted his hand, and the frumentarius stared intently at the red stone's carved face, nodding slowly. 'It looks authentic. But the fact remains that I don't know you. So why should I trust you?'

'Because your boss Sartorius does.'

The big man frowned, putting a hand on his dagger.

'None of you recruits are supposed to know his name. So how is it that you came into possession of that information?'

Marcus mentally rolled the dice, knowing that the wrong answer would condemn him to death no matter how many of the Nomad's men he managed to kill before he went down fighting.

'Because I fought in the battle outside Rhaedestus. I didn't see you there, so I can only presume you were too busy being a *nomad* to join the fighting?'

The frumentarius stared back at him, his hand still on the hilt of his dagger, his voice cold at the insult.

'Go on.'

'That battle was a disaster from start to finish. First our glorious generals let the enemy deploy into a defensive position, then they threw us at their line without thinking through the consequences, when we could just have starved them out within a day or two. And then, when we'd sweated and bled for a few hours and got nowhere, they tempted the gods with a display of our three legion standards, to show them our superior numbers. Which resulted in the gods having a right laugh at us by sending a real eagle to land on the other side's one and only standard. And that was the end of it as far as we were concerned, the gods had shown their favour to the enemy, that was that, so we called it a draw and marched away to lick our wounds.'

The big man curled a lip in scorn.

'Sounds like you're not the most loyal of men to your commanders? Does that disdain include the emperor, perhaps?'

Marcus smiled back at him, his face hard.

'That's just what your man Sartorius asked me when I voiced the same opinion to him that night, after the enemy had marched away and while our lads were trying to come to terms with the whole shit-show and how many of their mates they had lost in an afternoon.'

The Nomad shook his head.

'You were talking to Sartorius without an invitation? Unlikely.'

The Roman affected a shrug.

'I was centurion of the night watch. It was supposed to be one of my mates, but he was dead on his feet and carrying a flesh wound, and I was never going to sleep after a day like that, so I took his watch. Halfway through the night your man Sartorius came walking through the camp and got himself challenged by a bunch of nervy legionaries. He wasn't having it, not an important man like him, and they weren't fucking around after a day like that, with half of their mates dead or dying. I reckon he was as close to getting a spear through him as he could ever be without the actual bloodshed, but I'd seen him with the emperor earlier that day so I knew he was genuine. I pulled them off him, apologised for the legion, and offered him a drink of wine. He was magnanimous enough to accept, and we ended up having a talk about the battle and what we could have done better. Seems like he liked my style, because the next day I was called to my legatus's tent and told I was being put on detached duty working for the man.'

'He recruited you on the basis of a cup of wine and a bit of talk? Just like that?'

Marcus stared back into the Nomad's disbelief.

'Some men are just good judges of character, I guess.'

The big man shook his head in continued distrust of the story he was being told.

'Prove it. What does he have hanging from his belt?'

The Roman grinned knowingly, having seen Sartorius at close quarters on the battlefield.

'A miniature beneficiarius lance. He doesn't carry the actual spear, he's grown past that in his service to the emperor, but he likes to remind himself where he came from. Or at least that's what he told me.'

The other man nodded reluctantly.

'Perhaps you did meet him. So, you talked in the army's camp. Then what happened?'

'I was sent over to his part of the camp and briefed as to what was expected of me. I was to make my way west, get around the enemy legion we'd fought the previous day, find the enemy main force, get the measure of their strength and then report it all back to him.'

'And how were you supposed to report?'

Marcus took the risk he knew was unavoidable, making up what the executed spy he'd seen in Severus's camp was likely to have been instructed to do on finding the army marching east.

'By sending a message to Calchedon, on the eastern side of the straits. When I found the enemy army on the road from the west I paid a farmer with a horse a gold coin, and told him there were five more like it waiting for him when he found Sartorius or whoever he left waiting to receive the message, because that's where he told me Niger's army would be retreating to initially and where I was to send any messenger. And, having done what I was ordered to achieve, a report of the enemy strength, I headed back to the east to re-join my legion, managing to stay a day's march ahead of the enemy until they reached Rhaedestus.'

'Which was where you met this one, I take it?'

The note of disbelief was still strong in the frumentarius's voice as he jerked a thumb at Gracchus.

'Yes. We literally bumped into each other while we were both watching the enemy army march past the city. He was the chosen man of the century I was allotted to when I joined the legion, so I knew him well enough to know he would never have deserted. I made my way over to him to find out what he was doing, saw his ring and realised that he must have been given the same mission as me. Probably as insurance against my being killed or taken, or vice versa. And when I found out that he had a way to escape across the sea from the port and across the Propontis, rather than having to walk all the way to Byzantium and cross the Ox Ford, I joined up with him to save myself a lot of wasted time and miles.'

The big man turned away in thought, then gestured to his accomplices.

'Go and fetch the horses and get ready to ride, we'll send all this to Sartorius and let him make sense of it.' He waved a hand to the watery-eyed doorman. 'You can watch these two while I write some messages.'

He sat in a corner of the warehouse and busied himself with a pair of wax tablets, presumably inscribing the news that the Severan army was heading north towards the straits, along with the return of both Gracchus and the spymaster's apparent first recruit from the Third Legion, into two messages, at least one of which would be intended for his master. Marcus and Gracchus went to sit on the floor with their backs against a stack of amphorae of olive oil, the region's staple product.

'How did you know Sartorius is at Calchedon?'

Marcus smiled at Gracchus's whispered question.

'The ring you're wearing bears a stone of carnelian. Which is mined, among other places, in Chalcedon. Making it logical that he has some sort of base close to where the stones were cut and engraved. A lucky guess, I suppose.' He shot the centurion a questioning look. 'You realise he plans to kill us?'

Gracchus looked at him in disbelief, matching the Roman's low tone to avoid being overheard, but with a note of panic in his voice.

'Kill us? Why would he want to *kill* us? We've done exactly what was asked of us, haven't we . . . ?'

His indignant whisper died away, and the Roman smiled grimly as the truth of their situation dawned on his companion.

'Exactly. We've done what we were commanded to do, and now that we've reported back we have no further utility. Indeed, we might be an embarrassment, if the truth of our mission were ever reported. The upper level of Roman society, if you haven't already realised this, hates informers, having been terrorised by them off and on for the last two hundred years. Added to which their use is seen as ungentlemanly, a tool of terror against the ruling class used by emperors and never to be openly admitted so as not to undermine their dignity. Which means it would all be so much easier if you and I had never existed in the first instance, don't you think?'

Gracchus stared at the floor his face turning pale as the reality of his position hit him like a sickening blow.

'But I was promised early release from my contract, and a farm to retire to.'

'By Sartorius? You might as well have been promised a villa on the Palatine Hill! The only land in your near future is the small plot they'll bury you in, and if you think that betraying me will save you, think again. We're both dead men, unless we manage to give them a nasty surprise, because pleading for mercy will only excite that evil bastard's urge to kill, I've met animals like him before.'

Gracchus shook his head.

'But how? It's not as if we're armed with anything useful, and there are four of them with knives and swords.'

Marcus shook his head.

'Don't worry, we've got two things on our side that are more powerful than all that iron in the hands of men who have no idea what's about to happen to them: surprise, and what's in my pouch.'

He ignored the other man's incomprehension, watching with apparent detachment as the Nomad finished his message and stood up. At the sound of hoof-beats in the street the doorman looked out of the door, then ducked back in and nodded to the frumentarius.

'Horses are here.'

The big man finished sealing the tablets in which he had written the two messages, then beckoned to Marcus and Gracchus, his face carefully composed to avoid alarming them with the truth of their likely fate.

'You two, come with me. We're moving you to somewhere safer.'

'Safer? Where?'

The big man grinned, unable to contain his amusement at Gracchus's poorly disguised nervousness.

'Where? Somewhere a bit quieter, out of town and a bit less public than this. Somewhere you can rest for a while, nice and peaceful.'

Gracchus, unable to contain himself any longer, was starting to show clear signs of panic. Outside the warehouse the narrow street was empty other than for a pair of riders, and the Nomad handed one of the sealed writing tablets to the closer of them, who tucked it away in his saddlebag.

'Take that message to Sartorius at Calchedon. Tell him this, word for word. Tell him that we're closing up shop here, and that we'll re-join him in a week or so, once we've tidied up.'

The rider saluted and trotted his horse away, the big man handed the second tablet to his colleague.

'Take this to Legatus Augusti Aemilianus at Parium, and tell him the same message has been copied to Sartorius. He'll have to work out what to do with the information for himself.'

The second rider echoed the first man's salute and spurred his horse away to catch up with his comrade, the clatter of his mount's hoofs filling the street with noise and capturing the attention of the Nomad's men for a crucial moment. Taking advantage of the distraction, Marcus put a hand into his purse and wrapped his fingers around a metal item in the small leather bag. The riders turned the corner at the end of the street, and the frumentarius turned back to them with a predatory smile.

'Right, I think it's time we got you two precious flowers somewhere a bit quieter, eh?'

Gracchus was unable to control his terror any longer.

'No! I'm not going anywhere with you! Give me my money, and I'll be away to my family. Trust me, I'll never speak of this to anyone!'

The Nomad shook his head in affected sadness, but couldn't conceal his amusement at the centurion's fear.

'Can't do it, I'm afraid. My master told me to make sure that there were no loose thread ends left dangling, and trust me, you're a loose end that could end up unravelling into a major problem, months or even years from now.'

Marcus stretched his arms out slowly and yawned, rolling his head on his neck as if to manage muscle stiffness.

'Take it like a man, eh Gracchus? Sometimes you kill the lion, and sometimes the lion kills you.'

The centurion goggled at Marcus in outraged amazement, while the Nomad's face creased in puzzlement at the unexpected sentiment.

'But you—'

The Roman abruptly pushed him with both hands, hard enough to send him staggering back into the frumentarius and knocking the big man off balance even as he put a hand to the handle of his dagger. Feeling a hand on his shoulder, Marcus threw a swift elbow back into the thug's face, hard enough to break the bruiser's nose and momentarily disorient him. While the men around him were reacting to the unexpected turn of events he put the whistle that he had taken from his belt pouch to his mouth and blew it hard. Adding to the sudden chaos, he pivoted at the hip and drove a half fist into the stunned guard's throat, crushing his larynx, then pulled the pugio from the stricken man's scabbard and turned to face the remaining enforcers.

'Kill him!'

As he roared the command to his men, the Nomad pulled his own dagger out and sank the blade deep into Gracchus's back as the centurion turned to run. Bearing him to the ground, he ripped the knife free for the killing stroke while the other two enforcers focused their attention on Marcus. The closer of them lunged in, springing back with a shout of pain as the Roman blocked his attack with a raised arm and then punished him with a vicious slice of the blade across the back of his hand, severing the tendons and causing the knife to fall from his useless fingers. Stabbing the hapless Gracchus in the back of his neck to finish him off, the frumentarius got back to his feet and shot Marcus an evil look, the other thug at his side, while the doorman and the youth waited behind them with their own blades drawn.

'Whoever the fuck you are, you're a dead man!'

He raised the bloodied blade of his pugio, then looked past Marcus as Sanga and Saratos came around the corner of the warehouse behind the Roman from the gutter where they had been impersonating beggars, both raising swords ready to attack. In an instant the Nomad was away up the street in the opposite direction, sprinting for his life, and Marcus let him go, concentrating his attention on the closer thugs as the two soldiers made short work of them.

The frumentarius slowed, turning back to spit defiance at them.

'You'd better run, you cunts, because—'

He crumpled, smashed sideways by a blow to the head from a boarding club wielded by Skaiv's leading man, who had stepped out of the shadow of another warehouse as the fleeing frumentarius had paused at its corner. Staggering away from the attack with his jaw hanging brokenly from his face, he turned to face Marcus as the Roman stalked up to him, grunting with the sudden shock as the Roman drove the butt of his dagger's handle into his throat, stepping back to allow the stricken frumentarius to slump to the cobbles, choking noisily in his death throes.

'What about these two?'

He turned to find Sanga and Saratos eyeing the doorman and his young companion, both having thrown down their weapons rather than face the two soldiers' long blades in combat. Both men stared at him in mute supplication, but Marcus shook his head sadly.

'They have to die. If we let them live and they send the story of that man's death to Sartorius then this has all been a waste of energy, and the landings on this coast will be opposed far more swiftly than will otherwise be the case.'

The doorman dropped to his knees in desperate supplication.

'No! Kill me, but don't harm the boy! Take him with you, but don't take his life!'

The Roman realised what had been bothering him about the two men.

'You are father and son?'

The doorman nodded.

'My only son.'

Marcus thought for a moment.

'There is a way. But it'll need you to tell me everything you know, and if I think you're holding anything back I'll have no choice but to execute you both here and now.' He raised a hand to forestall the promise of immediate co-operation he was expecting from the other man. 'And you'll have to give up your freedom to earn the right to keep breathing.'

'Anything!'

'Very well. Tell me, why is Aemilianus at Parium?'

'I don't know much about it' – the doorman raised a hand to prevent Marcus from interrupting him – 'but I can tell you that Aemilianus is the emperor's favourite general, and that he marched past the city a few days ago with three legions. His men emptied the storehouses to feed that many soldiers, and the city was up in arms about it.'

'And where exactly is Parium?'

'Seventy miles to the west, close to the Hellēspontos.'

Marcus pondered the new information for a moment.

'We're going back to the boat we sailed here, and you two can come with us if you wish to live. But if either of you make any attempt to draw attention to us then I'll gut the boy and leave him to bleed out where he falls, and leave you with his corpse.'

Saratos nudged the closer of the dead men with his booted foot.

'What about these bodies?'

The Roman pointed to the warehouse.

'Get them in there.'

Inside the warehouse they found a roll of cloth in which to wrap Gracchus's corpse, winding the cloth around the body until the blood seeping into the weave was covered from view, and Marcus gestured to the captives.

'Carry him to the boat, and remember: one sign of trouble and these two will make sure the boy troubles the ferryman a long time before you do.' He nodded to Skaiv's crewman. 'Get ready to sail. I'll be with you shortly.'

He waited until the frumentarius's corpse and those of his men had been carried to the middle of the warehouse, and the party had returned to the boat, then went looking in the doorman's cupboard. As expected, the wooden box contained a lamp and a jar of oil, and he poured the oil in a trail from the door to a pile of cloth bales, unrolling a length of the nearest of them and soaking the material in the pungent fluid. Finding the amphorae of olive oil he'd leaned against earlier, he used an iron bar to smash the ends off them one at a time, pouring their contents out onto the warehouse floor until the slowly spreading puddles formed a lake across the building.

The offering bowl on the small altar was still perfuming the air with the ascending heat from the coals gently smoking in their bowl, and he blew on the embers to coax them back to glowing life. Offering a prayer of apology to Mars as he took the bowl to the door, he turned and flicked the coals onto the oil, waiting while the liquid momentarily fumed and then caught fire before shutting the warehouse door and heading for the boat.

Sailing out into the harbour, as Skaiv's men turned the boat towards the sea beyond, with a breeze to propel them away from the city, the Roman stared back at the shoreline, looking for the smoke that soon enough started billowing from the warehouse's windows. The shouts of the men who came running from neighbouring buildings to try to extinguish the blaze were barely audible over the angry roar, as the building's roof beams caught fire and the clay tiles collapsed into the blaze. He nodded satisfaction at the outcome of such a high-risk gamble.

'And that, I think, is enough for one day. Misleading information provided to our enemies, and their spy network on this coast decapitated, with the bodies all made unrecognisable.'

'Decapitated?'

Saratos grinned at his mate.

'It means that the head has been cut from the body.'

Sanga shook his head unhappily.

'My belly thinks my throat's been cut, never mind decapitated. Is there even any food left on that island?'

5

Marching camp of the army of Septimius Severus, Rhaedestus, September AD 193

'Rutilius Scaurus! I wasn't sure that we were actually ever going to see you again.'

Severus flashed a chilly smile to match the dismissive nature of his greeting at Scaurus and Marcus from his place on the gilded wooden throne in which he was holding court. The two men had been hurried into the imperial encampment once Laetus had realised that they had returned, the hard-eyed general clearly eager to see them before the emperor to recount whatever it was that they had achieved.

'We have accomplished the result that I promised you, Imperator.'

The emperor shot Scaurus a long questioning stare before replying.

'And did you bring my prisoners back?'

Laetus butted in with a note of triumph in his voice.

'They did, Imperator, but the interrogators may find them less responsive than would have been the case if they had they *not* been entrusted to the care of these two men.'

Severus switched his attention to the general, holding his stare until Laetus dropped his gaze, then turned his attention back to Scaurus.

'So, *both* of my prisoners are dead then?'

'Yes, Imperator.'

'I see. That is . . . disappointing. And in return for their sacrifice you bring me what, exactly?'

'Our actions have destroyed both the usurper's spy harbour and his base in Cyzicus, dismantling a spying operation that, had we failed to do so, would probably now be providing the usurper with full details as to your deployments, Imperator, and—'

Severus cut him off with a waved hand.

'You don't have to use my title in every sentence, Tribune, I'll take your undying respect for granted. I will call you Scaurus and you will call me "sir", unless there is a wider audience that needs to be shown the nature of the respect my throne demands. Now tell me more.'

'Yes sir. We located the tiny harbour on an island north of Cyzicus, from which the enemy spies were coming and going to and from your port of Rhaedestus. After we had captured the men operating this supply line we sent them back to our side of the sea. They are waiting with my men outside, ready to be questioned. One of the prisoners was killed in an attempt to escape, an attempt I allowed him to make with my men in place to kill him, in order to motivate the other man to support us in infiltrating their main base of operations.'

'I see.' The emperor's smile was almost reptilian in its pleasure at the information. 'How very cold blooded of you, Tribune Scaurus. And this "main base of their operations"?'

'Was in the port city of Cyzicus, sir, a warehouse in the docks. We gained access to it, killed the remaining spies and then burned it to the ground in order to hide the evidence that we had ever been there. Although we only did so after ensuring that false information with regards to your army's plans for an attack had been sent to both Niger's frumentarius spy Sartorius and his general Aemilianus, to deceive them and enable you to strike unexpectedly.'

The emperor leaned forward, his eyes narrowing at what might be construed as a dangerously independent course of action, and Laetus smiled faintly at the prospect of his potential wrath.

'And the nature of that false information, Tribune? In what way have you sought to deceive the enemy at the risk of constraining my freedom of manoeuvre?'

'I sent Sartorius a message stating that you have marched your army north to the Bosporus, where you will seek to force a passage of the narrows and advance into Asia on the far side.'

Severus's silent stare was an eloquent comment in itself, intended to intimidate, and the other men in the room held their breaths in anticipation of an outburst.

'That was . . . *presumptuous* of you, was it not? That might be exactly my plan, might it not?'

Laetus's eyes lit up at the possibility that the two men might yet fall foul of his master's ire, and Scaurus lowered his head in half-bow and half-supplication.

'Perhaps so, sir, and if you deem it to be punishable, I will bear the sentence lightly. My assumption was that you would never make such an obvious move if there were a better and less costly alternative than an attack on such a well-defended fortress available.'

Severus smiled thinly.

'Such as?'

'To use the praetorian fleet to ship your army across the Hellēspontos, sir. It would afford your generals the ability to build the army of Pannonia to its full strength quickly, before the enemy can bring their own to bear. Although I can tell you that Aemilianus was positioned at Parium with three legions as of two days ago, according to the men I interrogated when I heard his name.'

'And you have these men with you as well?'

Scaurus shook his head, allowing a hard smile to creep onto his face.

'No, sir. Lacking your expert interrogators' skill in such matters I managed to kill the two men in question – a father and son – while verifying that they were not seeking to deceive me.'

Severus nodded knowingly, and with a hint of pleasure at the news of such a robust approach.

'While such a loss is of course regrettable, and I would have relished the chance to have them questioned professionally, it speaks well for your zeal in the matter. And that is exceptional *scouting*, and to be differentiated, gentlemen' – he looked around the audience chamber – 'from the base acts of spying and informing of which the usurper is so very evidently guilty.'

Marcus kept his face emotionless, knowing that both of the supposedly dead men were now happy members of Skaiv's crew, albeit indentured for five years as the price of their lives, long enough that any knowledge they might be able to take to the enemy would be long out of date by the time of their release. The emperor pondered for a moment.

'So, you have spread false information that I am marching on Byzantium. Which will undoubtedly lead the traitor Aemilianus to send some part of his strength north to help repel such an attack, while remaining in place in Parium to watch for any attempt at our making a crossing nearby. And, of course, to wait for orders to abandon his position and follow those reinforcements. And an attack across the Hellēspontos is, I will admit, my favoured option. It would afford my army with options, either to march north and cut Byzantium off from any source of supply from Asia across the strait, or to take a bolder approach, and advance deeper into Asia in order to threaten the usurper's line of communication with the rest of what's left of his so-called empire. A well-timed landing while the enemy's attention is elsewhere might be just the thing we need to prevent Niger being allowed to dictate the pace at which we are able to advance even though his army is so inferior to ours. Very well, my decision is made. Send for the *dux exercitus Illyrici!*'

When the commander of the four Pannonian legions presented himself a few moments later, Marcus was glad to see that Tiberius Claudius Candidus had lost the faint air of bafflement that he had displayed on being assigned to the command of Severus's army of Illyricum, in the days after Severus's triumphant procession into Rome. Giving every sign of being a highly competent general, he nodded briskly on hearing of the raiding party's success, and the potential for a surprise attack it had unlocked.

'That's excellent news, sir. My staff have been working up options for whatever strategy you might order us to enact next, and our collective view is that crossing the Hellēspontos in force is the most likely to give us the initiative. Although we will also be at the most risk of being defeated, if the enemy manages to confront us in force before our full strength can be gathered. If what Rutilius Scaurus has told us translates to the usurper focusing on defeating a crossing of the Bosporus, then we might well be able to get all our legions ashore and into the field before he even knows we're there, by taking such an approach to the problem.'

The emperor nodded briskly, confident in his general's competence.

'And your plan for the crossing, Claudius Candidus?'

'We have made contact with the navarchus commanding the praetorian fleet that shipped our colleague Fabius Cilo's Fourth Legion to their glorious destiny, sir. It appears that his ships will be able to land two legions on the far side of the straits each day. Which means that on the morning of the third day we will be able to take the war to whichever part of Asia you think most appropriate.' He turned to Scaurus with a knowing, if friendly, smile. 'You know the navarchus, of course, Rutilius Scaurus, and you won't be surprised to hear that he was asking after you, when he heard about the battle that you fought outside Rhaedestus.'

'Indeed.' Scaurus nodded expressionlessly. 'And I look forward to telling him all about it in person, given his close personal interest in the matter of my success in battle.'

An aide entered the tent and whispered in Laetus's ear, the smile on the general's face broadening as he listened to what the man had to say. Severus raised an eyebrow at him, a tapping foot betraying his impatience.

'Well then Julius, what is it that your officer has to tell you? An interesting development, to judge from your expression.'

Laetus nodded, his amusement clear to see.

'It *is* interesting news, Imperator. The usurper has sent one of his underlings to sue for peace. Apparently, he is waiting at the gates of the camp under a flag of truce, and wishes to pass a message to you.'

'Who is it?' Severus stretched wearily. 'Which one of his treacherous dogs has he chosen to risk?'

'That's what made me smile, Imperator.' Laetus's eyes settled on Scaurus and Marcus. 'It seems that Niger has sent his former frumentarius, the master informer Sartorius, to make this offer.'

Severus's eyes narrowed in icy calculation.

'Very interesting. And a wise choice on my rival's part. I cannot be insulted by this, as the man is beneath my attention, a mere functionary, even though the role he plays in his camp is so repugnant. Whereas sending a man of the senatorial class would have risked that man being executed for his treachery in siding with an enemy of Rome. It's certainly a clever move on someone's behalf. Very well, bring him in. And you, Rutilius Scaurus, and your tame swordsman too, will both stand quietly and given no indication of enmity towards this man. I want to hear what he has to say, and I don't want you making wolf eyes at him and bringing my ability to respect a flag of truce into disrepute. Do you hear me?'

Sartorius walked into the audience tent between a pair of the emperor's praetorians, spotting Scaurus and Marcus almost instantly as his eye swept the small space, but if he felt any fear in their presence he refused to show it. Bowing his head low enough for the seated Severus to see his nape, he remained in the position of obeisance until the emperor commanded him to stand straight.

'What is it that your master the usurper has sent you to say to me, Frumentarius?'

Sartorius replied in a tone somewhere between respect and, as Marcus commented to Qadir and Dubnus later on, an obvious and very sincere desire not to be executed for any imagined slight.

'Imperator, I bring you friendly greetings from my master, Gaius Pescennius Niger Justus Augustus.'

Severus smiled with his mouth, but his eyes remained hard.

'Clever of you to omit the titles "Imperator" and "Caesar", but to leave in "Augustus", associating him with the throne without a formal claim of imperial power. Was that his choice of greeting or your own, I wonder? And what is it that my former friend and colleague is hoping to achieve by sending an envoy to me at this time, when I have his army on the back foot and the gods themselves have already delivered their verdict on which of us is the true emperor? I believe you were there when the eagle landed on my single legion's standard, rather than any of your *three*?'

Sartorius inclined his head again, in silent and therefore unrepeatable recognition of such undeniable facts, continuing his address in the same respectful tone.

'Imperator, my master has instructed me to make you an offer. He is magnanimously minded, and willing—'

'To share the rule of this great empire with me, with his half starting at the Bosporus and encompassing all of Asia, Syria, Judea and, no doubt, Aegyptus too, to give him control of Rome's bread basket? Yes? Plus of course whatever territory he can carve away from the Parthians, I expect?'

'In fairness, such a territorial division is no more than the current extent of his control, Imperator. He—'

Severus interrupted again, the smile on his face visibly hardening.

'Is willing to swear an oath to all the gods that he will maintain the supply of grain from his territory to Rome, and to act in concert with me in all matters pertaining to the empire's security? I expected nothing less. And in return for peace, of course, he will be allowed to rule as emperor east of the Bosporus, and doubtless there would also need to be some agreement as to the succession in the event of the first of us dying. Which is an interesting question in itself, given he has a great many friends in Rome, some of whom are both influential and, shall we say, *resourceful*? While my influence in Antioch is limited. Making my death rather more likely than his, I suspect. And is that the limit of his offer, or are there yet more concessions he seeks from me?'

Sartorius bowed again, his face mask-like in its composure.

'You have the essence of it, Imperator, an impressive prediction.'

Severus shook his head tersely, in contemptuous rejection of the obvious compliment.

'It was no harder to predict these details than it was to guess that he would make such an offer at this juncture. Indeed, I have been waiting weeks for him to get round to the realisation that his defeat is inevitable and sue for peace under terms favourable mostly to himself. This offer is exactly the same as the one I would make in his place, as the alternative to discussing a surrender that does not involve his execution and that of his family. And, master informer, his closest advisors.' He made a throwaway gesture. 'Which, let us face the truth of it, is all that he can really hope to achieve given our relative strengths. Take that back to your master as my only offer, his life, those of his family, and perhaps even yours . . . *perhaps* . . . in return for a swift and total capitulation.'

He leaned forward, his gaze locked on the spymaster.

'You can also tell him that I am aware of your deadly scheming against my army's advance, making you personally so close to being an informer that it is only the flag of truce, and my need to remain reasonable – if implacably opposed to any such peace deal – that prevents me from taking pleasure in your immediate and protracted interrogation. And, following that, the execution of whatever is left when the torturers are done with you.'

Sartorius held his stare, but Marcus noted a tremble in his knee, and wondered how firm his bladder control was under such a threat. The emperor nodded grim satisfaction.

'Yes, you do very well to remain silent, weasel, my patience is close to exhaustion. So tell your master of my last and final offer, that he may yet surrender and be allowed to relinquish the purple without the loss of his life, or those of his wife and children, or any punishment other than his exile to some island or other to live out his days in grateful and complete isolation, and with a generous guarantee that I won't order him to be starved to death, as was the habit among the Julio-Claudians. Those are *my* terms, the only terms that matter because they are the only terms that are on offer from the inevitable victor of this war, and even then for a very short time indeed. Once battle is joined again there will be no further discussion, and the result of his inevitable defeat will most assuredly be death, whether in battle or at the hand of my executioner.'

Sartorius bowed again and when he raised his head his expression indicated that he understood all too well the thin ice onto which he was about to venture.

'I understand, Imperator, and will convey this message to my master. There is, however, one more question I am *required* to ask of you, with my apologies, if you will indulge me?' Severus stared at him flatly for a moment before he nodded his head in a terse gesture. 'I am required to ask you, were you to respond as you have, whether you would be willing to extend the same fair-minded treatment to other members of his inner—'

'No.' The emperor shook his head, his lips pursed as if at the taste of sour wine. 'I know what game this is! You have been instructed to ask on behalf of Asellius Aemilianus, because Niger calculates that the death of such an influential man would break his power base in Rome for good. And I refuse for exactly the same reason! Beside, Aemilianus is no better than a traitor to Rome! He knew full well that if he sided with me the need for a civil war would be removed, as in him I would have an ally with a carefully nurtured network of the most influential of friends in both Rome *and* Asia. And that Niger would then have had no choice but to come looking for a pardon, rather than costing me thousands of *my* legionaries on both sides of a needless civil war! Instead of which that fool, that . . .' Severus groped for words, clearly now incandescent in his fury '. . . that *charlatan* Aemilianus followed the instructions of his cousin Albinus, who is my other rival and who has no more strength than the three legions of Britannia. He sided with Niger in order to force me to fight in the east, rather than being free to fight a swift and decisive campaign against his cousin's army, in a ploy of such disgraceful duplicity to Rome that I would have him publicly flogged in the forum and then executed in front of the curia, as an example for his fellow senators to consider at their leisure!'

He leaned forward and spat invective at the frumentarius, utterly enraged.

'So you can tell Niger, and Aemilianus, that the best thing he can do will be to die on the battlefield, hopefully in a way that will bring some honour back to his family! Because he is already a dead man to me, and if he is brought before me alive I will indeed have him executed in the bloodiest manner possible, as an example to others as to the penalty for such a crime. Now get out of my sight, before I decide to send you back to your master lacking your head!'

Sartorius bowed again, turned and exited from the tent as fast as he could walk with a modicum of dignity, leaving Severus glaring after him. After a moment he turned the grimace on Laetus, as if daring him to attempt humour on the subject, but for once the general kept his gaze on the emperor's feet until his master relented.

'Yes, I know, I did exactly what I warned your man Scaurus not to. His plea on the behalf of Aemilianus was too much for even a man as controlled in his passions as I am to tolerate.' He sighed. 'The nerve of the man, whose actions have condemned thousands of my soldiers to death at the whim of his cousin, to send that worm to ask for his life? He should die of shame.'

He turned to Candidus with a small smile, the fire of his anger seemingly burned out.

'And you, Legatus Augustus, can be the man to deliver Aemilianus's destiny to him. Take your army, cross the Hellēspontos, find his army and destroy it. Either bring me his head or preferably his living body, so that I can have him disgraced and executed myself. And if you can bring the usurper Niger to bay and either capture him or send him to meet his ancestors, so much the better!'

The Hellēspontos strait, Propontis Sea, October AD 193

It had been deemed inevitable that the city port of Abydus's watchmen would be in a state of high alert, given the high risk that their place on the narrowest part of the strait would make them the most likely recipients of any invasion force. Further, it was clear that, having seen the praetorian fleet's leading ships standing out from the western shore in the first light of dawn, they would immediately send messengers to the enemy army suspected to be lurking some way back from the city, positioned and ready to deal with an invasion at any point along the strait's eastern shore, before more force than they could throw back into the sea could be landed on the Severan invaders' chosen beach.

And so, when the plans were being laid for the invasion of Asia via the Hellēspontos's most convenient crossing, little more than a mile at its narrowest point, Scaurus suggested that Skaiv's *Neptune's Bride* be used to clandestinely put his familia ashore to the east of the city in order to prevent any such warning reaching the enemy and thus giving them additional time to react to the presence of the invading army. What he had not expected had been that his nemesis Titus, as prefect of the fleet, would insist on accompanying them across the strait, overruling Skaiv's reluctance to allow a senior officer aboard his vessel with the bluntly stated assertion that either the fleet's prefect would sail with them or he would have the vessel commandeered and put his own crew aboard.

In a break in the planning Candidus beckoned Scaurus to him, asking the question that his officers were clearly fascinated by, at least to judge from the way they had gathered around to hear the answer. Looking around at them, Marcus found it hard to avoid the conclusion that, other than Candidus himself, they were political appointees to a man, the sons of the influential men rather than experienced legion commanders.

'Tell me, Rutilius Scaurus, are the rumours true? Has the prefect of the praetorian fleet really put a death curse upon you?'

'Indeed he has, Legatus.' A member of the senatorial class himself, Scaurus replied frankly, as to an equal, as the army's commander was, at least socially if not in terms of military seniority. 'He had the curse written in Thessalonica, which I presume is no less effective than seeking divine retribution anywhere else.'

The general shook his head in bafflement.

'But . . . *why?*'

'Why would one imperial officer curse another?' Scaurus shrugged. 'I was indirectly, but very clearly, responsible for the death of his family under the rule of Commodus. Which means that I can hardly blame the man for wanting to be avenged on me for his loss.'

The legatus's expression betrayed his disbelief.

'Well that's very . . . magnanimous of you, Rutilius Scaurus, and indeed it is a salutary example to us all. But I have to admit that if it were me on the receiving end of such impertinence I'd have one of your frankly intimidating familia put the man out of his evident misery, if only for having the sheer bloody cheek to do such a thing to a man of *our* class.'

Scaurus inclined his head in acceptance of Candidus's entirely valid point, that Titus's placing a death curse upon a senator was entirely deserving of a brutal death.

'I have considered such an action, of course, if only to punish his lack of respect for my social rank. My decision not to do so was mostly based on his importance to the success of this campaign, which must of course take priority over all else. Besides which, as a priest of Mithras I am yet to discover whether his attempt at damnation will even be allowed by the gods. The curse was for me to die in the moment of my greatest victory, and our battle outside Rhaedestus was, strictly speaking, settled by divine intervention rather than by victorious force of arms, and so the question remains as yet unanswered.'

As the commander of an army, Candidus had been quick to proclaim that he would be aboard the first ship in the praetorian fleet, the flagship *Victoria*, and lead his men across the Hellēspontos at the head of his vanguard legion, the Tenth Gemina. The legion's first spear, a hard-faced veteran soldier by the name of Draco, was very clearly equally determined to claim his right to be the first man ashore when the time came.

'See these?' The hard-faced senior centurion tapped his medal harness meaningfully when the subject of who would have that honour was raised. 'None of these phalerae were awarded for letting some other bastard go first when it came to a fight' – he winked at the gathered officers without any hint of self-consciousness – 'or at least not one who lived to tell the tale and spoil my record. And I'll be buggered if I let the chance to be the first man ashore tomorrow go begging.' He tipped a nod to Scaurus. 'Or at least the first man from the army, at least, since I'm not allowed to come and play at pirates with you mad fuckers. Sir.'

Candidus, who had been half-listening to the conversation and half-studying the map of the Asian side of the Hellēspontos strait, waved Draco away with an amused smile.

'You can be first to get your feet wet, First Spear; now see if you can use your unique talent for inspiring immediate obedience to persuade the men serving the wine to hurry up and bring out another amphora?' He turned back to Scaurus with a graver expression. 'So it seems that you will have to wait for a genuine victory, if you are to find out if the curse will have any effect? If it does, then of course you may well be dead, and unable to take any action either way. And if it does not . . . ?'

Scaurus shrugged, opening his arms and raising his hands to the heavens.

'Then I will consult with my god and decide as to my future actions at that time. And as you say, Claudius Candidus, the whole question might be completely moot, if my next taste of battle's bitter cup is my last.'

Candidus bowed, a genuine expression of respect for the stoicism that the tribune was displaying.

'That's all very well and good, and, I suppose, worthy of dear old Marcus Aurelius himself. And it does you great credit as a Roman gentleman. But does an unopposed landing count, I wonder? It would be a damned shame for you to drop dead on the beach without having the chance to use your undoubted skills.'

The *Bride* sailed without fanfare in the middle of the night, slipping silently away from an unlit pier into the inky darkness of a moonless and cloudy night, Titus standing in silence alongside Skaiv as the wary navarchus issued orders to his crew in a loud whisper. Marcus and Scaurus sat in the vessel's bow with Qadir, a pair of his archers and three of Dubnus's pioneers. The remainder of the familia had been taken under First Spear Draco's wing, the veteran having recognised a kindred spirit in Dubnus himself and inviting the Briton and his companions to sail across the straits with him on the leading warship.

'We can only hope that our brother manages to keep Ptolemy away from Draco, for fear that such a ferocious officer might just put him over the side rather than tolerate one of his history lectures. After all, we are crossing one of the most historically significant pieces of water in the whole of the world.' Scaurus leaned back against the ship's side, trailing his fingers through the water that was lapping at the vessel's timbers as it eased through the strong current under the power of its black sails. 'For one thing, Troy is only a few dozen miles from here and the coast we're sailing towards is where the Trojan War happened, the whole thing caused by the Greeks' need to defeat Troy and stop them controlling all of the trade coming through the strait and strangling their grain supply. And the Persians under Xerxes crossed it from east to west on their way to Thermopylae seven hundred years ago, a favour that the Macedonians under Alexander returned a hundred and fifty years later. And we all know how both of those adventures ended.'

He laughed softly.

'In fact, Herodotus writes that Xerxes had two pontoon bridges built across the strait right here, at Abydus on the eastern shore, so that his army could cross from Persia into Greece, an act of hubris that seems to have attracted the attention of the gods themselves. The bridges were both destroyed by a storm, and Xerxes had their designers and builders beheaded. And then, and this is the part that defies belief, he had fetters thrown into the strait's waters to imprison the sea, ordered those waters to be given three hundred lashes and had them branded with red-hot irons, while his soldiers shouted insults and defiance at the very sea itself.'

One of the axemen accompanying them spoke out of the vessel's darkness in a tone of disbelief.

'Was he mad?'

The Roman shrugged at the pioneer's question.

'Herodotus says that while it was a questionable way to address the Hellēspontos, it was in keeping with his behaviour. He was, after all, an emperor, and absolute power can do strange things to a man's mind over time. And besides, he had an army to remind exactly who he was. If his men felt he had offended the gods then they might have lost their fear of him, and so he set out to prove his mastery of the elements, I suppose. And it seems to have worked, because they managed to cross the strait successfully enough on their way to their eventual defeats by both the united Greek army and fleet. Although it seems that another engineer came up with the idea to lash the ships together, with their bows facing the current, and to add two more anchors to each ship, which was the real reason why the army was able to cross safely. A combination of faith and engineering, perhaps. The Hellēspontos was also the scene of the story of Hero and Leander, in which Leander swam the strait every night to couple with the priestess Hero.'

The same pioneer guffawed softly at the thought.

'That must have been some woman, for a man to swim that sort of distance rather than just handing over a coin to one of the local girls.'

'Hmm.' Scaurus shook his head in fresh amusement. 'It really doesn't work like that in the old stories, relationships between men and women are usually somewhat less commercial. But I can see your point, and since the story ends with Leander drowning in yet another storm, perhaps he would have been better off sticking to your approach to romance.'

After a while longer the *Bride*'s crew hauled down her black sails, and stealthily drove her onto the eastern shore a mile to the east of the city under the power of her oars. The familia started to disembark onto the beach, fanning out to secure the landing point, but as Scaurus prepared to follow, Titus appeared out of the gloom at his shoulder. He muttered a question intended to be heard only by the man he had so viciously cursed, but the words were still loud enough for Marcus to hear.

'I heard tell of the battle that resulted, after we put you ashore on the Thracian coast. And that you only managed to escape with your life thanks to an eagle landing on your standard. Is that true?'

The Roman turned and smiled grimly at his would-be nemesis, seeing the disappointment in his face that such a powerful curse could have been ignored by such apparent divine favour.

'Indeed we did. I can only presume, that, as the result was no sort of victory but rather an honourable draw, the result wasn't favourable enough for your curse to strike me down.'

The navarchus nodded, his face expressionless.

'It seems so. And now you are about to go looking for more trouble, I presume?'

'That's why we're here.'

'Then perhaps my curse won't be needed. There will be plenty of unfriendly spears out there ready to bathe their iron in your blood, I would imagine.'

Scaurus shrugged.

'It's a continual hazard of my chosen path in life. And whether or not I die as the result of your ill wishes being enacted by the gods, even without your having achieved the revenge you so clearly crave, you can be assured that I will regret your family's deaths to the end of my days.'

Titus stared at him for a moment, then shook his head and turned away.

'You'd best get off this ship and go and find the enemy then, hadn't you? I hope not to see you again.'

Having worked their way silently off the beach and up the gentle slope that led to the coast road, behind Qadir and his Hamians with their bows strung and ready to shoot, they quickly found the road and set up in ambush. As the light steadily strengthened, the pioneer left to watch the beach made his way to Marcus, Qadir and the archers at the roadside, whispering as quietly as he could and ignoring the pained glances the Syrians were giving his attempts at stealth.

'The fleet is clearly visible now sirs, putting out from the other shore. It can't be long before their messengers come.'

The hissed warning of the archer standing beside Marcus silenced him.

'Hooves. Two, perhaps three horses.'

The Roman waved his friend back, gesturing to the Syrians to ready themselves. Shrinking back into the cover of the trees that lined the road they waited as the sound of the couriers' horses grew louder, their riders talking loudly to be heard over the clatter but their words indistinct. The horsemen came into view out of the light mist, less than a hundred paces distant, and as the Hamians raised their bows Marcus muttered a command, pitched low to avoid the words carrying in the fog.

'Wait . . .'

The riders were cantering their horses, which made him wonder just how close the legions to whom they were taking word of the landing were to the town, given such a profligate use of the beasts' stamina. The archer closest to him started to pull back his arrow, minute creaking sounds coming from the weapon as he forced his strength into its wood and sinew frame.

'*Wait . . .*'

As the riders closed within thirty paces he nodded at the waiting bowman, who drew his arrow back until the fletching was touching his ear, the broad-headed horse-killing head poised for a moment before he loosed it into the leading horse's chest, aiming for the heart. The shot instantly felled the horse, dead before it hit the ground, throwing its rider onto the road where he scrambled away from the dead animal's corpse only to find himself cowed under the axes of the waiting pioneers as they strode onto the road. Another of the messengers survived the fall from his own wounded mount, but the third hit the road's broad stones with his jaw, the impact snapping his spine and leaving him staring sightlessly at the roadside vegetation.

'Bring them here, and put those beasts out of their pain. You archers, move down the road towards the city a hundred paces in case there are more of them; and if there are, you shoot to kill.' Scaurus had emerged from the forest. 'These two will tell us everything we need to know.'

He waited until the two men were squatting before him before speaking again, looking down at them with a foreboding expression.

'You men have a choice to make. You can talk to me now, man to man with no shame attached, and tell me what I need to know nice and easily. Or, if you force it on me, I can hand you over to the commander of the legions that are making the crossing right now. He takes a torturer with him on campaign, and I can tell you for a fact that both he and the man in question are looking for the opportunity to exercise the man's skills. I've seen him castrate a man with a single stroke of the knife, it's his party piece. He used nothing fancier than a legion issue pugio that's been in the coals of a fire for a few minutes, only as a warm-up for the main event but still, it seems to get the attention of the men he does it to even before the iron is red hot. They stop shouting about what they don't know, and start shouting what they do know instead.'

He paused for a moment and both men practically fell over themselves to be the first to speak, the main thrust of which was to tell Scaurus they would do their very best to answer any questions he had for them. A few moments later the party were on the road east, marching for the city, which was only two miles away, the two captives walking under the close attention of the pair of Dubnus's axemen, who had already made it clear that they would be delighted were their prisoners to attempt escape. From a rise in the road they came in sight of the walled settlement, staring out at the massed vessels of the praetorian fleet which were spread out across the Hellēspontos in the act of shipping the first of Candidus's four legions across the narrow strait.

'And if that's not enough to put the fear of all the gods into them, wait until they see these two men and realise that their attempt to call for help will not be answered.'

Scaurus nodded at Qadir.

'True enough, but we'll have them out of sight for the time being, I think. Perhaps you could have our pioneers stand between them and anyone we meet? Speaking of which . . .'

A small group of men with spears and helmets, and bearing the stylised armour and shields of gladiators, were standing in the road; at the sight of the party approaching, one of them took to his heels back into the city. The remaining guards watched the approaching soldiers with an air of bemusement at men approaching them from an unexpected direction, apparently unable to decide whether to stand and resist them or melt away into the buildings on either side. Marcus stopped the party's progress up the road a hundred paces from them, dismounted and went forward alone, although Qadir deployed his archers to either side with their bows strung and arrows nocked to make sure that the guards understood the threat they were facing. After a moment's discussion the Roman ostentatiously turned his back on them to demonstrate his dominance of the situation and walked back to Scaurus.

'They're from the city's gladiatorial ludus, not that that will mean much in a city of this size, and they've been told to report to the council of elders if anyone approaches from this direction, so someone seems to have predicted the possibility of a landing to the city's east even if not quite this soon. I'd say they're jumpy enough to do something stupid if we try to march past them, and to be honest they look harmless enough that we might as well leave them to it, and wait here for someone with authority to show up? I see no point in us slaughtering these innocents when the city will surrender the moment they realise what's happening.'

The tribune agreed, and the party sat in the shade by the roadside while they waited for the guards' message to bear fruit. After a while a dignified-looking older man wearing a ceremonial toga arrived. He walked forward to talk with them, escorted by a pair of gladiators, both men carrying a good deal of weight in the usual manner of trained fighters.

'The toga is a good touch.' Scaurus smiled as the dignitary walked past the city guards and came on with one of his escorts on either side. 'Supposed to remind us that we're all Roman here, I suppose.'

Stopping a judicious distance from where they were sitting, the elder essayed a bow and called out a greeting, his voice only a little tremulous as he called out across the gap between them.

'Gentlemen, welcome to Abydus, a thriving commercial port and in no way part of any military preparations for war! Might I ask the purpose of your, ah, visit, which I would imagine is something to do with that fleet bearing down on us?'

Scaurus stood and walked out to meet him, ignoring the fact that the gladiators had their hands on the hilts of their swords. He waved a hand at the fleet clearly visible stretched across the strait, raising his voice to declaim their fate.

'Those ships signal a reinforcement of your city's undoubted allegiance to Rome's only emperor, and your expected rejection on behalf of your townsmen of any claim to the throne by the usurper Niger! I am Gaius Rutilius Scaurus, tribune of the imperial Pannonian army group and sworn to the service of the one true emperor, the Imperator Caesar Lucius Septimius Severus Pertinax Augustus! And I have been sent to your city as an advance guard of the legions which are currently engaged in landing on the beach to the south-west of your city! You will have noted their passage across the strait, which means that you will be aware that we have the support of a full-strength fleet, which will be shipping several more legions to join the men that have been landed over the next day or so! We have chosen not to attack Abydus itself, out of respect for its age and significance to the empire, and we will maintain that as our attitude just as long as your city gives the emperor's legions the same respect in return. Am I making myself clear?'

The dignitary nodded tersely.

'I am Prusias, leader of the city's council, and I am happy to commit to Abydus respecting the arrival of imperial forces. I cannot speak for the commanders of the army of Pescennius Niger though, as—'

'You do not need to make any such pronouncement on their behalf, Prusias. Simply promise that you will command the people of the city not to attempt to inform any local military forces as to our presence.'

'The very thought of such an idea had of course not occurred—'

Scaurus held up a hand, and Prusias fell silent as his messengers were brought forward from behind the wall of axemen whose bulk had hidden them until Marcus's signal to bring them forth.

'I thought you ought to see these two before protesting quite so forcefully that you have no thought of warning my colleague Asellius Aemilianus of our landing. I don't blame you for trying, of course, and if you promise to co-operate fully there will be no reason for the emperor – the *real* emperor – to hear of this. But let's be clear, we will be posting men on the road west to Cyzicus, and if we intercept any, *any*, communications originating from Abydus, then your city will be treated a good deal less leniently than is our current intention. Because when my general learns of so treasonous an act, he'll have no alternative but to send his men in to teach your inhabitants a lesson. And I'm sure you're well aware of what tends to happen when soldiers are allowed to forcibly occupy cities like this one. Just imagine how they see you, a whole city plump and ripe for the taking, and with your coffers probably fat with gold from all the traffic that comes up and down the strait whose navarchs have to pay taxes to you for onward transmission to Rome?'

Prusias went pale at the threat, and was about to speak when Scaurus continued.

'And yes, we know that Niger has already emptied most of your treasury into his own, but that won't stop our men from having fun rooting out all the wealth that has stuck to your fingers over the years, or from visiting their frustration on you *and* your families. Do I make myself clear?'

'I can assure you, Tribune, you will encounter no resistance to imperial rule from us!'

Scaurus smiled beatifically.

'In which case, councilman, I am sure there will be no need for any legionary to set foot inside your walls ... such as they are. I, on the other hand, will be accompanying you, with my men, back into the city, so that we can ensure that your people understand the risk they might run as well as I expect you now do.' He gestured to the road into the city. 'Shall we?'

'And you think it likely that no other messengers have ridden for Cyzicus with the news of our landing.'

By the time the party made enough of a swaggering show of force that none of the councilman's colleagues could be in any doubt as to their involuntarily changed allegiances, the afternoon sun was slipping towards the horizon, providing some relief from the late summer heat as they rode back towards the landing beach, leaving Qadir and his archers on the road to the east in order to ensure compliance with the edict.

'I can't see how they would have had the time to do so. Titus anchored his fleet out of sight of the city yesterday, and there's only one road to the east along which such a vital message could have been carried to Aemilianus. Which will hopefully leave him in blissful ignorance, waiting for a warning that will never come until it's too late, and provide Candidus with the time he needs to get the rest of his army across the sea and ready to fight. And in any case, I'd say it's likely that the city elders will refrain from sending any further information, given the promise of Abydus being looted and sacked if they fail to obey.'

Scaurus nodded at Marcus's opinion, looking out from his saddle at the strait, in which Titus's ships were to be seen ferrying another load of legionaries and their equipment and supplies across the narrow channel. The councilmen had listened with obvious concern to Scaurus's repeated warnings as to the revenge that would be visited upon the city, were any attempt to communicate their landing to Niger's generals. His statement that there would be men on the road that ran east from their city, first to the great port city of Cyzicus and then on to the great inland cities of Bithynia, had been made loudly and on several different occasions to ram the point home, and had been answered with much nodding and statements of agreement that indeed there was no way that any plea for assistance would be sent east in light of Abydus's abruptly changed allegiance.

A mile from the landing beach they passed a century of legionaries running east towards the city, Draco bringing up their rear and shouting gruff encouragements at the sweating soldiers. The bearded officer threw Scaurus a crisp salute as his men doubled towards the junction that split to take a traveller either to the city or to the east, and Scaurus bent over his horse's neck to speak to him. The first spear signalled to the detachment's centurion to keep their men moving while he stopped to talk.

'I'm not much for standing around and watching boats being unloaded, so I am taking it on myself to close the road east until we have the army ashore.' He raised a hammer and a handful of nails. 'And any fool that tries it on can be nailed to the nearest tree for his stupidity.'

He saluted again and ran after his men with his medal harness jingling, taking his vine stick to an apparently blameless man in the rear rank with a bellowed warning at the silently outraged soldier not to slack off the pace. Scaurus laughed as the legionaries ran out of view.

'A born warrior leader, that man. Today must be better than his birthday and Saturnalia rolled into one as far as he's concerned. Let's hope he finds the face of battle as enjoyable as he seems to expect when the time comes for us all to stare into its full terrifying magnificence again.'

The party found the First Legion already ashore, and busy digging out a turf wall and with a four-foot-deep ditch in front of it around the landing beach down to the high-water mark, a perimeter encompassing enough ground for four legions and all of their support equipment to be housed in relative security. The headquarters tent had already been erected at its heart, and Candidus was standing at a map table with his officers, looking at the best representation of the surrounding countryside that had been available on the other side of the strait.

'I can improve on that map, Legatus Augusti.'

Scaurus handed Candidus's staff officer a rolled-up map that had until an hour before resided in the Abydus treasury's tax office, and the young officer unrolled it across the table and moved the weights to hold it flat. The general stared at it for a moment.

'The only way that the enemy are likely to approach us is from the north-east, from wherever it is that they're camped. Perhaps that will be Lampascus, but more likely Parium, for its better port and swifter passage back to Cyzicus and Chalcedon by sea. From the comments you tell us that Sartorius's lieutenant in Cyzicus made to his messengers before he died, it seems likely that my former senatorial colleague Aemilianus – and I say former because the emperor has already condemned him to *damnatio memoriae* in his absence and declared him to be under sentence of death – is in command of an army sent here to repel any attempt to enter Asia by this route. And it is more than possible that he responded to that message by sending men north, back to Chalcedon, to deal with the attack across the Bosporus that you invented to sow confusion in their minds.'

The general pondered the map again.

'But while we hope that you have deceived him, Aemilianus is no fool, you can take that from a man who knows him from our time together in the senate. It was a hammer blow to Severus when a man of such gravitas and reputation declined to serve him, especially after so long dissimulating and pretending to be in his camp. And it's obvious that were he to have chosen to fight on this side, rather than throwing his lot in with Niger, he would be the one in command here, and not me.'

He looked at the map again.

'If I were him, with the risk of either a crossing of the Bosporus close to Byzantium, as warned of by your false dispatch to Niger's man Sartorius, or the alternative of a landing somewhere along this coast, I would have my legions positioned handily for either eventuality. There, I think.' He stabbed a finger at the map, indicating the city of Parium. 'Why there?' He looked around at his officers. 'Anyone?'

One of the legati nodded thoughtfully.

'A central position like that, is the best place to strike out at a landing at either Cyzicus or here, depending on where our army comes ashore. That, and I hear that the city is large enough to contain adequate diversions for the officers of his legions while they await something more martial to occupy their attentions. And if he has sent some of his strength back to the usurper, he will want to have some space to manoeuvre in the off chance that a stronger force comes ashore, rather than being too close to the landing beach when the time comes.'

Candidus smiled his agreement.

'I agree, it's where I would locate my army, if I had to wait a few weeks to find out where the next blow was going to fall. So I think that you should start your search for them there, Tribune Scaurus, a nice quiet scouting mission to find out what it is that we're facing, if you will?'

'We are to ride east, to scout for the enemy legion or legions that Candidus is sure must be camped nearby, waiting to attack any attempt at landing. Prepare to ride.'

On Scaurus's command the reunited familia started readying the horses that had been unloaded from one of the praetorian fleet's transports, but in the middle of their bustle one man stood stock still, with an expression of distress on his face.

'But . . . Tribune?'

They turned to look at the source of the plaintive interjection to find Ptolemy, with a look of pure anguish, pointing a hand away to the south-west.

'Scribe?'

'I realise that this is a time of war, Tribune, but surely we can make the time to visit Ilium?'

Scaurus frowned in puzzlement.

'A city on the coast close to the entrance to the Hellēspontos, proven to have been built over the ruins of ancient Troy. What of it? It has no relevance to our present task.'

'But . . . Ilium is Troy, Tribune. *Troy!* The remains of the greatest city in ancient history, the inspiration for the majestic *Iliad*?'

'It's really not all it's supposed to be.'

The Aegyptian turned in his saddle and frowned at Khabour, who was riding behind his master Dubnus.

'What . . . ? I mean, really? You are a slave, how can *you* even begin to make such a judgement of one of the greatest pieces of literature—'

The easterner shook his head, seemingly unbothered by such an offhand condemnation of his intellectual abilities.

'I do not speak of the *Iliad*, I loved that story as a child, before I knew the facts behind it. I meant Ilium. It simply would not stand up to your expectations of it. I visited the city when I was a younger man.' The Aegyptian gaped at such privilege, shaking his head in disbelief, but the slave merely smiled back at him knowingly, speaking softly but with no lack of confidence. 'You betray the preconceptions of your kind, scribe. You so-called free men who nevertheless work a lifetime in pursuit of the money you need to survive, as effectively indentured as I am, just without the honesty to admit to yourself.' He shook his head at Ptolemy's rising ire. 'I was not always a slave! There was a time when I was a free man, and I am as well educated as you, whether that is a comfortable fact for you or not.'

'I'd have you beaten for such insolence!'

Dubnus laughed uproariously at the Aegyptian's anger.

'Good thing you're not his master then, isn't it? As for me, I could listen to him all day, and I have a new-found respect for the man!'

Marcus turned in his own saddle.

'Tell us how you came to be here another time, Khabour, when we have the time to give your story the attention it deserves. But I would enjoy hearing you speak of Ilium, if you will?'

The slave gave him a dignified nod.

'By all means, Tribune. I was in the service of a rich man in Antioch, performing the role of what you Romans call a *maior domus*.' He smiled at Ptolemy's disbelief. 'I ran his estates for him, and ensured that his land was well farmed and produced a rich crop, and I was the master of his finances. And so when he travelled it was natural that I would go with him, to help ensure that his business transactions were profitable. We travelled to Byzantium, and on the return journey my employer paid our navarchus an additional fee to visit Ilium, having also read the *Iliad*. The ship's captain warned him that the experience would be a disappointment, as he had heard from other passengers, but he was not to be deterred from such an opportunity. And, I am sad to say, he was right in his counsel. Not that the city lacks a certain provenance, of course. You do know that the first settlement on the site dates back into a time before any recorded history, I presume?'

Ptolemy stared back at the slave as he spoke, his face a picture of mute outrage, both at the rubbishing of his dreams and Khabour's unexpected and unwelcome claim to intellectual equality with him. The Syrian continued, showing no sign of any discomfort at the scribe's enmity.

'There is much that could be made of such a site, were the inhabitants so minded, but sad to say, they are not. They have turned the place into their own little gold mine, in which they chip diligently away at the purses of visitors who have little alternative, having made such a journey, but to make the best of the whole dismal experience. They charge a hefty sum to see the ruins, with more thought for preventing anyone getting a look without paying than the actual presentation of such an important site, and seem uninterested in the preservation of what remains. They sell trinkets too, cheap rubbish made in their workshops, that aim to extort the maximum profit from the least effort. And they have an

Odeon, in which a family of actors, who pay handsomely to the city fathers for the privilege, play out the majestic story of Helen and Paris and Achilles to such a poor standard that it would make you weep bitterly, were we blessed with the time to visit. Which, it seems, we are not.

'So, my friend, take my advice, and reflect not on what you have been deprived of but rather the lucky escape you have enjoyed. Keep the *Iliad* in your head as you have always imagined it, and do not sully it with the cheap and tawdry version these hard-hearted chisellers would have you believe represents the truth. It is a facade, aimed at your purse and little else.'

With the Aegyptian reduced to a sulky silence they rode on towards Abydus, Dubnus turned to speak to his slave with a new-found respect in his tone.

'Is it really that bad, this Ilium place?'

Khabour nodded sadly.

'For the most part, yes. The people who live there genuinely are the most grasping and uncaring of creatures, concerned only with selling mementos and getting visitors to eat in their taverna rather than the one on the other side of the road.' He leaned closer to the Briton, lowering his voice. 'Although the ruins are something to be seen, freighted with the ghosts of a thousand years ago when living gods like Achilles walked among us. Just *don't* tell the scribe the truth of it, or you will have to tie him to his horse for the next week.'

After passing the city they encountered the same century of legionaries they had met on the road earlier. Half of the soldiers were wrapped in their cloaks and asleep in a ditch, prompting an envious stare and an insufficiently muffled opinion from Sanga.

'At least there are some officers with the decency to let their men . . .' His complaint trailed off, as he realised what he was seeing in the heart of the century's temporary encampment. 'Hang on, is that man nailed to a tree?'

Scaurus dismounted and returned Draco's salute, gesturing to the helpless captive, who was crouching next to an olive tree and softly weeping, staring at his left hand which was nailed to the trunk through the web of his thumb.

'You caught him trying to get past you, I assume?'

The grizzled officer grinned lopsidedly and nodded happily.

'Seems like some of the local hotheads decided that they had to get a warning away to the other side. He wasn't the only one trying to get past us and up the road to take a message to the enemy. We could hear them sneaking about in the bushes, trying to work out how to get through the line of men we had out to stop them. So in the end I got bored, took my helmet and armour off and pretended to be one of them. Which led one of them to make the mistake of getting too close, at which point I smacked him good and hard and dragged him back here while he was still seeing stars.'

He laughed softly, shaking his head at the cowering prisoner, who was staring in horror at the long nail pinning his hand to the tree.

'I showed him the hammer and nail, and he started shouting that I couldn't do it, he was a citizen and it wasn't right. Which was probably enough to put the shits up his mates, but when I banged that nail through his palm you should have heard the screams. A clipped bronze to a new minted gold the rest of them ran all the way back home to their mothers.'

'It *isn't* right!'

Draco half-turned and shouted back at the captive.

'Shut the fuck up, or I'll find two trees close enough to hang you up in the air! You'll run out of hands and feet before I run out of nails, you miserable cunt!'

He returned his attention to Scaurus, resuming his cheery disposition.

'Scouting for the enemy, are you Tribune?'

'Indeed so. The general is quite keen to know just how close the nearest decent sized force is, and he's decided that my familia are the best suited to go and sneak around this unending olive grove in search of them.' He gestured at the captive. 'What will you do with him?"

The centurion shrugged.

'If he stops grizzling then I'll probably pull the nail out and send him back to the city to tell everyone else what a gang of bastards we are. That, or cut his throat if he doesn't stop complaining, and then deliver him to the gates to *show* them what a gang of bastards we are!' He turned and looked at the prisoner, who sensibly kept his mouth shut and looked away. 'See? Who said the easterners were all stupid bastards?'

Scaurus smiled wryly and remounted, the infantry officer shouting a parting comment after the familia as they rode away.

'One thing to think about, Tribune, while you're out there looking for them?' Scaurus looked back, raising a wryly expectant eyebrow. 'Try not to let them see you first, eh?'

6

The familia rode east along the coast for several hours, sending the keenest eyed of the Hamians out to ride half a mile in front of them to check each fresh rise or bend in the road for any sign of enemy activity, but the countryside was quiet, and empty of any sign that there might be enemy legions waiting for them. Calling a halt to allow his men to take a swift meal at midday, Scaurus warned the scouts not to relax their vigilance.

'There still has to be at least one legion out here, and probably camped in a position that will allow them to react to either east or west, and they have to have their own scouts out, if they're to know when the landing they're here to react to happens. Unless of course they've chosen to wait for word from the men on the spot when it happens. Either way, you must assume that there are men out there looking for you and take the right precautions to avoid being seen first. You must find the enemy, but you must avoid being seen as you do so.'

They resumed their careful progress, sending a fresh pair of archers forward, and Marcus, tiring of both the boredom and Ptolemy's continuing stream of complaints about the opportunity of a lifetime to visit ancient Troy having been squandered, raised an enquiring eyebrow to Qadir, who nodded grateful agreement. The two men cantered their horses forward to join the scouts just as the two archers were carefully approaching a ridge over which the road's undeviating line rose and then fell. When they were still a hundred paces distant one of the bowmen turned and crouched on the road's flat-stoned surface, waving frantically for them to get off its hard surface. Hobbling their mounts to a tree the two men hurried along the road's verge to where the scouts were lying flat and peering over the ridge, the Hamian turning back and whispering at Marcus as if there were an enemy less than a dozen paces away.

'Legionaries, Tribune.'

Marcus took off his helmet, then slowly and carefully raised his head to look down at the flat plain on the other side of the ridge, on which what looked like a cohort strength of legion troops was busy digging out a marching camp. Qadir muttered a comment in his ear, a sardonic note in his voice.

'One is forced to be impressed by their perfect adherence to doctrine, if not by their timing. It is perhaps a little early in the day to be stopping for the night?'

The Roman smiled at the acerbic comment.

'It might be wishful thinking on our part, but it does rather seem as if our esteemed enemy has decided that the real fight is happening somewhere else, and is perfectly happy with that state of affairs. But it would be a mistake to interrupt them while they're making that mistake.'

They backed away from the ridge leaving the archers to maintain a watch on the enemy, and went back to warn the rest of the familia. Scaurus shook his head at the news, smiling wryly at the news of the enemy unit's apparent lack of any martial intent.

'One of Niger's less industrious tribunes must be in command of that cohort. That notwithstanding, I believe that we would be well advised to make a swift withdrawal from here back towards our legions, just in case they gather their wits and decide to conduct an effective scouting of the area and wake up to the fact that they're no longer alone out here. I expect that Candidus will be keen to snap them up without word getting to whichever legion it is that they were detached from.'

They found the general ten miles back down the road at the head of his vanguard legion, First Spear Draco marching alongside his horse having apparently politely declined the offer of a mount from Candidus.

'He says that riding is all very well, but to understand the state of a legion he needs to have put in the miles beside his men.'

The legatus leaned conspiratorially out of his saddle to stage whisper to Scaurus, deliberately pitched loudly enough for the centurion to hear even over the clattering of hoofs and rattling rasp of the legionaries' hobnails.

'I'm quite sure he secretly believes that we're all soft gentlemen and not fit to march with him and his men. And I believe he's probably right!'

Scaurus nodded his agreement, laughing out loud as Draco shot him a knowing wink.

'So, Tribune, what do you have for us? I presume your earlier than expected return from your scouting mission is based on your having found something of note to inform me about?'

When appraised of the lone cohort camped on the road ahead, Candidus thought for a moment.

'It is a stratagem straight from the textbooks. In the absence of cavalry with which to scout, one sends a vexillation forward to act as a trip line. This enables warning to be provided of the approach of any hostile force and allows plenty of time for a message to be sent back to the main body and thereby enable either attack or retreat, depending on the circumstances. I'd imagine whoever is in command has sent another such detachment to the east, in case we were to land closer to Cyzicus. So what we need to achieve now is to overwhelm this single cohort, which will be easy enough, but without their having the chance to get a message away, which will be a good deal harder, as they will be ready to send riders away with the news the moment they see us come over the hill.'

'I have an idea in that respect. There is a side track you will have passed a mile or two back—'

'Which might just be the perfect opportunity to put a force behind them?' Candidus flashed a knowing grin at his junior. 'Indeed it might, which is why I've already sent a force of cavalry along it to see where it leads to, led by my most junior and therefore also my most hungry cohort commander. Perhaps we ought to halt the march here and wait to see what he has to tell us? Apart from anything else it'll give those lazy bastards of the Second Adiutrix time to catch us up, eh Draco? Halt the column, First Spear, but no we'll have no horn signals for the time being please, just in case the enemy have scouts in the vicinity.'

The veteran centurion ran up the line of march to rein in the leading cohort, and the legion's soldiers, used to being marched at high speed for hours only to then be stopped at the roadside with no sign of any urgency to move on, cleared the road and drank sparingly from their bottles under the close supervision of centurions who knew that no refill could be guaranteed for many a mile. After a couple of hours, a single squadron of horsemen rode in from the direction of Abydus, their leader seeking out Candidus and dismounting with a swift salute.

'Ah, Acting Prefect Barbatus, that was quick! You really are a *very* keen officer, aren't you? So, what did you find, and where is the rest of your cohort?'

The man in question was old enough to have the effortless authority of a typical cavalry leader, but young enough for his beard still to be jet black, and with the look of a Dacian warrior from beyond the Danubius. He spoke quickly and with assurance, shooting a glance at Scaurus in calculation as to his place in the command structure, but his eyes lingered on the two Romans with the look of a man wondering if he knew them.

'I left them at the junction of the coast road and that track, Legatus, with orders to stay well out of sight. It's as you suspected sir, the track leads into the interior and meets another which runs back to the coast road.'

'And that comes out where?'

'At a guess, sir, fifteen or so miles from here.'

'And did you see any sign of the enemy?'

Barbatus grinned wolfishly.

'We saw no one other than the usual farmers, but when we re-joined the road I had my lads give it a quick search, and they came up with these interesting clues.'

He reached into a pouch and presented them with a pair of hobnails, which Candidus accepted, looked at then passed to Scaurus.

'You're well versed in all this sneaking around and attacking from the shadows, Gaius, what do you make of these?'

The tribune eyed them critically.

'They're freshly dropped, to judge from the bright and largely unrusted nature of the point where they rub on the road. I'd say you've found evidence of the cohort that's camped five miles to the east, Prefect.' Scaurus raised a hand to forestall any expression of disappointment that the cavalryman's discovery was lessened by the enemy force already having been discovered. 'And, in fact, you've just handed them to us on a golden plate, along with their general, if the dice I expect our esteemed legatus is about to roll land the right way up.'

Candidus reacted every bit as aggressively as he had expected, and an hour later Marcus and Scaurus were riding beside Barbatus along the country road's twisting path as it wound through the countryside to the south of the coast road.

'I can see why this wasn't chosen to be the route of the coast road, even if it does run more directly.' Scaurus shot the acting prefect a speculative glance. 'So, Prefect, Candidus describes you as his newest and most ambitious prefect . . . ?'

The Dacian grimaced.

'Acting prefect, Tribune. I was a decurion until the day before we crossed the strait, and I'm still trying to work out exactly what inspired him to temporarily promote me, rather than just picking out one of the keen young lads that have been sent here by their daddies to find out what war's like, and to lap at the two pools, of blood and glory.'

'How very poetic.' Marcus smiled encouragingly at him. 'But what happened to your prefect?'

Barbatus shrugged.

'He fell off his horse at dawn two days ago, still drunk from the night before, and broke his neck. Dead the moment he hit the ground. And the legatus decided not to replace him right away, for the fear of giving some clueless new boy no time to get to grips with how to command a gang of evil-minded roughnecks like my boys. So for the time being, at least, he's considering whether I'm fit to wear bronze, carry a silver-handled dagger and eat my dinner with a golden spoon, rather than the knife I usually use.'

He grinned, and Marcus raised an amused eyebrow.

'You talk like a veteran. Have you actually done this before? Been to war, I mean?'

The Dacian nodded happily.

'We were part of the army that put the Sarmatae down when they got too big for their boots ten years ago. I was just a trooper then, but we saw our fair share of the fun and games.'

'I recall it well. Tribune Scaurus and I were a part of it too, serving under Pescennius Niger, which is more than a little ironic.'

Barbatus laughed.

'I *knew* I recognised you both from somewhere! The two of you were in command of a cohort of auxiliaries, right?'

Marcus nodded ruefully.

'Yes, and we lost good friends in that war. One of them in a battle that convinced me never again to advance without doing the necessary scouting of the ground. And taught me that when you have your enemy's throat under your boot you press down. Hard. Which means that you and your men are going to need to be both stealthy and, at the right time, brutal.'

Barbatus nodded approvingly.

'In which case you teamed up with the right men, Tribune! There's sneaky cavalry, and there's nasty cavalry, but if it's sneaky, nasty cavalry you're looking for, you need the Flavia Brittonum.' He lifted his spear in the air and barked out a rallying cry. '*Flavia Brittonum!*'

The men riding behind them echoed the shout, and Marcus shook his head at Barbatus in amusement, unable to resist the cavalryman's infectious enthusiasm.

'Flavia Brittonum. Blondie's Britons? You are Dacians, am I right?'

'Yes, we are. Apparently, our cohort was shipped out to the province from Britannia a hundred years ago, and we've been there ever since, with son following father and those among the local lads who decided that they'd rather carry a spear and ride a horse than spend their lives breaking their backs farming or digging for gold.'

Scaurus nodded knowingly.

'The name Flavia Brittonum tells us that your cohort was founded in Britannia, by the emperor Vespasian of the Flavian dynasty. It seems one of his very distant ancestors had fair hair, and that became the family name as was the way of things back in those distant days. Once formed, the cohort was probably marched straight off to Dacia, at the other end of the empire, because a revolt in Germania Inferior by the empire's favourite auxiliaries, the Batavians, had just taught Rome a valuable lesson in a very painful way.'

'Really? Something bad enough to make them send men hundreds of miles from their homes?'

Marcus nodded, realising that he was playing the role usually accorded to Scaurus.

'Thousands of miles, as far as possible from their own people, posted to a province with a known risk of revolt and with men from Dacia sent to Britannia, which was and still is equally uppity, in return. And with good cause. The Batavians had enough men to make them the equivalent to a legion, and a very powerful one since they were made up of eight part-mounted cohorts. They also provided the emperor's German bodyguard on the Palatine Hill, but when a man called Galba succeeded Nero as emperor, he made the fatal mistake of humouring the praetorians who were later to kill him by dismissing them. He also sent all those cohorts back to their homeland at just the time that their people were being provoked beyond their ability to turn the other cheek by some inept local command on our part. The result was that they went on the rampage, pretty much destroyed a couple of legions and taught Rome not to leave well-trained and equipped men close to their own tribal lands, in case they get caught up in local disputes and end up making a mess of the regulars sent to sort it out.'

'Makes sense.' The decurion nodded agreement. 'Rumour has it that you and the other tribune already had a decent enough go at proving why it's not a good idea to set legion against legion a few weeks ago, on the other side of the water. So now it's our turn to teach these eastern arse stains some manners.'

They found the remainder of the cohort waiting close to the junction where the track re-joined the road. Their decurions saluted neatly, but Barbatus jumped down from his saddle with an impatient wave.

'You can forget all that "and at every command we will be ready" bollocks, boys, the tribunes here are a pair of murdering bastards just like us. What's happening?'

'Not much.' The man who answered was older than Barbatus, but clearly content with the younger man being his superior. 'A couple of legion cavalry messengers came down the road from the east an hour or so ago, and they haven't come back in the other direction yet. Apart from that, nothing.'

'And they didn't see you?'

The older man scoffed.

'No chance. I had a couple of my smarter lads on watch and they knew to keep their heads down.'

'Good, tell them I owe them a drink when we get the chance to wet our throats. So, Tribune Scaurus here has found a cohort of the legion road menders camped a mile or two up the road, apparently taking very little interest in anything other than getting their walls up and their dinner cooked. Which means that they're rats in a trap of their own making. Once the general has a legion ready to throw over the hill at them he'll have the horns blown, which is when we jump out of the wardrobe behind them with our gladiator costumes on and shout, "Surprise!" Although all we have to do, I'm a little disappointed to tell you, is ride down anyone trying to make their escape to the east down this road. And worse than that he wants them *alive*, and *able to talk*. So tell your boys this for me: no spearing, no scalping, no taking of ears, noses or heads neither. All prisoners to be kept alive, intact, and able to talk when encouraged to do so.'

The other decurion asked a question without going through the usual routine of a raised hand and permission to speak, both the informality and his question making Marcus smile to himself.

'Can we do the encouraging?'

'No, you fucking well can't, because if you do I'll be demoted back to decurion and then I'll have to take my annoyance out on you lot. Besides that, if we're good boys and do as we're asked then we'll get the chance to ride out in advance of the army again once this little sideshow is done with, and then you'll probably find you've got more ears than you can fit around your neck; but until then just pretend you're legion goat fuckers and behave yourselves . . . no offence intended, Tribunes.'

'And none taken. We're more your auxiliary cohort goat fuckers, as it happens.' Scaurus grinned and tapped his dagger. 'And some of our men were Britons, but shipped in from Germania as it happens, and they're equally partial to taking an ear or two, so we completely understand. But in this instance the prefect is right, Candidus needs intelligence, and he's not likely to get it from a man whose head is hanging from one of your saddle horns or whose ears are decorating your neck, is he?'

'See?' Barbatus shook his head at his comrade. 'I told you they're not all donkeys! Now, let's get the lads ready, shall we, and you make that last instruction nice and clear to them, eh? Because the man that gets a line drawn through my potential for promotion by killing the wrong enemy rider will find himself enjoying the pleasures of having my lance stuck up his arse. As will his decurion. Got that?'

The two men nodded meekly enough at their leader's pithy instructions that Scaurus was forced to turn away and affect to inspect his horse's bridle to hide his smile. With the cohort thoroughly and equally unequivocally briefed, with much careful explanation of what was and was not expected of them, and the dire consequences of disobedience, they deployed out onto the coast road in a column formation and walked steadily to the west until the leading riders who were scouting the way forward declared that they could see the enemy camp. Barbatus and the Romans went forward to the spot, and looked out through a screen of bushes at a peaceful scene, smoke rising from a dozen cook fires while the guards on the marching camp's walls were sitting in small groups, playing dice or knuckle bones from the look of it.

'Look at them. Still three hours to sunset and all they're bothered about is what's for dinner and who can catch the most bones. This lot don't deserve to have an emperor.' Barbatus grinned at Scaurus and Marcus. 'They tell me you commanded a legion in Syria. Were they as useless as those bastards?'

Before the two men had any chance to defend their former command's honour, in the face of the usual western army's bias against the east, a distant bray of horns removed the need to consider the question. Scaurus shrugged.

'That's Candidus on the attack. Shall we see what rats attempt to leave this sinking ship?'

The enemy camp was at once a scene of outright panic, as the leading cohorts of the Tenth Gemina came over the far hill and started to form up across the gentle slope facing them in battle formation. Their evening meal forgotten, the enemy force ran for their turf walls, and Marcus could imagine the dismay growing among them as cohort after cohort crested the hill and extended the battle line facing them until it was long enough to wrap around the entirety of their small perimeter.

The Dacian grinned wolfishly as a pair of riders exited the camp from the side facing away from the oncoming legion, spurring their mounts away to the east with the obvious task of taking a warning to Aemilius. Backing away from the cover of the bushes they hurried back to their horses just in time to witness the horsemen's' shocked reaction to riding over the rise only to find themselves within fifty paces of the waiting Dacians' lances. While they dithered, reining their mounts in and looking about them for an escape route, Scaurus called out to them in a loud and commanding voice.

'Don't try to run for it, gentlemen! These Dacians of mine will run you down in less than a hundred paces, and Legatus Augustus Candidus guarantees your safety *if* you surrender to his rightful command here and *now*!'

The two men looked at each other, the urge to flight visibly going out of them at the difficulty of their situation. The decurion looked to his junior for support, calling out to him loudly enough for their captors to hear.

'We had no choice, right?'

Scaurus walked forward to them, shaking his head in gentle admonition.

'I think what you meant to say was that you felt you had no alternative, that you recognise the obvious legitimacy of the one true emperor's rule, and that you took your first opportunity to surrender yourselves to his forces. Even a man as pragmatic as Candidus will be forced to treat you harshly unless you come to him entirely of your own free will. And, I will add, in case you had not worked it out for yourselves, freely offering the information he will expect of you, rather than making a show of having to have it dragged out of you. Do you understand?'

'One legion. That was all that my colleague Aemilianus chose to keep here in Asia, when your false information of an attack across the Bosporus reached him. And that legion with one cohort captured, another out to the east watching Cyzicus, and two more left to man their walls on the Euphrates. So Aemilianus has no more than three thousand men to face our four legions. What he was thinking to so denude his army of men, I can only imagine.'

With the two captured messengers having been appropriately submissive and informative, Candidus clearly found himself somewhat dumbfounded at the lack of opposition faced by his landing. He took a sip of his wine, adding another dash of water to the cup with a grimace.

'Gods below, but this is sweet and disgusting muck. Nobody could ever accuse this half of the empire of working hard to match the wine lands of the other half for quality. So, for reasons that are not immediately clear to me, my esteemed opponent and former colleague has chosen to send most of his army to assist Niger in resisting a purported invasion of Asia via the Bosporus, and yet he has personally remained here to face the possibility of an attack from the Hellēspontos with nowhere near enough strength to succeed in such a defence. One might even suspect that he has chosen to avoid putting himself into the path of what he believes to be our likely route of attack, in order to be able to spare his children from execution were he to further antagonise the emperor.'

He sipped the wine again and shrugged.

'No amount of water can make this any better. So, he is going to be faced with a stark choice when we unexpectedly arrive on his doorstep after a nice brisk battle march. He can preside over a mass surrender like the one that we witnessed today, when our four legions take the field against his own. He can lead his men to their deaths, and at least have the satisfaction of dying with his sword in his hands. Or, and this feels most likely to me, he can make an undignified and rather hasty exit to the east in the hope of re-joining his master Niger, wherever he is, to avoid being dragged before Severus and executed, at least for the time being. It seems to me that your informally devised stratagem worked about as well as could have been hoped, Rutilius Scaurus.'

'Surely he has another choice, Legatus?'

The older man nodded good naturedly at Marcus's question.

'Well yes, I suppose he does. He could act like an old-fashioned gentleman from the days before the empire, unsheathe his sword, commend his example to his ancestors and send a final greeting to his family, after all of which he could then proceed to fall on the blade.' His slightly acerbic tone made his views of the matter clear even before he proceeded to express an opinion. 'But I feel it less than likely, with this man. As long as there is a war to be fought he will strive to stay alive, and perhaps to fight, in hopes of turning the tide that has turned against Niger so strongly now. Which is why I have a particular task for you to perform, when we confront his legion on the battlefield.'

He nodded at Scaurus's raised eyebrow.

'I think you already know what I need you to do, in the event that my opponent decides either to make a run for it or to give himself up.' He shot a questioning glance at Scaurus. 'If he succeeds in surrendering, which he could well achieve with every man in my army seeing him as their path to a rich reward, I expect that our esteemed emperor' – he lowered his voice, looking around to be sure that they weren't overheard – 'will have him tortured to death in a protracted and exemplary manner. Quite possibly after keeping him alive for long enough to witness his wife and children being executed in front of him. Severus is not a man given to last-minute sentimentality, gentlemen, but rather to a somewhat cold-blooded and remorseless approach to any man – *any* man – he deems to have betrayed him. Which Aemilianus most certainly has. And my colleagues in the Senate, who communicated with me *privately* before I marched to war, made themselves very clear that they have no desire to have one of their number subjected to such indignity, if it can be avoided without putting myself at risk. I believe they fear that the emperor will be encouraged to more of the same violence, making victims of the men he believes plotted against him, when this war is over and he can give Rome his undivided attention.'

'And perhaps they fear that he will name names, under interrogation?'

Candidus grunted a laugh.

'You see through me, Tribune. Be careful not to advertise such perceptive abilities to the emperor, if you do not wish to attract his attention. Yes, that might well be a factor as well, although I was too wise to ask the question of them directly. I tend to find that the less I know the happier I am when it comes to the doings of the rich and powerful.'

'But you think it more likely that he will seek to flee?'

The general smiled faintly at Scaurus's question.

'Exactly. And you can believe me when I tell you that if he succeeds in making an escape from the battlefield, if indeed he hasn't already read the runes of the failure of his messengers to return, and ridden east, then I am likely to fall under our master's suspicion for having allowed him to do so. Which means that I suggest you don't fail at performing this task for me, if you wish to avoid the same fate as me should the esteemed senator actually escape us and live to fight another day.'

'So, let's make sure I understand you clearly, Tribune.' Barbatus adjusted his horse's bridle as he spoke, making the same preparations as the rest of his men to allow the beast its head at a full gallop. 'The last time we rode out, your orders were to make sure nobody got as much as a broken fingernail or I'd probably be a decurion again before sunset.' He removed the leather cover from his spearhead, folding it up and putting it into a saddlebag. 'Whereas this time we have to kill everyone who gets in our way until we find the enemy general and put a spear through him too. But if we fail to find and kill him . . .'

'Yes, the result would be the same. You could very well be a decurion again by sunset.' Marcus grinned at the quizzical Dacian. 'You wanted to command a cohort. Then you got lucky, and now you command a cohort. Except, quite possibly, it's the wrong cohort at the wrong time, if what you were hoping for was a quiet life from here on.'

Barbatus shook his head.

'A quiet life? Fuck that. It would be nice to enjoy a little consistency though.'

'Consistency?' Scaurus laughed tersely as he hauled himself up into the saddle. 'I think you're fighting in the wrong war if that's your dearest wish.'

'Hmm.' The acting prefect shrugged. 'We get to take ears, I presume?'

'You can take all the ears you want, as long as their owners have stopped breathing by the time you put iron to their flesh, with only one exception.'

'No, don't tell me, let me guess it. We can't have them off this general, can we?'

'Right in one. The emperor will want to see proof of his death, and quite possibly to put either his body or more likely just his head in a cask of oil and send it back to Rome, where it will be displayed in the Forum outside the curia, the building where the senators meet, as proof of the price of betrayal. His complete and recognisable head, that is.'

'You think that a small thing like a missing ear is going to be a problem for a man that'll do something like that? And you Romans call us barbarians?'

Marcus mounted, laughing at the Dacian's affected outrage.

'*Called.* We used to call you barbarians. Now we call you Romans.'

'At least until the gold in our mountains runs out you do.' Barbatus grinned back at him. 'Sir.'

Scaurus shook his head ruefully.

'I think he has you, Marcus. Better just to focus on our task perhaps?'.

The army had marched at the battle pace for twenty-five miles from sunrise that morning, the leading legion arriving within a short distance of the main enemy camp, scouted by their cavalry, soon after midday. Issuing orders for the first two legions in the column to deal with the pathetically small enemy force, Candidus had sent Marcus and Scaurus to issue his instructions to the Dacians, with orders to accompany the Brittonum and ensure that they fulfilled their task perfectly.

Barbatus waved two of his men forward, taking a pair of lances from the first trooper.

'If you're coming with us you're probably going to want one of these.' He passed them each a weapon, then called the second man, who passed them both a round cavalry shield. 'Of course, you might not be all that skilled at using these on horseback, but better to have them than not. Ah, they're playing our music . . .' Horns were sounding close by, the Dacians having been pushed up the order of march to be close to hand when battle was finally joined. 'Shall we? You're armed, I've told my lads not to take any part of anyone who's not already dead or wearing bronze, so I think we have the basics of it nailed down. Now it's down to what happens when we ride out in front of a half legion of eastern hand-holders.'

'You lead here, Prefect.' Scaurus gestured to the column's head. 'We're simply here to make sure we all get to avoid the irritation of an emperor denied the one thing he really wants from this excuse for a battle.'

Barbatus nodded to his standard-bearer, whose dragon standard's long tail was hanging limply in the afternoon's light breeze.

'When I give the word, get that thing singing! Trumpeter, sound the advance and be ready to sound the charge like you've got a proper pair of swingers.'

'You realise that when the man we're looking to take down hears all that commotion he's likely to run like a scalded cat?'

The Dacian shrugged at Marcus's gentle admonition.

'Let him run. We're the fucking Brittonum!'

At the horn's call the cohort started to canter forward up the advancing column in a four-horse-wide column, the legionaries they were passing calling insults and cat calls after them, the horsemen riding up the road's verge until they crested the rise and the enemy came into view. Already starting to fragment, with individual legionaries evading vicious blows from the vine sticks and swords of their centurions to flee, the hastily formed line facing the Severan army was visibly bowing, the men at both ends unconsciously predicting an encirclement by the much larger Severan force and pulling back to avoid being outflanked and cut to ribbons from both front and back. Barbatus raised his spear over his head and roared a command at the men of his leading squadron.

'*Follow me!*'

He led them out to the right of the enemy line, staring hawk-eyed across the embattled cohorts from the vantage point of his saddle.

'There!'

Marcus followed his pointing hand to see a small party of riders heading away to the east, their vivid red cloaks immediately identifying them as senior officers who seemed to have decided to abandon the soldiers who were depending on them for leadership. Barbatus grinned at him like a madman, shouting a question over the thunder of the cohort's cantering progress.

'Shall we?'

The Roman nodded, hunching over his horse's saddle like a jockey at the circus, while the Dacian turned improbably in his own saddle, holding his spear and shield out from his body in a masterful display of horsemanship as he turned to roar at his signifer and cornicer.

'*Sound the charge! And make that dragon roar!*'

The horn's peal split the air, and the draco's tail, released, allowed the wind of their passage to pass through it and over a vibrating reed to generate a low but piercing note that stood Marcus's neck hair up with its other-worldly droning call. The Dacians rounded the enemy line at the gallop with Barbatus at their head, Marcus gauging the distance to the fleeing horsemen and realising that, alerted by the noise and commotion of their rapid advance, their quarry was now making a run for it with their mounts pushed to an equal pace. Seeing the same signs of headlong retreat, the prefect shouted out to him with a gleeful expression.

'Don't worry, they can't escape!'

He bent low over his mount's back and spoke encouragement into its ear, and whether or not his communion with the beast had any effect, the Roman could see that Barbatus and his leading riders were gradually overhauling the enemy officers. A legion deserter running from the battle that was yet to start strayed unwittingly into their path, realising too late that he was in the path of four hundred galloping horses. He dithered momentarily, turned to run for the relative safety of his legion and was ridden down, speared by one of the leading riders with an exultant shout and then trampled underfoot by the beasts following close behind.

The riders around Aemilianus were looking back at them, less in calculation of their odds of escape than in simple terror at their impending doom. One of them broke away to the right, running for who knew what illusory safety, and a pair of Dacians vied to be the man to take him out of the saddle with a spear thrust. By a quirk of fate, neither of them backing away from the race to be the first to the fleeing officer, both of them put their long blades through him at the same moment, one from either side, and the dying man rode on for a moment more before the weight of the wooden spear shafts pulled him from the saddle and dumped him over his mount's tail.

The death lent the fleeing riders fresh urgency, but their frantic whipping of their horses with the loose ends of their reins had little effect on the inexorable progress of their pursuers. When the Dacians were little more than fifty paces behind them the man at their head threw up a hand and reined in his horse, calling on his colleagues to do the same. Barbatus's men rode around them, individual riders raising their lances in readiness to take such easy kills, but Scaurus shouted a command to the Dacian.

'Take them *alive*, Prefect! All of them!'

'What?'

Barbatus shot him an amazed glance, but to his credit did as he was ordered.

'Hold your spears!'

The half-dozen officers shrank away from the raised spear blades, looking at Scaurus in awe as he dismounted and marched into the heart of the horsemen surrounding them.

'I know . . .' The Roman raised a hand to forestall the prefect's ire. 'I promised you ears. But these men have surrendered.'

'Quite so! I demand to be taken to my colleague Claudius Candidus!'

He turned to the enemy general.

'You, Asellius Aemilianus, are in no position to demand any such thing. You are declared a traitor by imperial order, for having gone back on your word to the one true emperor, and siding with the usurper Niger at the urgings of your cousin Clodius Albinus.'

'How *dare* you accuse a gentleman whose boots you're not fit to—'

Barbatus leaned out of his saddle and speared the rider who had interrupted Scaurus through his throat, twisting the blade before pulling it free. The Roman turned to look at him in exasperation, while his victim tottered in the saddle for a moment, looking down at the blood sheeting down his chest in almost comical surprise. His eyes rolled up to show their whites as his consciousness left him, and he fell from the horse with a heavy thud to lie still in the road's dust in a slowly expanding puddle of blood.

'*Thank you*, Prefect, for such a graphic demonstration of the likely treatment of anyone else who chooses to argue as to whether I have the right to discuss such matters with Legatus Aemilianus. And for those of you tempted to join your colleague in his salutary example of why it's important to think before calling the odds, observe these two things.' He drew his sword and held it aloft. 'Tell me what you see? Anyone? I guarantee that the prefect here won't kill any of you for answering me.'

Another of the general's staff, a man barely into his twenties, spoke hesitantly but in a tone freighted with undertones of the same outrage.

'I see a sword. In the hand of a murdering—'

He struggled for a moment to find the right word to express his anger, and Scaurus rode over him in a harsh tone.

'The word you're looking for is senator. In the hand of a *senator*, tribune, whether murdering or simply bringing imperial justice to you traitors! Do you see my gold ring? It was given to me by Commodus himself, restoring my family's rightful place in society! So if any of you equestrian gentlemen feel like telling me that I'm not fit to clean the Legatus Augustus's boots, be wary that I don't request some further spear work by my esteemed

Dacian colleague here who, although you might not realise it, is equal to you all in his rank. Anyone?'

After a moment of silence he turned back to Barbatus.

'If your men want ears there are a good many of them back there, trapped between their own line and the inconvenient way that our rapid advance around them has blocked the road. I suspect you would be bringing the battle to an early conclusion while also allowing your troopers to enrich themselves considerably.'

The Dacian turned to his squadron commanders.

'Take your squadrons back to do as the tribune suggests. I want to see what happens here, and make sure that none of these honourable gentlemen gets any ideas about either fighting or running for mummy again. Your men can share the ears they take with mine evenly, so that we don't have any jealousy resulting from my feeling the need to make sure that our own gentlemen are safe.'

'I assure you that Tribune Aquila and I are perfectly capable of . . .' Scaurus thought for a moment. 'However, this is a generous gesture, and I thank you for it.'

Aemilianus spoke, in the authoritative manner of a man used to being listened to.

'Well then, if that's all now honey and roses, I am forced to renew my dem—' Aemilianus managed to control his temper in the face of Scaurus's obduracy as the younger man turned, hard-faced, back to him ' . . . my very reasonable *request* to be taken to Candidus!'

The general was still holding himself upright at the heart of his staff, as if he were riding in a victory parade, rather than captured and under the spears of his enemies.

'Dismount.' Scaurus waited a moment, then roared a further order. '*Now!* You too, Legatus Augusti, unless you'd rather die on horseback?'

The officers reluctantly got down from their saddles, surrendering the last vestige of their dignity, and he gestured with an open hand to Barbatus.

'Take these other men away please, Prefect, I need a quiet word with the legatus. Keep them safe from the soldiery, if the looting and killing gets as far as here, and only kill them if any of them show disrespect to you.'

'Any of them?'

The Roman smiled knowingly.

'Oh yes, any one of them can sentence them all to death, But I'd suggest that you use that freedom to kill them very sparingly, unless any of them really are stupid, and even then you might want to be sparing with such a valuable resource. I expect there will be some men of influence among them who might well be worth more alive than dead, so you might want to temper your eagerness to spear any more of them. Any ransom will of course be shared by you and your men. Perhaps you could content yourselves with administering a good beating to the first man to provoke you, and see what the impact on the others is?'

'Ransom?'

Marcus nodded with a wide smile.

'I thought that might get your attention. Civil wars are funny things, for the most senior men in society. Take the general a Roman senior officer's corpse and all he'll think is that he'll have to write a letter to the dead man's family explaining the circumstances of his death, and quite possibly make enemies of them for life. But take him a senior officer as a prisoner, and he can both be that man's new best friend and make the soldiers who captured him rich by agreeing a ransom with his family. Which might be worth bearing in mind . . . unless of course the idea of releasing these men in return for gold offends you?'

The Dacians led their captives away with the look of men who had made the realisation that the taking of battlefield trophies wasn't the only reward to be had from such a victory. Left alone with Aemilianus, who was glowering at them from beside his horse, Scaurus took a matter-of-fact tone.

'I understand your situation, Legatus Augusti. You have been deceived as to your enemy's intentions and left with no option but to surrender. Perhaps a prompter return to your master's side, while cementing your guilt in the eyes of our master Severus, would at least have spared you from having to witness this unfortunate defeat.'

Aemilianus looked bleakly past him at the scene of the battle playing out less than half a mile distant. The depleted legion that had only moments before been making at least some show of resistance had surrendered almost to a man, throwing down their swords and shields and cowering under the weapons of Candidus's men, who had taken their eagle from its aquilifer and were parading it up and down before them in the ultimate humiliation. The eastern legionaries who had initially fled from their advance, seeing the brutal way in which the Brittonum were treating those who had run first, were now running for their lives back to re-join their comrades. Their choice, to endure the abuse and beatings that would surely be administered to them, clearly seemed the better option in the face of the hard-faced cavalrymen's eagerness to kill and take trophies. The general nodded, his shoulders slumping.

'Yes. It is indeed a sad moment, and the end of my career. And I know that I must die. Not least for inflicting this shame on a proud Roman legion. I received orders to march east and re-join the army in Bithynia two days ago, gentlemen, and I ignored those orders.' Shaking his head in dismay at the disintegration of his command, the general sighed heavily. 'I did so in order to avoid taking part in any further fighting with Severus's army, in the hope of shortening this doomed war and perhaps mitigated the hatred for me that Severus has already made perfectly clear. I also sent my least effective tribune east with a cohort, expecting that Candidus would scoop them up, and I have generally failed to prepare for the inevitable battle. In short, I have tried to make amends for my rebellion, now that the gods have shown their disfavour for Niger. I know that I must die, but perhaps if I can explain my actions to my esteemed colleague Claudius Candidus, and seek his assistance in getting a message and my personal effects to my wife, it might ease my family's grief a little to know that I was well treated at the end of my life, and had the chance to set matters straight. And perhaps I might also leave my will with him, for delivery to Rome?'

'For all of your attempts to redress your treachery, your position is less well balanced than that, Asellius Aemilianus.' Scaurus spoke softly, but with the firm tone necessary to get through to a man who was still under some degree of misapprehension as to his remaining choices. 'You should not mistake my gentle treatment of you for respect for your rank, because from the moment you decided to run, rather than fight, you no longer had any rank. The emperor has declared that you are no longer a senator of *his* empire. It was only in Niger's service that you had any status, and by choosing to surrender you have made the decision that you are no longer in Niger's service. By rights I could beat and manacle you, and face no opprobrium from my peers, as you are no longer a gentleman. That I choose to refrain from doing so is only from a sense of decency.'

He tapped the hilt of Aemilianus's sword.

'And I have allowed you to retain that doubtless treasured blade only because you must now use it one last time.'

The older man stared at him in horror, looking about him at the scene of his greatest humiliation.

'Suicide, yes, of course. But *now*? And here?'

'Yes. Now, and here. You have one other choice, but I cannot in all conscience commend it to you. If you refuse to kill yourself, and if I choose then not to obey my general's orders to kill you if you're not able to do the deed yourself, then you would be taken with all haste to the emperor's headquarters. I doubt that Claudius Candidus would even allow you to speak to him, as treason is a contagious disease in Severus's opinion. Worse, Candidus strongly suspects that Severus would have you subjected to the most demeaning of tortures in the name of intelligence gathering before a very public execution, and that you would undoubtedly name other members of your clique in the senate. Is that really how you wish to die, in agony and in betrayal of your friends, when a private and dignified exit is being offered to you here?'

Aemilianus sagged visibly, shaking his head.

'No, clearly not. I had no idea his hatred for me was quite so visceral.' Making a clear effort to compose himself, he stood up straight and looked out into the distance to the west. 'Forgive me, Rome, I have acted in your best interests at every turn.'

He drew the sword from his scabbard.

'This is an honoured weapon, held by the oldest son of the family since the dawn of the empire. May it bring me honour now. Perhaps you might see a way to deliver it to my own son so that—'

Scaurus interjected in a soft but firm tone, shaking his head in refusal of the doomed general's final request.

'The weapon will necessarily be taken to the emperor with your body, Asellius Aemilianus. Anything else would put everyone involved at great risk of being seen to share your treason. I'm sure you can see the necessity of this.'

The disgraced senator looked down at the blade.

'A sad loss to my family.' He looked up at Scaurus with a sudden insight. 'My family . . . will be spared?'

The Roman shook his head.

'I cannot say. This example of your genuine contrition, and perhaps a suitably amended epitaph in support of such a noble example, might be enough to make the emperor consider sparing them more favourably. But there is no way for me to predict how his mind will work on this matter. I believe that all you can do is seek to influence him in this last moment.'

Aemilianus nodded.

'Thank you for such clarity, Rutilius Scaurus.' He looked up at the sky for a moment, and then smiled unexpectedly. 'It's true what they say about moments like these; the purpose of one's life is suddenly replaced with an understanding that it has all been somewhat meaningless. But as you say, I must perform one last task. Let my final words be reported to Severus as these: I sought to serve Rome, but erred in my choices, and now bitterly regret not siding with the man who was and remains the one clear answer to the empire's needs. Let my sacrifice be a beacon to draw all men to the service of our one true emperor. Do you think that will suffice?'

Scaurus bowed his head in a gesture of respect for the sentiment, and Aemilianus took a deep breath and blew out a gusty sigh, then untied the ribbon securing his armour and allowed the heavy chest and back plates of the cuirass to fall to the dusty ground with heavy thuds.

'Let's get this done then. I believe the accepted form is to place the point of the blade just so . . . ?'

He placed the sword's point against his sternum.

'With all due respect to those who have gone before us and suffered great agony in doing so, I would suggest a small change.' Marcus moved the weapon's point down an inch, then adjusted the angle of the blade to point upwards. 'This will ensure that your heart will be pierced, and that you do not suffer unnecessary pain. Neither of us is allowed to grant you a mercy stroke, and your body is expected to be complete when it is presented to the emperor to prove that nobody weakened at the moment of your death. It will also serve to allow Legatus Candidus to deny that he sanctioned your suicide, to protect himself from any hint of association with you.'

A rueful smile touched the corners of Aemilianus's mouth.

'Wise of you, and kind, young man. Very well!'

He braced himself, closed his eyes and allowed his body to topple forward so that the sword was driven through his body with an audible crunch as he hit the ground. The two men watched as his corpse twitched and spasmed in death, then lay still with the weapon's blade protruding through the fine tunic the general had been wearing. They rolled him over and pulled the sword free, wrapping body and weapon in his discarded cloak, then stood to watch the final stages of his legion's abject surrender while the column of Candidus's army continued to pour down the slope and around their dispirited huddle. At length the general himself, having accepted the surrender of the enemy first spear, trotted his horse over to them behind a screen of Barbatus's Dacians, many of them with freshly excised human ears hanging from their necks.

'Another walkover! At this rate we'll take Niger's entire army without any more casualties than we'll lose to disease and desertion in the next year.' He dismounted and walked over to look at his opponent's corpse. 'It was well done?'

Scaurus nodded.

'He died well, Legatus, and quickly, and said the right words to assuage the emperor's anger.'

'If it is to be assuaged, that is.' Candidus nodded, looking over at the corpses of the officers who had been speared by Barbatus's men. 'It seems likely to me that you learned of his last words from those two men, since he was of course dead by the time you found him and could not have been taken prisoner. His suicide was his last defiance of the emperor's wishes, and most definitely not sanctioned by any of us. And it is a shame that they were then swept up in the battle and lost their lives soon after having reported that epitaph to you.'

'I understand.'

Candidus put a hand on his shoulder.

'Very good. Write it all up for me if you will, Rutilius Scaurus, the report you received from the men who witnessed his obviously agonising death, as I believe that will go down better than his having died with a smile on his face? His last words were doubtless appropriate, but if that was not the case then feel free to make them so. I'll have Prefect Barbatus take the body back to Abydus for shipment across the Propontis on one of the fleet's fast couriers, so that our master can review the evidence of his death before the rot sets in too badly.'

He looked back at the scene of the brief battle.

'I could wish that the easterners had put up something more of a fight though. This sort of prompt and meek capitulation will be building the expectation among our men that this whole campaign is going to be like this, a march to accept the surrender of a defeated enemy.'

'Your concern being that when the enemy actually show their teeth it will be an unpleasant surprise to them?'

The general nodded at Scaurus's comment.

'Quite so. And under the wrong circumstances it could be utterly disastrous, if inexperienced men shrink from a proper fight and leave my legions at risk of a rout. Which means that achieving the advantage of effective scouting is going to be of the utmost importance. And not the sort of scouting where five hundred bloodthirsty cavalrymen roam the countryside pillaging the locals either; I have something a little more subtle in mind. I suggest that you reunite yourselves with your familia and make sure that you're all suitably mounted and supplied for a few days' riding. You can take a few of Barbatus's ear thieves with you to act as messengers, but I want you to quietly work out what it is that we're facing while I get the army reformed and march east along the coast behind you. Oh, and you can take a message to the city elders of Cyzicus while you're at it.'

7

Marcus led the familia out of the legion camp at first light the next morning, and they rode for most of the day without encountering anything more interesting than olive farmers tending their groves and the occasional traveller, none of whom had the look of enemy scouts and all of whom left the road to hide among the trees when they saw such a large party of armed men approaching. They continued on along the coastal road, other than to bypass the last eastern cohort in their unwittingly doomed vigil, until Cyzicus came into view as they crested a rise, the port built on an isthmus that broadened out into a brooding mass of land looming above the city in the late afternoon's dull light.

'That is the Arctonessus, the Island of Bears.'

Sanga looked around on hearing Ptolemy's knowledgeable statement.

'Bears?' He turned back to Scaurus with a hopeful expression, raising a hand to stifle the Aegyptian's explanation. 'You'll be wanting it scouting, will you, Tribune? We don't want to risk any bears—'

Scaurus shook his head at Sanga's eager suggestion.

'The bears are a story from history, soldier, rather than a present-day reality. And I'd imagine you're less concerned with scouting for bears than with the potential for there to be *beers*. So while I thank you for the offer, I think not. You gentlemen can stay here and get settled for the evening while I take a few of our number for a somewhat quieter look around.'

Accompanied by Marcus and Qadir, and taking pity on Ptolemy, who was desperate to see Cyzicus after the disappointment of his having missed the chance to walk the streets of Ilium, he allowed the scribe and Lugos to accompany them. They rode towards the city at a relaxed pace, hoping to create the impression of being an officer and his men on their way along the coast to the west and seeking a bed for the night. When they came within sight of the beach on the city's western side he reined in his horse and looked out over the strand.

'This sand was the site of one of the fiercest and closest battles in history, gentlemen, and perhaps one of the most unlikely for that matter, as it involved a war in which the Spartans were allied with the Persians, of all people, in their mutual enmity with Athens. Hard though that might be to imagine, given Athens and Sparta's previous alliance during the Persian invasion of Greece only seventy years before. You may well have read about it, if your tutor was that way inclined, and not too Greek to ignore the Spartans' part in that war for their country's very survival.'

He raised a hand to forestall Ptolemy, who was showing every sign of joining the conversation.

'Not now, thank you scribe. I know this small piece of history well enough not to require your assistance.'

Ignoring the sulking Aegyptian, he continued.

'The Spartans, having apparently got over the fact that Xerxes had decapitated their dead king Leonidas's corpse after the famous battle of Thermopylae in a fit of frustration, made common cause with the Persians against their oldest enemy, which was of course Athens. Sparta and Athens had already forgotten their alliance against the Persians, and were locked in a struggle to control the Hellēspontos, the Spartans looking to restrict Athenian trade and strangle the city to death, so to speak. In the course of which unlikely alliance, the combination of a Spartan fleet of sixty warships and a powerful Persian army combined to take that city, Cyzicus, forcing the Athenians to completely retreat from the Propontis. But the Athenians were commanded by Alcibiades, who was a man of great cunning, and who had an excellent pair of fleet commanders to do his bidding . . .' He shot an irritated glance at the Aegyptian, who was squirming in his saddle with an apparent need to contribute. 'And yes, Ptolemy, I know that you scholars believe that his subordinates, Thrasybulus and Theramenes, were the real source of the Athenian's genius, and perhaps they were, but the point of my story is not to provide a history lesson!'

He smiled kindly as the scribe slumped back onto his horse.

'Anyway, whoever it was that was really in command, they came back through the Hellēspontos at night, to avoid being seen making such a bold move, and camped on the Prokonnesos, the island on which we captured Niger's spies, ready to attack with ninety ships to the Spartans' sixty. Which would probably have been enough of an advantage even without their superior seamanship. Alcibiades's only problem was that he knew that when the Spartan commander Mindarus realised his numerical disadvantage he could simply refuse to come out and fight, which would make the Athenian naval advantage meaningless given the strength of the Persian army waiting onshore. And so he came up with a plan to fool the Spartans into fighting on his terms.'

Qadir nodded, his interest now engaged as his soldier's brain considered the long-dead Athenian commander's options.

'He employed a deception, I presume?'

'He did, Centurion. He took only twenty ships and sailed into view of the port, at which the Spartan fleet came out, eager to engage and destroy such a vastly inferior enemy and without pausing to consider the highly unlikely nature of such an unfavourable challenge. Once they were well out of the harbour, and their crews were tired from rowing against an unfavourable wind while the Athenians retreated before them in order to draw them out, the other two Athenian commanders joined the fight from behind the Arctonessus there, using the favourable wind to speed their approach before the Spartans could run for the safety of their harbour.'

'A naval encirclement resulted?'

Scaurus shook his head at the question.

'Not quite. The Spartans realised that they had been fooled, and they turned back to the south and ran for the port's safety. But their oarsmen were exhausted, and the Athenians, superb sailors, were able to catch up with them and block any retreat into Cyzicus. Which left the Spartans with only one alternative, to run for the beach beside the port with the Athenians at their heels, cutting out individual ships that were lagging and boarding them. The Spartans unloaded their crews and marines to make a stand at the water's edge, hopeful that their Persian allies would be able to join them and thereby snatch a victory out of the mouth of defeat. The fight was fierce, the Spartans and Persians seeming to have the upper hand as the Athenians tried to tow their ships off the beach, and struggled to fight their way out of the surf to give battle on dry land. But Alcibiades's second navarchus landed on one flank and simply rolled the Spartan army up, killing Mindarus and utterly defeating and scattering his men.'

'It's a good story, Tribune!' Lugos's booming voice was filled with the pleasure of learning. 'So that was the end of the Spartans, was it?'

Scaurus shook his head with a smile at the giant's almost childlike enthusiasm for history.

'Not exactly. They built a new fleet, very much like Rome did every time the Carthaginians defeated us at sea, and returned to the war with their ambitions unchanged. Athens eventually ran out of money, and was forced to come to terms which were highly disadvantageous. Which just goes to prove that it's often the fighter with the greatest stamina and the strongest jaw, rather than the hardest punch, who wins the bout.'

They approached the city along the coast, seeing the same small fleet as before still moored in the docks, and Marcus pointed out the distant but visible gap in the run of warehouses where the fire he had set had burned out the building from which Sartorius's spy operation had been run. But, their attempt to appear harmless notwithstanding, the party were still a hundred paces from the city's southern gate when a party of ten armed men came out to meet them, their somewhat disordered formation and old armour and weapons at once identifying them as some sort of citizen levy.

Stifling a smile at their grim faces and hostile, if somewhat inept approach, Scaurus reined in his horse and called out to them, while Qadir and Marcus nocked arrows to the bows that they were carrying and Lugos dismounted, menacingly hefting his Warhammer, made to be swung two handed by any normal man, and raising a small round gladiator's shield that looked toylike in his huge hands.

'Good afternoon, gentlemen! Have you come out to surrender the city to me, or are you looking for a fight that will not be of our seeking but most definitely within our abilities?'

An older man wearing a relatively pristine mail shirt and unbattered helmet by comparison with his companions walked on forward, signalling his men to halt thirty paces from where the horses stood. He came to a halt ten paces from them, close enough to be able to speak conversationally rather than having to shout, one hand on the hilt of his sword.

'Greetings. I am Socrates, the centurion of the city's militia as appointed by the council of Cyzicus. Are you Severans, or are you loyalists? It would be best for you be frank, as we're in no mood for half measures.'

Scaurus smiled sadly at him for a moment and then got down from his horse, initially keeping his hands away from the hilts of his weapons as he walked forward almost to within touching distance of the militia man. Bowing with equal gravity, he very deliberately put a hand onto the hilt of his own weapon.

'Greetings, Socrates. It is my hope that you will prove to be every bit as wise as the Socrates of old.'

The centurion laughed tersely.

'Just without having to drink the hemlock, right? Your words are warm, but I must repeat my question. Are you loyalists?'

'We are men who consider ourselves to be loyalists. As you clearly do as well. The difference between us is that we serve a man who has actually been declared emperor by the senate and the people of Rome. Whereas your man in purple has only the acclamation of the men of the eastern cities, and therefore no such authority. And, more practically, our emperor's general Claudius

Candidus has five legions within a short march of here, four that he landed at Abydus and one that he has taken from his rival Aemilianus. Whereas you have precisely none. You would be wise to capitulate, and to welcome us into the city as ambassadors of a victorious army.'

The centurion shook his head in a studied show of disbelief, although the trickle of sweat down his neck belied his outward confidence.

'You should know that there is a loyalist army waiting close to here, ready to engage and defeat any attempt at landing on this coast. And there is a fleet in our port that will be used to bring men ashore in your force's rear, and deny them any chance of retreat. There is no need for our council to consider any sort of concessions to you.'

Scaurus shrugged, and gestured Marcus to speak.

'Perhaps you can persuade our friend here as to the most sensible course of action, given your recent presence in the city? I am loath to make an enemy of a man of this fine city . . .'

Socrates shrugged.

'It seems you will have to, unless this man plans to surrender on your behalf?'

His eyes narrowed as the younger man leaned forward in his saddle.

'As a man of the city you will probably remember a fire in the docks some weeks ago? A warehouse burned to the ground, and dead bodies found in the ashes?'

Socrates nodded slowly at the Roman's question.

'Yes. But what—'

'We started that fire, with the aim of destroying the warehouse. We did so to conceal the fact that we had unearthed and dismantled a spy network that was sending men across the sea to Thracia, intended to gather information on our readiness to invade Asia and put an end to this nonsense. And when I say *dismantled*, I mean killed to the last man, all of them dead for their treason. Ask me how I can prove my part in this.'

'How *can* you prove it?'

'You found three bodies. Two of them died from stab wounds and so probably bore no discernible signs of violence once the fire was done with them, but the third was a big man who went by the name of the Nomad. He was a former frumentarius who liked to throw his weight around, and I'm betting that you found him objectionable in his overbearing nature. And before he died and was cremated in the warehouse he sustained a broken jaw, which would have been obvious despite his corpse being reduced to a remnant. It was, wasn't it?'

The centurion rallied valiantly, aware that the discussion was getting out of his control.

'This is all very interesting, but I fail to see what this story has to do—'

'Before we set the fire, we had managed to convince the Nomad that our main strength was going to be deployed elsewhere, rather than in an invasion of this coast. Which led him to order his messengers, who were about to ride north to report to their master, and east to brief your general Aemilianus, to pass that information on to both men. You will recall the troops that marched east a short time after that fire, no doubt, and you might even know that they had orders to join the army on the Bosporus to resist an attack there. An attack that was never in reality proposed to be made there, and which has now been landed down the coast from here, across the Hellēspontos. The four legions we landed have quickly overrun the single legion that remained to face them, and so effectively that no one escaped to bring you the news. And Aemilianus has committed a dignified and regretful suicide, stating himself to be mortified to have betrayed the empire by siding with a usurper. That single legion has added its strength to our own, which means that this whole coast is now back under the rule of the one true emperor.'

Socrates stared at him in silence, and after a moment Marcus continued, as if with an afterthought.

'Oh, and the fleet you claim will defend you, and even land a non-existent army in advantageous positions in our rear? I saw those ships when I sailed in right under your noses, and there were perhaps a dozen vessels. All sitting in port and none of them out patrolling, just as I see them today. Which is why you don't know what's waiting just over the horizon, a seventy-ship praetorian fleet strong enough to take this city with only its marines. You will already have realised that the only options that leaves you are either to surrender now – and do all you can to provide our army with supplies – or to wait until there are five angry legions outside your walls. I suggest you choose quickly.'

Scaurus remounted, and called out his parting comments loudly enough for the other members of the citizen levy to hear.

'We're going back to re-join our men! We'll be waiting for any messengers you try to send to Niger, and we won't be taking prisoners if we catch them. And from this moment on, unless you choose to side with the one true emperor here and now, your city will be considered hostile and will be treated as such, with our soldiers free to act as they wish in the course of its capture!'

He looked down at the centurion with a questioning expression, his tone softening a little.

'You look like a man who has served.'

Socrates nodded, keeping his face straight but straightening his back fractionally at the question.

'I was a centurion in the German wars, Tribune.'

'Which explains why you hold your position. And makes you the only man likely to be able to explain to the city's council the peril that Cyzicus faces, if it makes the wrong choice now. So trust me in this, under this emperor there can be no opportunity to surrender later. He expects either instant obedience or for the price paid for dissent to be the heaviest possible, one or the other and nothing in between. And the news of that likely retribution will be all over the city an hour after you march your men back in through those gates, while the sort of panic that it will inspire might even be as bad as having five legions running amok in your streets.'

The hapless officer shook his head in defeat.

'Very well. Wait here, please, and I'll have some water brought out to you. It may take a little while for me to communicate the full implications of your generous offer to the men of the city council.'

At dawn the next day the familia renewed their march east, having spent the night in the levy's barracks after Cyzicus's inevitable, if a little slow, decision to capitulate to Severan rule. Marcus had posted sentries overnight to guard against any thoughts of double cross, but with the dawn it became clear that not only had no such precaution been necessary, but that Socrates's men were actually standing guard on the barrack as well, to prevent any expression of dissent against their presence. Scaurus shook hands with the veteran centurion as they prepared to leave, smiling wryly at the presence of his men around the building.

'The legions will arrive late today, I expect, or possibly tomorrow, if Legatus Candidus moves as fast as I expect. I'll send him a messenger with the news that he can expect a friendly welcome from you.'

Riding away to the east, they sent a pair of keen-sighted archers forward to scout the road ahead as they pushed on out of Asia and into the province of Bithynia. Scaurus pointed a hand at the road down which the two men were riding.

'So, to our orders, to seek information as to the dispositions of the remaining enemy forces. There are two major cities in Bithynia, Nicomedia and Nicaea, which we will reach by passing the coastal city of Cius and then pushing on into the interior of the province. The closest of them is Nicaea, on Lake Ascania, so I suggest that we go and have a quiet look there first, to find out what strength is invested in the city and what it's people's allegiances are.'

They rode on late into the evening, seeing no more sign of any military activity, camped as the sun was setting again and resumed their progress at first light, riding through increasingly mountainous land until they reached the coastal city of Cius. After buying provisions they moved on, climbing up into a pass between two mountains, at the top of which the terrain levelled out into a gently sloping plain that ran down to the massive lake by which the city that was their destination was situated, Nicaea itself still out of sight at the expanse of water's far end, fifteen or so miles distant. Scaurus looked up at the sun, which was halfway between its zenith and the horizon.

'There are a few hours of light left, and I would estimate still twenty miles of road left to ride to the city. We'll get to within five miles and then camp for the night, and tomorrow morning Marcus and I will go and see what's to be seen.'

They rode on along the lake's southern shore, the road empty at such a late hour, with Ptolemy happily sharing his knowledge of the city's origins to all that would listen.

'Nicaea was named for the dead wife of the king Lysimachus, who reigned on both sides of the Propontis in both Thracia and Asia after the death of his master Alexander the Great. Ironically, he was killed in a war that started after he had been fooled into having their son executed, deceived by a false charge of treason engineered by his third wife, who wished her own son to inherit the throne. This so disgusted the cities of Asia that they rebelled against him, and defeated him on a battlefield somewhere around here.' He waved a hand at the city, now distantly visible through the haze at the eastern end of the lake. 'It is one of the two great cities of the region, the other being Nicomedia to the north, and they are in constant conflict as to which of them is the greater. Once Septimius Severus's presence in Asia becomes widely known, it is certain that one of them will declare for him and the other promptly take Niger's side, for they are opposed in everything.'

'Now that *is* interesting!'

Morban, overhearing the lecture, promptly rode up alongside the Aegyptian and engaged him in a whispered conversation that Marcus was able to hear due to his proximity to them.

'So which of the two will declare for Niger, do you think?'

Ptolemy shot him a baffled glance, disconcerted by the unusual show of interest from a man who had previously not seemed in the slightest interested in his historical knowledge.

'I really can't say.'

'You really can't say, or you really *won't* say?'

The Aegyptian shook his head in even greater confusion.

'Why would I not say, if I knew?'

Morban's expression turned to one of knowing certainty.

'Because, you little bastard, you know the answer and you plan to bet on it with me.'

'Bet on it? With you? Why would I—'

'Come on, you know exactly what I mean! You know that when it comes to making money from guessing the uncertainties of the future, I am the master. And I am the master because I specialise in removing the uncertainties from the matter *before* I accept as much as a clipped copper coin from a gambler. So just tell me which one of the two cities will declare for Niger and I'll split the winnings with you, eighty for me, twenty for you. Can I say fairer than that?'

'But I simply cannot—'

'Thirty for you!'

'But I—'

'Forty! My last offer! You're taking gold from my purse here!'

They rode on with Morban continuing to harass the hapless scribe until Lugos sent him to the back of the column with harsh words and a clenched fist, after which he and Ptolemy fell to discussing the wars that had followed Alexander's death, and in such detail that reaching a spot where they could camp for the night, still five miles from the city, was a relief to the rest of the party.

Early the next morning, and resolutely refusing to allow anyone else to accompany them – ignoring the protests of both Dubnus and Qadir as to their safety, and Sanga as to the delights that they would doubtless be enjoying without any poor soldiers having the opportunity to partake – Marcus and Scaurus rode on from the roadside camp. Both men were wearing the rings that Marcus had taken from the spies captured on the Propontis, enabling them to pose as Sartorius's men if challenged. Scaurus shouted a parting comment at his men as they rode away.

'You can come and look for us if we don't come back by evening tomorrow, but until then the last thing we need is an escort of bad-tempered men whose idea of an opening conversational gambit is an invitation to a fight. Until then, just stay here and do as I ask for once!'

They rode along the lake shore in companionable silence for a mile or so before Scaurus spoke again.

'Of course there's always the risk that someone will recognise us when we get to the city. All it takes is for one of the legions that fought in our battle at Rhaedestus to be stationed there, and for a man that saw us while we were negotiating with Niger and that rat Sartorius to catch sight of us and make the connection, and we'll be executed as spies without any hesitation at all.'

Marcus shrugged.

'Do you remember what we looked like by the time we were out between the armies? I was covered in other men's blood, and you weren't much better. And we were wearing helmets. I don't think anyone that saw us from fifty paces or more is likely to have any clue as to who we are.'

'Perhaps. We'll just have to trust that the gods see fit not to put anyone that knows who we are into our path.'

As they drew closer to the city the tents of a legion marching camp came into view, huddled beneath Nicaea's more imposing bulk.

'What strength are they, would you estimate?'

Marcus took a moment to assess the encampment with an expert eye before answering.

'There are enough tents for one legion, I'd say, plus their supporting auxiliary cohorts. No more.'

Scaurus nodded his agreement.

'We could turn around now and ride away, you know? All that Candidus needs from us is the knowledge of what it is that he's facing, not the flavour of the broth that's being served in the city's taverns this week.'

The younger man nodded.

'We could, but then if we did we'd know nothing more than the rough number of men we'll be facing when the two armies meet, no idea as to who they are, or their state of mind and readiness to fight.'

'Agreed.'

The two men rode up to the camp's gate, approaching the sentries whose duty centurion came forward with a look that told them that if the legion wasn't yet on a full war footing, their officers were in no way shirking their duty. He raised a hand, gesturing his men forward on either side, their spears ready to use.

'Identify yourselves!'

Marcus smiled easily down at him, gesturing to the ground at his beast's feet.

'You're happy for me to dismount, colleague? I've been in the saddle for three days and my backside feels like old boot leather. And I'm not sure that the tribune here is especially fond of having spears pointed at him when he's on a mission to speak with your commanding officer.'

The centurion stared at them for a moment, then waved his hand to indicate to his men that they should lower their spears.

'Yes, you can dismount. And my apologies, Tribune, we're all just a bit jumpy here, given we're getting ready to march out and fight.' He turned to his chosen man. 'Take these men to the principia, then fetch out Tribune Audax and tell him these officers are asking for him.'

Scaurus leaned closer to Marcus, lowering his voice.

'Audax? We might be in luck.'

They followed the soldier along the via principalis to the headquarters building, waiting patiently for the officer in question to appear and noting the higher than usual number of officers purposefully coming and going from the headquarters with writing tablets in their hands.

'They do seem busy. Perhaps the word of our landing has already arrived here.'

After a short wait the senior officer came out of the camp, a puzzled look of recognition crossing his face as he saw the two men waiting for him.

'Gentlemen, I believe you . . .' realisation dawned upon him. 'Gods below, is that *you*, Rutilius Scaurus?'

The two men embraced in the manner of old friends, and Scaurus turned to indicate Marcus.

'Titus Cornelius Audax, this is my colleague Marcus Valerius Aquila. Marcus, Titus and I are old friends from the days when we were both wet behind the ears legion tribunes with the Fifth Alaudae on the Rhenus.'

Audax laughed at the memory.

'Which was back in the days when we both imagined that we had something to add to the legion's function, and no clue at all that we were in fact a liability that required the most careful of management by our long-suffering centurions! But tell me Gaius, what are you two doing here? You do realise that enemy legions may come down the road from the west any day, now that they've landed in Asia? We have orders to march out and go to meet them in the morning, which is the reason for all the excitement.'

Scaurus's answer was delivered without even a hint of any pause to think. If he was suffering any qualms at lying to an old friend, they were in no way evident in his reply, framed in the knowledge that the enemy command were aware of their landing.

'Yes, we know. We heard the news on the road. We were overtaken by a messenger sent to your legatus from Niger's headquarters in Chalcedony. We have the task of reporting back as to your readiness to take the fight to the invaders.'

'You're working for Niger?' Audax shook his head in puzzlement. 'I haven't seen you in the camp at all.'

'No, not Niger.' Scaurus raised his hand to show his friend the ring that had been taken from one of Sartorius's spies. 'We're working for another man, who stands behind the throne rather than sitting on it.'

The tribune nodded slowly, his expression puzzled.

'But . . . you? Spying for Sartorius? I mean, men of our station acting as informers? You must know the man's reputation.'

Scaurus shook his head, affecting a horrified reaction to the question.

'Gods no! We may have been seconded to his command, but we're in no way to be compared with the rest of his informing scum. The task we were originally given was to come out this way, and then on to Cyzicus, and to make sure that the reports he received that the enemy army was marching to cross the Bosporus wasn't some sort of bluff. And to be fair it seems as if he was right to do so. We have orders from Sartorius not to make any contact with your legatus, by the way; he doesn't want it to seem as if he's spying on the army, given how touchy the emperor's generals can be if challenged by a man not of their class.'

Audax nodded.

'Our legatus? You won't see him, not in the camp and not in the city either. He has a private headquarters in a rich man's villa overlooking Nicaea, and he hardly ever comes down here to visit us mortals. Although he'll be roughing it with the rest of us soon enough, once we march out to go and find how much of Severus's army has washed up on this side of the sea, and hopefully to link up with Aemilianus's legions. The message from Chalcedony that arrived late yesterday said that the enemy were making a landing across the Hellēspontos, and that there were enough ships involved that it could be a full-sized fleet, and carrying one or more legions. Anyway, you have a job to do, and I'd imagine you'd like to get it done and be on your way to Cyzicus. But once you've done with looking around, join me for a cup of wine and something warm to eat. I'll show you the best of what Nicaea has to offer; you can spend the night here and ride on to the west tomorrow morning. And now if you'll excuse me, I'm the duty officer. Just come back to the gate when you're ready to enjoy some hospitality.'

The two men watched him walk away with mutual disbelief, Scaurus shaking his head in amused disbelief.

'You remember that fervent hope of mine that we didn't cross paths with anyone that knows us? Clearly the gods were listening, and equally clearly they do have a sense of humour. My old friend is going to allow us to roam the camp without so much as a centurion to keep an eye on us.'

They led their horses to the legion stables, paying the duty decurion handsomely to feed and water them, then made their way out into the camp. Walking around the encampment, Marcus was more than once struck by the feeling that there were eyes upon him, but in the absence of any obvious sign of surveillance in the camp's bustling preparations to march, he put it down to a natural wariness on his own behalf, under the strained circumstances. Their steady progress around the sprawling maze of tents and rough wooden buildings confirmed what Scaurus had been expecting to find.

'One legion, the Sixth Ironclad, and four auxiliary cohorts, two of them mounted, one of which is a five-hundred-strong cohort of horse archers and the other a full cavalry wing. All well turned out, and with their camp discipline nice and tight. And did you see all the men with the scars?'

Marcus nodded, having noted the number of legionaries and their officers with freshly healed facial wounds.

'We faced these troops outside Rhaedestus and taught them a lesson, and now they're battle hardened and looking for revenge. Which will make them doubly dangerous if Candidus's legions have to face them across a level field, because they're just as virginal as these boys were before that ugly battle.'

'Indeed. And with that noted I suggest we call it a day, before one of them recognises you from the battlefield and starts trying to get that revenge here and now? And besides . . .' Scaurus gestured to a centurion chivvying his men into a line for review of their turn out, presumably in preparation for their going on guard. 'It looks like it's time for the guard to change, so let's go and find my old comrade Audax and see what refreshment Nicaea has to offer.'

Scaurus's friend was good to his word, relinquishing his responsibility to the incoming duty officer and leading them back through the tents towards the city walls.

'We try not to eat the food that the legion cooks produce, it's all very well for men with iron constitutions like the legionaries have, but even their centurions prefer to dine in the city when they get the chance.'

At the camp's far end they exited through another well-guarded gate, and walked across the short distance separating camp and city. Nicaea's streets were much like any other eastern city, with the smell of cooking and both human and animal waste assailing their nostrils as they followed Audax into the warren of alleys. Although they were alert to their surroundings, neither man noticed the shadowy figure following at a safe distance in the street's shadows behind them, his face obscured by the hood of a soldier's cloak raised against the evening's chill. At length, in the quiet of a dead-end street, a pair of massive wooden doors set in a frame fully nine feet high presented the only way for them to proceed any further, a pair of heavily built doormen barring entrance to those unfavoured by wealth or position. Both men nodded to the legion tribune respectfully, opening the doors and allowing them to enter. After waiting in the doorway of a taverna at the end of the alley for a moment, the man who had been following them turned and walked purposefully away.

Inside the building's imposing entrance hall, Audax handed his cloak to a servant and turned to the two men with a smile and a gesture of welcome.

'This, my friends, is where a man comes to find the best food, the best wine and the best women that Nicaea has to offer! I presume it's food and a drink that are first on your mind?'

The proprietor, bowing at his command to show them to the army's reserved section of his establishment, ushered them into a carefully lit and artfully decorated space in which three officers were already refreshing themselves in preparation for what – Marcus assumed from their fine tunics and footwear, and their generally well-scrubbed appearance – was intended to be one last night of hedonism before their legions marched to confront the Severan forces. Audax raised a hand to them in greeting.

'I had feared this place might be a little livelier, with the collected officers of a legion and several cohorts looking for a chance to teach their sorrows to swim before we march to war!'

An urbane tribune whose appearance sparked a distant memory for Marcus looked up from the couch on which he was sprawled with a glass cup of wine in his hand.

'Most of the boys have already gone upstairs, but we can share a jug or two with you before our turn comes. Who are your friends?'

Audax gestured to Scaurus.

'This is an old friend of mine, Gaius Rutilius Scaurus, fresh off a horse from the north and come down here to see what's what, now that the Severans are ashore. He commanded the Third Gallica in that unpleasant business with the Parthians back in the 938th year of the city, so he knows all about a good fight.'

The lounging officer sat up, his expression changing in an instance.

'You're the man who gave those horse-fucking eastern bastards a bloody nose at Nisibis?'

Scaurus bowed slightly.

'I'm one of the men who managed to achieve that unlikely result. And I'm prouder of the shock we gave them in the desert before we reached Nisibis; but yes, that was me, or rather me and several thousand other men, including my good friend Marcus Valerius Aquila here.'

If Marcus had feared that his name might strike a chord with the officers, he was relieved to see a general lack of any reaction.

'Well you're both very welcome to join us. Tell me, Rutilius Scaurus, what do you think we can expect the enemy to do now that they've got their boots on our soil?'

They talked through first one jug of wine and then another, Scaurus careful to keep his story as detail free as possible while encouraging the officers to talk as much as they wished about themselves and their legion, a mixture of entertaining but mostly useless gossip shot through with some precious intelligence regarding recruitment, training, troop strengths and the usual supply problems. At length the officers were beckoned up the stairs and left, promising to re-join Audax and his friends when their needs had been satisfied in the brothel on the floor above, and the tribune took them into dinner.

'I can recommend the lamb, but I'm not so sure about the pork. Take my advice, get them to spice the food the way the locals eat it and you won't forget this meal for a good while.'

They ate, Audax quizzing them about recent events in Rome once he discovered that their cover story was that of having left the city to re-join the service of Niger, a man known to both of them from their time in Dacia.

'What's he like? We don't see much of him now that he's an emperor, and even when we do he's wrapped in purple with a dozen guardsmen surrounding him in case someone puts a knife in him and robs them of their meal ticket.'

'Niger? He's a little stolid, perhaps not an inspirational leader, but he seems to have—'

The dining room's door opened and a small party was shown in, several muscular thugs preceding a single man who was dressed in the finery of an imperial officer, a small gold replica of a beneficiarius's lance hanging from his belt. He stood for a moment in the doorway as his men fanned out to either side, a slow smile spreading across his face.

'I hardly thought it possible when the news reached me of two men unexpectedly arrived from the west, that anyone in Severus's service could be so foolish as to blunder into a city as firmly committed to Niger's rule as Nicaea is. But there was something about the description of these unexpected new arrivals that made me think. A pair of tribunes, brazenly wandering around the camp with an interest in anything and everything, my source told me, and so I wondered, just idly, if these potential spies might be you two. And had them keep an eye on you so that I could check up on you later, when you were boxed into whichever taverna you chose to eat in rather than take the risk of losing you in the camp's maze if we came for you too soon.'

Sartorius walked slowly across the room, his guards advancing on both sides in response to a subtle hand signal from their master.

'But this is perfect! The two men who swore to my face that they would kill me when we last met, and you have chosen to deliver yourselves to me so neatly that no operation I could have set up to ensnare you could ever have had any hope of such a tidy success.'

Audax looked at them in consternation.

'But you said you were in the service of this man?'

The spymaster smiled in evident delight.

'Did they really? How very clever of them, had I not already made a quiet and unheralded arrival in the city last night!' He shook his head in disbelief of such fortune, then waved his men forward. 'Take them, and watch the younger one like hawks, because if you give him even the ghost of a chance he'll have that dagger out and be among you like some kind of gladiator, from what I've heard.'

He smiled again as the bodyguards drew their own daggers and dragged the two men out of their seats, disarming them with swift efficiency.

'Welcome to Asia, Rutilius Scaurus. Although you might soon find yourself wishing you'd stayed on the other side of the Ox Ford!'

8

'How did you come by these rings?'

Any trace of Sartorius's amusement at capturing his sworn enemies had turned to icy hatred the moment that he had realised his captives were wearing the talismans they had taken from the bodies of his dead spies. He held the two rings that his men had pulled from Marcus and Scaurus's fingers out on his palm, placing them under the latter's nose so that, even with his head down, and breathing hard from a clinical initial beating administered by the spymaster's thugs, the tribune would be unable to ignore them.

'I don't need you to answer, Rutilius Scaurus! I *know* where you got these rings! I had them made specially with jewels mined close to Chalcedon, and I gave them to the men I recruited from the legions and sent across the sea to gather information as to the dispositions of the usurper's army, so that they might recognise each other in the field. And their intelligence duly flowed back to me, via my men in Cyzicus, telling me that Severus was planning to cross into Asia by forcing a crossing of the Bosporus! Information that has proven unreliable, to say the least! What I want to know is how you came to be wearing them?'

Scaurus looked up at him with a faint smile, his left eye already puffy from the swift working over that both men had received after being hustled up the stairs, and into a room hastily vacated by a legion tribune and his female companion at the spymaster's terse order.

'Forgive me if I'm amused at being interrogated in a room that still smells of sex. I presume Niger moved his legions according to your intelligence, leaving only this one in addition to Aemilianus's to bar the road from the southern coast of the Propontis; and even then at a distance, because you were convinced that Severus's main attack would fall elsewhere.'

Sartorius nodded tersely at his captive's pleasure at having deceived him.

'Yes, I did. Although I was already starting to wonder at just how easily that intelligence had made its way back to me when news arrived that my base of operations in Cyzicus had burned to the ground, and that both the men I sent across the sea and those who had waited for their reports in the city had gone missing without any trace. I suspected some interference, which is why I advised the emperor to move this legion here a week ago, to cover the risk of an advance from the Asian coast, and to send messengers to Aemilianus ordering him to withdraw from Asia and bring his legion here, to form an army in Bithynia that would be worthy of his talents.'

Marcus laughed hollowly.

'And just how well did that advice go down with Niger, when you had only recently warned him of an attack across the Bosporus? Might he be starting to wonder if promoting you to the position of his spymaster was a wise thing to do, given your schemes always seem to end in disaster?'

The leader of Sartorius's bodyguard reached out and took him by the hair, tilting his head to one side and raising a ring studded fist.

'You want us to smack them around some more, teach them to keep their mouths shut until you want them to speak?'

The frumentarius shook his head with a knowing expression.

'I suspect that you're keen to provoke me, in the hope that I'll have you beaten senseless, Tribune. Which makes it fortunate for me that I'm not a small-minded man. Because while having you both beaten half to death would be deeply satisfying, there are far better uses for you. I will not allow you to goad me into unnecessary violence that might lead to one of you being killed. But don't mistake my current forbearance for softness.'

Scaurus spat blood on to the floor at his enemy's feet.

'Unlikely, given the death of my friend at the hands of your murderous scum in Thessalonica.'

Sartorius shook his head, assuming a tolerant expression.

'Come now, Rutilius Scaurus; in war all things are fair, as a man with your known ability to use ruse and subterfuge knows all too well. You can hardly murder every man in my intelligence operation and then complain that I was responsible for the death of one of yours.' He leaned closer to his captive. 'And do I really need to make clear to you just how much freedom there is for a man like me, in time of war? I came here to check on this legion's readiness for war, and to receive the reports of their scouts as soon as they return from their missions, but now I have no need, do I? Because, Rutilius Scaurus, I have you to tell me everything I need to know.'

Scaurus shook his head.

'I'll tell you nothing.'

Sartorius beamed at him, positively delighted at the unexpected turn of events.

'Oh no, on the contrary, you will tell me *everything*. The first time you tell me what I want to know it will be laced with falsehoods, and you will be grimacing from the pain to which you will have been subjected. We'll start with one of your hands perhaps, peel the skin from fingertips to wrist, and then salt the raw flesh to cause you quite exquisite pain, as an introduction to the techniques of my interrogators. And you will think that you have given me just enough of the truth to confuse me as to what you have told me is honest, and what is falsehood.'

The spymaster smiled, and shook his head at the idea that he might be fooled by such an obvious ploy.

'Whereas the second time you answer my questions you will be roaring in agony, and any idea of trying to misinform me will have fled your mind from the moment that I tell my men to introduce you to a whole new world of pain. Your toes, perhaps, removed in delicate slices, one cleaver blow at a time. You will tell me everything, and more, so much more, to stave off the agony. And you will have no thought as to attempting to deceive me, as your mind will be filled with the pain, and the need to make it stop. But the third time . . .'

He smiled at the prospect, bending to speak in Scaurus's ear.

'The third time you answer my questions will be the time I will be sure that you have no means of dissembling. Because you will have abandoned any hope of surviving, and surrendered yourself to the inevitability of your death. You will be bargaining for a swift exit from this life, the need for which will consume your very being, as the interrogator breaks your bones, one at a time. You will tell me everything, not with a grimace, not in a roar of agony, but in a hoarse whisper through vocal cords ruined by the incessant screams of what has gone before. And you will beg me to kill you, quickly and cleanly. Which I will, of course, being a man of my word . . . eventually.'

He gestured to Marcus.

'Not that you'll be going first. I'll make you watch this impudent bastard make the same lengthy exit first, and without the option of a mercy stroke. You had the temerity to threaten me with death, Valerius Aquila, after the defeat from which you were rescued by the chance landing of a bird on your standard. Now the time has come for you to make amends for that insult.'

He straightened up and addressed his men.

'Tie them securely and put two guards on the door. We will ride for Chalcedon; once we've eaten and taken a few hours rest, I'll have these two strapped to the torturer's rack before the sun sets tomorrow.'

His men secured them even more securely to the chairs, their leader making to gag them until Sartorius shook his head and waved a dismissive hand.

'No need. Let them talk, they can spend the time working out the lies that they'll tell us while they're still capable of talking, rather than whimpering.'

When Sartorius and his men had left them alone, the two men sat helpless in the dark, the realisation of their predicament sinking in.

'Pure bad luck, I suppose. If that animal hadn't taken it on himself to come forward from Niger's headquarters, we would have been able to ride out tomorrow with no one any the wiser.'

Scaurus answered Marcus's gloomy statement after a moment's thought.

'Bad luck, or the result of the curse on me, I wonder? After all, perhaps what we achieved in destroying his spy network might have been my greatest victory, if it enabled Severus to steal such a strategic march on Niger? Perhaps this is the doom that Titus wished upon me, made worse by the scale of our success?' He leaned forward as far as his bonds would allow, whispering in the dark. 'And even if this is the end, Niger is still unaware of the loss of a legion and the death of his greatest general, which means that we still have a vital role to play, because it is knowledge that we must keep from them as long as we can.'

They sat in silence, alone with their thoughts in the darkness, until both fell into an uneasy and fitful doze. At dawn, Sartorius's men returned, untied them other than the bonds securing their wrists together, and took them down the stairs and out into the empty street, where a dozen horses were waiting in the half-light. The spymaster was already mounted, and he smiled gleefully down at them from his saddle with the delight of a man in complete control of the situation.

'You'll have to forgive me for dragging you from your sleep, gentlemen, but it's seventy miles to our destination, and if we are to be there before the end of the day we will need to make the most of the daylight. It will be a long day, and we might all be a little sore by the time we arrive in Calchedon, but I can distract you along the way with stories of the interrogations I've witnessed at the hands of my expert questioners in recent months. And, of course, sore backsides are going to be the least of your problems by this time tomorrow, aren't they?'

They mounted their horses, which had been retrieved from the legion stables, their reins tied to the saddle horns of Sartorius's escorts, and the party rode out of the city and along the road between the lake's grey expanse and the camp, which was alive with preparations for the legion's departure. The commotion of the men mustering for war was not lost on either Sartorius or his captives.

'A battle-hardened legion getting ready to march. What a sight to behold!' Sartorius looked across at Scaurus with a grim smile. 'Yes, that's the news you were supposed to be taking to your master Candidus, isn't it?' He laughed at the Roman's attempt to ignore the comment. 'Don't delude yourself, of course we know who it is that Severus put in command of his main field army, and a brave decision it was too! To select a man with no obvious qualifications, rather than opting for his close and proven associate Julius Laetus, that was quite an upset, I'd imagine.'

He waited for Scaurus to reply, but only smiled at his captive's silence.

'Don't worry, you can keep your thoughts on the gossip around the way he divides and rules his generals to yourself for now, Rutilius Scaurus. You'll be happy enough to share them once you can see the irons heating up in the torturer's brazier, and anticipate the scorching of your flesh. But I'll tell you this, his inconstancy with the men who commands his legions will be his downfall, sooner or later. If an emperor frustrates the expectations of too many of the men who command the loyalty of his legions, then he sets himself on a collision course with their ambitions. And history teaches us that that's not a thing that ends well for one or the other party, as a rule.'

He pointed out to the west, and the massive lake's distant far end, invisible in the dawn. At such an early hour the road was empty of the bustle of farmers and merchants that could be expected, once the sun's heat was sufficient to burn off the veil of early morning mist that had crept over the landscape from the water's cold silver expanse.

'And it's a shame for Severus that you're not going to be able to warn Candidus that this angry dog of a legion is waiting for his meek lambs to attack them. He might have *almost* won the war for intelligence, but he will lose the war on the ground, I have no doubt of that! It's one thing for a clever man like you to have prevented us from detecting your scheme to cross the sea, and to take us by surprise with such a bold move. And a good job you did of it too, I'm grudgingly forced to admit, in rolling up my entire spy network. But it's another thing entirely to take on a battle-hardened legion like this with men who've seen no fighting. Because whether Candidus bought three or even four legions across the Propontis with him, they won't stand against the men you blooded on the other side of the sea at Rhaedestus, not under the circumstances we have planned.'

He smiled at the questioning looks on their faces.

'I see no harm in telling you the truth of it, the knowledge will do you no good. Niger is marching, gentlemen, coming south with two legions, Apollo's Fifteenth and the Twelfth Thunderbolt, which will join with the Sixth Ironclad back there to form a battlegroup bestowed with both strength and experience. Two of them are legions which fought you at Rhaedestus, to their shame at failing to overcome a single legion, and those legionaries are positively slavering for revenge. And they'll have all the time they need to prepare the battlefield by the time your relative innocents reach them; it will be a slaughter. And do you want to know how I can say that with such assurance?'

Scaurus kept his gaze locked to his front, refusing to engage with the frumentarius, and Sartorius dipped a hand into his saddlebag, pulling out a message contained and waving it at the Roman.

'This is an order from the emperor, the real one, that is, which I have relayed to the commander of the Sixth, and which I am now carrying back to Chalcedon to prevent the imperial seal upon it being reused. Niger's messengers have strict orders to bring them back for destruction, myself no less than any other. So, can you guess what the emperor has ordered the Sixth's legatus to do, in preparing for the invasion of your army along the coast of Asia?'

He waited theatrically for a moment before continuing, evidently pleased with himself.

'As I told you, the news of your landing arrived in the imperial headquarters faster than you might have hoped, borne by a ship that sighted the ships of a large fleet crossing the straits and whose navarchus was both intelligent and loyal enough to sail for Chalcedon with the information. And when Niger received the news of your landing, he was quick to realise the danger it poses to our position in Asia if not dealt with promptly. Given the lack of any return communication from Aemilianus in response to his orders to withdraw to Nicaea, we are assuming that the single legion he kept in Asia to deal with what he expected to be an attempt to deceive us with a fake landing has been captured or destroyed. Along with the man himself, if he didn't die on the battlefield.'

Sartorius shot a swift glance at Scaurus to see if there was any reaction, but the Roman simply shrugged.

'I cannot say.'

'Or at least not yet. Give it time and you will be singing like a bird. The question of Aemilianus's fate is of no importance either way, the man had long since come to the end of his usefulness in any case. And he was starting to show clear signs of being more concerned with his family's survival than the fate of the empire, which I suspected he believed to be preordained by the events of the battle at Rhaedestus.'

The spymaster waved the message cylinder again and then pushed it back into the saddlebag.

'These are orders from Niger, issued following my advice as to how to deal with this invasion, whether it be diversionary or the whole of Severus's army. You've seen the road from Cyzicus to Nicaea for yourself. Typical Bithynia, all olive groves, hills and mountains, not nice flat farmland of the type you soldiers prefer to fight on. Ground that's easy enough for an army to traverse in the absence of any resistance, if the man giving the orders is careful with his scouting and throws a strong advance guard ahead of his column of march, ready for action. But when that army reaches Cius, and turns to the east to head inland for Nicaea, it will be advancing uphill, into mountains, and with no way to go around them without squandering a week's march and more. There is no option from there, no choice but to push up through the pass that separates the coastal plain from the interior of the province, and that's where I am proposing to set up our defensive line.'

He looked across at Scaurus.

'You are a field commander of some repute, Rutilius Scaurus, so you will immediately recognise the truth of the matter. An experienced legion like the Sixth, given days to dig into a narrow position between two mountains, will construct a defence that three times their strength will break on like waves reaching the shore. Candidus will know that, of course, when he realises the danger his men are marching into, but he will still have no option but to make the attempt in the teeth of resistance from all three legions that are marching to face him. And I wasn't exaggerating as to the anger in the ranks of two of those legions, after the way you handled them so brutally at Rhaedestus in the summer. We should be grateful to you for giving them such a rough lesson in the realities of battle, because that's what will bolster them to fight like animals when it comes to the decisive moment. Severus's much vaunted army of Pannonia will be broken and cast to the wind like chaff, its survivors hunted down and destroyed as they flee back towards Cyzicus. And your so-called emperor, a man who seized power at the point of a spear when all the senators of Rome wanted was for Pescennius Niger to come home and take his place on the throne, will be shorn of his ability to resist the empire's rightful master!'

'You don't think that Candidus will detect such an obvious trap, and march around it?'

'No, I don't.' The spymaster waved the question away. 'His scouts will be lured into carefully set traps, and their death or capture will poke his eyes out. Then his advance guard will come upon what will look like a hasty defence, some distance from the pass. They will attack, of course, and will manage to push a token force from their positions, a cohort of the most disciplined men we have, able to retreat uphill and retain their formation.

Emboldened, and seeking glory, your advance guard will pursue that careful retreat up the road and into the pass between the coastal plain and the lake. They will send runners back to Candidus for immediate support, and his leading legion will push in behind them to exploit this apparent victory, only to find the enemy units that were fleeing have seemingly turned to fight. The legions following up will pack in behind them, at which point archers on the heights on either side will start to pour arrows down into them, killing or disabling his men without their being able to do anything about it. Can you guess the result?'

Scaurus nodded.

'I know how you would like to see it: either a bloody battle of attrition which the attacker is likely to lose, bled by losses to the defending legions and their archers, or a rout with the defending legions counterattacking downhill and breaking the men facing them.'

Sartorius laughed tersely.

'More likely both, the second after the other has played out. Not that you'll ever know the outcome. Your only future is in a torchlit interrogation chamber.'

They rode on along the lakeside until the road's path took it away from the shoreline, curving away to the north, the road running first to Nicomedia and then ultimately the Bosporus. After another mile the early morning fog had become so dense that they could see no more than twenty paces, and Sartorius shook his head with an unhappy expression.

'You two, ride forward and make sure there are no bandits waiting for us in the bushes. It would be typical of this—'

The leading rider tensed in his saddle and then toppled onto the road, the sound of the bow that had shot an arrow into him dulled to a barely perceptible note by the fog's muffling qualities. More arrows flew, the archers who had loosed them invisible in the murk, and three more of Sartorius's men fell. The spymaster put a hand to his sword hilt, freezing as a massive figure loomed out of the murk from the olive trees to his right, an axe raised above his head and his eyes wide beneath a centurion's helmet, shouting a battle cry immediately familiar to the two Romans.

'*Tungriaaaaa!*'

The axe fell, cleaving the spymaster's horse's head from its neck, and the beast's decapitated corpse slumped to the cobbles, throwing him face first into the road's surface. Marcus jumped neatly down from his own saddle, ignoring the arrows flitting past in his haste to prevent Dubnus delivering a death blow to such a precious captive.

'Take him alive!'

As the frumentarius tried to get off his hands and knees, the Briton gripped his axe below its polished head and tapped his head with the blade's iron butt hard enough to drop him back down onto the road's wide stones. All around them his pioneers were assailing the few men in Sartorius's party who hadn't been felled by Qadir's archers from all sides, fending off the horsemen's swords with their shields before hooking them from their saddles with their axes and hacking at them as they sprawled on the road. Marcus offered his bound wrists to his friend's axe blade, and the Briton parted the cord binding them while the Roman looked around at the human and equine wreckage left by the ambush.

'Thank you, you've saved us from slow and agonising deaths. But how did you know?'

Qadir walked out of the mist.

'You really thought your friends were going to obey an order to let the two of you just wander into an enemy city without some careful oversight? And when I say "careful", I do of course mean the presence at your backs of a pair of whore-mongering soldiers and myself to keep their minds on the task of watching over you. We followed you around the camp, and watched you go into that brothel with the less cautious watcher who had watched from closer behind you for much of the day in attendance. And then we saw him' – he nodded at the spymaster, who had staggered to his feet and was standing under the guard of a pair of axemen – 'follow you in not long after. When you didn't come out it was obvious that you would need rescuing when he took you back to his master.'

Scaurus nodded.

'I have never been so grateful to have my orders disobeyed. Shall we get this mess cleaned up, before the legions march through? It would be a shame to lose the advantage you seem to have gifted us.'

The spymaster's dead bodyguards were easy to hide in the olive grove up the slope from the road, but the corpses of three horses were harder work, Dubnus settling for his men's grisly but practical suggestion that they would be more easily removed from the scene in pieces. The pioneers wielded their axes with gusto, then carried the results of their butchery away, although not before cutting out generous chunks of meat to be eaten later. The archers carried helmets full of water from a nearby stream to wash away the blood that had pooled in the seams between the road's cobbles, and the pioneers waded into the water to remove the blood from their tunics and skin.

'Well done, gentlemen; you'd never know that anything had ever happened here. And thanks to the earliness of the hour, we've not been disturbed while we cleaned up.'

Scaurus's praise was interrupted by a horn sounding in the distance, joined an instant later by the bray of every cornicer in the Sixth Ironclad, a nape-lifting challenge of the sort to be expected from a legion marching to war.

'Our enemy is on the move, from the sound of it. It's a shame that we can't prevent them from doing so, but at least we can warn Candidus as to the nature of the trap they are baiting for him.'

Marcus shook his head, gesturing to the still-dazed Sartorius who was sitting on a rock by the road with a Tungrian pioneer standing guard over him.

'I think we might well achieve somewhat more than that.'

'Riders coming in!'

The rearmost centurion in the Sixth Legion's order of march shouted a warning to his men, who cleared the role to either side at the sight of a bronze armoured officer and an escort of a centurion and four archers trotting their horses out of the lakeside mist behind them. Century after century made space for the messenger to pass through them as they progressed down the legion's column, taking to the verge as they passed the artillery wagons rumbling along in the wake of the leading cohorts before reaching the command group. Slowing his horse to a walk, the leading rider acknowledged the wary salute of a centurion who, to judge from the finery of his clothing and equipment was the legatus's first spear, tapping his saddlebag which, the centurion noted, was embossed with the symbol of an aquila.

'I carry a message from Niger for Legatus Renatus. I need to see him immediately.'

The senior centurion relaxed slightly, knowing the expected routine for such an eventuality.

'We will do what is ordered and at every command we will be ready! You carry orders from the emperor, you say?'

The tribune nodded brusquely.

'Quite so, First Spear. To be handed to the legatus, by myself, and the imperial seal to be reclaimed immediately.'

The older man nodded resignedly, but restrained himself from asking the courier any questions, knowing both that nothing good was likely to be contained in the messenger's saddlebag, and that the best way to find out their fate would be to escort him to the legion's commander with all due haste.

'Come on then, sir. You can leave your escort here, you won't be needing them until you take back whatever reply the legatus gives you. And you' – he gestured his cornicer forward – 'blow the signal for the halt. There's no point us marching off to the west until we know what it is that the throne commands of us, and I'm sure the men will be ready for a rest in any case.'

The tribune's Syrian escort, a centurion and several archers, dismounted and waited at the roadside while the horn call's notes sounded into the muffling mist, and were picked up and repeated by the cornicer's colleagues up and down the column. The legion halted, soldiers unslinging and leaning on their shields, each tent party a nest of gossip as to the cause of the unexpected break in the march. The first spear walked the messenger a short distance to where a half-dozen men in the finery of senior officers had also dismounted, the oldest of them turning to him with an expectant expression.

'Ah, First Spear, I was wondering why we've stopped. And who's this . . . ?'

'Imperial courier, Legatus.'

Marcus snapped to attention, proffering the message container that had been taken from Sartorius's saddlebag, waiting for any sign that the general facing him was able to recognise a man whose face had been painted with the blood of a dozen dead legionaries the last time they had been at close quarters.

'Did you have trouble on the road, Tribune?'

'Legatus?'

Renatus waved a hand at his bruised features.

'Your face man. You look like you've been brawling, and if there's one thing I won't tolerate in my officers it's the sort of lack of discipline that leads to fighting.'

Marcus nodded gravely, realising that the facial injuries inflicted by Sartorius's thugs were effectively disguising him from the potential of recognition.

'Quite so, Legatus, my father remarked on the same sentiment more than once. My horse . . . my previous horse . . . decided to throw me off yesterday, and I must have landed on my face from the feel of it today.'

But the senior officer's attention had switched to the cylinder in his hand, reaching out to take the message and breaking the waterproof wax seal on the wooden cylinder with a twist. He pulled out a scroll embossed with the aquila of an imperial military dispatch, the words *Senatus Populesque Romanus* heading the text to indicate the purported sender's assumption of imperial power.

'It seems there is a change to our orders, gentlemen.' The gathered officers collectively leaned a little closer to the general. 'We are no longer to establish a blocking position between Cius and Nicaea, and prepare to defend it against the legions commanded by my colleague and our enemy Candidus. We are now instructed to reverse our steps and march north with all due speed via Nicomedia to the Bosporus, where the usurper's main blow now seems to be about to fall. The legions that were being marched south to join us are now heading back to the north as well, to mount an early defence.' Renatus looked up from the parchment at Marcus. 'This is correct, Tribune? Severus has chosen to attack across the strait after all?'

Marcus nodded without any show of emotion.

'So it would seem, Legatus.'

The senior officer's gaze lingered for a moment on him, and the Roman waited behind a mask of imperturbability for the general to ask him who he was, perhaps puzzled by an unexplained but nagging familiarity with the unexpected messenger's face. After a moment he shrugged, handing Marcus the message's imperial seal.

'And the force we were told that landed on the Asian coast? I had assumed that they were the main thrust of Severus's assault.'

'Nothing more than a powerful ruse, it seems, Legatus. They burned out the fleet at Cyzicus, remained onshore long enough to draw our attention, and then returned to their ships and left.'

'Really? It's a masterstroke of strategy, if it's true.' Renatus shook his head in bafflement. 'How could we know that so swiftly?'

Marcus fell back on the story that he and Scaurus had prepared for exactly that question.

'It seems that Sartorius has made use of the ships taken from the Thracian shore as we retreated, and built a small navy of ships that are his eyes and ears, Legatus. Which is how he knew of the landing in Asia in the first place.'

The enemy general nodded at the mention of his master's frumentarius, turning an amused smile on his officers.

'What did I say? That bastard's so sharp he could cut himself. Doubtless even he was surprised by his own intelligence, given he gave us orders to fight this illusory invasion only yesterday!'

Marcus kept his face carefully composed.

'Quite so, Legatus. We met him on the road ten miles to the north of the city, and when he heard this fresh news he rode hard for Calchedon, and urged me to pass on these new orders with all possible haste. He believes that your legion will make the crucial difference in any battle for the crossing.'

Renatus nodded decisively.

'I see. Well, you may inform the emperor that the Sixth Ironclad won't let him down. We will march for the Bosporus, and with all due haste. First Spear Silanus, to me!'

He turned away to speak with his officers, and, realising that he had already been forgotten, Marcus saluted with just enough formality not to attract attention back onto himself and turned away. The legion's first spear was deep in an animated conversation with his superiors, seemingly having to make it clear to them just how fast his men would be able to reach the straits.

'Even the Blessed Julius only ever managed to get more than thirty miles out of his lads in a day, gentlemen, and he was a fucking god!'

He walked back to where Qadir and the other Hamians were waiting at the roadside. They mounted at Marcus's command, walking their horses north and away up the stationary column in the direction from which they had come, to the general disinterest of the legionaries squatting on the cobbles.

'Did your idea work?'

He nodded at his friend's question.

'It would seem so. I left the legion's tribunes arguing with their first spear as to just how long it would really take them to get to the Bosporus.'

Qadir grinned at the mental image of a soldier with twenty-five years of experience being forced to explain the realities of military life to men who clearly went everywhere on horseback.

'In which case we should head north ourselves and re-join the tribune.'

They mounted, spurred their beasts to a trot, and left the legion behind them, finding Scaurus and the rest of the familia at the agreed meeting point two miles to the north. Hiding deep in the grove, they watched as the two legions' long columns ground past them at the battle march, heading back towards Nicaea, waiting until the sound of their passage had died away before emerging onto the silent road.

'Should we follow, and make sure they head for Calchedon?'

Marcus shook his head at Dubnus's question.

'There is no need, they will keep marching until they meet Niger coming the other way. The moment that that legatus laid eyes on that imperial seal I could see that he was convinced it was from the hand of his master. It's ironic that such unquestioning trust in the emperor's will, which is a central tenet of our class's beliefs, is the potential downfall of the man.'

They rode south and then west along the southern shore of Lake Ascania, alternately walking and trotting their beasts to maximise their stamina and still cover some ten miles in an hour, riding towards the lake's far end where the road ran downhill towards Cius through the pass that ran through the mountains separating the lake from the sea. Scaurus looked about himself with fresh eyes as he considered the potential defensive positions that were tiered up the road's long climb from the city by the sea, hemmed in on either side by steep mountain slopes that would be impassable to heavily armed and armoured legionaries unable to match the nimbleness of Niger's auxiliary archers.

'Give me even a single legion and some good Hamian bowmen to position on the slopes to either side of the road and I could hold this place against three times their own strength for days. With three legions I would have the leisure of rotating my cohorts in and out of the fight to keep them relatively fresh, and could hold it for as long as supplies of food and arrows lasted. Which with the whole of the empire east of the Bosporus to call on might as well be indefinitely.'

Marcus nodded at his friend's sentiment.

'And at the end of that fight you'd be able to disengage at your leisure, leaving behind an enemy with the strength and the will to fight bled from them. Being taken prisoner by Sartorius was a matter of the purest luck, when I consider our great fortune in being able to send that legion off in completely the wrong direction.'

They reached the coastal plain by midday, with Cius only a mile distant, and sent men into the city to purchase supplies from the city's street vendors. Chewing on bread and cheese, Dubnus gestured to a pile of water skins besides which a disconsolate Sartorius, his face starting to bruise badly from its violent impact on the road's surface, was staring at them with an expression of hatred.

'Now there's a man whose world has crashed down around him.'

Scaurus turned to the disgruntled spymaster, smiling as the pioneer standing next to their captive put a hand on his shoulder, effortlessly preventing him from standing. The former frumentarius spat defiance at them both.

'I should have killed the pair of you while I had the chance!'

'Indeed so. Except you were rather more interested in having us tortured to death.' The Roman shrugged. 'I'd say you'll know better next time, except that with any luck we've just made sure there won't be a next time. And for the time being, at least, you can spend some time wondering if all the extravagant promises you made as to how we would be interrogated will instead become your fate, when we deliver you into the tender care of Septimius Severus. I seem to recall that he was close to having you killed the last time you met, so the gods only know how he will react to having you at his mercy.'

The familia mounted and rode south and west towards the city of Prusa, beyond which the road would turn west in its course to Apollonia and Cyzicus, passing the usual farmers and traders heading in the other direction, most of whom very sensibly vanished into the olive trees as so many heavily armed horsemen approached for the fear of being predated by bandits. In the middle of the afternoon, as they were watering their horses at a spring by the side of the road, one of the Hamians spotted a distant cloud of dust on the road to their west, the horsemen whose mounts were kicking it up vaguely visible at its heart in the pale afternoon sunlight. Qadir stared at the oncoming riders for a moment before venturing an opinion.

'Horsemen. But how many there are is a complete guess.'

Marcus nodded his confirmation.

'They could be Candidus's advance guard . . .'

'Or they could perhaps be the remnant of Aemilianus's last cohort, running from Candidus's advance guard. Let's not take the chance, even twenty men with cavalry spears would have the edge on us in a fight in the open. Into the trees, gentlemen!'

They followed Scaurus's command and dismounted, hurriedly leading their horses far enough into the grove as to be out of sight from the road, then used branches hastily cut from the olive trees to sweep away their tracks in the sandy soil. Scaurus surveyed the result with satisfaction.

'And now we wait. Let's see if we can work out whose men they are.'

He crawled forward through the trees with Marcus at his back until they had a clear enough view of the road without sacrificing too much of their concealment. Hearing the sound of approaching hoofs they flattened themselves against the grove's litter-strewn floor and waited, the clamour of the approaching horsemen growing to a noisy clatter as they swept into view. Identifiable as legion cavalrymen by their shields and long spears, they were riding at a fast trot, clearly pushing exhausted mounts to the limits of their endurance. As they passed the hidden watchers, the rearmost rider looked back over his shoulder with the nervous look of a man being pursued by an enemy who was closer to hand than was comfortable.

'So, eastern looking cavalry who appear to be running from . . . well, let's go and see, shall we?'

As he spoke, Scaurus got to his feet and walked carefully out of the trees, prompting Dubnus to sprint forward and push past him.

'For fuck's sake, Tribune, what if there are stragglers? One lance will kill you just as quickly as twenty!'

The two tribunes exchanged amused glances, although both knew the Briton was right. The road for a mile in both directions, however, was empty, the horizon to the east marked by a plume of dust from the swiftly receding horsemen who had just passed, while a similar ochre cloud was visible a way further off to the west. Scaurus pointed at the second group of horsemen.

'And here come their pursuers.' He looked from one plume of dust to the other. 'Judging from the dust they're kicking up, a substantial number of men, and perhaps two miles behind them. Bearing in mind your solicitous advice, Dubnus . . .'

Lugos spoke from within the treeline, his deep growl rich with glee.

'He means that he appreciates you being concerned for his safety.'

'I do indeed, enough that I think you're rather overdoing the impression of a book that explains words. Anyway, it might well be best if Marcus and I sit here and wait for them, rather than remount, in case they mistake us for the men they're pursuing. The rest of you can take up positions to fight from just in case we've judged this poorly, and these are also men of the eastern legions. Especially you, Lugos, as you'll be able to practise your Greek on them as you lay about yourself with that sword.'

The familia arrayed themselves in the olive trees on either side of the road, while the two officers waited for the oncoming horsemen to reach the point where they stood. Only the leading two ranks of riders were visible as dust rose from the road and obscured the riders behind them, rendering their shield insignia impossible to read. Scaurus turned to call an order to Dubnus.

'If they turn out to be more of Niger's men, make sure that you cut Sartorius's throat before they take us captive!'

The cavalrymen spotted them at a hundred or so paces, lowering their long spears and slowing their pace, walking their horses up to the point where the two men stood. Their faces were obscured by scarves covering their mouths and noses, their eyes almost invisible in the dust caked onto their faces. The lead rider pulled his horse up so close to Scaurus that his lance's point was inches from the tribune's chest, looking down impassively at the Roman from beneath the crested helmet of a decurion.

'What have we here then? More of Niger's traitors?'

Marcus took a step forward, pushing the spear away and drawing breath to bark a challenge up at the cavalryman.

'Your fucking face!' The horseman pulled down his scarf to reveal a familiar grin, the officer's black beard an instant giveaway. 'Apologies gentlemen, I couldn't resist the joke!'

Barbatus handed his spear to the man alongside him, dismounted and saluted Scaurus and Marcus, then turned to the mounted men behind him.

'Second and third *turmae*, continue the pursuit! I'll escort these fine gentlemen back to the safety of the legions!' He turned back to the familia and made a show of counting heads. 'All present and correct, I see, and you still have both the giant and the small child who accompanies him!'

They found Candidus twenty miles further back down the road from Cyzicus, riding in the heart of his bodyguard close behind the leading cohorts of his vanguard legion.

'Well now, Rutilius Scaurus, I was wondering when you were going to turn up! What do you have to tell us about our enemy's dispositions? And who's that dishevelled looking piece of unpleasantness trying to ignore the glares of your men?'

Scaurus swiftly briefed him on the events of the last day, and when the legatus realised just who it was that they held prisoner he shook his head in amazement at the close escape that Scaurus and Marcus had enjoyed.

'I think the question of whether the gods love you is fully answered! If you fell into shit you'd come out smelling of roses, wouldn't you?' He glanced at Marcus. 'And that goes for you too, Valerius Aquila; I'm well aware of your family's disgrace under Commodus, and your subsequent exoneration under Pertinax, but this is a new level of divine favour. But even for you, Rutilius Scaurus, the fact of your having been captured by this animal and then managing not only to free yourselves but turning the situation to our advantage is quite exceptional. Presumably you would recommend that we move forward and take the pass between Cius and the lake with all due speed? I have to warn you that we only have three legions, I was too desirous of getting to grips with the enemy to wait for the last one to catch up with us.'

Issuing a stream of orders to his tribunes and senior centurions, he issued orders for the army to advance at the battle march pace, smiling grimly as the legionaries grinding past the command group gritted their teeth and obeyed the trumpet calls demanding that they increase their speed to the maximum possible.

'We won't be able to get anywhere near the pass before nightfall, so I suggest you take Prefect Barbatus and his men and scout as close to Nicaea as you can, just to make sure that the enemy legions really have followed these fake orders you've given them on Niger's behalf and, I suppose, to delay their progress when they eventually meet with Niger's legions on their way south and get themselves turned around. As long as you're able to tolerate their bloodthirsty desire to collect enemy heads, of course. I can lend you an ala of *sagittarii* as well, so that you can give a decent account of yourselves in the event that you encounter any resistance.'

The *sagittarii* in question turned out to be a cavalry wing of mounted Hamian archers and so, leaving the remainder of the familia to ride with the command group, Scaurus and Marcus mounted fresh horses and accompanied Dubnus and all of his pioneers back up the road to the east. Barbatus ranged his horse alongside Marcus's as they trotted away from the leading men of the vanguard legion, curious as to why the Roman had chosen to include the big Britons in the party.

'Why do we need those axe-wielding monsters, when we have my boys and these Syrian bow benders to protect us?'

'Call it a precaution, if you like. And Dubnus, try to stop your bearded monsters making comments to the archers about their lack of manhood, could you? These Hamians haven't had ten years of incessant abuse to harden them up enough to give it straight back, unlike our own comrades, and I need them to be on our side rather than sulking at being called names? That goes for you too, Acting Prefect. It would be a shame—'

The Dacian rolled his eyes.

'If I were to have my temporary commission revoked because my men upset a cohort of eastern makeup wearers, Tribune?'

'Exactly that. Off you go and make that point to them, if it matters to you?'

The ala's prefect, a man in his late twenties, was clearly somewhat inexperienced in his role having only taken command of his men in the days before the orders to march east had been received, but he seemed keen to get forward and fight, if a little diffident in the face of the two battle-hardened tribunes. Reaching Cius by early evening, they found Barbatus's men watering their horses from a narrow stream running down from the rocky hills. His decurions came out to meet them, whistling appreciatively at the sight of eight hundred horse archers on the march and clasping arms with their comrade as his squadron trotted their horses off to join their comrades. The older of the two men pointed up the pass's steadily climbing road, its highest point out of sight among the hills on either side.

'Those boys we were chasing managed to stay ahead of us, so who knows what might be waiting for us up at the top? Want to go for a look while we still have a little light?'

After a brief stop to water their beasts, Marcus and Scaurus rode on up into the hills that rose on either side of the road in the orange light of an incipient sunset, accompanied by Barbatus and a squadron of his men, the acting prefect insistent that he wasn't about to let them scout the pass unescorted.

'See that comment you made the other day about my having the chance to lose my command by nightfall? It seems to me like this is another opportunity to do just that – if some bright boy manages to put an arrow in you – so me and my boys will be coming up there with you whether you like it or not.'

Alert for the slightest sign of an enemy presence, their caution swiftly proved redundant, as the eastern scouts had to all appearances long since left the pass behind them. Dismounting a hundred paces from the spot where they knew the road flattened out from its long climb, the two friends went forward on foot with Barbatus and a pair of his men, using the natural cover of the roadside vegetation to disguise their presence as much as possible. When they reached the top of the ascent the Dacian stepped out into the road, and Marcus waited for any lurking scouts to put an arrow into him; but after only a brief moment, the irrepressible cavalryman turned back to them with an exaggerated shrug, his shouted opinion loud enough to have been heard from half a mile away.

'Nothing! Looks like those boys are long gone, eh, Tribunes? They knew we were after them and they fucked off sharpish!'

The gently rolling country between the pass and the lake was empty, as far as they could see in the last light of the day, with the sun already behind the mountains at their backs, lacking any sign of either the cavalry who had fled from Candidus's oncoming army or the legions the two friends had sent away in the direction of Nicomedia and Chalcedon.

'They've ridden after the legion. Even if he doesn't run into Niger's army first their legatus will put two and two together smartly enough, once they realise that there really is an army marching east from Cyzicus, and orders or no orders they'll counter march to block this pass. It's the only place they can stand a decent chance of holding us off while they wait for reinforcements.'

Scaurus nodded at Marcus's opinion, looking up at the full moon rising over the mountains.

'Their legions have had ten hours, in which time they could have marched another twenty miles to the north. And those men's horses will be half dead, so they won't catch them up before darkness falls, but there will be moonlight enough for them to keep going. Assuming they do find the Sixth Ironclad sometime overnight, their legatus will turn his men around first thing and battle march them straight back here by the middle of the afternoon if he pushes them hard enough.'

The two men looked at each other, and after a moment Scaurus pursed his lips in decision.

'It's going to be a close thing. And if Niger gets his men to this piece of ground before our legions, then it might be more expensive for him to hold than if he'd had a day or two to fortify it; but he'll still have the whip hand over us. It seems to me as if one of us is going to have to go and speed up the army to get them here sooner, while the other uses the men we've been granted to mount some sort of delaying action tomorrow.'

Marcus nodded.

'Who's going to do the delaying is obvious enough. I'm the more junior of the two of us, so I'll take the job of holding them up while you go and bring the legions here, before they end up in exactly the trap Sartorius intended for them. Take one of Barbatus's *turmae* to escort you back to the legions, I'll use the others to scout for the enemy and get the *sagittarii* to within bowshot without being seen. With a little luck.'

Later, with Scaurus and the majority of the familia away down the road to the west for the second time, leaving Marcus with Dubnus and his pioneers to brief the horse archers as to what would be required of them the following day, the Roman went to talk to the archer's prefect, Verax.

He found the younger man eating his dinner with his senior decurion beside a watch fire, and accepted with gratitude the offer of a bowl of stew, bread and a cup of watered wine. Verax ate in silence, only speaking once he had emptied his own bowl and set it down.

'Perhaps you might like to do your rounds, Decurion, once you've finished your meal?'

Taking the hint, the older man scooped the rest of his food into his mouth with a piece of bread, winked at Marcus while Verax was looking the other way and walked away with a satisfied belch.

'Do you believe we will see action tomorrow, Tribune Aquila?'

Looking up, he found the prefect watching him with a look that combined nervousness with determination.

'I do. We will have to ride forward, make contact with the enemy legions that I expect will be hurrying back here, in the hope of occupying the pass' – he pointed to the looming bulk of the maintains to either side of the road up to the lake, silhouetted against the stars – 'and try to stop them from getting here as quickly as they might otherwise be able, and to the best extent of our abilities. Your men are ready for war, I presume?'

Verax nodded slowly.

'They are.'

'But?'

The younger man shot him a sideways look.

'We . . . I . . . haven't done anything like this before. Putting on displays of horsemanship in parade armour is all very well, and doubtless it trains our men as to how to fight, but this is . . .'

He shrugged helplessly.

'Much the same as practised, truth be told.' Marcus smiled into the prefect's uncertainty. 'Really, it is. You and your men have practised to perfection all the drills in the manual for mounted archers, I presume?'

The prefect nodded.

'My predecessor trained them to perfection, it seems. Shooting on horseback, both moving and stationary, the dismount, advancing on foot to a shooting position, rapid shooting at an advancing target, retiring to remount and moving to the next position, replenishing our quivers from supply carts . . . all of that.'

Marcus smiled encouragingly.

'Then you and your men have all the skills you need to make a success of what we're going to be doing today. And besides, I'll be riding ahead with the Dacians to find the enemy for you, and manoeuvring you and your men into the best positions from which to engage them. All we have to do after that is make sure that we don't overstay our welcome. Take position, shoot five or ten volleys into them and then pull out before the enemy have the chance to shoot back, or send their cavalry after you. You and your men will do very well, I expect.'

Thanking Verax for the food, he stood and went in search of Dubnus and his men, only to find the senior decurion waiting for him out of eyeshot from his prefect.

'Tribune, sir . . .'

He looked about himself shiftily, and Marcus chose to put him out of his misery rather than wait for him to summon up the nerve to voice his concerns, with the risk of being punished for insubordination.

'It's all right, Decurion, I'll say it for you. You're worried about your commanding officer. He's nervous about tomorrow, you and your men can sense it, but when you try to raise it with him he avoids the subject. Am I right?'

'Yes, sir. I'm worried about the effect he's having on the troopers. They've started thinking that he knows something that they don't.'

Marcus thought for a moment.

'Get them bedded down and tell them it's all going to work out perfectly. And make sure you're confident with them, because they're going to need every little bit of their courage tomorrow. I'll speak to Verax at dawn and give him something bigger to worry about than whether his men can shoot straight when the pressure's on. They can shoot straight, I presume?'

Scaurus reached the army's leading cohort soon after midnight, his pace having been reduced to a moonlit walk by the onset of darkness. Draco was waiting for him with a full century of men arrayed on the road behind him and in the grove on both sides, and the look of relief on his face when he recognised the men approaching from the east made Scaurus smile despite the gravity of the situation, the first spear's air of levity at seeing some action only days before having been replaced by that of a man with the responsibility for the fate of an empire on his shoulders.

'Am I glad to see you, Tribune!' He jerked a thumb at his centurion. 'Right, you lot can bed down again but stay where you are in case anyone else comes down the road. And you, Tribune, had best come with me, you'll never find the command post in this darkness.'

Holding up a branch cut from one of the grove's trees, he led Scaurus down a road that was littered with sleeping soldiers on either side.

'No way we can make any sort of marching camp in the middle of all these trees, so the legatus decided that the boys should sleep in their armour so they can be quick into action, if needed, and quick to get back on the march.'

Candidus was still awake, sitting with his officers by a fire with a cup of wine, and he handed Scaurus and the first spear one each like it and bade them to take a seat.

'Thank you, First Spear Draco, take a cup of wine with us? I've been waiting for you, Tribune. What news?'

'Nothing all that good, sir. The scouts your men were chasing managed to get away, and I'd imagine they'll be warning Niger's generals that you're on the march from Cyzicus sometime soon enough. Which means he'll realise he's been deceived, turn around and come marching back towards the defensive position he picked to use against you, and just as fast as his men can grind out the miles.'

He briefed the older man as to the nature of the threat posed by the pass between Cius and Lake Ascania, and Candidus nodded his understanding in the flickering firelight.

'So either we get there first tomorrow or I'll be forced to send three legions into a meat grinder? It doesn't sound like much of a choice. Which means that we need to get these animals on the road at first light, and hurry them along at the forced march all the way to Cius and up that pass.' He looked around the fire at his officers. 'Pass the word please, gentlemen, once you've finished choking down that execrable filth that passes for wine in these parts, because I want your men to be on their starting marks the very instant the eastern horizon shows the first hint of the dawn. By the time the sun sets tomorrow we'll either have won this half of the empire for our master or be trying to pull together the remnants of a broken army while they flee from a lost battle. Or quite possibly all be dead. And Niger's men will know all too well that the same applies to them. Only one side can be the victor in this situation, and there won't be any room for a tactical draw and a fighting retreat, because the first army to step back from tomorrow's fight will be the one that finds itself running!'

9

The Hamian archers had their horses saddled and ready to move soon after dawn, and Marcus found Verax taking a morning beaker of hot water and honey beside his mount, and chewing on a piece of bread toasted on the embers of a watch fire. The prefect saluted, ordering his men to offer the tribune the same, and the Roman accepted both gratefully, feeling the honey's energy invigorating him as he chewed at the warm bread. Drawing his sword, he examined the edge critically.

'I could wish I had the time to put a better edge on this steel. But war's not like that, you just have to get on with it with whatever you have. And what you have, Prefect, is a well-trained and disciplined cohort of the only sort of troops who, in the absence of any serious obstacle such as a bridge over a deep river we could set fire to, have any chance of delaying legions on the march. I suggest you gather your officers, and we can tell them how they're going to finish this war in a day's fighting.'

Verax called for his decurions to assemble, and they grouped around Marcus while their men readied themselves to ride.

'Good morning gentlemen!' He looked around at their faces, the usual combination of uncertainty, nerves, stolidity and determination. 'Some of your men want today to be an anti-climax, with the enemy failing to show up for the fight.' He smiled at them knowingly, drawing amused chuckles. 'Which would be nice, but which is also not very likely! A few of them – perhaps one man in ten – want nothing more than a battle, and the chance to prove themselves. And the remainder? They just want it all to be over, and to have their friends still breathing and their own faces and limbs intact. But it doesn't matter which of those groups they . . . or you . . . belong to, because what's going to happen here is so predictable that I can tell you now what will happen today.'

The collective intake of breath was audible, and he smiled wryly around at them to ease the moment.

'I genuinely can tell you what will happen today, but not because I have some mystical ability to see the future – and gods, gentlemen, what a curse that would be!' They smiled at the weak joke, just starting to relax a little. 'The reason I can tell you what will happen today is because I know what *must* happen today! The emperor needs us to ride out to meet the enemy legions, find them, harass them, delay and frustrate them! He needs us to end the day with empty quivers and with a century's worth of enemy dead and wounded for every mile they advance in the face of our opposition! And what he needs most of all is for us to delay Niger's legions for long enough that our army reaches the top of that pass' – he pointed at the road rising into the valley's murk – 'before they do! Our doings today might seem like a small matter when you compare them with the clash of armies that will happen later, but we, gentlemen, have by far the most important place in the order of battle today. Because if we fail, and our legions find themselves having to fight their way up that road into the teeth of shields, spears and arrows, the most likely outcome will be their defeat!'

He paused for a moment and looked around at them all.

'So that is what the emperor needs to happen, which means that it is what we are *going* to make happen! I *know* it! And now you do too. Prefect Verax?'

The younger man stepped forward, looking as if a weight had been lifted from his shoulders.

'As the tribune says, we will do as we are ordered, and at every command we will be ready! For the emperor!'

The senior decurion seized the moment, cannily ending his officer's speech while it was still short and to the point.

'For the emperor!' His decurions, quite possibly pre-warned, barked a swift echo of the war cry, and as they fell silent he spoke again with the assurance of his years of service. 'Saddle up! Keep your bow strings dry but be ready to string and start shooting at a moment's notice! The tribune's going forward with those Dacian animals to find us the best places to shoot from, but you never know who we might trip over!'

Marcus turned away to his horse, calling a final command over his shoulder as he led it away towards Dubnus and his waiting pioneers.

'Make sure you keep their pace to no more than a trot. We don't want your horses winded when the time comes that you're going to need all their speed!'

Scaurus stood next to Candidus as the First Legion took to the road east, watching as century after century of men strode out from where they had slept fitfully by the roadside overnight; tired, dishevelled but looking determined and ready to fight. Centurions and watch officers stalked alongside them, shouting commands to get their men's attention as they spelled out the day's challenge, as it had been explained to them in orders groups with their superiors moments before.

'There's nothing to it, is there Gaius? All we need to do is march what, thirty miles . . . ?'

'We counted off twenty-eight miles last night, Legatus, but it was dark.'

'No, I'm sure you're right. Twenty-eight miles at the double march, then climb up into a pass that's two miles further to the top. And then, with all that behind us, we need to deploy into battle order and be ready to take on a pair of legions with recent combat experience – thanks to the emperor kindly sending you forward with a legion to blood them for Niger – and avoid being pushed back down into the pass, bottled up and showered with arrows from the slopes until we're all dead. As I said, nothing to it!' He gestured to the road. Well then, shall we go?'

The Brittonum cavalrymen walked their mounts up the pass's long climb, Barbatus ranging his horse alongside Marcus's and saluting respectfully before asking the question that the Roman was waiting for.

'So, what are we looking for exactly, Tribune?'

'You'll know it when you see it, Acting Prefect; but put simply: legions. Three of them, I expect, and with all the auxiliaries that you would expect as well, some of them mounted. They'll be coming this way down the road from Nicomedia and along the lakeside, probably turned around first thing this morning after the scouts you were chasing finally caught up with them overnight.'

'So, your friend the tribune has gone to fetch the legatus augusti and all our men, and we're going to take those archers up the road to delay the enemy legions for long enough that they don't catch our boys coming up through the pass, with their breeches round their ankles and their pricks in their hands?'

The Roman smiled.

'A colourful image, but yes, more or less that.'

'Which means that you'll be wanting to find positions where those horse archers can dismount, fling a few arrows at the enemy to slow them down and then hoof it away to avoid getting speared by nasty bastards with spears like these?'

He waved his lance in the air to emphasise the point.

'Indeed.'

'And we're scouting ahead of them to make sure that they don't crest a rise to find themselves nose to nose with ten thousand legionaries? And you'd probably prefer it if we don't either?'

'You very much have the idea of it.'

Barbatus grinned infectiously, clearly full of confidence.

'In which case you teamed up with the right men, Tribune! Like I said to you the other day, there's sneaky cavalry, and there's nasty cavalry; we're the sneaky, nasty cavalry you're looking for.' He barked out the now familiar rallying cry. '*Flavia Brittonum!*'

The men riding behind them echoed the shout, and Marcus shook his head at the Dacian in amusement, unable to resist the cavalryman's infectious enthusiasm.

'Very well Acting Prefect, let's go and make sure we're not sending several hundred archers to unnecessary graves, shall we?'

Having climbed out of the pass, the small party rode along the southern lakeside towards Nicaea. The road ran through a flat, bare plain for the first few miles, gradually narrowing down to less than a hundred paces where the mountains looming over them to the south met the lake shore. Fingers of high ground reached down from the towering hills to the water's edge, forcing the road to rise and fall over their crests, a heavy forest girding their slopes all the way down to the narrow cleared strip on the road's right. Marcus could see the decurion looking up at the higher ground and then back along the road's undulating ribbon as it rose to meet each shallow ridge in turn. At length, with the city less than five miles distant and visible across the lake to their left, and as the road rose to crest the last of the significant ridges, the Dacian turned in his saddle to look back the way they had come.

'Here. It's perfect.'

Marcus nodded.

'I agree. But what is it that you see?'

Barbatus pointed at the road running down the shallow descent in front of them and curving away around the lake shore.

'From the city the road runs alongside the lake across a plain, perfectly flat and a mile or more from any high ground. To attempt any sort of ambush back there would not just be doomed to failure, it would be suicidal. The enemy general would only have to send his cavalry at your *sagittarii* to send them riding for their lives, or tear them to pieces if they stayed to fight. But here . . .' he raised a hand to point at the rise in the road. 'See how the mountains run down to the lake? Each one of those rises in the road provides us with a ready-made vantage point from which your Syrians can lob arrows onto any approaching force from beyond the range of any return shots. If the archers were to set up here, they could loose twenty arrows, mount and be gone before the enemy archers could get close enough to be able to shoot back. And with the lake on one side of the road and thick forest on the other, there's no easy way for them to flank us. Like I said, it's perfect, although your man Dubnus has the means to make it even better, I suspect. Is it true what his men told mine about him, by the way, that he's a prince back in Britannia?'

'Yes, he is; and yes, I agree, he has the means to make each of those rises into a fortress, of sorts.' Marcus stared down the ribbon of road running away across the undulating terrain into the distance back towards the pass. 'Give me your message tablet please.' He pondered the idea for a moment, then scratched some words into the tablet's smooth wax surface. 'Have some of your men ride hard to Cius and buy me these items. These' – he took five gold coins from his purse and handed them to the other man – 'should cover the cost. Warn them that if I can smell drink on them when they return that you will most *definitely* be at risk of being a decurion again by nightfall.'

Barbatus raised a weary eyebrow.

'Is this constant threat of being returned to my previous role going to be a feature of life until the day I take my citizenship and my discharge bonus?'

Marcus smiled at him, shaking his head.

'From the moment that the fate of the empire doesn't rest on your men's ability to go and buy some urgent items with the maximum haste possible, then the risk that they will fail to discharge their orders by taking unseemly advantage of them will no longer be a risk for you. So hopefully, if we're victorious today, this will be the last time I have to emphasise the high stakes involved for all of us.'

The Dacian nodded.

'I could do the task myself . . .'

'Ah, you could, but then you would not be performing your appointed role of commanding your cohort. Issue the order and make sure it is completely understood, and I'm sure all will be well. Welcome to the joys of command, Acting Prefect!'

'The emperor, gentlemen! Imperator Caesar Gaius Pescennius Niger Iustus Augustus—'

Niger pushed through the praetorians who had preceded him down the column of the legions he had marched south from Chalcedon, thousands of men standing immobile as the result of having met head-to-head with the single legion that was being marched in the other direction, and, amazingly, ostensibly under his orders. He walked angrily up to the legion commander waiting at his own column's head.

'Why in the name of all the gods are you marching north, Legatus? The real enemy threat is approaching us along the coast of Asia, legions ferried across the Hellēspontos days ago! Surely Sartorius made that clear to you?'

The legion commander – a respected senator who had survived Commodus's chaotic rule, and was therefore very much at home in dealing with men blessed and cursed with the empire's most exalted rank – was equally forthright, if respectful, in his response.

'Imperator, I am following the written instruction which I received from you yesterday, a clear and unambiguous order to change direction and march north, and assist in countering an unexpected threat from across the Bosporus.'

He passed Niger the order that the man he had considered to be an imperial messenger had given him the previous day. The emperor looked at it in puzzlement.

'No such order has been issued, Legatus, and this, I can assure you, is not genuine.'

The senator shook his head in equal bemusement.

'It was handed to me by a tribune, and I had to break a fresh imperial seal to open it. It could only have been any more credible if you had issued the instructions to us in person.'

'It bore the imperial seal?' Niger's response combined disbelief with incredulity. 'How in the name of all the . . .' His expression hardened as he sprang to the only possible conclusion. 'Sartorius. Is he with you?'

The legatus shook his head.

'No, Imperator. He sent word that he had a captive to bring to you, and left Nicaea early yesterday.'

The emperor nodded grimly.

'And we have seen no sign of him upon the road. Which can only mean that, assuming he was with his usual escort of former frumentarii when he left you, that he's either been taken by enemy scouts or decided to change sides and use his ability to scheme against me rather than for me. And given the unlikelihood of a scout having the wherewithal to perpetrate a forgery of this quality, even if they could overwhelm his gang of ruffians, I can only assume that my former master informer has gone over to the service of the usurper Severus!'

He stared up at the sky for a moment, his face dark red with anger.

'Very well, we must endeavour to make the best of this. He might well have betrayed me, but the plan we designed to lure Candidus's legions to their doom will still be just as valid. Get your men turned around, and off the road, I'll bring my Fifteenth Legion down your column and you can fall in behind as soon as I'm beyond your men. This is still the day we break the usurper's army for good! I'll feed every crow for a hundred miles back down the road to Cyzicus once we have then running, let our cavalry off their rope and have them hunt down the stragglers. Those men in the usurper's army who manage to escape from Asia with their lives will be able to tell Severus what it means to raise the ire of a real emperor!'

'So, Prefect Verax, your men are ready?'

The prefect looked back at his archers, sitting on the ground behind the impromptu barricade of freshly felled trees that Marcus's pioneers had built across the road at the top of the easternmost ridge. The Hamians were giving every impression of being as relaxed as they could be under the circumstances, talking quietly in their tent parties, perhaps helped by the fact they could not see the oncoming enemy legions. Five miles distant from their position, Nicaea crouched by the lakeside, smoke rising from its chimneys into the still air to form a thin brown haze above the city in the sky's otherwise cloudless blue vault. In the far distance, where the road from the north ran down to the lake, occasional glints of sun on metal indicated the progress of the eastern legions' vanguard as they approached the city's northern side at the battle march.

'They seem to be as ready as can be expected. I suppose we shall find out when the time comes to start shooting.'

He turned his gaze back to the next closest ridge, where the Tungrian axemen were repeating their feat of blocking the road by the use of their axes to drop trees from the forest, while the men of Barbatus's cohort using their collective muscle power to drag the trunks onto the road's surface and then turn them to present their bases, and nigh-on impenetrable foliage, to an attacker.

'How many of those barricades do you plan to build?'

'Three, I expect. I think it's all we will have time for, before those legions are upon us.' Marcus looked back at the second ridge, looking for signs that the men Barbatus had sent back to Cius were returning. 'Although I don't think that the second and third attempts will have quite the same effect as the first when it comes to holding the enemy infantry back. We're going to be somewhat dependent on the added deterrent I sent our cavalry colleagues to procure, if the gods grant that it's available in time.'

They watched in silence as the first enemy troops passed the city, Marcus casting a critical eye over the ground between Nicaea and the barricade.

'Perhaps another half hour, perhaps less. I suggest that you quietly warn your decurions that we'll be shooting soon. Have them carry out whatever last checks they feel are necessary, bow strings and the like, because once this fight starts it'll be non-stop.' He held a hand out to the prefect. 'And the best of luck. If the gods are willing we'll share a cup of wine as victors before the sun sets.'

'That's got Nicaea behind us, so I'm guessing we might reach the pass soon after mid-afternoon if we press on? What do you think, Silanus?'

The Fifteenth Legion's first spear shook his head at Legatus Renatus's question, looking down the road as it curved around the lake's silver expanse.

'It's at least another fifteen miles to the pass, so three hours even at the battle march. And the men need to take a water stop, they're run through their bottles already with the pace we've been pushing them at. I've given orders for each cohort to water at the next stream, rather than drink the lake water.'

Glancing sideways at the other man, and seeing the determined frown on his face, the legatus decided that his senior centurion was entitled to a little irritation, under the circumstances. Silanus had more than once only narrowly retained control of his temper, as the legion tribunes had enquired of him on more than one occasion during the march as to how he might make his men move faster. He nodded his reluctant agreement, working to keep his frustration controlled as he replied.

'Understood. Just make it clear to them that every moment we're not marching is a moment when the enemy could be beating us to the pass, and making this whole thing so much worse than it already is. And for that matter a moment when the emperor might take it on himself to come forward and provide us with his invaluable motivation.'

Looking back down the marching column it was clear that his men were already tired, their heads thrown back to gulp in the cool autumn air as they pounded down the road in the wake of the scattering of legion cavalry that were scouting the ground ahead of them; the auxiliary cavalry being held in reserve for the more decisive moment that was expected to arise later in the day. The leading cohorts had reached the stream at which their water bottles would be refilled, less than a mile distant, and he smiled grimly as the men marching alongside him started cheering at the thought of replenishing their own empty canisters. Suddenly Silanus was shouting orders, and for a moment the legatus thought he was warning them not to drink too much when their turn came, only to realise with a lurch in his gut that something unexpected was happening at the ridge line a mile further down the road from the river.

Shading his eyes, he saw the cavalry falling back at speed, the bodies of horses and riders telling of the unexpected but evidently effective resistance they had encountered. Silanus needed no instruction, shouting for the leading cohorts to attack, and Renatus watched in satisfaction as his men reacted as ordered, advancing in exactly the sort of hasty attack required to brush aside the sort of flimsy resistance that would surely be all that the enemy could offer on such a narrow frontage, and with no previous sign of their presence. The tribune who had ridden forward with the legion's scouts cantered up to the command group, pointing back at the point of unexpected resistance to their advance.

'They have archers up there, and there's no indication how many!'

The first spear was back at his side, shaking his head in irritation. They watched as the counterattack went in, a cohort of legionaries climbing a shallow slope towards the point of contact, and suddenly men started falling among their ranks as the defenders shot arrows into them at a range close enough to render shields and armour only partially effective, narrow-headed arrows punching through both to inflict horrific wounds on the men behind their inadequate protection. Centurions and their officers drove the assault home, roaring at their men to attack into the teeth of the archer's hail of iron, only to find themselves frustrated by the barrier of trees from behind which the archers were shooting. And with the attackers unable to reach them through the highly packed branches and foliage, the defenders shifted their point of aim to the following second cohort as they deployed into line to support the attack, efficiently shooting a rain of shafts high into the air to scatter random death among the following troops from out of the sky.

'It's a delaying attack. And they've managed to get some sort of barricade in place to shoot behind.' The legatus turned to listen to Silanus, who was staring hard at the high ground from which the arrows were flying. 'I can't see any infantry backing them up anywhere down the road behind them, so they have to be horse archers, most likely, or they wouldn't risk being so far forward. They'll most likely look to shoot a few more volleys and then retire back behind the next ridge and do it all again. And this bloody road goes up and down enough times that this could be a long afternoon, if they manage to do the same thing every time it crosses a rise!'

Renatus nodded agreement, turning to his trumpeter.

'Blow the signal for the attack to continue! We'll just have to do this with numbers!' He nodded to Silanus. 'I'm going with them. If I fall, tell broad stripe tribune Pelagius he's in command.'

'But—'

The centurion's protest fell on empty air, as his general spurred his mount and cantered away towards the fight.

'Fucking aristos, always feeling like they have to be hitting the enemy with their swords to have the right *dignitas* to show off to the others.' He raised his voice to a parade-ground bellow. 'Third cohort, follow first and second in!'

But if the legatus had been hoping to inspire a swift defeat of the ambushers by reinforcing his counterstroke he was to be frustrated. By the time Silanus reached the spot where the road crossed the highest point of the ridge, from which the ambush that had killed and wounded hundreds of the leading cohorts' men had been mounted, the enemy had made a swift exit and the remaining attackers were contemplating the barricade from behind which they had fought.

'They must have pioneers with them.' The disgust in Renatus's voice was palpable as he pointed at the trees that had been felled and dragged across the road, their axe-severed trunks facing away from the advancing legions so that his men were fighting their way into the mass of branches with nothing more effective than their swords, and no easy means of manhandling the trees out of the road. He turned and pointed at the next rise in the road, a mile distant. 'And look, the bastards are doing the same thing at the next ridge. This looks like a task for the archers, and for our artillery muscle men for that matter. Send word back to make way for the artillery to be brought up, and let's see if our archers can make these impudent bastards sorry they decided to get in our way!'

Marcus was the last man to ride through the narrow one-horseman-wide gap that was all of the road that was passable at the spot where the road crossed the next ridge. With a flurry of barked orders, the last of the felled trees was dragged and then pushed into place by his axemen, and he dismounted to look at the Hamians' readiness for the next round of the fight, forming ranks twenty paces behind the improvised barricade. Verax walked up to him looking, like a man with the weight of the world lifted from his shoulders.

'Not a man lost! And we must have killed hundreds of them!'

'It was a good start, but then they weren't expecting us to be this far forward. I'm guessing they'll lead with their own archers next time, or perhaps even artillery, so you'd best make sure your horses are far enough back from the archers not to get caught up in any sort of pissing contest.'

He turned as Dubnus walked up with a weary smile, the butt of his axe's head resting on one booted foot.

'Just like old times, eh brother?'

Marcus grinned at his friend's obvious delight.

'Not *quite* like the old times. There's no Julius to gurn at us all and do his best impression of a warrior king! Do your men have another two ridges' worth in you?'

'We might be slowing down a little by the time we're done, but you can count on us.'

'I know.'

He clapped his comrade on the shoulder as he turned away to head for the next ridge in the road's undulating course along the lake's southern side, where his men were already labouring at felling yet more timber, then walked over to the barricade of felled trees.

'Tribune! Your royal highness!' Marcus ignored Dubnus's snort of irritation and turned to find Barbatus pointing over the barricade. 'You're just in time for round two.'

The two men walked over to him to see the enemy finally breaking through the previous barrier and spilling out into the narrow corridor formed by the densely forested slopes on one side of the road and the lake on the other. After a moment spent watching Niger's men deploy, he called out to Verax, waiting for the officer to walk over to him before speaking quietly into the other man's ear.

'How far can your men loft a shaft?'

'Two hundred paces, give or take a few. Why do you ask? They'll need to advance a good four hundred paces before we have them in range, not that it matters, because once they're close enough we'll be able to do just the same—' The prefect fell silent as he realised what it was that Marcus was looking at. 'Oh.'

The enemy, rather than rushing to attack the next barricade, were making room for a column of similarly equipped soldiers to his own to pass through into the open space.

'Yes. You'd better warn your officers to be ready to deal with casualties. This round of the fight might be as much about standing and taking damage as inflicting it.'

'Get those archers into action! What's holding them back?'

Silanus cast an expert eye over the two cohorts of Hamians forming up in front of his legion, packed tightly into the fifty-pace gap between the water and the trees.

'Probably the fact that they're going to have to shoot uphill at targets they can't see, and which will be shooting back at them. Should I go over there and encourage them?'

Renatus shook his head.

'No, not yet. Let's allow their prefects a little longer before we submit them to the indignity of having to be told how to do their jobs, shall we? Ah . . .' he sat back in his saddle. 'They have it, I feel.'

The archers' commanding officers looked at each other and nodded, grim faced, both men turning to their senior centurions and barking the same order at them. The two cohorts lurched into motion at the same instant, using exactly the tactics that the legatus would have chosen if presented with such a potentially suicidal mission, starting with a steady advance at the enemy while they were still outside their adversary's bowshot. He watched as the two first spears paced deliberately forward in front of their men, smiling grimly at the encouragement and threats that their officers were shouting at the nervous bowmen as they advanced.

A single arrow arched over the improvised barricade of felled trees that filled the next gap that the army would have to pass, falling to earth twenty paces in front of the advancing Hamians. The men of the two cohorts' front ranks tensed in expectation of the order to raise their shields, but the two cohorts' officers had discussed their tactics beforehand in a hasty gathering around their prefects, and were refusing to play the opposing archers' game. They waited until their leading men reached the upthrust arrow shaft, and then waved them forward in a carefully judged gamble, shouting for them to run for their very lives. Renatus nodded approvingly as the cohorts sprinted into the space in front of the Severan force's barricade.

'A good move. Running into the beaten zone of those archers ought to minimise the impact on the front ranks, and enable them to run without the obstruction of fallen comrades. If whoever's idea that was survives this, I'll make sure he benefits from it.'

The first volley from beyond the barricade landed squarely on the hurrying cohorts' rear ranks, hundreds of arrows falling in an iron rain that reaped a savage toll of men whose small circular wicker shields were an inadequate defence against the sleet of heavy pointed iron heads. The front rank, having run another thirty paces, lifted their bows and started lofting arrows over the barricade as fast as they could, shooting blind in the hope of landing their shafts among the enemy archers.

'And now to put the real threat in place, while the enemy are distracted by shooting at the target we're so kind as to offer them. Bring those scorpions forward at your leisure, First Spear.'

The wagons of the leading legion's artillery train rumbled into position at Silanus's signal from where they had been waiting behind the archers, having been driven up the army's long column with legionaries scattering to either side to allow them to pass. Their heavily muscled crews leapt into action with the alacrity of men facing imminent combat, assembling the powerful bolt throwers from their component parts with practised speed. A hard-faced centurion with three fingers of his left hand missing saluted the two men with an expression that spoke as to his glee at having been ordered to batter his way up the length of a stalled legion.

'Legatus, First Spear, the bolt throwers are ready for immediate action!'

Behind him the crews were now labouring to wind their engines' bow strings back to the maximum possible tension, the sidelong glances that the sweating half-naked legionaries were giving each other hinting at some competition between them.

Silanus nodded at him and turned to face Renatus.

'You want them to start shooting at the enemy Legatus?'

Renatus surveyed the archery exchange that was heating up three hundred paces in front of them.

'Let's see if those Syrians can drive the opposition off first, shall we? Have your men aim their bolt throwers directly at the barricade, Centurion, and be ready to shoot and keep shooting as fast as they can wind their machines.'

Marcus peered through the branches and leaves of the trees that had been felled to form the second roadblock, pursing his lips unhappily at the sight of a dozen heavy bolt throwers being unloaded from their carts and readied for action.

'Oh, that's not good. Lend me your shield Barbatus, I need to go and talk to Prefect Verax. Stay here and shout me a warning once they're ready to shoot.' He hefted the layered wooden board over his head, hefting the unaccustomed weight experimentally. 'Oh, and you might want to find some hard cover that you think – or hope – might stop a bolt before it turns you inside out. I would suggest a tree trunk, anything less probably won't be enough. They're about to start using their legion artillery on us.'

The Dacian shot him an indignant look.

'What, you borrow my shield and *then* you tell me we're about to start being shot at by the grunt fuckers?'

Marcus laughed at his look of incredulity.

'If I thought this flimsy thing would be enough to stop a bolt then you wouldn't be getting it back!'

He turned and walked back to the archers, holding the borrowed shield over his head against the arrows that were being lofted high into the air above the fallen trees and then falling to earth in a random rain of sharp-edged iron. The Hamians were taking casualties, unable to both protect themselves and keep shooting, and there were already a score of men down with arrows in their upper torsos and, in one unfortunate case, through a cheekbone. Ignoring the thwock of an arrow whose head had suddenly appeared through the shield's layered wood, jerking the board in his hand, he made for Verax, deliberately ignoring the younger man's evident horror at the harm being done to his command.

'Now we have them angry! And I can tell you that your men are killing at least three times as many of them as you're losing to their unaimed shooting!'

'But they're killing *my* men!'

The Roman nodded.

'Yes, they are, but my point is that you're killing a lot more of theirs. It's the way of things in a battle, I'm afraid. And it will get worse, unless I can dislodge them from that slope. Give me your best two centuries and I'll see them off, and stop this infernal pecking at our ranks! Oh, and tell the rest of your men to lie down and use their shields to protect themselves as best they can, because that legion on the other side of the barricade will be shooting artillery bolts at us next.'

Ignoring the prefect's horrified reaction to his last instruction, he led the men detailed off to his command back towards the barricade, shouting instructions at their centurions as they ran alongside him, their round wicker shields far less protective than his borrowed oval cavalry board.

'Once we get to the barricade, have your men loose their arrows down the slope at the enemy archers; aimed shots, not indirect arrow lobbing! They're out in the open and won't have anything that can stop our arrows putting their men down, not shields and not their mail armour either! We loose ten arrows per man, aimed shots, we'll kill a half a cohort's strength and break their will to fight! And try to shoot the officers! If we kill them then the rest of them will run!'

Reaching the fallen trees, he supervised as the two centurions thrust their men into the tangle of branches, encouraging them to worm their way into positions from which they could see the men on the slope below them, but were themselves effectively camouflaged by the leaves in which they were wreathed.

'Now get them shooting!'

The first few shots were hesitant, as if the Hamians were still coming to terms with the idea of seeing without being seen; but when one of the first arrows felled an enemy centurion, the enthused archers started shooting with more gusto. Their countrymen facing them were defenceless against the unexpected attack, looking to their officers for some idea as to what they should do, but without any response as centurions and chosen men ducked for cover, discarding their crested helmets in an attempt to avoid being targeted by the aimed shots that were clearly directed at anyone in authority. A few of the enemy bowmen chose to stand and fight, but with most of their arrows being stopped or deflected by the foliage into which they were shooting, and the swift and ruthless prosecution of such obvious targets, their defiance was ineffectual. Their frustration was increased markedly by the fact that when their shafts did find a mark among the defenders, the success was impossible to discern in their leafy camouflage.

One of the enemy centurions strode out in an attempt to rally his men from their cowering helplessness, took one arrow in the thigh, staggered, and before he had time to sink to the ground was struck in the throat by another, tottering for a moment before he fell to the ground with blood spurting from the neck wound. It was too much for his men, those closest to him taking to their heels first while those further away were quick to follow their example. In an instant every man in the two cohorts was either running or, in the case of those officers who chose not to do so, watching their men flee from the unseen and seemingly invulnerable archers in the barricade. The Hamians cheered their retreat, clear victors of a field on which hundreds of dead and seriously wounded men were strewn; and Marcus, with one eye on the easterners' bolt throwers, shouted an order for them to pull back and re-join the rest of the cohort.

Renatus shook his head in disappointment at the rout of his archers.

'I suppose that was a little inevitable, even if we had to try it as a way to pick the lock of their defences quickly, but they were ready for us. Which is starting to make me wonder if I might know who's commanding those archers. But no matter . . . where subtlety has failed, we will have to resort to brute force, I believe. You'd better have the artillery try a little door knocking, to see if we can persuade them to back away from it before they get a faceful of wood as we kick the blasted thing off at the hinges!'

Barbatus grinned at Marcus triumphantly, nodding as the archers strolled back to their mates with the swagger of men who had drawn blood for no more loss than one of their comrades left slumped in the barricade and another being helped away with an arrow in his upper arm.

'This is a walkover! We can keep them at arm's length all afternoon at this—'

He flinched away with blood in his eyes as the trooper next to him was punched backwards in a spray of blood, his shield and then his armour effortlessly penetrated by the four-foot length of an artillery bolt. Three of the archers making their way back to re-join their comrades were hit by missiles that had whipped through the barricade of trees as if it wasn't there, and another two men in the cohort's ranks who were still standing were also smashed backwards into the men behind them by the bolts' colossal impacts.

'Lie down!' Marcus waved frantically at Verax. 'Prefect Verax, tell all your men to lie flat on the ground!'

He lowered himself to the grass, quietly counting down the time to when he expected the bolt throwers to shoot again, but still some of the Hamians, clearly not quite realising what was happening in their places at the rear, tarried long enough that one of them took a bolt from the next salvo through his head, in a freak chance of fate that had the men around him flat on the ground an instant later. Marcus cautiously raised his head to peer over the barricade, nodding his reluctant approval at what he saw. The bolt throwers were again being reloaded, their crews working like demons to wind back the finger-thick horsehair bowstrings that were capable of spitting a missile through the barricade with enough energy remaining to transfix an armoured legionary. Behind them the best part of a legion was mustering, crammed into the narrow corridor between lake and forest, and even at more than three hundred paces their purpose was unmistakable.

Barbatus stood up, wiping the blood from his face and looking down sadly at his dead trooper, then peered over the felled trees, and when he spoke his tone perfectly matched the conclusion to which Marcus had already jumped on seeing the forces lining up against them.

'Looks like it's time to leave, if we don't all still want to be lying here hiding from the bolt throwers and in fear of our lives when those rather angry looking legionaries come through that barricade.'

Renatus nodded with satisfaction as the third salvo whipped through the barricade as if it were not there.

'Very good. That's the door open, I'd say; now switch to plunging shots to keep them running and send the dogs in.'

Silanus turned to the officers staring intently at him and pointed at the distant barricade, repeating his general's command in more robust terms.

'*Attack!*'

With a collective roar the legion that had been waiting behind the artillery trotted forward at a disciplined pace intended to be sustainable by armoured men as they closed on the barricade. The legatus forced his horse forward through the crush, ignoring the legionaries shouldered aside by the beast as their indignation quickly changed to abashed apology when they realised who the animal's rider was. He watched intently as the leading ranks closed with the barrier of fallen trees, throwing themselves into the outstretched branches and using sheer collective muscle power to drag them away from the road, spilling into the space behind them with the general and his first spear close behind.

Of the archers who had punished them so cruelly there was no sign, other than the scattered corpses of the bolt throwers' victims and a few grievously wounded men with arrow wounds who were swiftly put out of their agony by vengeful sword thrusts.

'Shit.'

Renatus nodded his agreement with his senior centurion's sentiment, as he followed the soldier's pointing hand to look at the next finger of high ground running down from the mountains to the lake, culminating in a twenty-foot cliff at the water's edge. Where the road crested the rising ground another barricade of trees had been dragged into place, and the Hamian archers responsible for their delay in reaching the pass far beyond were trotting through a gap left for them to ride through.

'Indeed.' The legatus shook his head wearily. 'Get those scorpions moved up as quickly as possible. I'm going to talk to the man who I think is responsible for this disaster.'

'That's a commendably brave approach.'

Barbatus leaned out from behind the tree he was using for shelter from the expected barrage of bolts, now that they were behind the third line of defence, watching the lone rider coming towards them.

'Commendably brave? The man's clearly a stone short of a game of robbers!'

Marcus shook his head.

'No, that implies he doesn't know what he's doing. Whereas there is a sort of traditional Roman gentleman who understands the risks all too clearly, but chooses to treat them with the disregard expected of a man of his rank. And that, Acting Prefect, is what you're looking at.'

Marcus watched from behind his own tree as the lone rider trotted forward, eschewing any escort and choosing to trust that the traditional signal of his holding of a cavalry shield over his head would suffice to prevent the archers from using him as a practice target. He shouted a command that was swiftly echoed by the Hamians' officers.

'Don't shoot! The legatus is alone, and has come to talk.'

The senior officer ranged alongside the freshly felled barricade, looking down at the archers lining it with the disdain typical of his class, with no more regard for them than he might have displayed towards his own slaves. The question he barked was equally dismissive, the tone that he might in better times have used to address an insufficiently responsive subordinate, in no way threatening, but simply devoid of any niceties.

'Who is in command here?'

'I am, Legatus.'

Verax raised a hand, but before he could continue, the legatus shook his head dismissively.

'I doubt it, young man! A perfectly decent officer you may well be, but this is a tactic more likely to have been devised by a man with a good deal more military experience than I suspect you have under your belt!' He swept a searching gaze along the line of the barricade. 'Come on, show yourself whoever you are! I would very much like to speak with the man who came up with this idea, and who also had the wherewithal to actually make it happen!'

Marcus stepped out from the cover of the tree.

'You're looking for me, Legatus.'

Renatus turned his horse and trotted the beast until he was within a few paces of the waiting Roman.

'Yes, now that I see you again, I can see that I was right in guessing that you were the man responsible for this obstacle to my progress. Ever since you gave me what must have been a forged message yesterday your face has been at the front of my memory, nagging at me even as I obeyed the command you purported to have carried from Niger himself. Where is it that I know you from, Tribune?'

'Rhaedestus, Legatus.'

The general closed his eyes as the import of what he had been told struck him.

'Rhaedestus. Of *course*. I recall you now, you were in the party of men who came forward to negotiate the surrender of a single embattled legion, far from any support and lacking even rations for their next meal. A formality, we expected, since your choices had been refined to either surrender or death. Except that negotiation turned into a disaster, when an eagle decided to roost on your blasted standard. You were at the shoulder of that hatchet-faced tribune who was the real commander of your legion, decent enough man that my colleague Fabius Cilo is, weren't you?'

Marcus nodded impassively, and Renatus looked down at the barricade.

'Well played, young man. Well played indeed. But tell me, how was it that you managed to come into the possession of an imperial seal, either the real thing or a forgery of such quality that I was unable to tell the difference? Has that frumentarii animal Sartorius changed sides on us? I ask so that my master the emperor can issue an edict for his capture and execution.'

Marcus shook his head.

'While I share your distaste for the man, I cannot accuse him of anything worse than having employed his dubious talents in the service of the wrong man. And the answer to your question is simple enough. We captured Sartorius, with a little assistance from his own massive hubris, and he of course was in possession of an imperial seal.'

The legatus stared at him for a moment, Marcus's return gaze respectful but impassive.

'By the gods, but you're serious.' Renatus shook his head slowly. 'When all this nonsense is over, and Niger is triumphant, seek me out. I have employment for a man as talented – and as fortunate – as you seem to be.' He shrugged. 'But now your delaying action is at an end. This will be the last of your barricades, I suspect, as I think I've proven conclusively that I have the key that will open this door. My bolt throwers will brush you aside as easily this time as they did only moments ago, and I'm bringing up my cavalry to hunt you down the moment we can pull these trees aside. And so I suggest that you choose discretion over valour, and retire while you can? Allow the prefect there and his men the opportunity to fight another day, rather than dying here to no purpose. It's either that, or you must fight a glorious but doomed defence against overwhelming odds. What do you say, shall we call it honours even?'

The Roman smiled up at him.

'You're right, we can't hold against that sort of attack. But it will take your artillerymen time to break down those bolt throwers and bring them forward to shoot at us here. Especially with your army having crowded in to tear away the trees we left for you, making them too tightly packed to make way in a hurry. I'd bet that you can't have them shooting at us again in less than an hour; and that, Legatus, is another hour you won't have to use for the purpose you're marching here to carry out.'

Renatus pursed his lips.

'A good point. In which case you will just have to hope that when we do break through this defence, which we surely will, you manage to avoid the retaliation my men will be eager to visit upon you all!'

He turned and cantered away towards his waiting army, and Verax walked over to Marcus with a worried look.

'What do we do if he just sends his legions at us?'

Marcus shrugged.

'Shoot every arrow we have left into them and then ride for our lives.'

'But won't they just pull the trees away?'

'No. This is your first battle, and you can't be expected to understand what would happen under those circumstances, so I'll try to give you a feeling as to what that would be like. The thing is, a man shot through with an arrow isn't like a man with a sword or a spear wound. He probably won't die quickly, unless he's lucky, but he will rather find himself helpless and unable to move very far. He will bleed, and he's also likely to lose control of his bodily functions. So if they send a legion at this barricade now, and we were to wait until they were fifty paces away to start shooting, there would very quickly be hundreds of mostly wounded casualties getting in the way of the rest of them, bleeding, urinating and defecating.'

He pointed at the far side of the barricade.

'The ground out there would quickly cut up, and become tricky underfoot with all that bodily fluid. All of which would hamper any attack, and make the legatus's men even more vulnerable to our arrows. No, he's better off waiting for his bolt throwers to be dragged forward to clear us out and give his cavalry a straight run, I'd say, because he knows we can't stand up to that sort of barrage and will have to retreat. All he has to do is to repeat what he did back there, so that he can send his men at an unmanned obstacle, and probably break through here without sending hundreds of his men to their death and littering the road with bodies. And he's right in what he says, we can only hold this barricade for as long as it takes for them to start shooting bolts into us again. So we'll have to find another way to hold them up just a little longer.'

'Tribune?'

He turned to find Barbatus at his shoulder, accompanied by the men he had sent down into Cius for supplies, the latter struggling under the weight of their purchases.

'Your timing, Prefect, is nigh on perfect. Now, can you have someone light me a fire please? We have a little time to make preparations, but the immediate availability of flame is going to be of critical importance, when the time comes.'

'We're ready to shoot again, Legatus.'

Renatus had waited unhappily but with enforced patience as the afternoon had worn on, and his artillery officers had overseen the movement of their bolt throwers forward through the army's packed mass, centurions laying into their men with their vine sticks to force them out of the wagons' path. He leaned forward in his saddle to stare at the barricade, and was on the point of ordering the attack to begin when something caught his eye. A man was waving at him from behind the obstacle, and shouting something that was just too faint for him to hear over the wind's gentle sigh through his helmet's plume.

'What's he saying?'

Silanus, bareheaded from his exertions in bringing the bolt throwers forward, frowned at his general.

'I think he said he'll see us on the battlefield, Legatus.'

'That cheeky bastard is making a run for it now that we're ready to start shooting! Not that I blame him. Get the bloody cavalry forward, and drag those trees away! We can still beat Candidus to the pass if we double time it from here!'

He spurred his horse forward, leading the charge towards the barricade, catching sight of the retreating *sagittarii* over the fallen trees as he crested the rise, already a mile distant and completely uncatchable. The cavalry decurions ordered their men to dismount and to use the ropes wrapped around their bodies to prepare to drag the trees off the road as they had done before; but before they had the chance to start the task, Marcus stepped out of the cover of the trees to the right of the road alongside a heavily bearded pioneer centurion with a burning brand in his hand, shouting to the legatus over the hubbub of his men's activity.

'Apologies, Legatus, but I can't allow you to pass that easily!'

The big man tossed the burning torch into the barricade, an officer in the armour of a cavalry decurion on the other side of the road copying his action, both men stepping hastily back as whatever it was that had been used to make the freshly cut wood easily flammable, lit with a gush of smoke and flame. Renatus watched on in disdain as his men were beaten back by fire which spread through the roadblock in a moment, sending black smoke high into the air above in an unmistakable signal for anyone within ten miles. The men who had set the fire turned and ran to their waiting horses, clearly laughing and joking with the sheer joy of having frustrated their enemy one last time. Renatus shook his head in disgust as they cantered away, his eyes fixed on Marcus's back.

'I take it back. If we defeat Severus's men today I will have that young bastard's head before nightfall, or hunt him to the ends of the empire.'

10

Riding away from the blazing barricade, Marcus raised himself in his saddle with a flex of his thighs, staring over the open ground between the lake and the mountains to its west. A mile or so in front of the small party, Verax's *sagittarii* were trotting their horses in a loose formation, but of the rest of Candidus's army there was no sign at all.

'You did everything you could, Tribune.'

He turned to find Barbatus at his shoulder, his voice raised to be heard over the horse's hoofbeats.

'I know. And yet it seems as if it will not have been enough. At least your men fetched the oil and tinder swiftly enough that we were able to leave them one last obstacle to—'

'Wait. Look!' Marcus followed the decurion's pointing hand, and saw the familiar shape of riders on the road at the top of the pass, making the connection just as Barbatus raised his spear and roared a delighted challenge that the distant horsemen were never going to hear. '*Brittonum!*'

Upping their beasts' pace, they cantered past the archers and reached the head of the pass, where Barbatus's men were waiting, accompanying Candidus and his staff. Scaurus rode out to join them, greeting Marcus with a clasp and a broad smile.

'You managed to hold them up for a while then?'

'Verax's archers did most of the hard work.'

Dubnus snorted derision.

'Oh yes, it was that bunch of eastern flowers who cut down the trees to make a series of roadblocks.'

Barbatus nodded agreement with the sentiment.

'For once I find myself on the side of royalty.' He ducked Dubnus's attempted cuff. 'But who was it that dragged the trees into place, and fetched the oil and the kindling to set fire to the last barricade?'

'I was wondering what the fire was.' Scaurus pointed to the last dispelling hints of the column of smoke that had risen from the burning trees. 'Although with it extinguished, I presume that Niger's men will be on their way here just as fast as their feet will carry them?'

Marcus nodded.

'In less than an hour, without any doubt. His men are already going to be double marching, and the moment he can see this ground without any legionaries on it he'll make them run the last few miles.' The Roman craned his neck to look at the head of the pass. 'Where are our legions?'

His question was answered, even as Scaurus opened his mouth to reply, by the sound of a legion's horns braying in the narrow valley below them.

'A mile back, but it's an uphill mile after twenty-eight miles of hard marching. We'd better make sure that the centurions know what they need to do, hadn't we?'

They rode back into the pass, meeting Candidus and First Spear Draco on the road at its top. The two men listened intently to Marcus's description of the ground onto which they were about to emerge, and the tactics he was suggesting. Candidus leaned out of his saddle and extended a hand to his first spear with a grim smile, shaking the nonplussed centurion's hand with a nod of respect.

'Whatever happens here today will be my result to own, Draco, whether it makes my reputation forever or kills me. But we both know that if we manage to win this battle then it will be your victory, whatever the historians care to say in years to come. Earn a triumph for your emperor and I know that he will make sure that your successor will have stars in his eyes at the thought of being gifted the sort of rewards that will be heaped on you before a grateful emperor allows you to leave his service. And since this is your battle to win, and without the time for any of the usual riding up and down and shouting encouragement that we generals tend to go in for, I suggest you issue your orders and get your men deployed as soon as we reach the top.'

The grim-faced veteran nodded, but as he turned to go, Candidus put a hand on his shoulder.

'One thing though, I want you and the Tenth Gemina in reserve, behind the line. This has the potential to go badly, and your men are likely to hold up best in a difficult situation, I feel. I know you want to be the first into the action, but I need you to indulge me in this.'

Draco nodded slowly.

'You realise that means that two unblooded legions will be our battle line?'

'I do.'

The first spear nodded, then beckoned his leading legion's senior centurion forward to march alongside them.

'At the top of the hill there's a plain a mile wide, with a lake on the left and a mountain on the right! Double march your boys for five miles and you'll reach the point where the plain is no more than a mile wide, and narrows to almost nothing in less than another mile. That's where we stop them and that's where we beat them! Because if we can hold that line they'll have no choice but to push up into the pocket that will form between our line, the lake and the mountains to try to get at us. And when they do that we can shower them with bolts and arrows, and bleed them before they even get into the fight! I want you to deploy on the left side of that line, where the Tribune here tells you to, occupy half the plain with your left flank resting on the lakeside and leave space for the Twelfth who'll be coming in behind you and will deploy on your right! You occupy the left half of the battlefield, eight deep, with your boys packed in shield to shield! Use your auxiliaries for casualty replacement, I'll be close behind and I'll bring your artillery up behind and start shooting over your heads as the enemy approach, the same with the archers! Go!'

He dismounted, leading his horse to the side of the road and beckoning the officers to follow his example, then spoke directly to Marcus and Scaurus.

'If you're right about this, Tribunes, we'll just about get into position in time. And if you're wrong they'll be on our lads while they're still deploying. I suggest you go forward and make any adjustments to my chosen tactics as needed, eh? Better to have a wider frontage than to have the enemy in our faces while we're still trying to form a line.'

Candidus nodded his agreement.

'He's right, go and take control of things for me, and make sure that whatever else happens we have a decent start to the battle. And take that evil looking Dacian and his men with you to keep any scouts that might have a fancy to snap you up as prisoners off your backs.'

Saluting, they rode back up out of the pass with the leading legion at their backs, gathering up the Brittonum and ranging forward at a fast trot until they could see the enemy legions coming forward along the lake road miles distant. Scaurus used his thigh muscles to raise himself out of the saddle for a better perspective.

'Gods, but it'll be close. They won't be very much later to the choke point than we will. And look at that!'

Barbatus was the first to respond to the sight of what looked like a thousand enemy riders coming forward in advance of the main body of the legions.

'They look like *sagittarii*!' He stared out over the plain's undulations. 'He's sent them forward to camp on the ground we want, and to hold us off for long enough that he can get his own boots on it and then sit back and wait for us to come at him. But I can see a way to take them in the flank, if they keep advancing!'

'They're your men, Acting Prefect.' Scaurus gestured to the distant enemy riders. 'We'll come along for the ride though.'

The Dacian gathered his officers about him, issuing a stream of terse orders.

'No horns, no howling dracos; we go forward quietly, close to the shoreline where the ground falls away to form a false cliff and gives us concealment! When we're level with them, or as close as we can see, we turn right and loop around to their rear! With a little luck we can catch them just before they dismount, and slaughter them before they can get moving again, but we don't let them dismount if we can avoid it! Follow me!'

He led the first *turma* away, gesturing to his standard-bearer to keep the draco's tail furled for the time being. Riding down towards the lake, the horsemen followed a path close to the lake's shore that dipped into the cover of a ridge barely high enough to conceal his troopers, looking to his right for any sign that the higher ground was falling away to reveal their clandestine approach. Far back down the lake road the legions' horns were blowing, and Barbatus turned in his saddle and laughed at the faint notes, almost lost on the breeze at such a distance.

'Someone can see us! I wonder if that will be enough to warn their archers though!'

Riding along the ridge's slowly bending length for another mile until they came within sight of the point where it sank back into the plain, he raised a hand and reined in his horse, dismounting and beckoning Marcus to follow him.

'Another hundred paces and we'll be in view. Let's have a look and see where they are.'

He dismounted and climbed nimbly up the slope with Marcus at his heels, and the two men flattened themselves against the grass, raising their heads cautiously above the ridge top. The enemy *sagittarii* were closer than Marcus had expected, the right-hand end of their line barely a hundred paces distant, the smell of their horses discernible on the breeze blowing towards the two men. They were already in the process of dismounting and staking their horses' reins to the damp earth in preparation for a delaying action to dissuade the oncoming Severan legions, now visible to the west, from attempting to take the advantageous position that would allow them to bottle up the eastern legions.

'Perfect, their bows aren't yet strung. You know what they're like for keeping the strings dry, so we have a short time in which their breeches are around their ankles, because *they* won't get here in time to stop us!'

He pointed to the west, where a body of enemy cavalry was visible riding in advance of the legions but still two miles distant. Marcus nodded.

'Yes, but will those heavy cavalry get here before our legionaries?'

The Dacian shrugged.

'We ride this lot down, send them running home to mother and then I'll worry about whatever comes next.' He shook his head at the tribune with an amused smile. 'I think you boys in bronze worry too much about the big questions that nobody down here in reality can answer until the answer's obvious. But what we need to do now is as obvious to me as the fact that we could all be dead or in chains by sunset – we deal with this lot and worry about whatever comes next, next. Right, Tribune?'

They scrambled down the slope and remounted, Barbatus pointing at his standard-bearer and trumpeter.

'Once I order the attack, *you* let the Draco sing, and *you* blow that horn with all you have in you! I want these eastern bastards to know they're about to get a good fucking even before we show them how sharp our iron is!'

He raised a hand, knowing that his decurions would be waiting for the signal, then dropped his arm and spurred his horse forward in a canter with the five hundred men of his cohort close behind. Rounding the end of the ridge, riding up and over the remnant of the higher ground, he turned the beast to face the archers, lowered his lance and bellowed the order his men had been waiting for.

'*Attack! Brittonum!*'

Echoing his war cry the Dacians followed his example, the cohort's formation widening as each successive *turma* to make the turn rode to the left of the unit in front of them and picked a part of the enemy formation not yet threatened by their assault. With a blare of horns and the screeching wail of their dragon standards the leading lancers, Barbatus at their head, rode into the disordered archers, who were caught between stringing their bows without the time to do so and the need to defend themselves. Picking his target and holding his beast back from the full gallop the horse was trembling for, he rode into the body of the enemy with his long spear flickering out and back, out and back, each thrust either felling a man or forcing him to drop beneath the iron spearhead's deadly reach and render himself an easy target for the riders following behind.

The Dacian's men crowded in on both sides of their leader, forming a wall of horseflesh and stabbing iron blades that rode through the hapless archers with the ease of a training exercise, their opponents' ability to fight back shattered by the surprise and ferocity of their attack.

'Leave the survivors to the men behind! With me!'

Now Barbatus gave his horse the spur to run, galloping along what had been the front of the increasingly disordered enemy line, which was growing more fragmented with each Dacian *turma* that rode into its rear. Leading his men out to the left a few dozen paces, he raised his lance and pointed to the right, at a squadron of *sagittarii* at their line's far end not yet engaged, bows strung and shooting at the lancers attacking them with deadly results, but with their backs to his own men.

'*Brittonum!*'

The *turma* wheeled to the left in unison, presenting a wall of spear heads to men who until an instant before had not perceived their threat, then rode into them with the same ruthless efficiency as before, scattering the hapless archers and recommencing the slaughter they had already visited on their comrades.

'Kill them all!'

The decurion drew his spear back to thrust again into the panicking mob of men, but one archer, possessed of his wits where all around him had lost their own, put an arrow into his horse's chest from such close range that the flight feathers were all that could be seen of the deeply buried shaft. The beast fell to its knees with a grunt of pain, then toppled over onto its side, already dead. Barbatus was able to jump from his saddle but landed in a winded heap, his spear lost along with his wits from the fall's impact. Not hesitating for a second, Marcus dismounted, pulling up his horse and throwing his right leg over the horns of its saddle to land facing backwards to the oncoming Dacians who parted to the left and right around the two men. Drawing his swords, he turned swiftly to hack a swift stroke with the longer spatha, cutting deep into the spine of an archer with a gladius who had been poised to attack the fallen Barbatus. Wrenching the bloody blade free he struck at another man who was in the act of bending his bow to loose an arrow into the Dacian, the sword's point ripping open the hapless soldier's mail armour and sinking deep into his chest.

As the dying man slumped with the blade deep between his ribs, his collapse pulling the sword's hilt from Marcus's hands, he looked up to find himself staring into the hate-filled eyes of a bowman half a dozen paces distant, out of the reach of his spatha, staring at him down the shaft of an arrow with the string pulled taut and ready to fly. Recognising from his own Hamians' shooting drills the last instants of the archer's preparations to shoot, the Roman's instinctive reaction was to freeze, knowing that at such a close distance and with no time to defend himself, his only hope was to entrust his life to the tiny chance that the easterner might miss for some reason while knowing with instant certainly that no such reprieve was in any way likely.

And then, as the certainty of his death settled fully on him allowing him a fleeting moment of resignation and regret for a life lived not as he would have wished, he saw the easterner's right hand open to release the arrow's shaft, but then the bowman's face contorted with shock and pain as Barbatus stabbed his reclaimed spear into the Hamian's unarmoured thigh. The Roman felt a stinging sensation in his right ear, putting a hand to it to find the lobe torn and bleeding from the unaimed arrow's random flight. The Dacian turned to him, grinning maniacally over his beast's corpse while the insanity of the battle raged around them.

'A life for a life, Tribune! A moment ago I was in your debt, now we're level again!'

Marcus nodded his understanding, putting a foot on the corpse of the man in whom his spatha was lodged and pulling it free from between the rings of his mail.

'Shall we retake command of your Britons, before the enemy lancers arrive and take advantage of their disorder?'

The Dacians reformed gradually at the insistent bray of the cornicer's horn calls, gathering in their squadrons and looking around them at the scattered human detritus that only moments before had been a five-hundred-strong cohort. Fewer men were holding long spears than before, having lost them in the fray or broken them in the act of killing the Hamians, but the light of victory was in every man's eye and Marcus knew that they were subconsciously absorbing the fact that they had collectively passed an important milestone for any military unit: victorious combat. The remnants of the archers were a mile distant, riding away barely a hundred strong, while the Dacians' losses had been so minimal as to make those men who had fallen the subject of surprised regret from their comrades, for being unlucky enough to die or suffer a serious wound when all around them were celebrating victory and survival.

'Put the dying out of their misery, theirs and ours, we're all soldiers of the same army and there's no call for hatred!' Barbatus looked across the ranks of his men. 'You fought well, my brothers, and these poor bastards were never going to be able to defend themselves against wolves like us, caught as they were! And we'll mourn the men we lost later, when this fight is done with! For now, we have them to deal with!'

He pointed to the oncoming enemy cavalry, now a mile distant and showing no sign of slowing or turning away.

'They want this ground! They want revenge on us for sending those archers away, torn to ribbons! And those legions can only win if they can stop us from holding here! Who takes this ground wins the battle!'

Marcus shot a glance back at the advancing friendly legions behind them, closer than the enemy and coming on at the battle march. He leaned out of his saddle to speak in Barbatus's ear, pitching his voice low so as for his words not to carry to the men around them.

'There's no need to fight again.'

The Dacian frowned in confusion.

'But what if they take this ground?'

'Then they will be ejected from it with grievous losses by our legions soon after. They don't want this patch of grass, and they know they can't hold it. This part of the battle is already over, and you and your men are the victors. All the man commanding that cavalry wing wants is to destroy your cohort, and thereby restore his master's pride in his army's skill at arms. Niger's legati want to be able to point to your scattered dead, and tell their legions that we will not be able to hold against their irresistible force, that they are battle hardened and we are not, and that your five hundred dead men are the proof of that! And more than that, you need to preserve this precious force for later in the battle, when its use, and if necessary its sacrifice, will be of real value and might even win this war.'

Barbatus shook his head in reluctance.

'But there is a fight to be fought.'

'It is a fight that you win simply by not fighting. And I believe that you will have your time to fight again today, and if the gods demand it of you, to die as well.'

'You swear it?'

Marcus smiled sadly.

'Can I swear to it? No. But trust me, I believe I know how this battle will play out, and I know that cavalry will play a decisive role when the moment comes for the intervention that might win the battle. And so I am saving you and your men for the moment when you might be the difference between victory and defeat. I am saving you for your emperor, and so that your battle honour this day will read not that you fought and died magnificently, but in vain, but that you were the men who did your duty, defeated an enemy who might have disrupted our advance and then stood ready to do the same again. Now will you do as I command, and withdraw to the safety of our line, and ready yourself for that moment of glory, or will you throw away five hundred of the emperor's most valuable warriors?'

'And so after all the spying and deception, the marching and countermarching, it all comes down to this.' Legatus Renatus stared over the heads of his waiting legionaries from the vantage point of his saddle, watching with a bleak expression as the last of the Severan legionaries marched into their places in the battle line facing his own men. 'Perfectly calculated positioning on our opponent's behalf, you'd have to say.'

Silanus nodded sourly, running a critical eye across the two armies' dispositions. The two men were at the head of the Fifteenth Legion's leading cohort, at the point where the tight terrain on either side of the lake road opened out into the widening plain on which the Severan army was deployed in line of battle.

'I couldn't have done it any better myself. They have set out their stall to force us to come at them, if we wish to defeat them and push them back into the sea. We have to cross a mile of open grassland to get to them, continually lengthening our line to left and right under a hail of arrows, and their artillery will be ready to start shooting soon enough too, dropping bolts onto the choke point behind us to demoralise our legionaries as they march to join the battle. It's a pity our own archers couldn't have made more impression, but their cavalry saw to that. Someone over there knows what they're doing, that's a fact, because this is not anything like the starting position I would have chosen.'

The Severans had chosen a gentle rise in the ground, a mile or so from the point at which the strip of land on which the road ran along the lake's southern side opened up from little better than a hundred paces wide to a mile in width in no more than the same distance. The eastern legions, waiting down a three-mile length of the lakeside road from Nicaea behind them, were making room for their cavalry to move back down the road to get out of their way, having tried and failed to claim the line on which the enemy infantry was now firmly established. A series of frustrated attacks when their prefect, denied a chance to attack the enemy cavalry that had slaughtered the eastern horse archers, had ridden his cohort at the enemy line, had left dozens of their number strewn across the open ground between the two armies, victims of Severan archery and obdurate defence by the advancing infantry.

Renatus looked back, stiffening to attention in his saddle as the imperial party, having pushed through the crush of men, cantered up to join them. The emperor positioned his mount alongside theirs, looking grimly out over the prospective battlefield.

'Legatus, First Spear, what is your assessment?'

Renatus answered.

'Candidus has managed to thwart our intended plan, to meet them in the pass with the advantage of the high ground. And our only choice now is to go forward, deploying under the lash of their archers and artillery, take the fight to them and beat them in a straight fight to the finish. There is enough time, if we start the attack now and be swift about it, to have them running before darkness falls, and we have the advantage of experienced troops where Candidus has done little more than march in triumph from Cyzicus. We can still do this, but we must either attack now or set ourselves to hold this narrow place and allow the rest of the army to escape and fight another day, under better circumstances.'

Niger grimaced.

'Better circumstances? There won't be any. From here we would have to retreat all the way to the Taûros mountains, four hundred miles, to regain the defensive advantage I hoped we might fight with today, and that would cede the initiative to the usurper and allow him to bring yet more legions to face us when we can only ever muster half his strength at best. No. It has to be now, and that means it has to be here. Can you win this fight for me?'

Both men nodded grimly, Silanus answering for his legatus.

'We can, Imperator. But it will be a bloody matter, and the victory, if we gain it, will feel much like a defeat when we count the dead and wounded when the dust settles.'

The emperor sighed.

'No one ever stops to consider the potential butcher's tally when they place the purple on a great man's shoulders, do they. But here we are, come to this point of decision, and if we fail to step up to the fight we might as well surrender now and face Severus's judgement. So yes, gentlemen, I need you to attempt to win this battle, and carve your names in the roll call of Rome's famous generals when you succeed. You both know that I will reward you richly for such a triumph.'

'We do, Imperator.' Renatus pointed to the rear. 'And now I must request that you ride back a way, to brief your other legati and remove yourself from the likely aiming point for the enemy artillery. Tell my colleagues to report here if you will, and Silanus and I will work their men into our plan of deployment.'

Niger shook their hands and turned his horse away, the praetorians closing around him as he rode back down his army's long column.

'You really think we can do this?'

Silanus nodded at his legatus's question.

'There is a chance. And we have no choice but to take the initiative, only without the room to manoeuvre to a flank or try to do anything other than just go at them with our teeth bared which at least plays to our lads' strengths and capitalises on their weaknesses. Which means I'd better get this lot deployed, and the quicker the better if we're going to have their bolt throwers pecking at us.' He turned to look at Renatus questioningly. 'You know all the famous battles from history, where you lot always make a speech beforehand that gets the troops pulling at their leash and eager to be at the enemy? I hope you've got a good one for us today, because we're in a tough corner unless our boys can manage to break their line and get at the soft meat behind all that armour.'

*

'How would you rate our chances, Tribune?'

Scaurus pondered the question for a moment before answering it.

'I'd call them fair, Legatus Augusti. But no more than that.'

Candidus nodded, turning to the legion commander saddled alongside him.

'You see? That's why the emperor sent Rutilius Scaurus along with us. Not simply because he's book learned and calculating where the rest of us are just talented amateurs by comparison, but because he's never anything other than ruthlessly honest.'

'Come now Tribune Scaurus, how can this be anything other than a victory?'

The Fourteenth Legion's legatus, a man still in his twenties and to Marcus's eye lacking the military experience usually required for his role, inclined his head in question, genuinely puzzled. Scaurus nodded his understanding of the other man's bafflement.

'I know, it looks perfect does it not? They have to advance a mile, with their ability to deploy limited by the bottleneck of the lake road, forcing them to constantly adjust their line as the front they have to cover gets wider and wider with every pace forward. And worse, they have to do so under constant attack from our artillery, and then our archers will join in as they get closer. And of course there's the fact that while both of our armies are three legions, theirs took more casualties in our battle with them at Rhaedestus than they will have been able to replace. All of which tilts things our way.' The legion commander smiled despite his efforts to present a martial facade, satisfied to have his judgement reinforced. 'However . . .'

The other man started slightly, and leaned closer in his saddle as Scaurus's tone grew reflective.

'Of the four legions that fought on that day, three of theirs and one of ours, only two of them are here. And they are both on the other side of the field, fighting for our enemy. And their commander will lead with those two legions if he has the sense to do so, because they are battle-hardened veterans, whereas none of our legionaries has seen anything much worse than a training accident and non-events during the march from Abydus, fights that were over before they began. I have fought in more than my share of battles, gentlemen, and I can tell you with absolute sincerity that the worst of them by a country mile was the first. It was more of a squabble than a proper fight, but it nearly killed me, and I was exhausted from the terror of it within minutes despite my understanding that I either fought or died. Our men will be terrified all the way through this fight, for the most part, scared half to death. Niger's men will know fear, of course, but they will master their urge to panic because they have seen these sorts of dreadful events before and survived. Put simply, most of our legionaries will be in terror of their own death, whereas most of theirs will have got past that and will be thinking about how to survive. And, more importantly, how to win.'

Candidus nodded sagely.

'Well expressed, colleague, and the mirror of my own thoughts exactly. So see to your men, gentlemen, and be ready to bolster their courage with your own personal examples of heroism, because it would be a long run back to Cyzicus with their cavalry's spears at our backs, and I for one am not in the mood after the distance we've already marched today.'

He dismissed his officers to their legions, but gestured to Scaurus to stay behind.

'Those Dacians masquerading as Britons. What did you think of them Gaius?'

'I was impressed. Their stand-in prefect is a leader of men, and an animal for a fight, and his men will follow him wherever he points his spear.'

'Good.' The general nodded his satisfaction at the answer. 'Because I have an idea as to how we might deploy them if the tide of this battle turns against us. And perhaps a way to both bolster their determination to take such a perilous role and to reward them for their successes to date.'

Scaurus rode back to the place behind the line where the Dacians were standing beside their horses, allowing them to drink from the narrow stream that flowed across the land between the mountains and the lake. Barbatus walked over to him as he dismounted, his face still speckled with the blood of the men he had killed earlier.

'Candidus sends you his thanks, and indeed his respect, for the way in which you saw off those horse archers, *Prefect*.'

The Dacian's eyes widened in surprise.

'Are you serious? He has confirmed my position.'

'As serious as the blade that nearly killed you an hour ago. You are hereby formally promoted to the rank of prefect, a battlefield promotion which is entirely within our legatus augusti's powers to grant as a permanent role. Your salary will be adjusted accordingly, if you live long enough to see the military bureaucracy grind that finely, and you will command your cohort until you either die in action or reach your age of retirement. Further, you are free to select your own officers and generally treat this cohort as your own. Go and tell your decurions the good news and then I'll tell you what part the general has decided you will play in this battle.'

He remounted his horse and rode to where the familia were waiting, reunited with the arrival of the legions. Marcus greeted him with a weary salute, clearly every bit as dog tired as his friend.

'What do you think of all this?'

Scaurus shrugged.

'The same as you, I'd imagine. On the face of it we should win, we have all the advantages after all. And in reality . . . who can tell? But we'll know soon enough.'

With a screech of horns the enemy line was in motion, disciplined infantry coming on at the battle march with the evident intention of getting to grips with their opposition as quickly as possible.

'See? Whoever is in command over there knows just what they're doing. Our boys will be nudging each other and asking why it is that the other side are so keen to get face to face, what it is they know that we don't? And look at the way they're deploying, feeding centuries onto the flanks as the frontage increases. It's masterful control under the circumstances.'

A mournful trumpet note sounded from the command group at the Severan line's centre in response to the advance, and the two legions' artillery, set up and ready to shoot a hundred paces behind them, responded with a volley of bolts shot over the defenders' heads to plunge down into the massed ranks of the oncoming easterners. Men fell, were lost underfoot to cause momentary confusion in the enemy ranks, then were left dead or incapacitated by their horrific wounds in the wake of their comrades, scattered detritus left by the artillery's pitiless scourge. Another horn command set the archers to shooting from close behind the Severan line, lofting their barbed shafts high into the air to fall back to earth in a deadly sleet that rattled on the shields and helmets of their targets. Most of the arrows either lodged in the wooden boards held up to obstruct their flight, or rebounded harmlessly, if disquietingly, from armoured heads and torsos, but with every volley men fell, or staggered out of the line unable to take any further part. Marcus, having remounted his horse to gain the vantage point needed to see over the defending line, shook his head at the impact on the enemy advance as it was battered by the combined attack of bolt throwers and bows.

'It looks impressive, but it's nowhere near enough, or at least not against veteran troops. And they'll be too close to shoot at too soon for it to make any real difference.'

'Yes. It will come down to an infantry fight.'

The horns sounded again, and, having achieved the required frontage to match the Severan line, the enemy legions covered the last hundred paces of their advance at a trot, obeying their officers' commands to halt when they were so close to the Severan line that neither the artillery nor the archers behind the legions facing them were able to shoot into them. Marcus looked across at the command group behind the Fourteenth Legion, waiting for the horn to sound the advance.

'We need to go at them now. Come on . . .'

But no signal was given, giving the breathless enemy legionaries a moment to regroup and prepare themselves for their inevitable attack while the defenders stood and watched, inexplicably allowing them time to prepare for the assault. Incensed, Marcus bellowed a command at the men of the legion in front of him, an expression of frustration aimed more at their failure to react than at any man in particular.

'Now! You must attack them *now*!'

If the young legatus heard him he didn't respond, although Marcus was sure the legion's centurions would have been shouting at their men to prepare themselves to carry out the obvious pre-emptive attack. And while Candidus could see what needed to be done, the command group's horns blaring out the command for his legions to attack while they still had the time, the order was a moment too late. Even as the legion commanders behind the line realised their error in failing to send their men forward, some of their centurions shouting orders for an attack without waiting for their legati to do so, the enemy line was coming forward behind a volley of thrown spears that caught the Severans between attack and defence, and without the benefit of either a well-set line of shields or an answering volley of spears.

'Shit, this looks bad!'

Marcus nodded at Barbatus's horrified comment as the assault was delivered at the run by the attacking legions, their front rankers storming in with their swords flickering out and back in disciplined sword drills, each sword thrust following a blow hammered at the men facing them with the iron bosses of their shields to throw them off balance. The defenders, caught flat-footed, suffered grievously in the first moments of the attack, second and third rankers finding themselves thrust into the fight faster than expected as first the men facing the enemy and then their immediate replacements staggered and fell with spear and sword wounds. Scaurus shook his head in frustration.

'Textbook tactics. Their fast advance negated our artillery advantage, now they're making the most of their greater battle experience to put our men on the back foot! And they'll plan to keep us that way too!'

The Severan line was already starting to give ground, battle-shocked legionaries stepping back in the face of their enemies' remorseless attack even as their centurions shouted at them to hold fast. With another blare of horns a party of horsemen was pushing up behind the enemy line, a strong escort of praetorian cavalrymen sheltering the man at its heart from arrows with their raised shields. Sitting upright in his saddle as if he were on parade, reviewing his forces, rather than within fifty paces of his enemy, Niger himself had chosen to face the risk of the Severan archers and inspire his men by his presence. Marcus could just about hear him calling out to his men, imploring them to enact the will of the people of Rome and unseat his rival for the throne, and bring themselves glory and gold in the process. The enemy soldiers fighting in the front ranks of his legions, alerted to their master's proximity to the battle line by the men behind them, joined the swelling chorus of adulation for a man so willing to put his life in danger in order to show his support for them.

'*Niger! Niger! Niger!*'

Barbatus stared hungrily across the hundred or so paces separating him from the emperor.

'I could take my men through that lot and have his head.'

Marcus shook his head.

'No, you couldn't. You would all be dead before you got within twenty paces of him, those legionaries are packed too tight to push aside, and they are raving mad for blood to honour him with. We need to get some life back into our legions before they start turning and running for their lives, but that's not something that can be done from the back of a horse. Wait here, and be ready either to exploit the chance to attack if it arises, or to cover the retreat if the line collapses!'

He turned to Scaurus.

'I'll go and put some fight into the Fourteenth, if I can!'

'And I'll do the same with the First!'

The two men rode to left and right, Dubnus and his axemen following Marcus as he spurred his horse across the back of the left side of the battle to where the commander of the Fourteenth Legion sat in his saddle watching the battle with a look of helplessness. Ranging his horse alongside the senior officer he looked into the man's eyes and implored him to act.

'Legatus, we *must* counterattack! If we do not attack now, we condemn our men to defeat without them ever really fighting!'

The young officer senator turned to look at him with an expression that told Marcus all that he needed to know about his state of mind, and the Roman dismounted, stalking across to the legion's aquilifer who was standing and watching the fight in a state of uncertainty no better than that of his commander, the cornicer alongside him looking no more confident.

'How far do you think you can run carrying that eagle?'

The veteran turned to him with a look of incomprehension, his scarred face pale with fear.

'What do you mean, how far—'

'You've fought in battles before, right?'

The question got him a nod.

'Then you can see that this one's going against us, which is why you're only just holding onto your shit.'

Another nod.

'You're a veteran of the German wars, a man with a reputation for having balls the size of apples, that's why you ended up carrying your legion's eagle! And you swore an oath, a blood promise to Rome and to the gods, to hold that eagle aloft for as long as you have breath in your body. Which means that you have a choice! You can do nothing, and end up getting a spear in the face when the line collapses and you stand to fight or you throw it away and run for the rest of your short life, probably still getting killed in the chaos, and wait to find out what happens to oath breakers in the next life. Or *we* can go and do the right thing, you and I . . .'

Marcus drew the longer of his two swords, and the aquilifer, seeing the grim-faced pioneers behind him, swallowed as the realisation of what he had to do struck him hard. He nodded slowly, with the knowledge that his choice was no choice at all written in the determined expression on his face.

'I have to face those bastards with this fucking eagle held high.'

'Yes. You do. You can be the man who makes this legion fight for its life, a hero who will be rewarded with gold by the legatus augusti when I tell him the story later this evening. Or you can be a man who dies with his honour intact, and face the judgement of his peers and his ancestors with his head held high. Either of those options has to be better than running.'

A slow smile spread across the standard-bearer's face.

'A quick and honourable death, or victory and glory, is that it Tribune?'

'You'll be the hero of the army, and your name will go down in the history books.'

'Fuck that, I'll just take the gold.' The aquilifer grinned at Marcus, his fear forgotten in the dark humour of the moment. 'And you're coming with me, are you Tribune, you and those axe wavers? I'd hate to find myself on my own in that boat across the river.'

The Roman shook his head in amusement.

'Trust me, if we die today, the crossing to Hades will be as crowded as the Hellēspontos the day we invaded Asia.' He turned to the cornicer, who was watching open mouthed. 'Will you come with us, and blow that horn so that our men know that the eagle is with them?'

The trumpeter shook his head resignedly.

'If this mad old bastard is up for it, who am I to spoil the party? And what's the point of you pair sacrificing yourselves if no one knows you're doing it?'

The Roman strode purposefully across to the rear of the battle line with the standard-bearer and his comrades at his back. He gestured to the slowly retreating soldiers.

'From here the only person who can make a difference to these men is *you*, brother. Do what you need to do, and I will make sure you live to tell the tale, if I am able. And you, cornicer, blow that horn like you have a pair! Let's order the legion to salute its eagle, shall we, and keep on doing it until everyone knows what's happening here?'

The trumpeter, momentarily taken aback to be ordered to blow such an incongruous command for a battle, nevertheless drew breath and blew two piercing notes long and hard – one high, one low – the parade command to salute the legion's eagle that in time of peace would have every man rooted to the spot and shouting their salutations to the legions' sacred symbol of imperial power. The aquilifer took a deep breath, squared his shoulders and roared a challenge at his comrades.

'Not another step back, you whoresons!' Ignoring the incredulity of the rear rankers closest to him, turning to stare at him he pushed his way into their midst with Marcus and Dubnus clearing a path ahead of him. 'If you want to turn and run then you go ahead, and be named as fucking cowards! Me and this eagle are going to fight though, and if you've got the balls for it then you can join us!'

With the cornicer blowing the same two notes again and again behind him he pushed through to a place right behind the front rank, the men in front of him glancing around in horrified amazement at the sight of their legion's precious standard so close to them. The enemy facing them were baying at the sight of such a prize, every one of them knowing that the capture of an enemy eagle would see the man who took it rich beyond his dreams, such would be the reward bestowed upon him. A pair of legionaries in the line facing the Severans glanced at each other and then launched themselves from their places in the enemy line, swords raised ready to fight, and the Severan line actually flinched back a pace, leaving Marcus and the aquilifer open to their attack.

'What's going on over there?'

Candidus was staring out to his army's left flank, narrowing his eyes in an effort to discern what was happening behind the

Fourteenth Legion. Draco, who had been cursing non-stop with each step back his legions took, nodded approvingly.

'Someone in that legion has decided that it's better to go down fighting. Look, they're taking the eagle into the front line! If our legionaries are willing to lose their eagle, then nothing we can do will help. And look, your tame tribune is doing the same with the First Rescuers on the right!'

The general nodded decisively, pointing to the aquilifer standing in front of the Tenth Legion behind them.

'They're taking the eagles into the battle to shame our men into fighting. And they're right! Come with me, First Spear, it's the moment I held your men back for. We'll show these men how a Roman general either triumphs with his men or dies with his men!'

The closer of the two attackers died with a spear point in his throat, Marcus having grabbed the weapon up from the ground a moment before. While the first man staggered back with blood spraying from the open wound the Roman pulled the spear back and then tossed it up into the throwing position, caught it perfectly at shoulder height and slung it into the other legionary's chest. He drew his gladius, setting himself to fight, Dubnus's axeman pushing into the line and positioning themselves on either side of him, and roared a challenge at both the enemy soldiers and the men behind him.

'Severus! Severus and the eagle!'

After a moment's silence the ranks of men behind him recovered from their surprise and shouted in response, stepping forward to reclaim the ground they had momentarily surrendered and pushing Marcus and the standard-bearer back behind their reformed front rank, chanting the name of their own emperor in defiance of the calls from Niger's men.

'*Severus! Severus! Severus!*'

To the legion's rear the horns were sounding the order for the attack, and up and down the line its centurions were taking up their challenge with calls for their men to ready themselves for the counterattack. The aquilifer shouted another challenge at his comrades.

'Come on you bastards, there's an emperor for the taking over there, and me and this eagle are going to go and get him!'

'Spears! Ready!'

The closest centurion's command galvanised the legionaries, men setting themselves ready to throw their spears at the enemy line while the legion's front rank held the opposing legionaries at sword's length. As the legion's men raised their spear ready to throw, a forest of pointed iron heads rising out of their line, the enemy soldiers showed their first signs of fear, the front rankers starting to shrink back as individual Severan legionaries stared at them with obvious intent. The horns sounded again, and up and down the line centurions were screaming the order that every man was waiting for.

'Spears! Throw!'

Stamping forward, the legion's line erupted in a shower of thrown pila, the volley ragged and unevenly delivered as individual centurions gave the order, but no less deadly to the men facing them, who were packed so tightly into their battle line that many of them were unable to do anything more than cringe down behind the men in front of them. Hundreds of the thrown weapons found a target, the long iron spearheads punching through armour or striking flesh; and as the enemy legions' ranks shivered under the assault, Marcus looked at the standard-bearer beside him.

'Now is the moment for your glory! The men of this legion are in the palm of your hand for one brief moment! Take them forward, and earn your place in history!'

The veteran aquilifer nodded determinedly, shouting a command over his shoulder at his comrade the trumpeter.

'Sound the eagle advances! Blow that fucking horn until your lips bleed!'

The cornicer did as he was bidden, and started blowing the command to advance, his single horn joined a moment later by a chorus of his fellows. With the familiar command to go forward pealing behind them, and sensing his fellow legionaries' eagerness to retake the initiative, the standard-bearer roared three words at the men around him as he took a decisive step back into the front rank.

'*WE! GO! FORWARD!*'

With a collective roar the legion surged into the gap that had opened between the two armies, the advance rippling down the battle line as centuries on either side saw their neighbours advancing and obeyed the collective urge to fight themselves. In a moment the battle was re-joined, the Severans attacking in the familiar shield punch and sword stab method that was instinctive from years of training repetition, while the men facing them, their bloodlust blown out by their sudden reversal of fortunes, found themselves on the back foot and fighting for their lives.

'We have them shitting themselves!'

The aquilifer needed no more encouragement from Marcus, leading the men around him forward and effectively dragging the legion into an arrowhead formation as the centuries on either side followed the example set by the men following him. Looking over the heads of the enemy legionaries it was clear that the cavalrymen around Niger were urging him to retreat from such an abrupt reversal of his army's fortunes, and after a moment the group started to turn their horses to pull back. With his soldiers already on the back foot and looking over their shoulders it was the only sensible choice for the emperor, but a catastrophic decision for legions suddenly fighting for their lives and seemingly deserted by their leader. With the grim inevitability of a battle sliding away from the men who a moment before had been in the ascendancy, the enemy line started to unravel from the rear, men running after the fleeing imperial party shouting pleas and imprecations after their emperor. A centurion close behind the Roman shouted the two words that presaged a rout:

'They're running!'

His men cheered, surging forward with fresh purpose as the legions facing them began to disintegrate, the legionaries in the front rank facing them caught between the deadly peril of facing an enemy with their blood up while the men behind them deserted the line, and the equal if not greater risk of turning their backs to run. With a sudden and almost simultaneous collective decision the legion facing them disintegrated, soldiers stampeding away from the battle line in terror, trampling the dead and wounded underfoot. Over to the right of the line the First Legion was enjoying the same sudden collapse of their wing of the enemy army's resistance, and in the centre he could see Draco's Tenth Legion's standard being carried forward into the line, as the reserve legion shouldered its way into the impending slaughter. Barbatus's Brittonum were also riding forward to join the pursuit, their lances stabbing out to reap the lives of the rearmost among the fleeing legions.

Turning back to the scene close to hand, Marcus stood and watched as the legion that had only minutes before been at risk of just such a disaster rampaged forward in the wake of their retreating foe, blood-crazed soldiers stabbing down at the living and the dead alike in their urge to wipe the shame of their own near rout from their collective memory.

'We . . . we seem to have them beaten.'

He turned and looked up at the Fourteenth's legatus, realising that the man's words were as much a question as a statement, the younger man's capacity to comprehend the swift passage of events overcome by both their sheer speed and his own inexperience. Trembling, as the fierce fire of the battle burned out of his blood to be replaced by the emptiness of a battle's aftermath, Marcus looked around him at the scattered corpses of the dead and the struggles of the wounded to stand or even simply to breathe and he clamped down on the urge to pull the man down from his saddle and kill him in recompense for the near disaster his inexperience had visited on his legion, and had resulted in so many of the casualties surrounding them.

'Yes, legatus. Your aquilifer has rescued the day for you. I suggest you ensure that he is rewarded as handsomely as you would hope will be the case for you and your colleagues when the emperor hears of this victory. And for now, much as you might wish to join Claudius Candidus and celebrate such a great victory, your first duty is to get the *medicae* to tend to your wounded, after which you should consider the dignified handling of your dead. Your first spear will know what to do, all you have to do is go and find him in that' – he pointed to the pursuit of the fleeing easterners, starting to slow as the retreating enemy were forced into an ever-decreasing perimeter forcing them to turn and fight for their lives – 'when both sides of this disaster are too exhausted to fight any longer.'

The legatus shook his head uncomprehendingly.

'Disaster, Tribune? Surely this is a great—'

'A great victory?' Marcus shook his head. 'Not for Rome.'

11

'So, the battle you fought outside Nicaea was a great victory, as I read in the dispatches, was it, Claudius Candidus?'

Marcus watched from his place behind Candidus, having been unexpectedly required to attend the legatus augusti's audience with the emperor along with Scaurus, the reason for their inclusion still being disquietingly unclear even as the emperor had swept into the room with his praetorians. The general straightened from his bow to address Severus's blunt and unheralded opening question, sentiment seemingly stripped of any respect for the circumstances of their triumphant reunion.

'It was certainly a victory from where I was standing on the battlefield, Imperator. As to whether it was great or not, better and wiser men than me will have to be the judges.'

The emperor waved a dismissive hand. He was sitting in judgement of his leading general's performance in fighting the war in Asia and, to Marcus and Scaurus's disappointment, if not their surprise given his penchant for unpredictability, was giving his legatus augusti a hard time of it.

'I believe that I will be the judge in that matter, thank you Legatus.'

The emperor had moved swiftly after Niger's decisive defeat at Nicaea, crossing the Bosporus with two legions and moving inland into Bithynia with the intention of joining up with his victorious army, leaving another two besieging the rebel city of Byzantium which was stubbornly resisting being taken on the not unreasonable grounds that the city fathers expected it to be sacked if they surrendered after having supported Niger. Having followed in the wake of the army of Pannonia's pursuit of their defeated enemy, as the broken army sought to escape to Syria across the provinces of Bithynia, Galatia and Cappadocia, he had caught up with Candidus's legions within sight of the mountains of the Taûros range that separated the high Asian plain from the fertile lands that bordered the Middle Sea. With the enemy forces having finally managed to regroup and turn at bay, defending passes on the mountain range's line with renewed tenacity, Severus had assumed control of the entire force with an attitude that seemed not entirely favourable to his leading general.

'So the facts as they have been presented to me are these. You effected a successful landing on the shores of Asia, thanks to the use of the praetorian fleet. After which you defeated the traitor Asellius Aemilianus outside Cyzicus . . .' Severus paused significantly. 'Defeated him and then allowed him to escape from imperial justice by committing suicide, it has to be said.' The emperor's frowning stare eloquently signalled his disapproval. 'Whereas I would have greatly preferred having the chance to enquire of him exactly what he thought he was achieving for the empire in siding with the usurper. And then to have him publicly executed to make the point to others who might still harbour the same misguided sentiments.'

He stared in silence at Candidus for a long moment before resuming, the general very wisely choosing to remain silent given that he had indeed ordered Scaurus to force Aemilianus to kill himself in order to prevent his being interrogated before execution.

'And then we come to the matter of the battle of Nicaea. Billed as a victory in your dispatches after the event, but, the truth be told, something of a let-down when the facts are considered.'

He stared hard at Candidus again, but to Marcus's eye the senator had now firmly concluded that he was unlikely to win any arguments with his irascible master, and was keeping his mouth firmly shut in expectation of a less than generous interpretation of the facts of the battle they had fought some weeks before. At length the emperor continued.

'You wrote that after a forced march of thirty miles, your men engaged a numerically similar force which was forced to attack you. You eventually managed to overcome their attack by means of the bravery of your standard-bearers in leading the two engaged legions into the teeth of the enemy, and so discomfiting them that they turned and fled. All of which – the long march, the difficult battle fought by a weary army and the example of your aquilifers – is all very much as I expect my armies to perform. It also makes me wonder what your legati were doing, if things were so dire that their eagles had to be placed in a position of extreme risk in the battle line to inspire their legions to victory. Perhaps you and I can discuss their conduct later, and in private?'

Candidus bowed his head, already planning, as Marcus knew all too well, to petition the emperor for new legion commanders for both the Fourteenth Twin and the First Rescuers given their legates' dismal showing at Nicaea. Severus continued in the same frosty tone.

'And, as I am always grateful to my legionaries for their golden examples of duty and sacrifice, you are commanded to reward the key men involved richly in the name of a grateful emperor. Make sure my insistence on their being properly recompensed for their sacrifices is known to them, Claudius Candidus. But, that said' – he shook his head in the manner of a disappointed parent – 'I cannot avoid asking how it was that Niger avoided capture in such a rout as the one you describe, and how it was that he escaped with so many of his men to retreat into the east, and continue to present a threat to our rule?'

'A combination of factors, Imperator.' Candidus, having remained silent, knew that he had reached the point of at least having to make clear the facts of the matter so as to hopefully avoid an accusation of treachery. 'As I have noted, our men were exhausted from a day spent at the battle march. And the enemy had the advantage of retreating down a long road between an impassable forest and an unfordable lake, making their escape route impossible to outflank and preventing the use of our cavalry. A cohort of their infantry under the leadership of Publius

Ampius Renatus managed to block the road at the point where the battlefield narrowed to the width of that road, and no efforts by our men, exhausted as they were, could force them from that position before the onset of a dark and moonless night. It was all we could do to bring our scattered legionaries together, and to retrieve the wounded for what treatment could be provided. And I should respectfully point out that we managed to kill three of the enemy for every man—'

'Enough.' Severus waved a hand to silence his general, affecting the air of a weary patrician whose underlings were a constant source of disappointment. 'I have heard these reasons already, and while I do not find that I am inspired by them I am willing to accept them, in order not to seem churlish to my most valued allies' – he paused for effect, but Marcus had already guessed what would follow – 'by which I mean of course the men of my army's legions. However, with all of these thoughts in mind, I have decided to make a change to the command structure of my army.'

He stood, extending a hand to Candidus.

'Tiberius Claudius Candidus, you have served the throne faithfully and well, and I thank you for your loyal service. You have defeated the usurper Niger twice on battlefields in Asia, and you have prosecuted the pursuit of his army, and the punitive measures required to remind those cities which supported him in whose service they are now permitted to continue their existence, with appropriate diligence. Those errors you have made have been well intentioned and innocent, and the throne remains grateful for your service. From this moment you are relieved of the burden of the position of being the principal commander of the army, a role that will be assumed by my dear friend and colleague Publius Cornelius Anullinus. Although I will still require your service in commanding two of my legions, as a legatus augusti.'

Candidus inclined his head in a respectful bow, having already expressed his expectations on the subject of his role to Scaurus and Marcus the previous day on discovering that the emperor's favourite had joined the army before it had crossed the Bosporus.

'Severus served as a quaestor under him when Anullinus was governor of Hispanic Baetica, and they have known each other from their earliest days in Rome.' He had shrugged, sipping at his wine with the usual expression of distaste before continuing. 'Which means that it is most likely that Anullinus is accompanying Severus in Asia to be promoted to a senior command role, hopefully the one I currently hold. Don't look so surprised, it's just the way that he operates. He will find faults in the conduct of the war in Asia with which to criticise me tomorrow in our audience, giving him all the reason he will need to remove me from senior command in order to so favour his best friend. Just as he did to Laetus last year before we left Rome, to take him off his pedestal. He does it to ensure that no one general ever reaches the height of power that men like Corbulo managed to attain before Nero ordered him to kill himself, and so avoid the emergence of another Julius Caesar to destabilise the empire, and either seize power or pave the way for another young genius like Augustus. And such is entirely his right. So make sure you display no emotion when he does so, and all will be well and as expected.'

Severus stared intently at Marcus and Scaurus in their places standing behind Candidus, but, forewarned, neither of them gave any sign of being perturbed by the matter of their general's demotion. Nodding to himself in apparent satisfaction, the emperor spoke again.

'And in fact, we will not need to speak again regarding the command of the Fourteenth and First Legions, which are the force that I wish you to command within the newly structured army of the *expeditio Asiana*. I have already made that decision ahead of time, on receiving your dispatches. These two young men who have been so active in your service seem to have a generous share in the successes that you have achieved, do they not?'

Candidus bowed again.

'Indeed they do. Imperator, just as they were a major part in your general Cilo's de facto victory over the legions outside Rhaedestus to boot' – he paused for a moment and then decided to take a risk – 'and the blessing of his standard by the alighting of an actual eagle might well be interpreted as some small measure of the gods' favour to them both in addition to its ringing endorsement of your rule.'

'Much as I surmised myself.' Severus played a hard gaze over both men, seemingly having generously decided to share the glory of that moment with them. 'Which is why I have decided to honour those same gods by promoting both of these men. You, Rutilius Scaurus, will henceforth command the Fourteenth Legion, Martial and Victorious. May it bring honour to your name and finally restore your family to greatness.'

Scaurus bowed deeply, even his usual imperturbable mask creased into an expression of surprise.

'Thank you, Imperator, I will endeavour to live up to your expectations.'

'Of course you will.' The emperor's attention shifted to Marcus. 'And you, Valerius Aquila – who I am told went by a false name in the decade after your father's execution for treason, a charge that I am also told may well have been false, motivated by a high-ranking official's personal greed and unrepresentative of your family's dedication to the empire . . .' Severus paused and looked around the audience chamber to allow anyone with a contrary opinion to make a comment, but the gesture was greeted with utter silence. 'You will also be elevated in life from this moment. I hereby use my power of *adlectio* to return you to the senatorial class from which your father's execution . . . or perhaps I could say extrajudicial murder . . . excluded you. There are formalities to be dealt with on another day, when we have all returned in triumph to Rome, but for now you will be needing this because I have decided that you will perform the role of *tribunus laticlavius* to Rutilius Scaurus's *legatus*. A legion commander needs a broad stripe tribune that he can trust, and you will play this part in the service of your emperor. Perhaps your fellow senators in Rome will be informed by your valour, and concentrate their efforts on making my reign a golden age for the city!'

He held out a hand, a slim gold ring glinting in the torchlight between thumb and forefinger.

'Approach the throne, Valerius Aquila, and reclaim your birthright, the prize you have won for never relinquishing your love for Rome and her empire through the years when that love went unrequited.'

'Don't forget to bow, young man.'

Hearing Candidus's muttered instruction as he passed the legatus, Marcus stopped short of the throne by two paces, bending at the waist to bow extravagantly and holding the position until Severus spoke again.

'Take the ring, Aquila. You won't get a broad striped tunic on your back by standing there looking at your boots, will you?'

Later, the audience complete and Candidus having taken his leave of the emperor and invited his protégés to join him for dinner, he and Scaurus gently teased Marcus for his continued state of wonder and bafflement at the unexpected turn of events. At length, Scaurus good naturedly shrugged in the face of his friend's continued state of perplexity.

'I know exactly what the problem our young friend is having boils down to.'

The older man raised an eyebrow at Scaurus.

'And that is?'

'I've known him ever since he was a centurion in a very unfashionable auxiliary cohort at the other end of the empire, the sort of unit that a young Roman gentleman would have to have fallen a good distance to have to go through the difficult process of actually becoming worthy of the title "Centurion", which, as we all know, is a good deal harder both physically and in terms of relationships with one's fellow soldiers than the much simpler role of tribune. He was being protected by his previous tribune, a man who had been promoted to the command of the Sixth Legion on the death of his predecessor in a local revolt. I discovered his secret soon enough, of course, it wasn't hard to discern given the news coming out of Rome as to his father's death and his disappearance. And I made what felt like an honourable but dubious decision to support him, and to keep his presence in my cohort to myself. And it is a decision I am yet to regret.'

Candidus shrugged in his turn.

'Interesting, and commendable in you both. But how does that shed any light on his problem with being adlected into the senate and promoted to *laticlavius*?'

'Ah, but if you only knew the lengths he has gone to in order to take his revenge on the men who wronged him – on *all* the men who were responsible for his family's slaughter and his exile – then you would understand. In the decade since the day I met him, Marcus Valerius Aquila, for a while under the assumed name Tribulus Corvus, has first fought to survive wars and continuing imperial intrigue, and latterly schemed his way to that vengeance. He killed a man last year whose death I expected to be the last step in his journey of revenge, and we were seeking the safety and peace of a province far from Rome when Severus's army happened to scoop us up by sheer chance, delaying our retreat into obscurity but not killing that dream. But with this one simple change to his army's command, Severus has condemned us to live this life for a good while longer.'

Candidus shrugged, taking a sip of his wine and wincing a little less than usual.

'This stuff seems to be getting better the closer we get to Syria, so perhaps by the time we're in Antioch it will be as good as it seemed the last time I served out here. But seriously, what is it that represents the fly in the butter here? You two have earned your promotions, and the security that goes with them, the money and the power. What more is there that either of you could possibly wish for from life?'

Marcus stirred himself from his torpor, raising his own wine cup in salute.

'Put that way, *Legatus Augusti*, how could I possibly argue with you? Here's to the rest of this campaign, and to Niger's capture and presentation to the emperor in chains!'

Candidus and Scaurus drank, and the conversation moved on to matters of preparing their legions for the push into Syria to end Niger's rule by taking Antioch, and discussion of the professional military officer's perennial concerns of recruitment, training and the vagaries of supplies in the face of a logistics structure populated for the most part by the venal and incompetent. At length the senior officer excused himself, and Scaurus, waiting until he was sure that they were alone, lifted his cup again.

'I know the real problem, one that we both have. That while these new positions are making us part of the elite of our society, the people we care about the most – and whose safety we fear for the most deeply – are either forced to accompany us or are living in who knows what conditions in Rome. And that one of them bears the curse of having been fathered by the emperor you killed to start this civil war. But all we can do until the day we are able to return to Rome is serve this emperor to the best of our abilities, and pray that we do not fall foul of his ill humour one of these days.'

Marcus lifted his own cup in salute.

'I cannot argue with your logic, Legatus.'

His friend laughed.

'And neither should you, *tribunus laticlavius*! Because as long as Niger's legions hold out in the mountains, our work will be cut out for us; and the expectations of this emperor of us will be as high as any we could cut ourselves, with a steep penalty for failure. So here's to victory, Marcus.'

'To victory. And survival.'

Historical Note

I always like to recommend a book for the reader to look into in the event that they want to know more about the period once they've read the story I've created around the history. In this case I feel the need to recommend several. David Potter's *The Roman Empire at Bay AD 180-395*, Michael Kulikowski's *Imperial Triumph: The Roman World from Hadrian to Constantine*, Anthony Birley's *Septimius Severus: The African Emperor* and Michael Sage's *Septimius Severus and the Roman Army* are all very well worth a look.

In writing this follow-up to *Storm of War*, in which our heroes were sent forward with a single legion to disrupt Severus's rival Niger's plans to attack the western half of the empire over the Bosphorus, I came up against a lack of absolute clarity as to exactly how Severus's plans to invade the east actually manifested themselves. It's clear that an invasion somewhere across the Propontis (the modern day Sea of Marmara) succeeded in establishing a beachhead for the landing of a sizeable chunk of the Severan army. Although whether this took place across the Hellespont, which would have been logical given the narrow nature of the strait that led into the northern Aegean (a crossing barely three kilometres wide), or elsewhere is not clear. The pirates and spies action of the first section of this story before that landing is completely my own invention. If it seems far-fetched, perhaps it is!

What we do know is that the Severan army under Tiberius Claudius Candidus, a man who later proved himself to be what

Kulikowski calls 'a loyal Severan butcher' for his bloody proscriptions of the emperor's enemies in Hispania later in the decade, brought Niger's most influential general Asellius Aemilianus to battle somewhere 'near Cyzicus'. Perhaps this was either at or close to the Hellespont, as stated by the not always reliable *Historia Augusta*. Wherever it happened, Niger's most important general, a man so influential that Severus believed it was his support that had facilitated Niger's claiming of the throne, earning him the emperor's implacable hatred, was soundly defeated, captured and then killed in some way. 'My' treatment of Aemilianus here is once again speculation on my part, as the ancient sources only refer to his being slain rather than the precise manner of his death.

We also know that the geographically proximate and fiercely rival cities of Nicaea and Nicomedia to the north-east of Cyzicus declared for Niger and Severus respectively. While I have for reasons of brevity avoided some of the potential manoeuvring around Bithynia that may have resulted, the battle of Nicaea, fought 'amid the narrow passes of Nicaea and Cius' is a hard fact and one of the pivotal moments in the campaign in which the Severan cause might have been set back sharply or even significantly derailed (the act of getting an army across the Propontis successfully being the other in my opinion).

Dio tells us (spoiler alert) that 'At first the followers of Severus, commanded by Candidus, were victorious, for they had an advantage in fighting from the higher ground, but later, when Niger himself appeared, the pursuers became the pursued, and victory rested with Niger's men. Then Candidus seized hold of the standard-bearers and forced them to turn round facing the enemy, at the same time upbraiding the soldiers for their flight; at this his men were ashamed, turned back, and once more got the upper hand of their opponents. Indeed, they would have utterly destroyed them, had not the city been near and had not a dark night come on.'

I have endeavoured to stay true to this account, written by a man born in Nicaea around AD 165, who would therefore have been about thirty years old at the time of the battle, and whose sources we can therefore expect to have been impeccable.

What followed, however, was a well fought and disciplined retreat by Niger back into Asia, a leader still very much in control of his remaining legions. And with the formidable barrier of the Taurus mountains between the oncoming Severans and his base in Syria, he must have still felt that there was much to play for, despite his enemy's preponderant strength. We will see what becomes of his remaining hopes in the next book in the series.

The Roman Army in AD 182

By the late second century, the point at which the *Empire* series begins, the Imperial Roman Army had long since evolved into a stable organisation with a stable *modus operandi*. Thirty or so legions (there's still some debate about the Ninth Legion's fate), each with an official strength of 5,500 legionaries, formed the army's 165,000-man heavy infantry backbone, while 360 or so auxiliary cohorts (each of them the rough equivalent of a 600-man infantry battalion) provided another 217,000 soldiers for the empire's defence.

Positioned mainly in the empire's border provinces, these forces performed two main tasks. Whilst ostensibly providing a strong means of defence against external attack, their role was just as much about maintaining Roman rule in the most challenging of the empire's subject territories. It was no coincidence that the troublesome provinces of Britannia and Dacia were deemed to require 60 and 44 auxiliary cohorts respectively, almost a quarter of the total available. It should be noted, however, that while their overall strategic task was the same, the terms under which the two halves of the army served were quite different.

The legions, the primary Roman military unit for conducting warfare at the operational or theatre level, had been in existence since early in the republic, hundreds of years before. They were composed mainly of close-order heavy infantry, well drilled and highly motivated, recruited on a professional basis and, critically to an understanding of their place in Roman society, manned by soldiers who were Roman citizens. The jobless poor were thus provided with a route to a valuable trade, since service with the legions was as much about construction – fortresses, roads and even major defensive works such as Hadrian's Wall – as destruction. Vitally for the maintenance of the empire's borders, this attractiveness of service made a large standing field army a possibility, and allowed for both the control and defence of the conquered territories.

By this point in Britannia's history three legions were positioned to control the restive peoples both beyond and behind the province's borders. These were the 2nd, based in South Wales, the 20th, watching North Wales, and the 6th, positioned to the east of the Pennine range and ready to respond to any trouble on the northern frontier. Each of these legions was commanded by a legatus, an experienced man of senatorial rank deemed worthy of the responsibility and appointed by the emperor. The command structure beneath the legatus was a delicate balance, combining the requirement for training and advancing Rome's young aristocrats for their future roles with the necessity for the legion to be led into battle by experienced and hardened officers.

Directly beneath the legatus were a half-dozen or so military tribunes, one of them a young man of the senatorial class called the broad stripe tribune after the broad senatorial stripe on his tunic. This relatively inexperienced man – it would have been his first official position – acted as the legion's second-in-command, despite being a relatively tender age when compared with the men around him. The remainder of the military tribunes were narrow stripes, men of the equestrian class who usually already had some command experience under their belts from leading an auxiliary cohort. Intriguingly, since the more experienced narrow-stripe tribunes effectively reported to the broad stripe, such a reversal of the usual military conventions around fitness for command must have made for some interesting man-management situations. The legion's third in command was the camp prefect, an older and more experienced soldier, usually a former centurion deemed worthy of one last role in the legion's service before retirement, usually for one year. He would by necessity have been a steady hand, operating as the voice of experience in advising the legion's senior officers as to the realities of warfare and the management of the legion's soldiers.

Reporting into this command structure were ten cohorts of soldiers, each one composed of a number of eighty-man centuries. Each century was a collection of ten tent parties – eight men who literally shared a tent when out in the field. Nine of the cohorts had six centuries, and an establishment strength of 480 men, whilst the prestigious first cohort, commanded by the legion's senior centurion, was composed of five double-strength centuries and therefore fielded 800 soldiers when fully manned. This organisation provided the legion with its cutting edge: 5,000 or so well-trained heavy infantrymen operating in regiment and company-sized units, and led by battle-hardened officers, the legion's centurions, men whose position was usually achieved by dint of their demonstrated leadership skills.

The rank of centurion was pretty much the peak of achievement for an ambitious soldier, commanding an eighty-man century and paid ten times as much as the men each officer commanded. Whilst the majority of centurions were promoted from the ranks, some were appointed from above as a result of patronage, or as a result of having completed their service in the Praetorian Guard, which had a shorter period of service than the legions. That these externally imposed centurions would have undergone their very own 'sink or swim' moment in dealing with their new colleagues is an unavoidable conclusion, for the role was one that by necessity led from the front, and as a result suffered disproportionate casualties. This makes it highly likely that any such appointee felt unlikely to make the grade in action would have received very short shrift from his brother officers.

A small but necessarily effective team reported to the centurion. The optio, literally 'best' or chosen man, was his second-in-command, and stood behind the century in action with a long brass-knobbed stick, literally pushing the soldiers into the fight should the need arise. This seems to have been a remarkably efficient way of managing a large body of men, given the centurion's place alongside rather than behind his soldiers, and the optio would have been a cool head, paid twice the usual soldier's wage and a candidate for promotion to centurion if he performed well. The century's third-in-command was the tesserarius or watch officer, ostensibly charged with ensuring that sentries were posted and that everyone knew the watch word for the day, but also likely to have been responsible for the profusion of tasks such as checking the soldiers' weapons and equipment, ensuring the maintenance of discipline and so on, that have occupied the lives of junior non-commissioned officers throughout history in delivering a combat-effective unit to their officer. The last member of the centurion's team was the century's signifer, the standard bearer, who both provided a rallying point for the soldiers and helped the centurion by transmitting marching orders to them through movements of his standard. Interestingly, he also functioned as the century's banker, dealing with the soldiers' financial affairs. While a soldier caught in the horror of battle might have thought twice about defending his unit's standard, he might well also have felt a stronger attachment to the man who managed his money for him!

At the shop-floor level were the eight soldiers of the tent party who shared a leather tent and messed together, their tent and cooking gear carried on a mule when the legion was on the march. Each tent party would inevitably have established its own pecking order based upon the time-honoured factors of strength, aggression, intelligence – and the rough humour required to survive in such a harsh world. The men that came to dominate their tent parties would have been the century's unofficial backbone, candidates for promotion to watch officer. They would also have been vital to their tent mates' cohesion under battlefield conditions, when the relatively thin leadership team could not always exert sufficient presence to inspire the individual soldier to stand and fight amid the horrific chaos of combat.

The other element of the legion was a small 120-man detachment of cavalry, used for scouting and the carrying of messages between units. The regular army depended on auxiliary cavalry wings, drawn from those parts of the empire where horsemanship was a way of life, for their mounted combat arm. Which leads us to consider the other side of the army's two-tier system.

The auxiliary cohorts, unlike the legions alongside which they fought, were not Roman citizens, although the completion of a twenty-five-year term of service did grant both the soldier and his children citizenship. The original auxiliary cohorts had often served in their homelands, as a means of controlling the threat of large numbers of freshly conquered barbarian warriors, but this changed after the events of the first century AD. The Batavian revolt in particular – when the 5,000-strong Batavian cohorts rebelled and destroyed two Roman legions after suffering intolerable provocation during a recruiting campaign gone wrong – was the spur for the Flavian policy for these cohorts to be posted away from their home provinces. The last thing any Roman general wanted was to find his legions facing an army equipped and trained to fight in the same way. This is why the reader will find the auxiliary cohorts described in the *Empire* series, true to the historical record, representing a variety of other parts of the empire, including Tungria, which is now part of modern-day Belgium.

Auxiliary infantry was equipped and organised in so close a manner to the legions that the casual observer would have been hard put to spot the differences. Often their armour would be mail, rather than plate, sometimes weapons would have minor differences, but in most respects an auxiliary cohort would be the same proposition to an enemy as a legion cohort. Indeed there are hints from history that the auxiliaries may have presented a greater challenge on the battlefield. At the battle of Mons Graupius in Scotland, Tacitus records that four cohorts of Batavians and two of Tungrians were sent in ahead of the legions and managed to defeat the enemy without requiring any significant assistance. Auxiliary cohorts were also often used on the flanks of the battle line, where reliable and well-drilled troops are essential to handle attempts to outflank the army. And while the legions contained soldiers who were as much tradesmen as fighting men, the auxiliary cohorts were primarily focused on their fighting skills. By the end of the second century there were significantly more auxiliary troops serving the empire than were available from the legions, and it is clear that Hadrian's Wall would have been invalid as a concept without the mass of infantry and mixed infantry/cavalry cohorts that were stationed along its length.

As for horsemen, the importance of the empire's 75,000 or so auxiliary cavalrymen, capable of much faster deployment and manoeuvre than the infantry, and essential for successful scouting, fast communications and the denial of reconnaissance information to the enemy, cannot be overstated. Rome simply did not produce anything like the strength in mounted troops needed to avoid being at a serious disadvantage against those nations which by their nature were cavalry-rich. As a result, as each such nation was conquered their mounted forces were swiftly incorporated into the army until, by the early first century BC, the decision was made to disband what native Roman cavalry as there was altogether, in favour of the auxiliary cavalry wings.

Named for their usual place on the battlefield, on the flanks or 'wings' of the line of battle, the cavalry cohorts were commanded by men of the equestrian class with prior experience as legion military tribunes, and were organised around the basic 32-man turma, or squadron. Each squadron was commanded by a decurion, a position analogous with that of the infantry centurion. This officer was assisted by a pair of junior officers: the duplicarius or double-pay, equivalent to the role of optio, and the sesquiplarius or pay-and-a-half, equal in stature to the infantry watch officer. As befitted the cavalry's more important military role, each of these ranks was paid about 40 per cent more than the infantry equivalent.

Taken together, the legions and their auxiliary support presented a standing army of over 400,000 men by the time of the events described in the *Empire* series. While this was sufficient to both hold down and defend the empire's 6.5 million square kilometres for a long period of history, the strains of defending a 5,000- kilometre-long frontier, beset on all sides by hostile tribes, were also beginning to manifest themselves. The prompt move to raise three new legions undertaken by the new emperor Septimius Severus in AD 197, in readiness for over a decade spent shoring up the empire's crumbling borders, provides clear evidence that there were never enough legions and cohorts for such a monumental task. This is the backdrop for the *Empire* series, which will run from AD 182 well into the early third century, following both the empire's and Marcus Valerius Aquila's travails throughout this fascinatingly brutal period of history.

The Chain of Command
Legion

Legatus — Legion Cavalry (120 horsemen)

Broad Stripe Tribune

5 'Military' Narrow Stripe Tribunes

Camp Prefect

Senior Centurion

10 Cohorts
(one of 5 centuries of 160 men each)
(nine of 6 centuries of 80 men each)

Centurion

Chosen Man

Watch Officer   **Standard Bearer**

10 tent parties of 8 men apiece

The Chain of Command
Auxiliary Infantry Cohort

Legatus

Prefect
(or a Tribune for a larger cohort such as the First Tungrian)

Senior Centurion

6-10 Centuries

Centurion

Chosen Man

Watch Officer   **Standard Bearer**

10 tent parties of 8 men apiece

From Ancient Rome to the Tudor court, revolutionary Paris to the Second World War, discover the best historical fiction and non-fiction at

Visit us today for exclusive author features, first chapter previews, podcasts and audio excerpts, book trailers, giveaways and much more.

Sign up now to receive our regular newsletter at
www.HforHistory.co.uk